Agent from Hell

Agent from Hell

JOHN PHELPS

Matador
5 Weir Road
Kibworth Beauchamp
Leicester LE8 0LQ UK
Tel: 0116 279 2299
Email: books@troubador.co.uk
Web: www.troubador.co.uk/matador

ISBN 9781848764101

A Cataloguing-in-Publication (CIP) catalogue record for this book
is available from the British Library.

Typeset in 11pt Sabon by Troubador Publishing Ltd, Leicester, UK

Matador is an imprint of Troubador Publishing Ltd

Printed in Great Britain by the MPG Books Group, Bodmin and King's Lynn

CHAPTER 1

THEO'S CAR LEAPED into the air on hitting a bump in the road.

Then it turned almost half-circle after the front wheel on the passenger side made contact with yet another pothole.

"Slow down! Patience can be a virtue!" Theo said to himself aloud.

The opening of Salter's Estate Agents can wait a while longer. A new beginning was round the corner.

So, too, though he did not know it just then, was a life-changing drama …

He reminded himself that there were even more deaths on fenland roads than on the notorious A14. During the last year, more than 60 people had lost their lives on them in Cambridgeshire alone. Four vehicles had plunged down steep banks, with victims meeting watery graves.

But it was so frustrating …

Before reaching the road to Camford, his newly acquired second hand Ford Escort had been taken round rural paths that twisted and turned both ways while connecting a series of villages and hamlets. Hairpin bends had been the norm for well over an hour.

Now the road was arrow straight. But it was narrow, too, with barely room for two cars to pass each other from opposite directions. The sun glinted and glared through low-hung clouds, meaning that visibility, at a squint, was for a matter of yards rather than miles.

Theo had had to slow to almost a halt twice already, when first a Mercedes and then a tractor approached from the opposite direction.

Apart from being almost impossibly narrow, the road was so riven with cracks, potholes and loose chippings and stones that it had clearly not been treated for years.

Most hazardous of all, though, were the steep banks that dropped down to a canal on one side and, for much of the time, deep ditches or drains on the other. The banks' height varied from eight to 15 feet and, more often than not, there was enough water to drown in down below. Only yesterday, Theo had read in the local press how police had warned young people in particular not to race along fen roads.

"Motorways are far, far safer," was the police spokesman's observation. "You are much more likely to crash on a rural road. There are lots of causes. Many are down to inappropriate speed and people don't realise fen roads have their own hazards. There are lots of fenland roads in Cambridgeshire and some are not very wide. It is not like driving down a dual carriageway with central reservations. You are putting yourself at risk if you travel at speed if there are no barriers."

Theo had memorised the warning almost word for word. It was as if he knew that a major event in his life was about to take place...

Almost simultaneously, his foot touched the brake as the Escort's front left wheel caressed a small boulder. The car lurched but remained straight. Then, all of a sudden, a series of loud bangs could be heard.

At the same moment, a beam of sunlight forced its way through a cloud so massive and dark that it resembled a giant bruise. Theo was almost blinded. He reduced his speed to a crawl. A few seconds later, part of the cloud seemed to melt. But, just as he started to accelerate, he could see a human outline. He slowed once more. The figure was waving frantically.

The sunbeam suddenly weakened and Theo was able to see that it was a woman ... unmistakably a woman, although she was as tall, if not taller, than himself. Her shape was ultra-slim, the type that tended to grace fashion magazines. She had long, flowing blonde hair and Theo could not fail to notice how elegantly dressed she was. High heels ensured that she stood at over 6ft tall.

This was hardly the sort of vision to be expected to emerge on a deserted fen road. Yet there she was ... a vision of cool beauty. The aura of coolness was quickly shattered, though. "Help!" the woman shrieked. Her poise had deserted her. "Please help! Wayne's in the canal! Wayne's car has crashed. It's left the road and gone into the canal. Please, please help me!" Not knowing why, Theo asked: "Wayne who?" The vision of beauty became more desperate still. "My husband ... Wayne Benson. Please, please help me!"

The situation was indeed desperate, and, despite his seemingly irrelevant inquiry, Theo could see that urgent action was needed.

Yet, despite this, he was still able to observe brown eyes made even more appealing by the vulnerability caused by her predicament. He noticed, too, a sensual mouth and a dress that clung to contours which were perfectly in proportion despite their slenderness. He also recognised the name Wayne Benson. And he could sense that Mrs Benson was shivering.

A tweed sports jacket was draped over the Escort's passenger seat. Theo grabbed it, leaped out of the car and threw it over her shoulders.

Then he looked down the grassy bank to see a partly submerged sports car. It looked like a Porsche. The front part was still just above the surface and facing the bank, indicating that the Porsche had turned full circle after the driver lost control and before the car careered down the slope. There was no sign of the driver.

Theo bounded down the 12ft slope until he reached the water's edge. Only the power in his legs, coupled with the athleticism of a gymnast, prevented him from tumbling headlong into the canal.

He estimated that the water closest to the bank was around 3ft deep but suspected, correctly, that it took less than a car length for the depth to increase to 10ft.

Theo's first instinct was the dive in. But, remembering his life-saving training and having no idea what else besides car parts might lie below the surface, he bent his knees and jumped.

The water was unexpectedly cold for the time of year. It was if the spring and early summer sunlight had basked the roads and surrounding arable land but failed to find its way down the banks. Theo then realised that the Porsche was open-topped. So hopefully

3

his rescue mission would be simpler as a result. Yet there was still no sign of Benson.

Both the front seats were empty. As Theo peered through the water, made murky by reed beds and silt, he spotted a seat belt lying dormant on the driver's side. He made a grab for the back of the driver's seat and propelled himself towards the section of the Porsche that was totally submerged. The water became murkier still. Visibility was about three inches. However, Theo was able to discern a few shapes. There was a brief case, a set of weights, two cricket bats, two cricket pads and a long, flat bag of the type used by top-flight cricketers. Then, at last, he saw the shape of a man.

By this time, Theo lungs were yearning for air. But this was no time for seeking respite. Benson was lying face down across the back seats.

Theo grabbed his left foot, the part of him that was nearest, and pulled. There was little discernible movement, and the reason was simple. The cricket bag was lying across Benson's back. Resting across the bag was a barbell with a 30-pound weight at each end. And, to make matters worse still, a 25-pound dumbbell had wedged his right ankle between the cricket pads and back seat.

With one desperate movement, Theo planted his feet on the floor near the front passenger seat and, while facing the back, grasped the barbell, pulled it towards him and, with all the might his right arm could muster, hurled it out of the right hand side of the car.

Had the Porsche not been open-topped, such a manoeuvre would have been impossible. As it was, Theo had to surface at this point.

Three hurried gasps of air sufficed, though, and Theo plunged below once more, to move first the cricket bag and then the short, compact dumbbell.

Finally, he was able to move Benson. This was itself a far from easy task. By this stage, Benson was, at best, unconscious, and Theo was faced with the prospect of having to move a dead weight of about 14 stone ... firstly from the car, then towards the water's edge and finally up a steep 12ft slope coated with slippery grass. Theo slid his hands under Benson's armpits from behind and, adopting a life-saving position, clasped the fronts of his shoulder blades before using the floor of the car as a springboard … enabling rescuer and rescued to be propelled upwards.

On surfacing and taking in a few gulps of air, Theo found that a smidgeon of the strength that had started to ebb had returned. Somehow he managed to sling Benson over his right shoulder before clambering up the bank. Halfway up, his feet slid on the grass and all the power in his legs and hips were needed to prevent a tumble back into the water.

Once Theo neared the top, Mrs Benson was able to grab one of her husband's arms and pull while Theo pushed.

The woman and the two men ended up in an ungainly heap on the narrow verge above the slope. Theo was all in. But the rescue mission was far from over. He was acutely aware that if Benson was still alive, he had to be resuscitated without delay. It was no use, though. He was unable to move. Luckily, however, help was on hand.

Mrs Benson had recovered her composure enough to telephone 999 on her mobile phone and now the siren of an ambulance arriving could be heard. Only barely aware of what was going on around him, Theo could hear the ambulance come to a halt, the sound of men's voices and then Mrs Benson's.

The temperature was beginning to fall and Theo was shivering. However, at this stage, all the attention was focussed on Benson. After what seemed to be an eternity but was only a matter of seconds, one of the men was heard to say: "He's breathing!" And Mrs Benson exclaimed: "Thank God!"

By the time Benson had been resuscitated and carried by stretcher into the ambulance, Theo was able to get up. One of the men asked him if he was all right. Theo replied: "Tired but otherwise fine, thanks." The ambulance man said: "That's good. But you'd better come with us anyway. We need to be absolutely sure you're OK and, in any case, you're going to have to get into some dry clothes." All this meant leaving the Ford Escort where it was and collecting it later but Theo was in no mood to argue and, uncharacteristically for him, he welcomed the helping hand that guided him into the ambulance. Within two minutes, he was asleep.

A few hours later, when he woke up, he found himself in a bed at Elmsleigh Hospital, which he learned later was about 10 miles from the crash and rescue scene.

He was one of four in a row of patients. But it soon became apparent that he was the ward's centre of attention. A young but authoritative-looking doctor appeared, strode up and sat on a chair close to Theo's pillow. "How are you feeling?" he asked. Then, without waiting for an answer, the doctor said: "We're just keeping you in overnight to stay on the safe side. You've been through quite an ordeal but you're clearly extremely fit and, because of that, you've come through it well. However, what you went through must have been a shock to the system and I want to keep an eye on you for a while to make absolutely sure there's no reaction. The likelihood is that you will be going home tomorrow. So tomorrow morning ..."

At this point, Theo felt compelled to interrupt. "How's the bloke I rescued from the canal?" he demanded.

"Mr Benson should be fine, too ... thanks to you," the doctor replied. "He's got a sprained ankle, which will heal in time, and there's a slight bump on the forehead, which we'll need to keep tabs on for a bit. After all, you never really know with head injuries ... even minor knocks can, on occasion, turn out to be dangerous, even fatal. But, if all things are equal, he will be out and about pretty soon. And that's thanks to you! If you hadn't acted so promptly and with such selfless courage, the picture would almost certainly be entirely different." Theo managed a grateful nod.

"You know you've become quite a celebrity, don't you?" the doctor added with an approving look. "As you're doubtless aware, Wayne Benson is quite a folk hero, especially in these parts. "And if you're a friend of Wayne Benson, which you're undoubtedly going to be, you can do no wrong round here."

Theo smiled and there was then a pause. "Anyway, right now you need to rest and I'll see you tomorrow morning," the doctor concluded before leaving him. Theo closed his eyes, in readiness for the sweetest dream to be enjoyed to years. He just could not believe his luck.

CHAPTER 2

THERE WAS NO SHORTAGE of visitors the following morning. Elmsleigh Hospital seemed to be heaving with journalists and well-wishers.

Most had come to see the larger than life Wayne Benson, who was still good for a news story now and then. His sporting exploits continued to be talked about, of course, and so, too, were the transgressions.

Benson's prowess on the cricket pitch and, to a lesser extent, on the rugby field, was "Boy's Own" stuff. The various scrapes and past dalliances were meat and drink for the tabloid press. A colourful, flawed hero, he could not stay out of the limelight for long.

However, on this occasion, the reporters also wanted to talk to Theo. News of the canal rescue drama had spread rapidly and everyone wanted to know about the mystery man who had saved a sporting icon's life.

All but a handful of people were turned away.

Theo received the two visits he wanted. One was from Mrs Benson, the other from Kelly Cheatham. Wayne Benson was recuperating in a different room and, after visiting him briefly, his wife sought out and called on the ward where Theo was resting. Theo observed that she was still wearing the same dress. There was a line of soil down one side of it, and she also had a slightly grazed knee. Even more noticeable, still, were those soft brown eyes that indicated a vulnerability not in keeping with the high-profile lifestyle he knew she must have led.

"I don't know how I can thank you enough," she cooed as she entered. "I…"

Theo cut the speech of gratitude short. "You're Lisa Sam, the model, aren't you?" he asked.

"Yes, that's right, though it's Lisa Benson these days," she replied as matter-of-factly as she could, though she still sounded a little shaken. "I have given up modelling almost entirely and I am mainly just a housewife now... and you are Theo Salter, I'm told." Her voice was soft and sensuous. Her composure was beginning to return. As it did, Lisa took the opportunity to study her "knight in shining armour."

Although Theo was half sitting, half lying on his bed, Lisa could see he was about 5ft 11in tall ... about the same height as her. She observed broad, sloping shoulders, a thick neck and powerful arms. And she could not resist making the assessment that the bedclothes concealed muscular thighs.

In point of fact, Theo's athletic build very much resembled that of Wayne, though her husband was slightly taller and had a waistline that had thickened in recent years.

The main difference was in the eyes, though. Wayne's were clear blue and exuded passion, determination, impulsiveness and abandon all at the same time. Theo's were blue-grey, shrewd, almost steely. Lisa could see that her husband's saviour had an athlete's determination and passion all right. But there was something more ...

"As you can imagine, Wayne's mightily grateful, too, and he'll be telling you so personally before long. That's for sure," Lisa told Theo. "Is there anything I can do to help YOU in the meantime?"

"You could find out if my car's all right," Theo said a little ruefully.

Lisa replied: "I'll go one better than that. Lend me the key and I'll arrange for it to be brought back for you. That's the least I can do. And I can tell you, in the meantime, that, whether you like it or not, Wayne is going to be your friend for your life. As sure as eggs are eggs, he's going to bend over backwards to return the favour you have done him. He's that kind of man." Then she asked: "You are a stranger in these parts, aren't you?" And, without waiting for an answer, she added: "Well, let me tell you, it won't be long before you're well known here. There will be no end of people, some of them well known people at that, who will want to get to know you."

Theo nodded and then, almost curtly, asked: "How come you weren't in the canal yourself at the time of the accident?"

Lisa told him that everything had happened so quickly that she could not remember everything. However, as far as she could recall, Wayne had been driving too fast … as was his wont … despite her pleas for him to slow down. He had also failed to fasten his seatbelt … another habit that constantly worried her.

The car had hit a pothole, a stone or some other object left lying in the road before spinning round and careering down the canal bank.

"I remember Wayne shouting at me to undo my seatbelt while he was braking," she said. "I did this and he then leant across me, opened the passenger door and pushed me out just before his Porsche left the road.

"I almost fell down the bank myself but somehow managed to cling on to the top and stop myself. I then phoned 999 on my mobile, saying what had happened. An ambulance did come quite quickly but the next thing that happened was you turning up … thank goodness! Thank God you did! The ambulance men reckoned Wayne would have drowned if he had been under the water for just a few seconds longer."

Theo asked how Wayne was now. "He's got a bit of a bump on the head and his broken ankle's a bit painful," Lisa told him.

Then, with a flicker of amusement, she added: "But the ridiculous thing is that he's much more put out by the fact that he won't be able to play in the annual cricket match, which is between the Camford estate agents and the building societies and banks." Each side was allowed to field a guest player, Theo heard. Wayne had filled that role for the estate agents for nearly 10 years. And, needless to say, he was the star of the show who never failed to draw in the crowds.

"Wayne absolutely loves to play in this match now that he's no longer a professional sportsman.

"God only knows who's going to take his place at such short notice."

All of a sudden, Theo could feel goose bumps and adrenaline surging through his veins in a way that he did not think possible any more. For he sensed that another opportunity to shine was about to be served on a plate. "I'll play!" he exclaimed, almost blurted. He realised later he must have sounded like a child who had seen a new toy in a shop and knew that he had to have it.

"Let me play!"

Lisa could not conceal how taken aback she was. Drafting in a total stranger at short notice was unheard of. Even including a new local hero would, to put it mildly, be frowned upon in some quarters.

But Theo would not be denied. "I used to play quite a bit of club cricket, and fast bowling is my forte. You asked me a minute ago how you could return the favour. Well, this is it. I MUST play." The vehemence and urgency in his tone could not be ignored. A pause followed, during which an embarrassed Lisa struggled to think of a diplomatic way out.

"I'll have to ask the estate agents' captain about this," she replied finally. "He might already have a reserve lined up ... but I'll certainly do my best to find a way of getting you into the side. I can't make any promises but ..."

Just then, the bulky form of Wayne Benson appeared and Lisa's sentence was cut short.

"He's GOT to play!" he bellowed while pointing towards Theo's bed.

"We've got a new hero here! This man's the talk of the town already and nobody knows him yet. The crowds will love him!! And you never know, if his ability to pull a bloke of my size out of a car submerged in water is anything to go by, he might even be able to play cricket a bit!" Then, to Theo, he said: "I guess I owe you my life, and believe you me that's something I value in spades ..."

Now it was Wayne Benson's turn to be interrupted.

A nurse suddenly appeared and demanded, in traditional matronly fashion, to know what he was doing out of bed. Theo could not help noticing that the nurse's trim, prim appearance accentuated Benson's larger than life persona. The region's favourite folk hero was burly, bulky and powerful-looking. However, a much thickened waist and a slight floridity of complexion served as a tell-tale sign of years of hard drinking. There was nothing fictional about those stories of carousing that occasionally got out of hand. However, the big and sometimes belligerent Benson began to look tired and was meek enough in accepting the nurse's implied order to get back to bed at once. Not before insisting on shaking Theo's hand, though. "Rest assured, you'll be in that team and I'll make sure you're well looked after in and around Camford. I'll be in touch soon."

His booming voice was magnified by Theo's deceptively high-pitched tones when Theo replied: "Great! I look forward to that."

No sooner had Wayne departed than a second nurse appeared to announce the arrival of another visitor. "A Miss Kelly Cheatham is here to see you," she said.

Theo said to the nurse: "That's excellent! Could you show her in, please!?" Then to Lisa: "You will forgive me if I cut you short, won't you?"

"Of course," Lisa replied. "But please believe me, Wayne and I are both so very much in your debt. Oh, and before I go, could I have your car key?" Theo got the nurse to hand it over. "And your address, too?" Lisa added.

"You'll have to ask Kelly that," Theo replied. At that moment the slight figure of Kelly Cheatham appeared in the ward. Kelly was as slim, if not slimmer, than Lisa and also six or seven inches shorter. The difference in poise was even more marked. Kelly smiled shyly and jotted down an address on a paper tissue from her handbag and handed the tissue to Lisa as the latter expressed pleasure in meeting her ... and, once more, heaped praise upon Theo. And, as she departed, Lisa flashed the sort of smile that was once seen on magazine covers throughout Britain. However, once Lisa was gone, Kelly came up with a grin that more than matched it.

As always, her hair was shoulder length and straw coloured, her skin on the sallow side, her skirt several inches above the knee and her grey eyes filled with adoration. The teeth were white but slightly crooked and the smile she reserved for Theo only these days conveyed a message that was unmistakable. In short, she was sex on legs.

"How are you feeling?" Kelly asked simply.

Theo's eyes twinkled. "Never mind that, come here!" he half commanded. Kelly moved forward obediently and when she was close enough Theo slid his hand up her skirt, grasped her by the thigh and pulled her onto the bed.

Kelly shrieked and cried "Stop it!" and …as always … Theo knew she meant "Whatever you do, DON'T stop!" as he pulled the skirt up to about waist height and put his hand inside her knickers. "Stop!" Kelly called out even louder. Almost inevitably, at this point, the nurse who had ordered Wayne Benson back to bed a while ago reappeared. Then, with a disapproving tone but a wry smile, she pronounced: "I think we can fairly say you will be able to pack your bags first thing tomorrow morning."

CHAPTER 3

ANGELA TRIMMINGTON, as her name turned out to be, was as good as her word. Theo left hospital at the earliest possible moment. Lisa had arranged for his car to be parked nearby and ensured that Kelly had possession of the key.

And when Kelly turned up to collect her patient, no one could fail to notice a dress that was even more figure-hugging and revealing than the clothes worn the previous day. Doctors, nurses and patients all had good reason to remember her presence.

"Something tells me Camford's not quite ready for all this," Staff Nurse Trimmington whispered to a houseman standing by her side. But the houseman was not listening ...

Theo's hand was caressing Kelly's buttocks long before the couple were outside. "The car's just across the road and around the corner," Kelly said, once they had reached open air.

Theo wrapped his fingers around an upper arm, almost propelling her along, as they threaded their way through semi-stationary traffic and chose to ignore a zebra crossing just 50 feet away. On reaching the Escort, which was parked in a side street, Theo asked for the key.

But Kelly surprised him a little by sounding something suspiciously close to assertive and insisting on doing the driving herself.

"You're only just out of hospital, you're probably not feeling quite yourself and you don't know where we're going ... I do," she said with maternal firmness.

A short pause, during which Theo gave her a speculative look, followed. Then his eyes twinkled. "Bless you!" he said softly. Yet, even before the key was in the ignition, Theo's right hand was stroking her left thigh.

"And while we're on this journey you can keep your hands to yourself and behave! The traffic's heavy and I need to concentrate!"

Her coquettish firmness was almost irresistible. The pair had been parted for several weeks, and Theo was hard put to contain himself. However, from then on his hands remained obediently in his lap. Fortunately for him, the car ride was a mere 15 minutes long. The couple's new abode was a first floor flat on Camford's outskirts.

Theo followed Kelly upstairs, enjoying once more a full view of her long, slim legs. Kelly turned her head, smiling knowingly. Then, as the key turned in the door of the flat, Theo lifted her up and carried her into a small hall.

"Well, what do you think to it?" asked Kelly, looking up at him. Theo put her down gently and glanced around. He could see straight away that the flat was small and sparsely furnished ... certainly no place for entertaining clients with cocktails. But at least it was clean and neat, and would more than suffice as a first place to live in a strange town.

Kelly started to adopt the tone of an estate agent showing a potential buyer around a much more palatial property. "This is the kitchen," she announced. "It comes complete with an oven, sink with draining boards and two cupboards with doors that open and close ... as long as you push and pull hard." Then Kelly took Theo by the hand and continued the "conducted tour." "This is the bathroom. It has a bath in it. Next door is the little boys' room. And here is the lounge/diner. As you can see, it comes with a carpet, curtains, settee, two armchairs and a desk. Any questions so far?"

Theo, entering into the spirit of things, replied: "Yes, what about the most important room in the entire property?"

Kelly's eyes lit up. She turned the handle of the next door along and opened it with a flourish. "And here is the bedroom," she murmured. It contained a double bed, wardrobe, dressing table and just a few narrow shelves. A threadbare carpet looked as if the task of touching all four walls had stretched it to the limit.

"Well … well done, my sweet," Theo said softly. "This place should do fine … for now, anyway." Theo and Kelly gazed at each other for a few seconds, before a playful glint appeared in two pairs of eyes.

Theo kissed Kelly lightly on the forehead. Then he made to kiss her on the mouth … but his lips made contact with a cheek instead. After that, he kissed her on the neck, nose, eyes, ears, mouth and forehead again. Each kiss followed a "feint." None landed when or where Kelly expected. The couple's antics almost resembled a boxers' sparring session, with the dominant one picking out openings and scoring points when least expected by his opponent. For Kelly, the unpredictability, the uncertainty of it all, was a large part of the excitement.

Then, without warning, Theo seized her arms just below the shoulder blades, bent forward and kissed her long and hard on the lips. Before long, tongues were rubbing together and Theo's hands were inside the top of Kelly's dress.

One hand ran along her breasts, the other undid her bra. Kelly gasped when, with one quick outward movement, Theo used both hands to exposed small, curved contours … before moving his hands inwards to cover them up.

Theo repeated this action four or five times with Kelly whimpering increasingly volubly each time.

Seconds later, she was wearing nothing but knickers. Theo's hand soon located the warm moisture inside. The caresses turned into one long, ferocious massage and before long Kelly was lying naked on her back on the bed. She held her hands forward, beckoning Theo to come to her. Theo moved forward enticingly, looking more than ready to oblige.

But, at the last moment, he lifted her up, turned her over and entered her from behind. Theo made love to Kelly for the rest of that day. At times the intimacy reached such intensity and ferocity that Kelly screamed with pain as well as joy. She felt kisses, squeezes and bites, as well as caresses, almost everywhere. And all the time there was that almost frenzied bucking motion of immense power. Eventually the intensity subsided.

Theo whispered into Kelly's ear: "Bless you!" he said, and the love-making ended with Theo kissing and stroking every part of her body. It was three in the morning before the couple fell asleep, locked in each other's arms.

Four hours later, Theo was rummaging for breakfast in the kitchen. "Bless you!" he murmured again on discovering that Kelly, although limited for time, had had the foresight to buy some cornflakes, bread, milk and coffee. He took these items out of the cupboard and fridge as quietly as possible and started to have breakfast.

As he ate, he became aware, for the first time, of the lumps and bumps he had sustained during the canal rescue. On loosening the cord around the waist of his robe, he was able to see a particularly large bruise on his left shoulder and a welt on his left upper arm.

These must have been the result of scraping that occurred while he was pulling Wayne Benson out of the submerged car, Theo mused. Then he realised there were a couple of scratch marks on his back … acquired during a different and more pleasurable activity! But, before having a chance to reflect on this, he could feel his robe being opened and pulled downwards.

Kelly was standing behind his chair. She kissed his neck and began to caress the points of pain. Then she began to kiss those points. A moment later, she pushed the table back a foot or two so that that there was room for her to move between it and Theo and sit astride him. "I've got business to attend to, Theo protested mildly. "You certainly do!" Kelly responded with mocking relish, while disrobing. And it was a good hour before Theo entertained any more thoughts about the office that needed to be opened and the country house that he was to due to inspect.

CHAPTER 4

APRIL MAY WAS FEELING the heat ... and it was far from flaming June. Dark clouds overhung fenland fields, and droplets were dancing on the dashboard of her open-topped MG. But the weather wasn't the reason for her being flustered. A Landrover was on her tail and the driver wanted to overtake. "Fuck off, you pig!" she muttered as the horn honked yet again. April was not used to being overtaken ... least of all by a Landrover.

But accelerating rapidly and leaving the driver behind for dead was not an option.

The road was narrow and it twisted and turned every 20 yards or so. Some of the bends were hairpins and, by fenland standards, there were hills that undulated steeply. A sudden increase in speed was simply impossible ... except perhaps for the Landrover. April May was not accustomed to being browbeaten either. Tall, athletic and feisty, she was known as someone who would not stand for nonsense from anyone.

Her thick dark mane of hair, flashing black eyes and deep, rasping voice added up to a persona not to be trifled with. Woe betide anybody in her office who might suggest she talked too loudly on the telephone. Under other circumstances, she was more than equal to the task of dealing with a truculent motorist.

Not this motorist, though.

April could see through her front mirror that her tormentor's shoulders were almost as wide as the Landrover's bonnet, his appearance was rough and his red face was contorted with rage. There was nothing for it but to keep going until there was room at the side of the road for the MG to stop and let the Landrover overtake. Meanwhile, the intermittent honking continued. At times, the Landrover was so close behind that it looked as if it was about to ram the MG.

At one point, when the Landrover was not within ramming distance, the road straightened a little, and April slowed down slightly, in the hope that she would be overtaken.

But, as luck would have it, a large van moving at great speed, then appeared from the opposite direction.

This enraged the Landrover driver even more, and the horn-honking became more frenzied than ever. More twists and turns in the road followed until at long last there was an opportunity to stop. After a few more miles, a small lay-by, close to a farm, appeared from seemingly nowhere, and April pulled in.

Then, to April's consternation, the Landrover stopped, too, after drawing parallel with the MG. The big red-faced man glared across and said: "You need to learn how to drive." April instinctively glared back and responded with a virtually silent "Fuck off!"

She then looked away but could feel the red-faced man's gaze before he drove off a few seconds later.

April stayed put for a while in order to regain her composure. However, as all her friends and colleagues knew, losses of composure and words were generally foreign to her! The only real problem this feisty young lady had was a beguiling belief in the best of people, sometimes with unfortunate consequences.

She used this unscheduled stop as an opportunity to consult her road map, which showed that her destination, Aggammenmon Hall was just a couple of miles away.

In fact, despite all that had just occurred, she was slightly ahead of schedule. In addition, the owner had indicated that he might be delayed and had issued April with a set of keys to enable her to start inspecting the property on her own if necessary.

After about a mile and a half, vegetation that flanked the road on either side started to give way on the left to a high barbed wire fence.

"This must be it," April mused. The fence twisted and turned with the road until, all of a sudden, the road straightened.

After about another half a mile, April could see Aggammenmon Hall's giant wrought iron gates. She parked outside, got out and fished for the keys in her handbag. One of the keys resembled the type that tended to be associated with clanking prison cell doors, and April assumed that this was the one that would get her into the grounds. But she was wrong. The gates were electronically controlled and they opened as soon as she was within two feet of them. She then recalled having been told that the opening and closing of the gates would be arranged in advance. They closed as soon as she had driven the MG through them.

Aggammenmon Hall itself was still half a mile away, though, and the route to it was via a wide gravel path flanked by conifers.

The path curved slightly and it was some time before the main house came into view. A number of outbuildings, including a small barn, a potting shed, a couple of empty stables and a dovecote were there to be viewed on the way, however.

The conifers gradually thinned out to be replaced by bushes, shrubs, flower beds, lawns and finally the house itself.

The final approach took in a croquet lawn, a disused bowling green, an overgrown lawn tennis court and an empty swimming pool. The fence designed to screen the pool had collapsed.

Immediately in front of the house were a fountain, still in a use, and a circular parking area.

The house itself was massive, even for its setting.

It had four storeys and, despite an incongruous mix of period styles, it was magnificent … a gem of a property that oozed prestige and one that would take pride of place in any estate agent's portfolio.

The only problem for estate agents and vendors was arriving at the right price and identifying the right kind of buyer.

The central part of Aggammenmon Hall was classically Tudor in appearance with a white frontage and exposed timbers. To the left and right were Victorian and Georgian additions, and, as April was to discover after walking round the outside, there was a red brick extension built within the last 10 years at the rear.

A steep gabled roof with dormer windows was modern, too.

"Just as well it wasn't listed," April thought. "It could never have been changed so many times then."

But she reminded herself that, although the house had been built in separate stages, it was, in fact, mock Tudor, mock Victorian and mock Georgian … and something that would be mocked by the purist among house buyers who disapproved of any kind of style reproduction.

Then she noticed that there were lampposts with electronically operated lights, mahogany doors at the back and leaded light and sash windows at the rear and side. At the front of the house were two pine doors with brass handles and a heavy oak main door in the middle that came with a brass knob, large keyhole and two metal bolts.

April undid the bolts and used the long iron key she had been given to gain entry.

The inside was even more impressive.

The main door led to a hall big enough to be used as a ballroom or for a banquet. And, as rumour had it, the hall had been used for both these purposes many times and for a variety of other revelries as well.

The floor was of oak, as was one of the walls, though both had a faded, slightly battered look about them and had clearly seen better days. A 10ft long coat rack to the left of the door was almost off its hinges, a patterned red carpet covering part of the floor to the right was expensive-looking but threadbare, and there was evidence of damp in one corner of the hall's high, corniced ceiling.

April was impressed nonetheless. Everything about the room exuded quality, even though there was need for renovation work.

Much of the hall's aura could be attributed to the mahogany staircase at the back, which faced the door and came into view immediately on entry. It had been taken from a manor house a few miles away and installed at Aggammenmon Hall just a decade ago.

Before moving on to the other rooms, April stopped to admire a partly rebuilt chimney breast to the right and, to either side of it, some hand-made wallpaper that had been created especially for this property. Its brightness made other areas look positively jaded.

It was almost as impressive as the shining staircase and balustrade. April was so engrossed in the detail of what she saw that she did not hear the sound of tyres on gravel outside.

The inspection continued. April looked forward to viewing the newly-fitted kitchen she had heard so much about. But, as she always did, she opted to go upstairs first.

In this case, this meant walking round a galleried landing from which another, narrower staircase led to the top of the house. There were also a wine cellar and several basement rooms to be looked at later on.

She looked up towards the landing and ascended. The landing was rectangular and overhung all four sides of the hall. Its wooden railings were solid but in need of several licks of paint. A series of doors, most of them pine with brass handles, were ranged round the perimeter at more or less regular intervals.

At this point, she decided to break from her usual routine and look at the rooms at this level before going to the very top.

Immediately facing the mahogany staircase from the ground floor was the main bedroom. It measured about 30ft by 20ft and was empty save a massive four-poster bed protruding from the far wall and directly facing the door. The door itself was pine with a brass handle. The ceiling was high and slightly stained in one corner, and April noticed that the room's pale floral wallpaper was faded and, in several places, about to fall off. There were signs of woodworm in the floor and even the cast iron fireplace had cracks in it and had a small section missing.

The room was imposing ... but in need of attention. April moved on to another room, to the left. As she did so, a door handle was turning downstairs and the main front door of Aggammenmon Hall was opening ...

The second room was a bedroom, too, smaller and smarter than the first Not long ago, it had been painted in a variety of colours. To one side was a small stage with a frame that clearly once supported curtains. April could see no toys but had no doubt that here was an ideal haven for creative children. Only a slight unevenness in the floorboards in one corner marred the overall impression. April then recalled from the property particulars she had taken down that the next room for inspection, again to the left, was the newly-fitted main bathroom

Suddenly footsteps could be heard on the stairs.

April walked out on to the landing, expecting to meet the owners of the property. However, the person she saw was about to put her composure to the test for the second time that day. It was Ray Williams.

"What are you doing here?" she asked the new arrival coldly.

"The same as you, I should imagine," was the reply. "You'd be amazed at the number and variety of friends and associates Mr Benson has out there. And, incredible as it seems, that even means me."

April found it impossible to conceal her contempt for the bulky, dark-suited man standing between her and the stairs. "Yes, it certainly is incredible, and I'd be most interested to know how his list of associates could possibly include you!" she snapped.

The big man's face darkened, and April could sense that Williams was undressing her with his eyes in an attempt to unsettle her.

"Now then, April, or whatever your real name is, that's not very friendly, is it? We're both estate agents, and even if we're rivals we should make the effort to get on with one another."

By now, Williams was beginning to lisp and stutter a little. April ignored what she could have realised were warning signs.

"Estate agent is might be what you call yourself, but the truth of the matter is that you are nothing but a crooked thug and the rest of us have to live you down!" she retorted angrily.

Williams ran a meat plate of a hand over his battered face, and his eyes hardened. "You really shouldn't speak to people like that," he said. The menace in his tone was now unmistakable.

A short pause followed, in which the pair exchanged unflinching gazes. Then Williams offered a half-smile.

"However, since you are so keen to know and I'm in such a magnanimous frame of mind, I will tell you something of why I am the agent most likely to secure the sale of this property … and why you are not in the picture." The lisp had become more pronounced.

"Wayne Benson and I have come to an understanding," he said.

"And what sort of understanding might that be?" April asked, as contemptuous as ever.

Williams' eyes hardened even more, and, after another pause, he said: "It's not hard to guess what you're thinking, you know. You were expecting your rivals to be the more toffee-nosed operators, such as Gathercole, Pike or Pinkerton. Well, Nathan Pike, as you well know, is never in the office and Ian Gathercole is so stuck up that even an easy-going cove like Benson can't stomach him. And Reg Pinkerton, again as you know, is not quite so toffee-nosed as Gathercole, but he's too pushy for words."

"April's lip curled. "And you are not pushy at all, are you?" she said sarcastically

Williams chuckled humourlessly. "You're one feisty lady, aren't you," he observed.

"But you're missing the point," he went on. You're refusing … or at least not trying very hard … to grasp the fact that Wayne Benson and I have a special understanding. We have an understanding that's both commercial and personal. I'm TERRIBLY, TERRIBLY sorry, but the understanding is so strong that you have made a wasted journey."

All of a sudden, April's anger got the better of her completely.

"Oh yes," she rasped, "I've heard of the sort of understandings YOU have with people. What you mean is that you have some sort of hold over Wayne Benson. What is it you've got on him? We all know about Benson's weakness for gambling and booze. Is that why he's selling this property … because he's racked up debts, or has he become involved in one of your grubby little scams. It wouldn't surprise me if you were blackmailing him if you had the chance!"

"Oh April, April, calm down," Williams mocked. "All right, you don't like me. I've got the message. But that sort of outburst is so … unseemly, unladylike. Which is surprising, when you obviously don't think I'm enough of a gentleman.

"All right, I come from a working class background. And I used to make my money as a professional boxer. But, whether you like it or not, boxing paid better than working at Billingsgate Market.

Perhaps it's the boxing that makes you so uptight. Yes, that must be it. It's not aesthetic enough for a lady from up-town New York to entertain the idea of granting me approval as an acceptable person."

Now it was Williams' turn to curl a lip. "Is that what it is?" he inquired with feigned curiosity.

April's temper was reaching boiling point. "No, it bloody well isn't," she shouted. "It's because you're scum! Do you hear me, nothing but scum! The likes of you are nothing better than the scum of the earth, and you shouldn't be allowed to mingle with ordinary decent people!"

Williams' face blackened. "Speaking to people like that is really quite inappropriate … to say the least." The lisp was stronger than ever. "Speaking in this way is especially inappropriate when you're standing at the top of a long staircase with lots of stairs!"

April went pale as she experienced the stare of a prize-fighter who knew he was getting the upper hand.

But, then, all of sudden, another voice could be heard. "And why's that?" the voice asked. It came from halfway up the stairs.

April and Ray Williams both turned just in time to see a smart-suited man bound, in three paces, from stairs to landing. "What the hell's going on here," the stranger demanded.

"Who the hell are you?" Williams fired back.

"I'm an estate agent who's here on business," was the reply. "I've come to view a property and meet its owner, and I certainly did not expect to meet a thug like you here."

Williams was both rattled and angry: "Just who the hell do you think you're talking to!?"

"I'm talking to you," the stranger said coolly. "I heard some of what you were saying to this lady . .. and it's quite clear to me that you're nothing but a thug!"

Williams stared hard at the stranger and clenched his knuckles. April could not help having a feeling of exhilaration concerning the possibility of what might happen next.

She noticed how the new arrival had moved up the stairs with muscular grace. She could see broad shoulders, a strong neck, slim waist, powerful arms and legs … and eyes like fists. Williams was both taller and wider. But his waistline was sagging and his cheeks puffy. Although she would never admit it, the prospect of a brawl between the two sent April's pulse racing,

However, the confrontation was to be interrupted, unwittingly, by two more arrivals … the property's owners, Wayne and Lisa Benson.

Lisa was the first to speak. "Sorry to keep you all waiting. We were held up because Wayne needed a quick check-up at the hospital and it took a bit longer than we expected," she said. "But at least you've all had a chance to meet and have a chat."

April then said: "Hello, Lisa. Yes, we have all met, though we haven't been properly introduced yet."

"Well," said Lisa, turning to the stranger, "these two are April May and Ray Williams, who are both local estate agents. "And this," she continued, pointing towards the stranger, is "Theo Salter. I dare say you have heard something about him by now."

"We certainly have," April replied, clearly impressed. "However, I have a horrible feeling that his act of heroism has put all the rest of us out of the running when it comes to the sale of Aggammenmon Hall."

Lisa looked embarrassed, and Wayne, who was positively sheepish, said to Salter's competitors: "Sorry about this, but we are talking about a man who has saved my life."

Nobody noticed that he could not look Williams in the eye. Lisa then added: "I'm sure everyone will understand how we are indebted to Mr Salter, and putting a slice of business his way seems to be the very least we can do." April, resigned to the fact that this just was not her day, admitted ruefully that she would probably do the same in their position.

Ray Williams looked less resigned. But he said nothing.

CHAPTER 5

INTEREST IN THE ANNUAL two-day cricket match between the local estate agents and the bank and building society personnel was as strong as ever.

Word had quickly spread that Wayne Benson would not be playing this year. Not surprisingly, his illustrious sporting past, and to some extent his colourful lifestyle, made him a major crowd-puller.

Yet his absence made little difference. The teams had been announced and everyone knew who was to be his replacement. The agents' line-up was to include a new local hero and man of mystery rolled into one, and the spectators were eager to get a sight of him

Nathan Pike, the agents' captain, was in a flat spin, though. A man who both thrived and suffered from living on his nerves, he fretted over the loss of both Benson and his star bowler, Phil Brown. Wayne Benson, a swashbuckling former Test Match batsman who could also bowl a bit, represented the team's best chance of winning. Phil Brown, who could test any club batsman with his nagging medium pace, had just left the area.

Pike himself and Reg Pinkerton were both fine batsmen who had, in the past, represented their public school teams with distinction. George Bowes and Rob Ward, of Bowes & Ward, were outstanding all-round sportsmen, too, though cricket was not their forte. They could, however, be expected to make some sort of contribution with both bat and ball.

The erratic Barny Kentford had been known to knock up a quick 20 or 30 on occasion … and then there was Theo Salter, an unknown quantity who had at least said he had played cricket at club level. The others were basically there to make up the numbers and there was no escaping the fact that Wayne Benson, when playing, could counter the banks and building societies' advantage of having more people to draw on when it came to making up a team.

With a sigh, Nathan Pike jotted down his batting line-up on a memo pad. It read: 1 N Pike, 2 R Pinkerton, 3 G Bowes, 4 R Ward, 5 B Kentford, 6 P Phelan (placed high in the batting because of his seniority in the estate agency world), 7 T Salter, 8 I Gathercole, 9 B Ratcliffe, 10 L Hatcher, 11 E. Knight. The inclusion of Evelyn Knight made him wince.

He took another look out of the pavilion window and saw that spectators, who had arrived in ones, twos and threes two hours before start of play, were entering the Camford Cricket Club ground in a steady stream.

Now there was just over half an hour to go.

"Well, at least the whole team has turned up in time," he said aloud in an attempt to console himself. "Most of them are even wearing whites!"

The notable exceptions were the flamboyant but un-athletic Ratcliffe and Hatcher and the notorious Evelyn Knight. Even Theo Salter had managed to rustle up the right kit, thanks to several offers of help.

The agents' team was still sartorially inferior to the banks and building societies line- up. The latter also included fewer "rabbits" and only one team member, a young woman, was not attired in the traditional manner.

Nathan Pike then reminded himself that the situation he found himself in was far less serious than his predicament a few months ago when gambling debts nearly led to him having his legs broken. Even Wayne Benson would be unnerved by that … Nathan went downstairs to the dressing room to talk to the team and discuss tactics, field placings, who would bowl and who were the opposition's "danger men."

Most of the team knew already that the agents would bat first if the skipper won the toss. The pitch could be pacey at the outset but tended to crumble quickly and suit the opposition's formidable spin bowling attack … or, to be precise, the wiles of Joyce Turner … later on.

Nathan's players seemed to be more in the mood for carousing than taking part in a competitive event. Banter was rife from all directions, with newcomer Salter playing more than a small part in the jocularity. Theo was getting on particularly well with the muscular George Bowes and the podgy Bernie Ratcliffe. Several of the team mates were, with ribaldry, speculating on how they would get to know Evelyn Knight, who was sitting demurely outside wearing alarmingly tight ski pants.

Not long after Nathan had somehow managed to get his team's attention and offer a few words that he hoped would be meaningful, it was time to spin the coin.

Nathan and his opposite number Lance Perry stepped out into the middle to perform the annual ritual in public, and Nathan duly won the toss and said the estate agents would bat first. An announcement to this effect was made on a loud-hailer.

By now, the ground was almost full and a buzz of expectation could be heard from around its edges. The sun had begun to bathe the lush green cricket field and its surrounds, and just one corner, furthest from the pavilion, was still under shadows. The emergence from the pavilion of the fielding side was greeted with sustained applause, which was amplified when Nathan Pike and Reg Pinkerton appeared and made their way to the stumps.

Pike and Pinkerton, along with the absent Benson, were the undoubted perennial stars among the estate agents. As an opening pair, the two ex-public schoolboys, with their classical batting strokes, could almost invariably give their side a good start … not to mention provide an incentive for cricket fans to arrive early. With no back-up from Benson this year, a sound opening partnership was more important than ever.

As expected, the bank clerk Neil Thomas opened the bowling.

A dour opening batsman and accurate medium-fast bowler, Thomas was another key performer. As a bowler, he was particularly dangerous early on, because of his ability to induce false strokes from a batsman before he got his eye in.

Aware of the importance of a good opening stand, Pike was more watchful than ever and made no attempt to attack during the first over which was a maiden. Bowling from the other end was another bank clerk, William "Woody" Allen, a different proposition altogether, who relied on sheer speed. He was fast by any standards. But he was erratic and potentially expensive, too, and was often removed from the bowling attack after just three overs if conceding a lot of runs.

His first delivery, to Reg Pinkerton, was wide, bounced high and flew past the wicket-keeper for four byes. A couple of balls later, Pinkerton stroked a ball that fell slightly short outside off stump for four. The last ball of the over was slightly short, too, and Pinkerton clipped it off his legs for a single.

The second over from Thomas conceded two runs from Pinkerton's bat. The score was 11 for no wicket.

Nathan Pike, still to get off the mark, prepared to face his first ball from "Woody" It was a bouncer, and Nathan needed to duck. Allen tried to repeat this delivery. But this time it was shorter and failed to lift so much and the batsman caressed the ball to the boundary with a perfectly time cover drive. Allen's next ball was slightly slower, and it kept low. Nathan, anticipating it beautifully, drove it majestically past the bowler for another four. Two more runs followed via a clever nudge past third man.

Just one ball in the fourth over to go, and the score was 21-0. A perfect start appeared to be on the cards.

By now, Allen was angry. One more sloppy delivery, and he knew he would be taken off early ... even perhaps after just two overs.

He added two extra strides to his run-up, charged in at express pace and pitched the ball slightly short on the leg side. As Nathan shaped up to hook, the ball reared up to head height and in towards the batsman without warning. Nathan could only "shoulder arms" and see the ball, flying off a glove and into the slips where Joyce Turner took an athletic diving catch.

Reg Pinkerton, now joined by the former rugby professional George Bowes, played the next over, another maiden, from Thomas watchfully, and at the other end Bowes smashed a four and a six off Allen.

Pinkerton's containment of Thomas continued at one end, while the muscular Bowes hammered the hapless Allen, whose bowling duties were taken over by skipper Perry.

Before long, the score stood at a healthy 67-1, with Bowes on 40. Then disaster struck. Medium pacer Perry, chauvinist though he was, gave way to Joyce Turner. Perry's bowling had proved innocuous and only Thomas had been able to stem the flow of runs.

Joyce Turner, a humble building society clerk during office hours, was an outstanding all-round athlete outside them. Her achievements on the football field and tennis court were especially well known.

Today, it was her solid middle order batting and mesmerising leg spin bowling that were to the fore.

Bowes, no mean sportsman himself, shaped up to her first delivery with confidence. Pitched high and slow, the ball seemed to hang in the air for several seconds before landing on the leg side of the wicket and spinning towards off so alarmingly that it missed the wicket-keeper and slips for two byes. The second ball was slightly quicker and straighter. Bowes misjudged its line completely and turned to see his stumps clattered. The score was 69-2.

Bowes' business partner Rob Ward, a one-time Formula 2 racing driver who still indulged in rally driving, was next to take strike. Although smaller in stature than Bowes, he possessed similar athletic ability and rarely failed to make a contribution with either bat or ball. Today was not his day, though. Another delivery, pitched high outside leg stump, spun in sharply, found the edge of the bat and flew to silly mid-off.

So in came Barny Kentford, intent on stopping a hat-trick. There was only one way he knew how, and that was to hit the bowling attack out of sight. His adversary, well aware of such intent, placed her fielders accordingly and got a mistimed drive to find safe hands at extra cover.

Next up was Paul Phelan. A competent golfer and ardent cricket lover, he could never recognise that his talent with the bat nowhere near matched his aspirations. Now semi-retired and leaving most of his estate agency duties to the much younger Ian Gathercole, he was generally considered a bit past it anyway. Yet somehow his up-market estate agency record, combined with an aristocratic bearing, had led to the belief that he should be no lower than No 6 in any batting line-up!

The last ball of Joyce Turner's first over was straight and low and hardly spun at all. Phelan lunged forward to make a forward defensive push and patted the balled upwards and into the bowler's waiting hands.

Four wickets had gone in a matter of minutes and suddenly the score stood at a perilous 69-5. However, groans over Phelan's latest failure soon gave way to buzzes of expectation from the crowd as Theo emerged from the pavilion.

The epic rescue of Wayne Benson from a watery grave had been heard about all round town by now. And rumours were beginning to abound that the new local hero had, in addition, saved a lady in distress and seen off a well known local villain. Were there more heroics afoot? This time on the cricket field?

Theo Salter's stride to the crease gave no hint of anything but confidence. Earlier on, there had been a few butterflies. But Theo knew he was on a roll, that he could do nothing wrong that day, and he was determined to go with the flow as long as he could. He did listen carefully to Nathan Pike's advice, a little earlier, on how a batsman should tackle the spin of Joyce Turner. The directive from Reg Pinkerton, on his arrival at the wicket, was more to the point: "For Christ's sake, stay in while I make a few runs!" Theo was told. Pinkerton, who was then on strike, made his intentions clear by smiting one boundary from a shorter ball from Thomas and then taking a single from the last ball of his over.

Pinkerton's policy of shielding Theo from virtually all the bowling continued for 20 minutes and the score moved up to 81-5. However, the inevitable eventually came with Theo having to face a full over from Turner's spin.

The first ball, pitched well outside the off stump, spun into the middle alarmingly and Theo was hard put to block it out. The second ball was a little quicker and straighter, the third, given more air but still comparatively straight. The fourth had more bounce in it, and spun viciously the other way, while the fifth was more or less a repetition of the first. Theo, who managed to cope with all these deliveries by employing a watchful defence, then saw that the final ball of the over was a little shorter than the others, and he was able to step out of his crease and smite it to the leg-side boundary. The crowd roared in approval and Pinkerton gave the sort of smile and nod that acknowledged a partner who could be trusted to share the batting workload.

As time went by, the opposition's two key bowlers began to tire and had to be rested. The two batsmen's confidence grew and the runs became more plentiful. The partnership put on 120 before Theo was caught behind the wicket for 52, bamboozled at last by a "doozra" from the returning Joyce Turner. Reg Pinkerton went on to make a dashing, undefeated 145 out of a total of 280. The rest of the batting folded quickly, though, and was noteworthy only for its ineptness. The innings ended with the arrival amid wolf whistles of Evelyn Knight and the clattering of her wicket first ball. Overall, this was one of the most exciting fixtures between the two sides for years, nonetheless, and the result could still go either way. The estate agents' total of 280 looked healthy enough but the banks and building societies' batting line-up had a much more solid look about it, and the agents' bowling attack relied too heavily on Pike and Pinkerton. Just 30 minutes remained for play on the first day, during which time Ian Shawcross, a building society bank manager and stylish left-handed batsman, and the more dour but ever dependable bank clerk, Neil Thomas, scored 18 without loss. The batting line-up read: 1 I Shawcross, 2 N Thomas, 3 P Green, 4 L Perry (capain), 5 T Catchpole, 6 W Allen, 7 J Turner, 8 P Smith, 9 J Needham, 10 J Clegg, 11 D Black.

Only Diane Black, who was Paul Green's secretary, could be considered a true "rabbit." Day Two was awaited with keen anticipation by players and spectators alike. For the players, there was the traditional carousing session when members of both sides congregated around the pavilion bar. However, the two captains, especially the punctilious Perry, reminded all concerned that it was important to be in a fit condition to play the next day and that the drinking should not get out of hand.

Theo was keen to get back to his new abode, where the attractions of Kelly exceeded those offered by liquor! So, along with fitness fanatic George Bowes, he left after downing just a half of bitter.

The flat was about 20 minutes walk away and, as George lived in the same direction, the pair made their way together along a route which consisted mainly of narrow streets and short, cobbled alleyways.

After about 10 minutes, Theo and George turned down an unusually narrow lane flanked by tall terraced houses that made it abnormally dark.

All of a sudden, the pair could hear raised voices and scuffling noises, and then they saw two large human shapes. As they drew closer, they could see that one man was pinning another against a wall and was about to strike him with a raised fist.

Then a lisp-laced voice could be heard, and Theo recognised it instantly.

"It's about time you realised that a deal is a deal, and that if you welsh on it there's a price to pay!"

The man pinned against the wall was Wayne Benson and he was half doubled over and gasping for breath, as if he had just been punched in the stomach.

"Oi!" The interruption came from George Bowes. Williams loosened his grip on Benson and turned round. He eyed his squat, powerfully built estate agency rival Bowes, and then the athletic-looking Salter. "You again!" he said, the voice high-pitched and the lisp more pronounced than ever. "It seems to me that there's more than one person I'm going to be having unfinished business with ... and sooner or later, you are going to be on your own!"

Williams then released his grip on Benson entirely and half-walked, half-ran towards a busier street.

Theo and George both considered, for a moment, pursuing Williams and demanding to know what was going on. But instead they turned to Wayne Benson. "Are you all right, Wayne? What was that all about?" asked George Bowes. Wayne managed to regain some of his composure, though he was not able to look either of his rescuers in the eye. "I'm sorry, I can't tell you, I really can't," he sighed. "I am glad to see you, though, believe me!"

CHAPTER 6

NATHAN PIKE CONTINUED TO FRET.

The 280 runs posted by his side looked pretty healthy on the face of it. However, the problem was how to stop the opposition surpassing that figure without Phil Brown or Wayne Benson.

Phil Brown's medium pace bowling was so accurate and probed for mistakes so unerringly that he had become known as the Glenn McGrath of Camford.

Wayne Benson's leg spin tended to be too expensive to be employed to any great extent in Test matches. But it was highly effective at club level, and had bamboozled many a batsman in previous years. Now Nathan was going to have to rely on George Bowes, Rob Ward, Reg Pinkerton and himself, with possible back-up from the erratic Barny Kentford and from Theo Salter, an unknown quantity.

Nathan felt he had no option but to turn to Bowes and Ward to open the bowling on Day Two, despite the fact that Ian Shawcross and Neil Thomas had made them look innocuous during the closing 30 minutes of Day One.

Bowes, a former hooker in his county's rugby team, could bowl at a brisk pace but his line and length were often faulty, enabling opposing batsmen to simply block his deliveries until the inevitable loose one came along ... which it did at least once an over.

Ward bowled at little more than medium pace and, although more accurate than Bowes, lacked the penetration to unduly trouble good club batsmen. Before long, the scoreboard showed 50 runs without loss. It was time to make changes.

Nathan decided to take a chance with Kentford at one end and the slow left arm deliveries of Pinkerton at the other. Kentford's bowling was, if nothing else, genuinely fast.

His first ball to Shawcross reared up to an alarming height and flew past both the batsman's head and the wicket keeper to hit the boundary fence. The second ball was a wide. The third was short and to the leg side, and Shawcross cracked it to the square leg boundary. Ball number four was well outside off stump, and Shawcross simply left it. Number five was short and just outside off stump, and the batsman was able to caress the ball through the covers for another two.

The score was now 57-0. The final ball of the over was straighter than the others and bounced higher than expected. This led to a lofted drive and Bowes, sprinting round the edge of the boundary, held a spectacular running catch. It was now 56-1 and Nathan's spirits rose. However, the new batsman, Paul Green, a bank manager, quickly showed an appetite for Kentford's bowling and smote a succession of fours in all directions. Pinkerton was less expensive but never threatened.

Nathan came on himself for a few overs of medium pace but made no impression. Bowes and Ward were brought back but only Bowes looked remotely threatening. When the dour Neil Thomas added to his tally of singles and brought the banks and building societies' score to 100-1, Nathan Pike decided there was nothing for it but to relieve Ward of the ball and hand it to Salter. "Perhaps you could find a way of separating this pair of buggers," he said to Theo despairingly.

The latter grinned: "I'll do what I can." Unknown to his skipper, Theo was highly experienced at club level and his bowling could strike terror into the opposition.

All his deliveries were brisk. Some were fast, seriously fast. In addition, he could produce a ball that could bounce steeply or rear up at an angle and strike the batsman's hand or rib cage. There were occasions, though, when his bowling was off-line or length and therefore expensive. But Theo was still far more accurate and consistent than Barny Kentford.

The first ball, a loosener, was slightly short and offside and Thomas pushed it away easily for a single.

Ball number two was close to express pace. It was pitched well up and flew off the bat as Green tried to cope with the sudden extra bounce, and sped to the boundary. The next ball landed on knuckles, and Green was forced to drop his bat and wince with pain.

A moment's pause followed, after which Theo sent down a delivery that was slower but straight. Green was just able to block it, and, still feeling pain in his hand, somehow saw through the over.

Theo started his second over with a ball that was slightly short and reared up menacingly. A clearly disconcerted Green ducked for cover. Then came a fast full toss, which should have been stroked through the covers for four. But Green's defence had become so disorganised that he backed away and trod on the stumps behind him. It was now 109-2.

The hapless banker was replaced by Lance Perry, deputy manager of the Camford Building Society, skipper and arguably the team's star player. In the past, many a winning partnership had been forged by the bats of Perry and Thomas … with Thomas dropping anchor while Perry produced an exhibition of thrilling strokeplay. Perry's arrival at the crease was greeted with a bouncer, which the batsman avoided easily by swaying backwards. Perry had studied his adversary carefully from the pavilion and decided to bat cautiously at the outset.

The run rate almost ground to a halt for four overs before Perry started to play his natural attacking game. The much more cautious Thomas was able to pick off some loose deliveries from the tiring bowlers, too.

Theo Salter was a player who liked to bowl in short, explosive bursts. He could be expensive if kept on for too long at a time, and this was beginning to prove to be the case now.

Ward replaced Bowes, but he, too, was conceding more and more runs. Before long, the banks and building societies' total was just short of 150 and Nathan Pike had no option but to make changes again. Bowes came back, as did the skipper and Kentford, and Reg Pinkerton bowled a few overs of slow left arm. But only Bowes looked even remotely likely to make the much needed breakthrough.

The 200 mark was passed when Perry produced a glorious cover drive off the wayward Kentford. Perry's score now stood at 115, with Thomas on 46. Nathan Pike was beginning to reach his wit's end. "Perhaps it's time to give Salter another go," he mused.

And, at that very moment, there was Theo Salter standing in front of him so close that he almost reading on his feet.

"Let me have another crack. I've got my second wind now, and I'm sure I can sort this pair out," Theo said waving his hand towards the two batsmen. His whispered tone was persuasive to the point of implying: "Ignore my wish if you dare!"

Nathan stepped back a pace and sighed. "Why not?" he replied after a pause. "Why not?" Theo did not wait to be given the ball. He simply plucked it out of Nathan's hand.

The first ball of his first new spell was straight, short and little more than medium pace. But the ball bounced unexpectedly steeply and nearly found an edge to Thomas's bat. "Good grief!" Pike said to himself. "Why didn't I think of that before…?"

The estate agents' skipper recalled how five years ago the groundsman had been beset by health problems and had not prepared the pitch so thoroughly as usual. On that occasion, rough patches had appeared in several places on the second day and led to bowlers producing startlingly bouncy deliveries. Yet nobody had seemed to notice that this was happening again. Nobody apart from Theo Salter … Theo could see that there was a patch just over halfway down the pitch, along with another outside off stump and yet another to the leg. He could feel the surge of newly-found adrenaline.

His second ball was the fastest of the day. It landed on the patch just outside the off stump, reared up to neck height and swung inwards. Even Thomas was flustered, producing a rare streaky short to the boundary just past third man.

Then a bouncer threatened to decapitate the startled batsman … whose stumps were clattered by an in-swinging yorker the next ball. The score was now 218-3 … just 62 behind but with batting looking increasingly difficult.

The next man in was Tim Catchpole, a competent club cricketer but nowhere near as talented as Lance Perry, who now had strike and had no difficulty in dealing with an over from Bowes and added six more runs to the total.

The first ball of Theo's second over was fast and pitched outside leg stump. It induced a streaky shot from Catchpole but shot out of the reach of fielders and earned him four lucky runs. However, Catchpole was unable to cope with the bowler's pace and the inconsistent bounce and the fifth ball, which was straight and kept low, trapped him lbw. 228 for 4.

Next up was "Woody" Allen, whose whole attitude to cricket could be summed up in one word … attack.

Allen had already seen what was happening to the pitch, and was more determined that ever to take on the bowling.

Delivery number six of Theo's second over was pitched outside leg stump. As the ball reared upwards, Allen swung the bat with all his might and lofted the ball over the leg side boundary for six. Sensing danger for his team, Perry decided to be more aggressive, too, smiting two fours in the next over from Bowes and then getting a quick single to give himself the strike against Salter … and protect his partner.

It was now 243-4, and the banks and building societies' team needed just 38 to win. Theo's next over yielded just two runs from the now watchful Perry. Allen followed this by smiting a four to leg off Bowes. However, a lofted drive two balls later cost him his wicket and the score line stood at 249-5. Next in was Joyce Turner, who was dependable with the bat, possessed an organised defence and had in the past forged a number of useful partnerships with Perry. The pair put on 12 careful runs in the course of five overs to put the side just 20 short of victory. Theo Salter and George Bowes were both beginning to tire. In an attempt to make scoring difficult, Ward was brought on in Bowes' place. But who could take over from Salter.

Nathan considered bringing on Barny Kentford as a

desperation measure aimed at achieving a breakthrough. "It might work," he thought to himself. "But, on the other hand, it could be a disaster... and a batsman of Perry's calibre should easily prosper by defending until the inevitable loose delivery comes along. No, that's not the answer!

After a few moment's thought, he turned to Theo and asked: "Can you keep going for just a bit longer? The situation's getting critical and I need your help."

Theo nodded. He could see that drastic measures were needed. Perry was looking composed as he waited for him. His batting had become increasingly majestic, and at this stage looked indomitable. His contribution towards the total was 164 and he was almost winning the match on his own.

Theo, with nostrils flared, thundered in to produce a ball pitched outside leg stump that reared up and smashed into Perry's elbow. Perry cried out in pain and dropped his bat, and a couple of minutes elapsed before he was ready to resume batting. Theo then produced an off side delivery that swerved into Perry's rib cage ... and caused a further stoppage. The third ball was faster than ever and hit Perry's ribs on the left hand side. Ball number four bounced off a glove and careered to the boundary fence behind. Theo then bowled a slower ball that kept low and straight, and Perry was just able to stop it hitting his stumps. But the shot lacked his usual control. The ball went down the pitch and slightly upwards and Theo ran forwards and took an athletic diving catch. The watching crowd erupted and Lance Perry was applauded all the way back to the pavilion. The excitement was then followed by silence as Paul Smith, the banks and building societies' number eight, made his way to the crease to face the final ball of Theo's over.

Smith was a competent batsman but notoriously nervous against quick bowling. Theo, a stranger to Camford, had no way of knowing this, though he could sense that he had a psychological advantage. And he had the bit between his teeth to such an extent that all feelings of fatigue had disappeared. Theo thundered in and produced a devastating Yorker that flattened all three stumps. The score was now 265-7. The match had become a genuine cliff-hanger.

The B&B side needed 16 to win with three wickets still to fall. The dependable Joyce Turner was still there and, of the three remaining batsmen, only Diane Black belonged to the "rabbit" category. On the other hand, the pitch was deteriorating and Theo Salter, the man who had burst in on the Camford scene in such dramatic fashion, was on the rampage. Meanwhile, It was Joyce Turner's turn to take strike against the economical but comparatively innocuous Ward. She was now the senior batter, and it was her responsibility to steer her side to safety. She would probably have to score most of the remaining runs and, in particular, tackle the menace of Salter. That was easier said than done. Ward, although never regarded as a front line bowler, was often able to get among the wickets when batsmen felt the need to attack. The estate agents set a defensive field. Ward bowled two balls just outside off stump, giving away nothing but inviting Turner to make a false stroke. Ball number three was much the same. But this time Joyce Turner charged down the wicket, swung the bat and smote the ball to the off side boundary.

Then, a couple of balls later, she cleverly nudged the ball slightly to the left of third man and she and her partner scampered for all they were worth for three more runs. The final ball of the over was blocked. The victory target was now just nine runs away.

Theo was now in something of a quandary. Should he send down the sort of deliveries that would "rough up" a woman? He was also tired and was not at all sure he could muster the energy to produce another successive over of such menace. After deliberating for a moment or two, he decided to reduce the pace and bounce and concentrate on accuracy. Joyce Turner still had to be watchful, though, and the over turned out to be a maiden. At the other end, John Needham managed to score two with an off side push, so that when Turner faced Theo again just seven runs were needed to win.

However, Theo was now feeling comparatively refreshed and he was able to produce a delivery that swung in at express pace from outside the off stump. The ball found the edge of the bat and the wicket-keeper took an athletic diving catch. The next man in was Jeff Clegg, no great shakes as a batsman but totally fearless and, a little like Barny Kentford, believed a cricket ball was there to be hit hard. Theo steamed in, Clegg swung his bat and missed, and the ball landed in the keeper's gloves. The next ball was loose and to the leg side, and was clear evidence of a flagging bowler. Clegg took a mighty swing, the ball sailed into the air and landed just short of the boundary. It was 278-8. Just three runs short of victory. Theo's next ball was straighter and more controlled. But Clegg was still able to crack it past cover point and start to run for a single. His luck was out, though. Joyce Turner, at the other end, hesitated, and Nathan Pike swooped in from the outfield and, in one movement, picked the ball up and threw it on to the batsman's stumps. A disconsolate Clegg skulked back to the pavilion, to be replaced by the plump, bespectacled and non-athletic Diane Black, who was Phil Green's secretary and had been drafted in to make up the numbers.

Rather unnecessarily, Nathan Pike walked up to Theo and said: "All you need is one that's on the wicket!" Theo duly obliged. He was too tired to argue, in any case! The ending was something of an anti-climax, with the ball, pitched straight and at medium pace, removing the bails as Diane Black wafted he bat as if trying to swat a fly. After a moment's silence, there was thunderous applause. Speeches were made by local dignitaries and the Mayor of Camford presented the Man of the Match award to Theo Salter.

There were those who argued afterwards that Lance Perry should have won it. A few observers had silent misgivings over Theo's tactics in unsettling batsmen. But, at the end of the day, who could ignore the new local hero?

As the players finally made their way back to the pavilion to shower and change, Bernie Ratcliffe sidled up to Theo to ask: "I trust you're going to the party tonight?" Theo, whose main thought was of returning to the arms of Kelly, replied with as much enthusiasm as he could muster: "You bet!"

CHAPTER 7

SHERRY MUNRO'S HOUSE was even more prestigious than Aggammenmon Hall. Not quite so large, perhaps, and not tucked away in such awesomely spacious grounds, but the location, in central Camford, was regarded by estate agents and anyone else connected with property as prime with a capital P.

The house, known simply as Sherry's, featured lawned gardens that sloped down towards the river at the back. Its next door neighbour, about 50 yards away, was the Exchange Hotel ... named after Camford's once prosperous corn exchange and still viewed as being almost on a social par with The Ritz in London.

Sherry was a shrewd local girl with humble origins who had made good as a pop singer and actress. She was a contemporary and great friend of Lisa Benson, who, apart from a convent school education, had much in common with her. Sherry, now in her 30s, had burst onto the pop scene with a string of hits about 10 years ago. Unlike many others in a similar situation, she had invested in property rather than squandered her gains on drugs or excessive drinking. The house named after her had been built to her specification five years ago and, not surprisingly, was seen as a monument to her success.

Almost every year, it was used as the venue for the post-cricket match party. Aggammenmon Hall had been used for this purpose once in a while in the past. But, as Lisa was forced to concede, Sherry's was a much more accessible venue and generally more suitable. Evening dress for guests at the party was optional, though, in practice, everyone considered it to be obligatory.

Wayne and Lisa Benson made sure that, as far as they could,

Theo and Kelly were both appropriately attired by referring them to Camford's most exclusive clothes hire outfitters ... and insisting on footing the bills.

So both Theo and Kelly were clad in the most expensive material possible, though Kelly's dress could be more easily described as "minimalist" rather than "appropriate."

Wayne had also loaned them his second favourite car, a Volvo, which he felt was more fitting for the occasion than his saviour's rather battered Ford Escort.

The couple arrived about an hour after the party's official starting time.

Part of a small team of security men, wholly or partially clad in luminous yellow, were standing by the tall, stained wooden gates to the front of Sherry's to greet the guests. Theo and Kelly, like the others, were directed towards a wide expanse of floodlit lawn where they could park.

A gravel path from the lawn to the pine front door was illuminated with the aid of lanterns. The door was approached via steps, a patio and a porch ... all of them marble.

On reaching the porch, Theo showed his invitation to a security man who smiled in recognition, opened the door and said "Please go in, Sir. You are most welcome." Theo was half expecting a toastmaster to be on hand to announce the arrival of "Mister Theo Salter and Miss Kelly Cheatham!" But there were no such formalities ... and, in any case, none were needed to herald the couple's arrival. The main hall, accessed via a smaller hall and a cloakroom, was half full already. It featured oak panelled walls, high beamed ceilings, massive chandeliers and a floor that resembled a giant chess board. As they entered, Theo could recognise quite a few faces.

Standing a few feet away was Nathan Pike, looking as rakish as his reputation as he puffed on a cigarette in a holder and had hanging on his arm a female companion with a backless dress and a slit down one side that revealed a long, slim leg. Nathan was part of a group of 10 youngish aristocratic men and women who were all quaffing sherry. The men all looked decidedly foppish. Just beyond this group were Evelyn Knight, who was clad entirely in black, and a male companion. Lance Perry was there, too, with Neil Thomas, Diane Black and Joyce Turner, whose sleeveless top showed her to be more muscular than most men.

Barny Kentford, Rob Ward and the portly Bernie Ratcliffe were present with partners. They were all cheerfully quaffing punch and looking close to merry already!

Before Theo and Kelly could make a beeline for anyone, Wayne Benson could be seen, half bounding, half hobbling towards them and wearing a beaming smile. "There you are!" he roared. "Come and join us." Wayne motioned the couple towards the hall's far left corner, where Lisa was standing with April May and another man and woman. "Look who I've got here," Wayne said to Lisa, on reaching the group. "Why don't you do the introductions while I go and get some punch for these two lovely people."

As Wayne marched off on his mission, Lisa flashed the sort of smile that would delight any fashion photographer, and gave both Theo and Kelly a hug. "It's great to see you both," she said. Then, turning to Theo, she added: "I hope you're feeling all right after all that's been happening. You certainly look all right, and the way you performed on the cricket field suggests that there can't be anything much wrong with you!"

Theo's eyes twinkled. "How could I feel bad after that?" he quipped.

"Anyway," said Lisa, "let me do the introductions. I would like you to meet Sherry Munro, our hostess for the evening and an old friend, and Edmund Rooker. And this," said Lisa, turning to the other member of the group, "is April …. who, of course, is already known to you, Theo."

The three women greeted both Kelly and Theo politely but formally, though all three looked at the latter speculatively. Edmund Rooker, the head of a firm of insurance brokers, as it turned out, was Sherry's latest "beau."

Sherry had had a long line of suiters, many of them regarded by friends as anything but suitable, and she had never settled with any of them for any great length of time. Edmund, grey haired and in his mid-50s, had been seeing Sherry for an almost record-breaking six months. A widower and widely respected as a businessman, he was seen as the epitome of honesty, propriety, security and respectability.

He eyed Theo a little suspiciously before saying: "I've been hearing a lot about you. You've managed to become famous in double quick time!"

"And quite rightly so!" chipped in April.

Then Sherry, smiling warmly, added: "Well, yes! It's not often that someone saves a man's life, sees off a local thug and then wins a cricket match … and all in the twinkling of an eye." Sherry's own eyes were twinkling as she made this observation.

It was not hard to see how she had managed to wow those pop fans. Short, blonde, buxom and showing plenty of cleavage, she could not fail to be noticed at any party, even though her waist line had thickened somewhat of late. Pop pundits often referred to her as the English Dolly Parton.

Lisa flashed another of those model girl smiles. She was dressed a little more conservatively than Sherry but was still able to display contours that Theo couldn't fail to notice.

The athletic looking April was comparatively dowdy in a trouser suit but, in her own way, managed to look the most devastatingly attractive of them all. She had the figure to make many a man feel weak at the knees and, although she would never admit it, made many a heart melt enough to lead to a place in her estate agency books

"The saving of Wayne is something I will never forget, as long as I live," Lisa said softly. And then she added, almost in a whisper, "not once but twice."

At this point, Wayne reappeared carrying a tray laden with drinks. "There we go!" he boomed. "But drink up fast, the band's about to get going and it's up to us to take the lead in tripping the spotlight fantastic!" Wayne then proposed a toast, among his group, to Theo. "Welcome to the local hall of fame!" he bellowed.

"We were talking about Theo's exploits just a second ago," said April. Then, with a wry smile, she added: "Lisa was highlighting the rescue in the water … though I personally think the way he dealt with that obnoxious Ray William at Aggammenmon Hall was his top deed!"

Wayne's face darkened for a moment. And then, grabbing Lisa by the hand and almost spilling her drink, he said: "Come on, love, let's carve up the dance floor!" The two disappeared through double doors the other side of the hall.

After a pause, Sherry said: "Perhaps someone should join them. Don't you agree, Edmund?" Edmund Rooker nodded and then, rather nervously, asked Kelly, who had had little opportunity to contribute to the conversation, to have a dance with him.

As the two headed off, April went back to what she had said a minute before. "You must admit I had a point about Williams, mustn't you?" she said to Sherry.

"Yes, by all accounts he's a thoroughly nasty piece of work," she agreed.

Theo then cut in, saying: "I'm curious. What exactly has he done?"

"Well," said Sherry, "nobody knows exactly but there are all sorts of rumours. And there are some things we are almost certain about but can't prove."

"Like what?" Theo asked.

"One thing we know for sure is that he likes to go around pulling down other estate agents' 'For Sale' boards," said April vehemently.

"OK," said Theo, "but he's not the first agent to have done that … and it's not exactly first degree thuggery either. There must be more than that."

"Oh, don't worry, there is," said Sherry. "There's been a lot more," said April. "And if we could prove any of it, he would be behind bars."

"Now you've got me really intrigued," said Theo.

"Well," April continued, "he's reckoned to have played every dirty trick known in the world of estate agency.

"And more besides!" added Sherry.

"Oh, do elaborate, please. I'm all ears!" Theo's interest had gone well beyond idle curiosity at this point.

April and Sherry tried to expand on what they knew, or thought they knew. Malpractices by Ray Williams had included giving misleading descriptions of properties for sale, "forgetting" to return deposits, charging higher fees than had been indicated, intimidating other estate agents and their employees, "ring fencing," money laundering and pressurising householders into vacating their premises so that he could act as agent for the builder wanting to develop the site the householder happened to live on.

"That's quite a list," Theo admitted. "Williams is a thug all right but how can you be sure that even half of what you have just said is true?" he asked.

"OK, let's start with the ring fencing bit," said April. "A couple of years ago, a friend of a friend who lived at the other end of the country inherited a house a few miles outside Camford and asked Williams to put it on to the market for her. She did not know the area and knew nothing about Williams. He just happened to be the first estate agent she came across when she come over to sort this all out. And she was too naïve to think about making any checks on him or seeing what terms any other agent might have to offer.

"Williams said he would handle the property but he made no attempt to publicise its availability. A handful of prospective buyers called in on him and expressed interest. But, on each occasion, Williams was able to deter them from taking the matter any further by falsely implying that there were major structural defects.

"Nothing was ever committed to paper, though, and all this happened while this poor woman ... Mrs Violet Emmington was her name if I remember correctly ... was waiting to hear about news of a sale from somewhere like Northumberland. Eventually Williams told his hapless client that he had found a buyer with great difficulty but could only secure a sale by drastically reducing the price.

"The sale went through and it was not until several months later that Mrs Emmington learned that the buyer was, in fact, one of Williams' shady associates. And, by then, the property had been re-sold at a thumping profit.

"Mrs Emmington was understandably furious but she was an

elderly widow with failing health and did not have the will or energy to take the matter further. She might well have been afraid of Williams, too, though that's something we will never know because she died not long afterwards."

Now it was Sherry's turn to chip in. "The money laundering episode is even harder to prove but the rumours are so strong that they won't go away," she said.

Then, just as Sherry was about to go into detail, Nathan Pike loomed behind her and tapped her shoulder.

Nathan grinned rakishly at Theo and, after welcoming him to the "annual cricket bash", said: "I suppose it's inevitable that the hero of the hour is going to be with the two most attractive women present. However, I'm here to break it all up, old boy. I would like to have a dance with our esteemed hostess. I hope you don't mind." And, without further ado, Nathan propelled Sherry towards the ballroom.

"Perhaps that's the cue for you and I to have a dance?" April suggested after a moment.

"That'll be my pleasure," said Theo, and the pair duly followed suit.

The ballroom was similarly designed to the main hall, though it was slightly smaller and had a stage-cum-bandstand at one end. A four-piece band was playing traditional dance music and about a dozen couples were on the floor. The music was soft, the light half off and the atmosphere intimate.

Theo looked out to see if Kelly was all right and was surprised to notice how well she seemed to be getting on with her staid companion. Not only did the conversation appear to be animated; the pair even appeared to be flirting!

April interrupted his train of thought. "We've done a lot of talking about Ray Williams but none about you," she said as they took to the floor. "Yet none of us here really knows anything about you."

"Oh, there's nothing to tell really. I'm just boring and ordinary," Theo said, tongue in cheek.

"Now, come on! You're anything but boring," April said,

looking him in the eye. "I want to see the real Mr Theodor Salter stand up!" she smiled.

"It's not Theodor, it's Theobald," Theo replied with mock indignation. "My full name is Gustav Theobald Salter. But, for some reason, nobody has ever called me Gustav since I was a toddler. That's absolutely fascinating, don't you think?!" he chuckled. "Anyway, what about YOUR name. April May can't be for real, can it?"

"That would be telling!" April replied playfully, while squeezing Theo's arm.

"Well," retorted Theo, "if you're going to keep the truth from me, there's nothing for it but for me to call you November December until you come clean!"

April pressed her body against his. "OK," she whispered." It's Alison Joyce McCardle, and I simply chose the name April May to attract business. And then she slid her hand along the front of Theo's trousers and felt his crutch.

At almost the same moment, the music stopped and a voice from the bandstand could be heard saying: "Now it's time for a gentleman's excuse me dance." A big hairy hand tapped Theo on the shoulder and its owner, Wayne bellowed in his ear: "How about a straight swap, my friend?" Wayne proceeded to push Theo towards Lisa and take April in a dance hold before anyone could express assent or dissent. The music re-started, and Theo noticed out of the corner of one eye that Kelly was still dancing with Edmund.

"Sorry about that," said Lisa, "but that's my husband all over. Big, generous, often brilliant, often stupid, often flamboyant and now and again putting his size twelve foot in it!"

"Don't apologise on my account, it's my pleasure," Theo replied. It was not unduly difficult for him to sound convincing! "Wayne strikes me as a great character ... even greater than how he's portrayed in the press." Then he added, a little more seriously: "However, I can imagine that a larger than life character like him could get into a bit of trouble now and then ... couldn't he?"

Lisa sighed. "Oh yes, I'm afraid that's true. He's been in debt and he's made a mess of some of the tasks he has been given to perform as a local councillor ... and he's been mixed up with Williams!"

"Has he now?" responded Theo. "I can imagine that being quite a recipe for trouble."

"Oh yes," said Lisa. "You've met Nathan Pike, haven't you? Yes, of course you have! Well, one of the worst kept local secrets is that Nathan once spent a night playing poker with Williams and a couple of his friends, and ended up owing Williams thousands ... some have said it was tens of thousands. There was a strong suspicion that Williams had cheated, and, at first, Nathan refused to pay up. But a couple of days later, he received a visit from a pair of local hoodlums who asked him if he would like to have his legs broken.

"Nathan is well known in these parts for his love of gambling on the horses and anything else he thinks might be worth betting on ... and equally for wine, women and song. But luckily he has plenty of wealthy friends and relatives ... and someone was able to bale him out."

Theo then asked: "Are you about to tell me that Wayne has had similar problems with Williams?"

"Yes, I'm afraid he has, said Lisa almost tearfully. "Not with cards, though, but with a scam involving Williams and a shady builder, and I don't know all the details."

"Who was the builder?" Theo asked. "I have had dealings with a few in my time and it's possible that I might know him, or at least something about him."

Lisa hesitated for a moment and then said: "I think the name's McAvie. Yes, that's it, McAvie. Sean McAvie."

Theo felt a chill down his spine.

"Do you know him?" Lisa asked.

"Hmm! The name rings a bell," Theo replied gravely.

The music stopped again. Wayne Benson reappeared, closely followed by Bernie Ratcliffe.

"Now then, my friend," Wayne said, placing his hand on Theo's shoulder, "you haven't seen the games room yet, have you?

Bernie and I are just about to play a spot of billiards and have a quick tipple and you must, of course, join us."

Theo, who would have far preferred to continue dancing with Lisa, replied: "That sounds fun but I'm not much cop at billiards."

But Bernie, who was arguably even louder in his ways than Wayne, countered: "That's no problem. You'll be with the best tutors in Camford ... and we're not bad at billiards either!"

Lisa squeezed Theo's hand and kissed him lightly on the cheek, saying: "You go ahead and have your game. There are one or two things I need to discuss with Sherry."

Lisa glided away towards the main hall. Wayne motioned Theo and Bernie towards a polished mahogany door that led to oak wood steps and a small, blue wallpapered room on the first floor. The room housed a small bar, a few easy chairs and a brand new billiard table

"Right! First things first!" Wayne said as he went behind the bar. "How about some good old fashioned neat Scotch, gentlemen?"

Then, without waiting for an answer, he poured some whisky into three glasses and handed two of the glasses over.

"Here's to us!" said Bernie. "And here's to good cricket, good whisky, good billiards, good women and, above all, good friends," he bellowed.

"And that especially means you, Theo," Wayne added smiling.

Theo smiled, too, though he felt an urge to ask Wayne about his troubles with Williams. Before he could do so, Wayne and Bernie were brandishing billiard cues and urging him to drink up and play. Theo was telling the truth when he said billiards was not his game and he was beaten all ends up. Wayne was competent at any sport or game that involved the use of any kind of ball, while the far from athletic Bernie turned out to be a maestro with the cue.

After what seemed to be almost an eternity, but was, in fact, just under an hour, Theo made an excuse to extricate himself.

"I need to see if Kelly's all right," he told his two new friends.

CHAPTER 8

THEO RETURNED TO THE BALLROOM, which was now packed.

The band was performing with panache and the party guests dancing with gusto. Sherry was bopping away with Nathan, as were most of the cricketers and their partners. April May was gyrating athletically with the more sedate Lance Perry. Evelyn Knight was shimmying sensuously with her much older-looking male companion. Theo had heard on the grapevine that the Knights estate agency office doors were frequently closed because of a tryst she was having with a leading local councillor and businessman. But there was no sign of Kelly, or of Edmund Rooker.

Theo threaded his way through the dancing couples, hoping to catch sight of Kelly's slim but shapely form, and made his way back to the main hall.

The hall was almost full, too. Three long tables, all laden with mouth-watering buffet food, were now lined up along one of the walls. Wine waiters and waitresses were moving around ceaselessly in their quest to keep glasses topped up and guests satisfied. Laughter filled the air, and the conversation was deafening.

A number of guests tried to stop Theo and engage his attention for long periods as he continued his search, and Theo needed all his wit in eluding them without causing offence. But Kelly and Edmund were nowhere to be seen. Sherry suddenly loomed in front of him to anxiously ask if he had seen Edmund. Theo could only shake his head. By this point, he was seriously concerned.

"What on earth can have become of her?" he wondered. Kelly was a quiet, shy, somewhat clingy person, who tended to get out of depth in conversations … and was never away from his side for any great length of time.

Theo walked round the side of the main hall and eventually noticed a door that led to a library. Three revellers were in there, holding glasses and plates of food. A little later, he came upon a small study. A couple were canoodling inside. Then he went back to the small hall, through which he and Kelly had originally entered, and finally went outside.

Theo was almost in a state of panic by now. A few couples could be seen strolling in the gardens, and Theo walked all round the house and covered almost every blade of grass. Then he went to the car park and saw that the Volvo he had driven to the party was still there.

Theo went back inside. On entering the main hall again, he espied Sherry and asked if she had yet seen Kelly or Edmund.

"No, and I've looked all around the house," she replied. "Unfortunately I have spent more than enough time doing that and I really must attend to the other guests."

Theo promised to let her know if his search bore fruit. He went back outside and told a security man he was temporarily leaving the premises to look for his lady companion.

Music and merriment could be heard from within Sherry's from quite a distance. The sound gradually faded as he walked away from it, though, and eventually little could be heard save running water from the river and a hedgehog scurrying for cover.

Theo walked along the river toe path for a while. He ducked to get under a narrow footbridge and, just after he did so, the river and path turned sharply to the right. A minute later, the Exchange Hotel came into view. It was massive and dominated the skyline.

Theo was so enthralled by how imposing it was that he forgot his anxiety about Kelly for a moment. The hotel's majesty also contrived to muffle the sound of footsteps a few feet away. After a few seconds, he put his hands up to his eyes and took a long, hard look around. Then, as he approached the hotel, he passed a massive oak tree.

A second after, that, Theo grunted as something heavy

descended on the back of his neck. As he fell to his knees, a huge fist crunched into his jaw.

Theo could only see stars as he lay on the ground. He felt a kick that just missed his groin, and then another in the small of his back … and another just above his left eye. Theo found enough presence of mind to roll himself into a ball to protect his head and genitals as far as possible.

But three pairs of heavy boots continued to sink into his ribs, back, stomach and anything else they could find. Thump…. thump … thump … thump! The pain was excruciating and there was no knowing when the torment was going to end. Eventually Theo thought he heard the sound of someone shouting "Oi!" in the distance. But it was at this point that he lost consciousness.

CHAPTER 9

IT WAS THREE O'CLOCK In the morning, and Mary Groves was having another disturbed night. Tap! Tap! Tap!

The sound of something like a broom handle being tapped on the floor of the room directly above her could be heard again. A minute later, a heavy item of furniture was being dragged across the same room.

Silence followed for about a quarter of an hour before an alarm clock bell sounded. And there were heavy footsteps. Mrs Groves lay there wondering if that was the end of it for that night, or whether there was more to follow. Sometimes there was, sometimes there wasn't. Occasionally, though not very often, there was no disturbance at all. By now, she was beginning to wish she had accepted that out-of-the-blue offer to quit her home. By now, everyone had moved out apart from Mrs Groves. The young couple who once occupied the flat above had quit three months ago.

Benson Lane was now empty ... save Mrs Groves's flat and the one above, where the mysterious Drummond now lived

Benson Lane was a cul-de-sac containing just 12 houses. It was reached via Benson Street and was part of a leafy suburb on Camford's southern outskirts. Benson Lane and Benson Street were, of course, named after the celebrated Wayne Benson.

Mrs Groves was 70, single following an acrimonious divorce 10 years ago, and was now beset with arthritis in one knee and a catalogue of mental health problems that included bouts of depression. Her problems were known to doctors but not considered serious enough to warrant hospital treatment. She had a stubborn streak, too, and had resolved that nothing would part her from her flat. It was all she had.

She had not seen her estranged husband for more then five years, she rarely saw her grown up son and had just two casual friends. She had even lost her beloved cat as a result of a recent road accident.

Ownership of the Benson Lane properties, which were all rented out, had changed hands within the last year. The new owner had secured planning consent to replace the flats and some redundant land into a development consisting of an up-market hotel, restaurant, casino and a block of prestigious apartments and penthouses. Chairing the council's planning committee at the time was Wayne Benson.

However, the existing properties had to be vacated before any redevelopment work was allowed to begin. Over the last 12 months, 11 of the 12 houses, many of them split into ground and first floor flats, had become empty. Some of the occupants, who were bound by six-month tenancy agreements, were leaving anyway. The others had been offered financial inducements.

Two months ago, there were two people living in Benson Lane... Mary Groves and a semi-retired odd job man, whose name, George Wimpey, had caused Mrs Groves much amusement. Mary Groves lived halfway down Benson Lane, while George Wimpey, a confirmed bachelor, had occupied a house at the far end, on the other side.

The pair had both tended to keep to themselves, and it was only when the exodus from Benson Lane was well advanced that they had had anything much to do with each other.

However, as the visits to their homes from representatives of MAC Developments increased in number, with the representatives becoming increasingly pushy, Mary Groves and George Wimpey forged an alliance, a bond. As time went on, the pushiness was accompanied by hints of menace.

"The area's becoming more and more rundown and deserted ... and it's so dimly lit. Surely there MUST be somewhere else where you're likely to feel SAFER at night!" a MAC man once suggested. His pinstripe suit did little to offset the impression given by an ugly scar that a moustache could only partly conceal.

"There's been a spate of break-ins in the area lately. What would you DO if you were confronted by a burglar in your hall?" a burly man in a sky blue suit and with a broken nose asked on another occasion.

"I can't help NOTICING that Benson Lane is getting more and more holes and cracks in both the road and pavement. Someone's BOUND to have an accident one day," the pinstripe-wearer once said. However, the pressure put on Mary Groves and George Wimpey only served to make them more resolute in their desire to stay put. "We won't be bullied," Mary would say to George. "If they think they can get their way by putting us under duress, then they've got another think coming!" her neighbour agreed.

Then, two months ago, George Wimpey suddenly capitulated. The pinstripe-wearer and the sky blue-suited man appeared on his doorstep together one day. The pinstripe-wearer pulled a photograph out of a big brown envelope and showed it to George Wimpey as soon as he opened his front door. The burly sky blue suit-wearer pushed Wimpey backwards into the hall. The two callers entered the property and pulled the door to. Mary Groves could only guess what was then said. George Wimpey left Benson Lane the same day, never to be seen again.

The following day, the two men from MAC called on Mary Groves. "I don't approve of your choice of friends," the pinstripe-wearer announced once she had opened her door. The sky blue suit-wearer waved the big brown envelope he had carried the previous day and pulled out several photographs. "Just take a look at these," he said, leering. "Don't you find them disgusting?" The pictures showed George Wimpey naked and in various uncompromising positions with various young boys.

"Absolutely DISGUSTING!" echoed the pinstripe. "Perhaps you're better off without such an unsavoury neighbour!"

"Even if it means you're all on your own in Benson Lane!" the sky blue suit added.

May Groves could feel four steely eyes boring into her. "What do you mean all on my own?" she demanded, unable to totally conceal her alarm.

"You mean he left without even saying GOODBYE?" the pinstripe asked, feigning a sense of amazement and horror. "Oh dear, oh dear, oh dear! Well, yes! It looks as if he's left in a really big hurry ... never to be seen again!" Then, after a pause, the sky blue suit said: "So now you're all on your own!" Mary Groves felt a chill down her spine, quickly followed by a surge of anger.

"Get out! Get out! Get out!" she screamed at the two men. "Get out! I don't care if I am on my own. Nothing you say and suggest is going to happen is going to make me move away from my home ... and you can both go to hell!"

After a moment's silence, the two callers looked at one another, turned round and moved quietly towards the Mercedes that they had left parked a few yards away. Mary Groves slammed the door once the car had disappeared. She was shaking and sobbing simultaneously. But she was also consumed with a feeling of pride. "That's told them!" she said to the umbrella stand in her hall.

For just over a week after that, all was quiet. The postman delivered mail to the house once, the milkman was round twice. On two occasions, Mary Groves went shopping ... once to a small corner shop some 10 minutes walk away in Benson Street, and once to a supermarket which was a short bus ride away. Most of her daylight hours were spent cleaning, dusting, hoovering and tending to her collection of potted plants. The outside of the house was beginning to show signs of wear and tear. But the inside was as clean as a new pin. Evenings were spent watching television, listening to the radio, reading or sewing.

Mrs Groves was beginning to feel able to put her confrontations with the "men from MAC" behind her. She was even entertaining the idea of stopping taking her medication for the first time in years.

Then, one evening, Derek Drummond arrived. The clock in Mary's front sitting room had just struck seven, when a taxi could be heard stopping outside. A small, ginger haired man emerged with three suitcases and three wooden boxes. Two cactus plants sat at the top of one of the boxes.

The ginger haired man handed some money to the cabbie, the taxi left, a key was produced and the front door of the property was

59

unlocked by someone other than Mary for the first time in two months.

The new arrival entered the front porch that separated Mrs Groves' flat from the one above, and the first suitcase could be heard being dragged up the stairs. Bump! Bump! Bump! Bump! A key turned in a lock at the top, a door creaked open and then a pair of heavy feet could be heard tramping on bare floorboards.

Mary Groves froze. What was she to make of all this? Why was someone appearing to move in above her at a time when nearly all the residents of Benson Lane had been persuaded or pressured into leaving? And what sort of person was her surprise new neighbour likely to turn out to be? Mary peered through her net curtains in an attempt to make an assessment.

She reckoned the man was just 5ft 5in tall … 5ft 6in at the most … and he looked compactly built. He was wearing a blue blazer, open necked white shirt, neatly pressed grey trousers and well polished brown boots. His hair was long, flaming red and striking. It had been impeccably cut and carefully combed. For one silly moment, Mary could not help observing how handsome he looked … from a bit of a distance, anyway. "Oh, if only I was 30 years younger!" she chuckled to herself. But then the feeling of unease returned. At this point, two of the three suitcases, along with the three boxes, were still sitting outside the front door. The ginger-haired man picked up another suitcase and dragged it up the stairs. Bump! Bump! Bump! Bump!

Mary Groves could hear slow, heavy, measured footsteps as the newcomer paced round and round every room in the top floor flat. This went on for 20 minutes. The next sound was that of the ginger-haired man bounding down the stairs, reaching the bottom in three strides. On stopping outside, he picked up the two cactus plants, after which his heavy footsteps could be heard once more. Mary was now beginning to feeling decidedly irritated. More walking round the flat followed and it seemed to go on forever. "For goodness sake, shut up!" Mary called out angrily. Several seconds of silence followed. Then, as the ginger-haired man could be heard walking slowly downstairs, Mrs Groves could only guess what would happen next. There was a knock on her front door, and Mrs

Groves made sure her chain stayed fastened when she opened it.

"The name's Derek Drummond. How can I help you?" the new arrival asked.

He had taken his blazer off and the short-sleeved white shirt he was wearing showed that he had broad shoulders and muscular forearms. What was alarming about his appearance, though, was a pair of clear blue eyes that had the cold, steely sharpness of daggers. But he was quite good looking nonetheless!

"Well, I'm just a bit concerned about the noise, and am wondering how long it's going to go on for," Mary said as calmly as she could. Then, after a couple of seconds, she added: "Welcome to Benson Lane, anyway."

Derek Drummond's eyes bored into her for a moment. Eventually he said: "Thank you, and I'm sorry about the noise. But I didn't know there was going to be anyone living below me. Rest assured, I will complete my move-in as quickly and quietly as possible." He spoke with an attractive Edinburgh lilt. "Who am I speaking to, by the way?" Mary Grove introduced herself.

"It's a pleasure to meet you," Derek Drummond said. "I look forward to us being happy neighbours and would like to invite you up for tea as soon as I get everything straightened out. In the meantime, however, I must attend to the rest of my belongings outside. They're a bit heavy, I'm afraid, but I will be as quick and quiet as it's humanly possible ... so I'll leave you to it for now and look forward to us talking again soon."

A somewhat flummoxed Mary Groves could barely manage a "Goodbye, see you later" as her new neighbour went outside to pick up his third suitcase. She felt a little more relaxed now ... but not for long. Bump! Bump! Bump! Bump! Bump! Bump! The suitcase's journey upstairs was longer than ever. So, too, was the walkabout above her ceiling.

After about half an hour, Derek Drummond tramped his way downstairs and picked up one of the wooden boxes outside. The sound of it being dragged upwards differed from that of the suitcases. Scrape, bump! Scrape, bump! Scrape, bump! The noise was repeated 20 times ...one for each stair!

Once at the top, the box was dragged forward and back, forward and back across one of the rooms. Then it was moved to another room … and dragged forward and back, forward and back. And then the same occurred in a third room. Yet another heavy-footed walkabout followed. Mary's blood was boiling by now. "Oi! What on earth do you think you're doing?" she called upwards. A pause was followed by heavy footsteps and a series of punches on Mary's front door. Drummond's blue eyes were blazing with anger. "What's the matter now?" he roared once the door was open.

"What do you think's the matter?" Mary shouted back. "It's the infernal noise you're making. I thought you said you were going to move your things as in quickly and quietly as possible, and you're doing anything but!"

Drummond'e eyes flashed and he bared his teeth like a fox. "I'll do what I like with my own belongings, and you can go to hell, you silly old bag!" he screamed. "That's what you are, a silly old bag!

"And let me tell you something, you stupid, fucking bag, I own half the property in this street, and if you don't treat me with some respect you might just find yourself thrown out on your fucking ear! You silly, stupid, fucking bag!"

Drummond stomped upstairs, slammed his door and then jumped up and down for a full 10 minutes. Mary Groves was so taken aback and so alarmed that she feared a ceiling would collapse. Once the jumping up and down stopped, there was still the matter of moving the second box, and the mixture continued as before … though for even longer this time.

It was not until the small hours of the morning that various bangs, bumps and footfalls finally stopped. By then, Mary's nerves were so frayed that sleeping ceased to be an option

Mary spent the night sitting in her armchair in the front room. The only time she moved was to go to the bathroom to take her medication. All thoughts of eschewing it vanished and she even considered taking the ill-advised step of increasing the dose. At eight o'clock in the morning, the front door could be heard slamming shut, and, through the net curtains, Drummond could be seen marching towards Benson Street. Mary gritted her teeth, picked up the telephone and called the police. She was told there was nothing they could do.

"What can we charge him with?" a bored-sounding voice asked. Then, a little more sympathetically, the voice added that she could get in touch again if she continued to feel frightened.

A call to her son, John, followed. John, who lived in Cumbria, said he was so inundated with work that he not possibly travel to Camford in the foreseeable future. However, after some hysterical pleading, he agreed to spend a couple of nights in her home in a week's time.

"Well, I suppose that's better than nothing," Mary said to herself as she hung up. The next thing she did was go to bed. At just after seven o'clock the same evening, a white van drew up outside the house. Mary, who had slept fitfully all day, woke up to hear the engine running. Derek Drummond was at the wheel. The small red-haired man was now wearing a tee-shirt, jeans and black boots.

Drummond jumped out of the van, slammed the driver's door shut and made his way to the back. Two doors were flung open and Drummond could be seen pulling out two tables, two armchairs, two smaller chairs, a single bed and a television set.

The front door of the house was unlocked noisily and thrown open. Drummond picked up the TV set and took it up to his flat, stamping on the stairs as he did so. A heavy-footed walkabout followed for the next 10 minutes. The same process took place with each item of furniture, though the bed and armchairs were dragged rather than carried upwards.

Mrs Groves did manage to sleep soundly for almost four hours … after which a bell could be heard from above, and then the sound of something like a broom handle being tapped onto the floor. All of a sudden, the bell of an alarm clock rang, after which hand bells could be heard. One of them reminded her of a school bell that told all the children that playtime was over and lessons were due to commence once more. The other bell had the sort of lighter tinkling sound that could be associated with the opening of a shop door and giving notice that a customer needed attending to. For the rest of the night, peace was disturbed either by a broom handle, one of the bells or a combination of all of them. On rising at eight in the morning, a furious Mrs Groves decided there was nothing for it but to confront Drummond and demand what he was playing at … and drat the consequences! But, just as she was steeling herself to do this, the front door slammed shut and her adversary was marching towards Benson Street. A feeling of desperation began to grip her. The police couldn't help her, her son could do nothing for the time being … there was no one she could turn to, it seemed. "Perhaps a trip to the doctor's will be of some use," she mused. "At least, he might help me find a way to calm my nerves."

An appointment was made for that afternoon. Dr Eckersley-Wade was an urbane Old Etonian. He was highly qualified and took a pride in his bedside manner, his ability to make patients feel at ease. Now in his mid-30s, he had some years ago turned his back on a possible high-flying career as a surgeon in favour of a post that enabled him to be an integral part of a community.

"Good afternoon, nice to see you," he said smiling benignly as his latest client entered his consulting room. "Do come in and sit down, and tell me how I can help you."

Mary Groves faltered for a moment, and then said: "Well, I suppose it's that my nerves haven't been so good lately," she said, her voice trembling. "And there's been trouble." She was close to tears.

Dr Eckersley-Wade, looking slightly less benign, glanced at his watch and matter-of-factly said: "Well, you'd better tell me all about it."

Mrs Groves described the problems she was having with her new neighbour, and pointed out that there was nobody else living in Benson Lane and that there was no one in Camford she could turn to. The doctor nodded and made sympathetic noises as the story unfolded, though a look of incredulity came to his face at the mention of bells and broom handles. He did not know what to believe, let alone what to do. "The sounds of bells could be the result of tinnitus," he suggested after a long pause.

"It's not tinnitus!" his patient shrieked. "I'm not stupid. I know what tinnitus is, and I'm telling you these bells are coming from the flat above and not from inside my ears!"

Dr Eckersley-Wade winced and waved a hand from left to right a few times, as if in despair. "All right, all right, all right, you've persuaded me!" he said, looking a little pained.

Then, after another long pause, during which he had a long look at his notes, he said: "I think the answer is to give you some stronger medication. I will prescribe you something that will make it much easier for you to sleep. However, it is important, especially important with this new prescription, not to exceed the stated dose. And you must, of course, throw the old tablets away." Once the prescription was written out, the doctor offered his patient a beatific smile and ushered her out.

CHAPTER 10

"WHAT ARE YOU DOING HERE?" On the receiving end of the question was Jenny Fitch, and she was not entirely sure how to take it. She looked down at the bed where Theo lay bare-chested and flat on his back. "That's nice, innit it!" she said. "Anyone would think you weren't pleased to see me after all this time!"

Theo didn't move. He knew it was best not to at the moment. The swelling around his left eye had gone down quite a bit. But his ribs and side were still sore and he knew that even the slightest movement needed to be made gingerly. "Sorry, Jenny. No offence meant," he said ruefully. "It's just that I've had one or two surprises too many lately! It's good to see you, really."

Jenny grinned. "That's better!" she said. Theo looked up at the squat figure with close-cropped auburn hair and clad in jeans and the usual top that enabled a tattoo of a scorpion to be seen on her left shoulder. He had employed Jenny on an ad hoc, cash-in-hand basis from time to time during the last couple of years. Now aged 21, and with a history of convictions for shoplifting in her teens, she had certain aptitudes that were useful to Theo. One of her talents was an ability to find things out. "So what ARE you doing here?" he asked again.

Jenny grinned broadly. "I got a phone call to say you were in need of help," she replied. "And you know what they say about a friend in need, don't you?"

"Who was the phone call from?"

"From Kelly, who else? She sounded quite concerned."

"Where is Kelly now?"

"How the hell should I know?! If you don't know, how can you expect me to know? All I can tell you is that Kelly phoned me to say she'd heard you'd been hurt and that I should get in touch with the Bensons. They're quite a couple, and they're concerned, too. Anyway, it was Mrs Benson who arranged for me to have a key to get into your flat ... so here I am."

Theo managed a semblance of a smile himself. "There must be some truth in what they say about bad pennies always turning up," he quipped.

Then, more gravely, he added: "Seriously, though, it IS good to see you. You couldn't have timed your visit better, and I might well have a job or two for you ... such as helping me get my new office in Camford up and running."

Jenny grinned again. "That's already in hand," she said. "I've got two sets of keys, one for you and one for me, and I've got hold of a picture of a massive great property, Aggawhatdoyoucallit Hall or something, in the window. Mrs Benson gave that to me, and she also said there were a couple of other people wanting to sell houses through you."

Theo was genuinely impressed. "That's fantastic," he told Jenny. "I can't wait to get started, and with a bit of luck I will be up and about in a couple of days. But there is just one thing ... When I asked if you knew where Kelly was, I meant it." Theo told Jenny about the party at Sherry's and how he and Kelly had lost contact with each other.

"Blimey!" said Jenny. "Now I've heard everything! I never thought Kelly could ever be away from your side for more than five minutes at a party."

"Well, there you are," Theo replied. "The man she was with when we parted company was Edmund Rooker. He runs a local firm of insurance brokers, I'm told. He's a friend of Sherry Munro and a respected local businessman. So it shouldn't be hard to track him down, and with a bit of luck he'll be able to tell us of Kelly's whereabouts."

Jenny grinned again and gave Theo a salute. "I'll get on to it," she promised. And then she added: "I do also have the job of looking after you just now."

Theo closed his eyes and started to doze. He'd been doing a lot of that during the last three days and could only barely recollect that George Bowes and his wife Susan had taken him back to his flat after the attack near the hotel.

Theo's assailants had been disturbed by hotel staff members who happened to be outside at the time. At almost the same time, George and Susan, who had been at Sherry's party but had opted to break away for a while to have a riverside stroll, had appeared and offered to look after their new friend.

A doctor had been round to check on him, and various well-wishers, including Wayne, Lisa, April and George had popped round to see how he was. Theo was hardly aware of these visits. And, at some point, Kelly had contacted Jenny ...

The sound of the front door bell brought Theo out of his semi-comatose state. He heard Jenny talking to April May, and his spirits soared immediately. April entered the bedroom looking more magnificent than ever. There she stood, all 5ft 10in of her, in a figure-hugging white cat suit and white shoes. The colour of her attire was accentuated by a mane of thick black hair, flashing brown eyes and shapely sun-tanned arms. "Hi!" she said with a smile that revealed a row of gleaming white teeth. Her eyes appeared to be dancing as they looked down on where he lay. They seemed to be saying to him: "Touch me if you dare ... but only if you're up to it!"

"Great to see you," Theo said.

"Great to see you back in the land of the living," April replied. The other two times I was here, you didn't seem to know if it was night or day ... and you certainly didn't recognise me!"

"Well," Theo said, "all I can say to that right now is that it's impossible NOT to notice you!"

April smiled warmly. "That's more like it!" she chuckled. "That's more like the cheeky THEOBALD Salter I started to get to know at Sherry Munro's party! You're sounding like your old self again. Are you feeling like your old self, too?"

"Not quite, but I'm getting there" was the reply. The reality was that April's presence was quite a tonic for him, and he was becoming increasingly hopeful of being out and about within two days at the most.

April turned to Jenny. "Is he being a good patient?" she asked. Jenny grinned one of her cheeky grins.

"Oh, he's OK. He has to be. He knows that if he steps out of line, I'll sort him out!" The two women laughed.

"Tell you what, "April said to Jenny at length. "If you feel like a break from nursing duties, I'll take over for a while. You must have been stuck with looking after this man for so long that you deserve a rest, or at least a chance to catch up on other things that you probably need to do."

Jenny eyed April speculatively, grinned again and then asked, tongue in cheek: "Yes but will you be safe if I leave you alone with him?"

"Oh, I'll cope somehow," April answered ironically.

"In that case, see you both in a while," said Jenny.

"No need to rush back!" was April's reply.

Once Jenny had gone, April walked over to the bed and looked down on her "patient." She could see there were contusions around the ribs and stomach, though these were clearly receding. Theo was a fit man, probably ultra-fit, and would doubtless recover quickly from the beating he had received. Meanwhile, he was undoubtedly in pain. She bent over and kissed him gently on the mouth. "Do you know something, THEOBALD? You just can't keep out of the limelight, can you?" she said softly.

"Cheers!" said Theo, half-smiling. "This last little entry into the limelight was just what I was looking for!"

"Sorry, Theo." April was cooing now. "I was really concerned when I heard you had been hurt. Have you any idea who your attackers might have been?"

"I can't imagine!!" Theo replied ironically.

"Hmm, Williams!" April murmured. "A number of us have been thinking it might have been him. Lisa has said as much, and George Bowes has said that if you needed some assistance in settling scores, he would be only too glad to help!

"If there's piece of good that's come out of all this, it's that

William has lost virtually any credibility he might have had as a respected citizen of Camford. He is not liked in the business community. People like bankers and builders have for a long time been regarding him with increasing suspicion, and the other estate agents have been resenting having to live him down. At the end of the day, Williams is a thug ... even though he has more brain cells than some other thugs."

Theo's eyes were flint hard at this point. But all he said was: "Hmm! And here I was thinking he should have been running a charm school!"

"That's the whole point," April added vehemently. "At the rate he's going, he won't be running anything. The only running going on will be people running him out of town!"

Then, after a moment or two, April's face softened. "As for you, the opposite is the case. Everyone seems to want to know you, shake hands with you, do business with you ... maybe even make love to you!"

The hardness in Theo's eyes melted a little. "You know," April continued, "the news that you had been attacked has spread like wildfire and people have reacted with both anger and horror. I have received phone calls from people asking how you were, and Wayne, Lisa and Sherry have all been inundated with inquiries. Jenny, too. You probably don't realise it but Jenny has been kept pretty busy fielding phone calls and turning away callers at the door. Every member of the estate agents' cricket team has been asking after you. So have half of the people in the other side!"

April looked down and Theo looked up. Two pairs of eyes were filled with desire. He could see that her jaw was a little too square and her nose a mite too long and pointed for her to be universally regarded as beautiful. But those eyes ... those dark, flashing eyes ... and those full red lips made her irresistible to him.

April sat down on the side of the bed, leaned forward and kissed him again. "What am I going to do with you? How can I restore you to full health?" she asked softly.

Theo was about to say, almost involuntarily that she had made a pretty good start, when she put a finger to her lips and the fingers of her other hand over his mouth. April kissed him yet again … firstly on the forehead and then on each side of his neck, and then hard on the mouth. She caressed his shoulders and arms and kissed the front of his neck. Her hand slid across Theo's broad chest and caressed his nipples. Her tongue followed a moment later.

Theo winced a little as the sore areas of his body started to receive similar attention. But the hand movements were slow, gentle and sensual, and any hint of pain quickly disappeared. He even found he could arch his body without discomfort as April hands and lips strayed around and below his naval. ?

Then, without warning, April pulled the bedclothes back and pulled down his briefs. She proceeded to kiss his crotch area while running a hand down his right thigh. Theo had started to have an erection some time before this and just as he began to come, April took his penis and put it into her mouth and sucked.

Her tongue caressed his manhood, and her mouth opened just once to release his cum. Theo had previously thought he had experienced every sexual pleasure he could have possibly desired. He was wrong. Eventually, after what seemed to be a glorious eternity, April stopped what she was doing and stood up. She was not finished with him, though. A hand went to a half-hidden zip at the side of her cat suit, and in an instant she was standing before him naked.

Her body was even more magnificently toned than Theo had imagined. Her shoulders were broad, shapely and strong looking, as were her arms. Her breasts were so large and perfectly formed that her waist looked even tinier and her stomach even flatter than they actually were. The hips were wide, however, and her buttocks big but firm. Her legs were long and her thighs powerful and slightly muscular. Her figure was Amazonian, yet the persona was utterly feminine. Her lips and tongue felt more heaven-sent than ever as April started to kiss and lick him all over. Before long, his penis was in her hand again. This time, April shook it about and squeezed it until it was erect once more. Then, sitting astride him, she came down on him.

There was no pain involved for Theo, just a new kind of

euphoria as he managed to keep in time with the thrusting motions coming from above.

Yet, although he remained lying on his back, both his hands were allowed to explore April's contours. He felt her buttocks, her breasts, her thighs, her six pack stomach and her arms. The muscles in her upper arms were taut, as she took care not to weigh down too much on the parts of Theo that were sore. The love-making went on for two hours, after which April and Theo fell asleep while still embracing.

CHAPTER 11

SLEEP HAD RARELY BEEN such a wondrous experience. When April was making love to him, Theo almost felt he was dreaming. Now he was re-living that dream, along with all the other events that he had experienced during the last few days. The rescue of Wayne Benson from a watery grave, the encounter with both April and Ray Williams at Aggammenmon Hall, the cricket match, the party at Sherry's, the beating and, above all, the most exciting of all sexual encounters.

Even the attack near the hotel was allowed to be enjoyable in Theo's dream, as he was able to mete out a particularly humiliating form of retribution on the man he knew to have been behind it. Immediately after the beating Williams senseless with his fists and then torturing him with a chainsaw, he was back at the scene of the water rescue, making love to Lisa on the grass bank near the canal crash scene.

There was just one disconcerting part of the dream, though, and that concerned the loyal, faithful Kelly. It sought to solve the mystery of her disappearance at the party, and Theo didn't like the possible outcome. Nor did he believe it. He was taken back in time to the party and his attempt to find her after the game of billiards. The lights were low, the music muted and all conversation garbled, as he pushed his way between party guests in the course of his search. Eventually he came to a room to the side of the ballroom that he had not discovered before. It was barely bigger than a box room and contained just a mattress on the floor. The sound of love-making could be heard. The wonderful dream was beginning to turn sour. Theo turned on the light to see Kelly naked on the mattress with a trouser-less Edmund Rooker. On seeing Theo, Rooker fled, still naked from the waist down, into and through the ballroom and out into the garden. Kelly just lay there giggling.

"What do you think you're doing?" Theo asked in disbelief.

"What does it look like?" was the mocking reply.

"But ... but ... but ... why him? What do you see in HIM?"

Before Kelly could reply, April entered the room and ordered her out. Kelly left meekly without making any attempt to get dressed, and then April started to disrobe. Suddenly Theo woke up in a cold sweat. Without thinking, he sat bolt upright in his bed. The feeling of bemusement in his dream was followed by relief that he had at least this level of mobility. The bedroom door opened gently and Jenny appeared.

"Ah! Good to see you're able to sit up!" she said smiling.

"What day is it?" asked a confused Theo.

"It's Wednesday, and you've been lying there for four days," Jenny replied.

"Where's April?"

"You might well ask!" Jenny was now grinning more broadly than ever.

"She left last night, saying she had some business to attend to, and that she would be in touch soon. I gave you plenty of time to be alone together yesterday, and, as it turned out, it wasn't enough! Never mind! When I got back, I hid myself in the kitchen ... and blocked my ears! Didn't want to disturb anyone!" Theo tried not to look sheepish. "Anyway, how are you feeling now?" Jenny asked.

Theo looked down his body and noticed that the marks left on it had all but disappeared. Then, much to his surprise, he noticed that his briefs were on. So April ... well presumably April ... had put them back on before she went out.

"Why don't you try getting up and walking about a bit?" Jenny suggested.

Theo pulled back the sheets, which had also been carefully put back into position, swung his legs sideways and slowly stood up. The pain had gone, apart from a little soreness in the left side of his rib cage. Jenny stood there watching. "Enjoying the view?" Theo asked.

"Don't you flatter yourself. I was just looking to see how your eye was!" Jenny quipped. "The swelling's almost completely gone, and you'll be as good as new in no time."

Theo looked around for some clothes and put on a pair of jeans and a tee-shirt. They were the nearest items to hand. "I feel almost there right now," he said smiling. "I might just pop over to my new office and open it up for business a little later on."

"That's great," said Jenny. "But it wouldn't do if you went there looking like you do now. You're in need of a shave, not to mention a bath. You haven't had either since you were at that party."

"Oh, sorry about that!" Now it was Theo's turn to grin broadly. Jenny grinned again, too.

"Tell you what, you go and have a good bath and shave and I'll fish out your best togs."

Theo picked up a bathrobe that was lying on an armchair, went into the bathroom and turned on the taps.

"Give your hair a good wash, too!" Jenny called out. "Take your time, you need to be sure you're smelling of roses!" The running water drowned the sound of Jenny picking up the telephone and making a call. Jenny knew Theo liked to wallow, often for an hour or more, and this time the latter allowed himself the luxury of some expensive bath salts. He knew from previous occasions that a hot bath with salts could be the ideal tonic after he had taken a knock at rugby, boxing or some other sport, and this time it was better than ever. As he lay there, he could feel the last hint of pain ebbing away, and even, yet again, went to sleep for a while.

After about half an hour, there was a knock on the door. "Allo, what is it?" was the dreamy response.

"Come on, rise and shine! Chop chop!" Jenny called. "You've got your best suit, a white shirt and clean underwear just outside. I've even polished your shoes for you."

Theo murmured his thanks, and then asked what the hurry was.

"It's time for you to open up your new office, and there are people who want to see you there … and, by that, I mean soon. Not in a fortnight's time!" he was told.

"All right, all right, all right, stop bullying me! I'm coming!" Theo got up, stepped out of the bath and towelled himself down. He moved less gingerly this time and felt almost as good as new. His clothes were neatly piled outside and he put them on and looked at himself in a mirror. Apart from a red, patterned tie, everything he wore was dark and smacked of sobriety. "Good grief!" he said to himself. "If I can't look like a pillar of respectability in this lot, I never will!" He turned to see Jenny standing there with a look of approval on her face.

"You'll do," she said. "All you need before I take you to your office is a comb through your hair."

"All right, little Miss Bossy Boots," Theo retorted. But he did what he was told. Jenny drove Theo to his new work place, handed him the keys to both his office and his car and told him she had some shopping to do. Theo stood outside for a while, observing that "SALTER'S" had been painted in large red letters on a board above the plate glass shop window. Much of the window was taken up by a massive photograph of the front of Aggammenmon Hall, along with some smaller pictures showing internal and side views of the property and its gardens. In the midst of all the pictures was a placard bearing the words "The Property of the Year."

Theo felt a glow of extreme satisfaction. The Bensons were friends in every sense of the word. He had never previously imagined that any chance encounter could be so productive.

Then he noticed that there were two other house pictures in the window, in less prominent positions. One of the pictures was of a small detached bungalow in a village a few miles outside Camford. The other was of an inter-war town semi.

What a way to get started!

Theo moved to the front door of the Salter's premises, put the key in the lock and was slightly startled to feel the door opening before he could turn the key.

Not knowing what to expect next, he pushed it open wide and bounded inside.

A tumultuous cheer followed by hand-clapping greeted him.

Assembled near the back of the main sales office, so that they could not easily be seen from outside, were all the estate agents who had played in the cricket match. Most of the spouses were there, too, as were most of the opposition players and their spouses.

Standing at the front of the gathering were Wayne and Lisa Benson and April May. Lisa walked up to Theo and gave him a kiss so tender that Wayne looked alarmed for a second, and said: "Welcome to Camford. We all felt it was time you were given a proper welcome."

Wayne shook him by the hand and added: "And so say all of us!"

April moved forward and pressed her body against Theo's and whispered in his ear: "You've only had a first taste of how welcoming I can be! It's good to see you looking so well. You've obviously started to get on top of things!"

Theo then whispered back: "That's something I'm really looking forward to!"

All the women in the room took it in turn to kiss Theo, and all the men queued up to shake his hand. A bottle of champagne was produced and opened and everyone handed a glass.

"Right!" said Wayne, at the top of his voice, once all the glasses were filled. "You all know why we're here and you all know what I think of this fellow," he said putting an arm round Theo's shoulder. "This is the man who saved my life … and, come what may, he is my friend for life. This is a subject I could go talking about for hours! However, by now you all know what happened in the canal. You also know about his heroics on the cricket field, and you obviously share my disgust at the way my friend was attacked and beaten up a few days ago. It's great to see you looking fit and well again, Theo."

Some members of the gathering called out "Hear, hear!"

"So," continued Wayne, "we thought it fitting that we should welcome you to the community of Camford, especially the business community, in a tangible way. This is why we are here now. So I now have great pleasure in asking everyone present to raise their glasses with the toast of 'Welcome to Camford, Theo.'"

"Welcome to Camford!" everyone said.

Assorted canapes were then brought in from the back by a firm of caterers especially hired for the event, and these, along with champagne and wine, were consumed for the next three hours.

"You know, it's not every day that a new estate agent on the block is given such a greeting," Theo was told. The observation came from George Bowes, though it could have come from anyone.

"And do you know something else? There's only one estate agent in Camford who's not represented here," George added.

"Yes," said Theo grimly. "But you can rest assured that I will be seeing him some other time!" The party went on all day, and well into the evening.

A number of customers did call in. They were politely turned away and asked to call in the next day. By the time the last guest had left, Theo had been invited by almost everyone present to dine at their home.

It was well past midnight by the time all the plates, cups and glasses had been washed up and cleared away, all traces of crumbs removed and any risk of stale wine permeating the atmosphere the following morning extinguished.

April, Lisa and Lance Perry's wife, Hannah, helped with the tidying up. Eventually, Theo was on his own with April.

"I don't suppose you've had a chance to take a proper look at your work place yet," the latter said.

"Well, not really, though the first impression, with all those house-for-sale pictures in the window is great," Theo replied.

"Yes, that was the work of your little assistant, Jenny ... she's quite an asset for you, you know ... and a little help from some friends. And, by the way, you know those two smaller houses pictured in the window? Yes? Well, they were originally going on the market through Ray Slimeball Willams. However, the two sellers learned about Williams' dubious reputation on the grapevine, and also heard about your exploits ... and hey presto!"

Theo put an arm round her waist and kissed her. "You're quite something, aren't you?" he said.

"Well, not bad for a business rival, perhaps!" April replied, smiling. "Anyway, she said, "you've seen the main office, you've seen the kitchen and you've seen the loo. You have yet to take a proper look at the parking area at the back, the consulting room and the board room."

April took Theo by the hand and led him up a narrow flight of carpeted stairs. At the top were two doors. One led to a small office with a desk and three chairs. The room was ideal for bringing in clients seeking a confidential chat. The other belonged to a larger room with a polished oblong table in the middle. The boardroom was simply and sparsely furnished, though, with six tables ranged round the table, a cupboard, a small cocktail cabinet and a picture rail, it was adequate for Theo's needs.

"Well, what do you think?" he was asked.

Theo, who had, of course, made a point of having taken a quick look round already, did not answer. April was standing in front of him in a little black dress with a plunging neckline and a zip at the front. He pulled the zip downwards and, in a moment, the dress was on the floor.

The front door of Salter's remained unlocked all night. If anyone had entered and gone upstairs they would have seen April spread-eagled across the table as Theo made love to her ... again and again and again.

CHAPTER 12

"WHERE THE HELL HAVE YOU BEEN … as if I need ask?!" The irony in Jenny's voice could not disguise her irritation.

Theo, who had had to dash to the telephone with trousers at half mast, said the first thing that came into his head: "I had some paper work to catch up with!"

"Is that what they call it these days?" was the caustic response. "Do you know what time it is?" Jenny asked severely. "Yes, that's right, it's 20 bloody minutes past eight and you're supposed to be open for business in 10 minutes time!"

Theo was not one to get flustered as a rule but on this occasion he was in a state of near panic. "Oh God! I'm really sorry! I was going to tell you exactly what was going to be happening today, what with the office opening and so on, wasn't I? I'm so sorry! The party did disrupt things, though. Did you know there was going to be a party."

"What if I did?" Jenny answered angrily? "You've got an office to open and you need to tell me what you need and when you need me to be in there."

"A clean shirt and a razor wouldn't go amiss," Theo suggested.

"Get lost!" Jenny answered before slamming down the receiver. Theo hung up, too, and, as he did so, April, now fully dressed and with not a hair out of place, brushed past him and made for the office's unlocked front door.

"See you later," she said, blowing a kiss at him. Theo pulled his trousers up, had a quick wash in the basin that came with the loo, combed his hair and made himself look as presentable as possible. The desire to shave was acute, and he just hoped that the growth on his chin could pass as designer stubble. The front office contained two desks, each with a telephone, a dozen small chairs, a coat rack, two filing cabinets, a computer with a printer and a series of boards on the walls, to which property for sale particulars could be attached. Theo paced behind and in front of each desk and ranged the other chairs round the walls near the door. He then sat behind the larger desk and looked out towards the street. Salter's was located in Avenue Road, a curiously, for its name, tree-less cul-de-sac off the High Street. The High Street was Camford's most prestigious road for shops, and very much the main magnet for estate agents. Avenue Road was one step down and, because of this, rentals for premises there were lower. Avenue Road consisted of a few shops with flats above and half a dozen terrace houses.

The biggest shop was a mini supermarket, which sold everything from milk and newspapers to blankets and underwear. Next to it was an old fashioned tobacconists that displayed a range of pipes, cigarette lighters and ashtrays. A second hand book store, a charity shop and a deserted Christian Science premises could be found in Avenue Road, too.

The only other estate agency in the street was Knights, run by Evelyn Knight and also deserted ... or at least closed for business for much of the time. Why this was so was open to speculation, though it was strongly rumoured that Miss Knight had been far more preoccupied with conducting a string of affairs than running a business that she had inherited from her father two years previously. There was little activity in the street at present. What there was consisted of a few people popping into Wilkies, the supermarket, and a few more leaving their homes to go to work. Theo looked down at his desk, and saw a note pad in one corner. It had a few messages scribbled on it. Jenny, bless her, had jotted down some names and telephone numbers of potential clients. What a find she had been for him!

Theo recalled how he first met her three years ago, when she wandered into his premises in Gloucester and unsuccessfully tried to steal some stationery from under his nose. After being caught red-handed, she begged him not to tell the police. He discovered that she had a string of convictions for shoplifting and drug abuse and realised that her latest misdeed could mean a spell behind bars.

Theo could also see she was bright and ended up offering her a job!

A few discreet inquiries uncovered the fact that her academic ability was impressive and that her school head had regarded her as graduate potential until she started to keep the wrong company. So he had taken her on as an assistant, even though she had never passed an exam in her life. "She's passed every test I've given her since then," Theo mused. Jenny had kept out of trouble and was everything an employer could reasonably ask of her ... and more besides. His thoughts were interrupted by a young couple entering Salter's and asking what homes he had for sale. Theo took down their details and promised to get back to them once he had something suitable on his books.

A minute later, an elderly man came in and said he had a thatched cottage he wanted to sell. Theo promised to call round, take photographs and measurements, and have a set of particulars printed for would-be buyers to look at. A number of Theo's rival estate agents, including George Bowes, Barny Kentford, Nathan Pike and Reg Pinkerton, popped round to say "Hi!" Evelyn Knight called in, too. "Good to know we're near neighbours," she drawled, with just the hint of a smile.

"Ditto," said Theo. "It's always good to know there's a friendly face nearby."

"Uh, yes," said Evelyn, suddenly sounding unsure of herself. Theo sensed that she had something other than socialising on her mind, though he had no idea what. The two gazed at each other for a moment or two without either saying a word.

Evelyn Knight was about 5ft 4in tall, auburn haired and shapely. She was currently clad in a twin set that clung to her contours, suggesting there was little or nothing worn underneath. Theo also noticed that her shoulder length hair had been carefully combed, that her lipstick, powder and eye liner had been fastidiously applied, and that her fingernails had been painted red.

"I have a business proposal to put to you some time," Evelyn said eventually. Perhaps we can talk about it when you are less busy?" Then, without waiting for a response, she turned and left.

Theo sat at his desk and gazed into space for a while. His hand went up to his chin, and he could feel the unwelcome profusion of stubble. "What a day!" he said aloud. "What a first day for business in Camford!" He now believed that the proposition Evelyn had in mind was going to be productive, perhaps in more ways than one ... However, time was marching on, and Theo was not sorry that it was now approaching 6pm. There was still another surprise in store, though.

The clock had just turned 5.30, when in walked the last caller of the day. He was tall, slightly taller than Theo, and slim and wore a pinstripe suit. His hair was jet black, laced with grease and brushed back. He had a bent nose, close-set eyes and a moustache that partially concealed a scar. Theo took a pride in his ability to assess people quickly and accurately, and it was pretty apparent that this particular visitor was not a church social worker! He was polite enough, nonetheless. "Good evening," he said. "Are you Mr Salter, by any chance!"

Theo nodded: "Yes, that's me."

"Delighted to meet you," the caller said, shaking his hand. "My name is Chris Doman, and I am here to represent the head of MAC Developments. I believe you know Mr McAvie already ...?" Theo nodded again.

"Well, Mr McAvie is extremely interested in buying Aggammenmon Hall, and would like you to show him round. He is prepared to make a cash purchase, so a quick sale is assured if he decides to go ahead ... and that will doubtless help you get your new estate agency venture in Camford off to a flying start."

Theo's eyes narrowed. McAvie was not the kind of purchaser he had in mind, nor the kind a person he particularly wanted to inflict on Camford, though the point Doman had made about a cash sale was a valid one. Doman paused for a moment, then added: "Mr McAvie also has another proposition to put to you, and this could be even more lucrative."

"Tell me more," said Theo.

"Ah, I can't do that," said Doman. "Mr McAvie wants to talk to you about that in person. The purpose of me being here is to take the first step in fixing a time to view Aggammenmon Hall."

Theo consulted his diary. "How about eleven o'clock tomorrow morning?" he suggested. Doman took a notebook from his breast pocket, glanced at it and said: "Yes, that will be fine. "And Mr McAvie will be delighted to renew old acquaintances."

CHAPTER 13

AN IMMACULATELY POLISHED Rolls-Royce drew up outside the front door of Aggammenmon Hall at ten past eleven. Theo, who had been waiting for exactly 10 minutes, having left Jenny in charge at the office in Camford, was back in his Ford Escort. His car had received a service and a thorough clean-up following the canal rescue. But it still looked as if it did not belong in the same driveway as the Rolls. Chris Doman was at the wheel. Ray Williams was next to him, and in the back was a small red-haired man. The three got out, and, once Doman had held a rear door open for a few moments, Sean McAvie emerged.

McAvie was an imposing figure of a man in his mid-fifties. He was 6ft 5in tall, stood as straight as a ramrod, and was as lean as a whippet. His shoulders were broad, however, and he had a full head of white hair. McAvie was clad in a three-piece grey suit that fitted so well that it must have been made to measure by a top tailor.

What made him more formidable than anything else, though, was his face. It was lean and pink and featured a nose that was even more bent than Doman's. A smile revealed a row of white dentures, which, according to rumours, were fitted 30 years ago to replace those lost in a fracas in the Gorbels. His lips were fleshy and frequently puckered. The pupils of his eyes were coal black and the whites appeared to be permanently bloodshot. A stare from those eyes had been enough to strike terror into some of the hardest hearts in Glasgow. "Hello, Theo. Nice to see you again after all this time," McAvie said with a handshake. His voice was deep and melodious, and it sounded cultured, too. "However, I expect my presence in these parts has come as something of a surprise to you," he added.

"Just a little bit," Theo agreed.

"Well, I guess it's a matter of learning about business opportunities, wherever they might be, from contacts," McAvie went on, waving his hand towards Williams. "I believe you have already met Mr Williams."

Williams half grinned, half sneered. "I hear you haven't been well lately," he said mockingly. "How are your ribs just now?"

Theo, remaining as cool as he could, replied grimly: "I'm fine, thank you. How's your jaw?"

"Now, now, now!" said McAvie. "I detect a hint of animosity. Let us all remember why we are all here. We're business associates, and perhaps, if it's all possible, friends."

"Friends?!" Theo snorted. "OK, let's settle for business associates just now." His feud with Williams could wait for a while, and his rib cage would probably benefit from such a wait.

"That's better!" McAvie said to Theo. "Now you've already met my valued assistant Chris Doman. The other member of my team present is Derek Drummond," he said motioning a hand towards the small ginger-haired man.

Theo made a quick study of Drummond's cold blue eyes and thought to himself: "He looks like a bit of a psycho to me!"

Drummond stared at Theo without either a word or a handshake.

"Right!" said McAvie. "Let's have a look round this wonderful property. I would have gone round earlier had it not been for the fact that Mr Williams who once had the keys in his possession went and handed them back to the Bensons. Still, that was after Mr Williams lost the job of selling Aggammenmon Hall to your good self, and that is one of two reasons why we're doing business now."

"What's the other reason?" Theo asked.

"We'll come to that a little later on, if you don't mind. Let's have that tour first."

Theo Salter and Sean McAvie spent the next hour or so wandering round the big house, while Williams, Doman and Drummond sat in the main hall and played cards. McAvie showed he was quick to spot both the good and bad points in a property, especially where repairs or improvements were needed. He indicated that he was seeking somewhere that would serve as a monument to himself... a luxury home in a secluded location and a place where he could entertain important clients. He had come a long way both educationally and financially since his days as a feared Gorbels hooligan. "This property's got a wee bit of potential about it." McAvie's excitement was such that his clipped and cultured tones gave way to a touch of Glasgow for a second! "Yes, this is quite a place," he went on. "Now let's have a look at the grounds and gardens."

Theo's suggestion of a tour in his Ford Escort met with approval. "I reckon this fits the bill perfectly," McAvie said at length. "At least, it will once I have finished with it. What I want is somewhere that I can use as a place to entertain and also as a bolthole that I can retreat to ... and not be disturbed without plenty of warning. It's a pretty good retreat already, mind you. However, my plan is to install a few extras, such as a swimming pool, a gym, a sauna and a games room ... perhaps a new tennis court and croquet lawn, too." McAvie was becoming increasingly animated. "Yes, this is the place for me!"

"That's excellent news," said Theo, who was finding it hard to conceal his own excitement over striking such a lucrative deal. "You must let me know how I can be of service." Theo's car was now back outside the front door, next to the Rolls-Royce. Williams, Doman and Drummond were standing outside, waiting.

Once the two men had got out of the car, McAvie slapped Theo on the back. "Yes, without doubt you're the man I want to do business with here!"

Doman smiled, Williams looked sour and Drummond remained impassive. "What's more, I will pay the full asking price and Benson will have it in cash. So there will be no delays, no pissing about." A broad, cadaverous grin revealed his full set of dentures. Then, after a few seconds, the grin disappeared and McAvie looked serious once more. "Now," he said. "You will recall that I said there was a second matter I wished to discuss with you. I have a proposition to put to you that will probably be even more lucrative than Aggammenmon Hall."

"I'm all ears," Theo said, not knowing what to expect next.

"Right! Well here it is. A little while ago, I acquired a portfolio of properties and land in Camford that I want to develop. I want to build on the land and improve or replace the properties and then sell them on at a nice fat profit. And, at some point in the near future, I am going to need an estate agent to market them." Theo could detect a look of surprise on Doman's face and, at the same time, see Williams was livid.

"Just a minute!" said Williams. "If you're talking about Benson Lane, I'm your agent for that. You've already said the job was mine and we've shook hands on it!"

McAvie puckered his lips and his eyes looked more bloodshot than ever. "That may well be," he sneered, "but you've blotted your copybook somewhat, haven't you?" I've been hearing reports of various acts of bad behaviour, including thuggery and upsetting Wayne Benson … the most popular man in Camford. The way you have conducted yourself has not done much for the image of MAC Developments, has it? Mr Salter, on the other hand, has become something of a local hero. And he's achieved heroics on more than one occasion … making him just the right sort of person to raise the profile of my company."

Williams began to look pale as McAvie went on: "From what I have heard … and, believe me, I take steps to make sure I have the correct information at my fingertips … you have lost any credibility you might have ever had as a respectable local estate agent … and I am beginning to wonder what use you can be to me in my set-up." Williams hung his head, not knowing what to say.

Theo could not resist gloating. "The toilets could do with cleaning!" he quipped.

Williams looked up and spluttered: "Why, you …"

McAvie laughed mockingly. "Now, now, now! Calm down, Ray! And Theo, you must learn not to be so unkind! Ray, perhaps it would be best if you disappeared for a while until you've cooled down a bit? Why not take a walk round the gardens? You can keep an eye open for a good spot for a tennis court or a croquet lawn."

Williams, whose face was now crimson, walked away without

saying a word. McAvie turned to Theo once Williams was out of earshot and said: "Williams was right, of course. I was talking about Benson Lane. At the moment, the street is a rather run-down-looking cul-de-sac off Benson Street. Both streets are named after Wayne Benson, of course. And there's huge potential. Both streets are within a few minutes drive of a new motorway that will be running from south west Camford to London. The motorway will also run past Carstairs Airport."

"So," said Theo, "if the project goes ahead property prices in that part of Camford will almost certainly soar because of its attraction to commuters."

"Absolutely!" McAvie went on. "And it will be especially so if the area is spruced up and the right kinds of properties are built on it. Now, that's already happening to some extent in Benson Street, which has seen a prestigious new office block, a number of up-market shops and a row of executive- style homes built there in the last few years. Benson Lane, on the other hand, has been allowed to become a bit run-down." McAvie went on to outline his plans for Benson Lane. "It's a potential goldmine," he said. "I am going to change the whole character of the street, and, when I'm finished, it's going to be one of the most sought after spots in town."

Theo was told how a new hotel, restaurant and casino would bring extra business, and therefore extra wealth, to Camford. Some of the redundant land would be built on and some would be replaced by new landscaping, and the 12 houses would be demolished and replaced by homes of a better quality. "And I want YOU to handle the marketing of these new properties once they're up for sale. We've already got the green light." McAvie was becoming increasingly animated. "Wayne Benson is the big noise on the council's planning committee… at least he was at the time the planning application was being considered. He liked the idea, and he made sure it went ahead."

Theo gave a wry smile. "I have a feeling there's a 'but, but, but!' coming up."

McAvie flashed his dentures. "You're quite right, my friend. There is, though the problem is a pinprick and not insuperable.

"We've just had a bit of a delay. MAC Developments has got the planning consent to go ahead, that's the main thing, but your friend Wayne Benson did express some concern about the position of the tenants living in the 12 houses. So, in the end, the planning permission was made subject to a Security of Tenure clause. The clause basically means that no one can be forced to leave their home while a tenancy agreement is in force. A lot of the tenancies were for just six months, and these have been no problem. The tenants have simply moved out once the six months was over. However, there have been three or four long-term tenancies, and we have been obliged to offer the tenants concerned financial inducements to quit. The Security of Tenure situation has slowed down the process somewhat, as you can imagine. But we are getting there.

"We have come to a settlement with everyone bar one, and I believe negotiations with the one person remaining will come to a satisfactory conclusion soon."

McAvie turned to look at Drummond, whose impassive expression disappeared momentarily for the first time. "Aye, the matter is in hand," he said smirking.

CHAPTER 14

"GET OUT OF THE WAY, you silly old bag!" Mary Groves stood up and let Drummond pass on his way to the front door. "And clear up that fucking mess!" he bellowed, as he bared his teeth. The front door slammed shut and heavy footsteps could be heard as Drummond headed for Benson Street.

Mrs Groves knelt down again and finished wiping away the puddle of urine that almost filled the small porch that she shared with her new neighbour. She knew the urine could have only come from one source, the sheepdog that Drummond had bought a few days ago. Or, on reflection, perhaps it was Drummond himself!

She had brought the matter up on a previous occasion and, for her trouble, received a volley of foul-mouthed abuse that lasted a full 10 minutes. No, there was no point in saying anything. To do so would only make matters worse.

Her main hope now lay in her son, John, who was due to arrive later the same day. Surely John, who was several inches taller than her tormentor, could do something to defuse the situation! The new medication, prescribed by Dr Eckersley-Wade had helped to some extent and, although the bangs on the floor above and the sounds of bells were becoming more frequent, Mary Groves was becoming better at sleeping through these disturbances.

Unfortunately there were other things going wrong in the meantime. Two dead rats had been delivered to her in the post, the pint of milk that was on order twice a week had been spilled all over the pavement, and, on one occasion, a pile of bricks and rubble had mysteriously appeared outside the front door.

The bricks and rubble incident had led to Drummond

accusing Mrs Groves of putting them there on purpose, just to cause trouble! The accusation, laced with every possible expletive imaginable, could have been heard several houses away, if anyone had been living in any of them, but not in the bustling, traffic-laden Benson Street. "Oh, please God, I hope John will be here to help me soon!" she said to herself, as she put away her mop and bucket. Then the next tirade started. "About bloody time, too! Don't let it happen again, you stupid bag!" Drummond was back in the house.

"You silly, stupid, fucking old bag!" he shouted as he stomped upstairs.

The door to his flat closed and, after a few seconds silence, Mrs Groves was subjected to the sound of stamping on the floor, more expletives and items of furniture being hurled around Drummond's floor. This went on for about half an hour. Half an hour's silence followed, after which heavy footsteps on the stairs and the slamming of the front door led Mrs Groves to hope that she would be left in peace for a while, at least. She would have liked to go out herself, even if just for a short shopping trip to the town centre, to gain some sort of respite from the atmosphere that prevailed in Benson Lane. But there was uncertainty over her son's time of arrival. John was a junior partner in a firm of solicitors in the small Cumbrian town of Appleby-in-Westmoreland. John Groves and his partner had fought hard to build up the business, and the list of clientele had grown rapidly during the last few months. The workload had almost doubled, and extra staff were being sought.

Further expansion was on the cards, though the immediate priority was to consolidate. The firm could not afford to make mistakes, and the idea of anyone taking a holiday in the foreseeable future was out of the question. It was the worst time possible to take even a couple of days off. John had battled hard to win his senior partner's approval, which had only been gained after he had promised to take work with him on the train. The journey to Camford, which entailed changing trains twice and two taxi rides, took around seven hours.

John used his portable computer and opened up his files as

much as he could, though, in practice, all three trains he travelled on were full and cramped, making it difficult to work effectively.

He felt tired, jaded and queasy even before his journey started. A sagging waistline served as evidence that long hours in the office, hurried meals, poor food and virtually no exercise had been the order of the day for day after day. During the last week or two, he had been suffering from intermittent headaches, palpitations and even chest pains

John Groves arrived at his mother's home at 7pm. As the taxi that transported him from Camford railway station disappeared and John went to the door to ring the bell, he saw a light and a slight movement of curtains upstairs. Although moved by the urgency of his mother's request to find the time to come over and see her, he had given less thought than he might have to her predicament. Now, for the first time, the needs of his Cumbrian business began to fade into the background. He had yet to grasp the full extent of the crisis he was about to become involved with but realised that there could be real unpleasantness ahead.

He heard the sound of the inner door opening, followed by shuffling footsteps, before the front door opened and his mother appeared to welcome him. Mary kissed and embraced her son warmly. "Do come in, it's wonderful to see you," she said, her voice quivering. "It's great to see you, too," John replied. An offer of a cup of tea, once inside, was gratefully accepted.

John noticed that his mother had aged markedly since he last saw her just under a year ago. She had put on weight and was slower and more deliberate in her movements, suggesting that the arthritis in her knees had worsened. Her face was pale and more lined and a nervous tic had begun to manifest itself. Yet, although he felt unsettled by these observations, he fell asleep in the armchair where he was sitting before he could finish his tea. Forty-five minutes later, his mother grabbed a shoulder and gave him a shake. "Sorry to wake you up but I've got some supper for you," she said, smiling. Yes, she was actually smiling! One possible reason was that, although she knew he was in, there had been no disturbance from Drummond since her son had arrived. Perhaps the presence of a man in her home was all that was needed to keep him under control, she thought. What a nasty little man! What a coward!

Mary and John Groves went into the kitchen to eat. The meal consisted of lamb chops, boiled potatoes and peas, followed by canned fruit. It was simple but acceptable and had not required much preparation. After they had eaten and cleared up, they moved back into the sitting room with more cups of tea.

Mary then went into detail about how Benson Lane had become empty, how representatives of MAC Developments had tried to persuade her to move, and, in particular, the problems she had had with Drummond.

"That's absolutely terrible!" John said wearily, once she had finished. "But what can we do? What on Earth can we do? It almost sounds as if this fellow Drummond is in league with the building company and helping them to get you out!"

"Oh, my goodness!" said Mary Groves. Do you really think so?" She had, in fact, considered such a possibility and then chosen to dismiss it.

"Do you remember the 1960s and the days of Rachmannism, when there were stories of tenants being harassed in all sorts of ways until they had no choice but to leave their homes? Thugs with Alsatians were used to intimidate people, and another way to get people out was to enter the premises while the occupants were out and remove essential items such as lavatories and kitchen sinks. At least you haven't had that."

"Well, I suppose that's true," Mary Groves agreed. "If Drummond really is playing that sort of game, he's being a lot more subtle about it. He's been extremely rude, unpleasant and anti-social but no crime has been committed. I wish there had been in a way, because we would then involve the police."

At that very moment, the door bell rang. Mary Groves gave a start. She knew who it was right away. The bell rang a second time, this time for longer and more stridently.

"Don't worry," John said, sounding as calm as he could. "I'm here and I'll come to the door with you."

When Mary opened the door to the porch, Drummond was standing just a few inches away. His pose was unmistakably confrontational.

"Would you mind clearing up those messes you keep on making in the porch," he said, glaring at Mrs Groves. "I've just had to bring down a mop and bucket to attend to the latest one ... and I'm getting a bit fed up with having to do it."

John took this as his cue to stick up for his mother.

"She hasn't made any mess," he said with cold indignation. "There was no mess when I arrived earlier this evening and neither of us have set foot outside the flat since then."

Drummond switched his gaze away from Mrs Groves and looked into the eyes of the man standing beside her.

"I'm not talking to you, I'm talking to Mrs Groves," he half-whispered, half-stuttered. "Mind your own business!"

Then, a little more loudly and in a high-pitched tone that was laced with menace, he added: "It would be far better for you if you minded your own business, because if you don't you're liable to get your teeth kicked in!" Drummond bared his teeth and his eyes began to resemble blue knuckle-dusters. "I'll kick your teeth in!" he screamed. "Do you hear me? I will kick your teeth in! I will kick your bloody fucking teeth in!"

John Groves froze. He was dumb-struck. Drummond then turned his attention to Mrs Groves once more.

"You need to think what you're doing, you silly old bag. You're turning this whole house into a rat hole ... and I'm not standing for it! And you know what the cause of all the trouble is, don't you? It's because you're a silly old bag! A silly, stupid, fucking bag!" Drummond continued in this vein for another minute, until John Groves was moved to intervene.

"Don't you talk to my mother like that! How dare you? Who do you think you are?" His voice was raised, though at nowhere near the volume that Drummond had reached.

The two men stared at each other. John Groves was a good five inches taller than the man in front of him but the height difference was no indicator of who was the more confident or where the more venom came from.

"So you are Mrs Groves's son," Drummond said softly. "Well,

well, well! That explains everything. And how alike you are! I can now see why you didn't listen to what I said to you a minute ago ... and it explains why you are so STUPID! Either you're as STUPID as that old bag of a mother of yours ... or you really want to have your teeth kicked in!" The volume was now increasing rapidly. "You stupid, pathetic prick! Do you WANT me to kick your teeth in! Well, come on, tell me! Do you really WANT to have your teeth kicked in?"

Drummond turned his attention to Mary Groves again. "Look at all the trouble you're causing, you silly bag!" A volley of expletives followed until John's hackles rose enough for him to lunge forward and give Drummond a push in the chest.

"Now that's enough!" he was really shouting this time.

Drummond snarled: "Don't you push ME," and he grabbed John by the throat and pinned him against the wall. "You fancy your chances, do you? Well, let me tell you, you don't have a chance!" The pressure on John's throat increased until he could hardly breathe. "You're pathetic, just pathetic ... just like your mother! There's only one way to deal with a pathetic creep like you ... and that's to kick your fucking teeth in!" Drummond removed one hand, his right hand, from his victim's throat and made a fist.

John Groves was gasping for breath and he sank down into a sitting position. Drummond removed his left hand from John's throat, shook his right fist at him, glared at Mary and stomped back upstairs to his flat.

John did not move for a minute or two. He thought he was going to throw up. His mother was sobbing silently. Eventually he got up and the pair went inside. "There's no point in calling the police," Mary Groves said. "They won't be interested."

Her son agreed, saying: "They couldn't do anything even if they were. For them, it's just a domestic dispute on domestic premises and, in any case, no one's been injured, and, even if someone was, there's no proof that Drummond caused it."

So, with more questions to be answered than even a hint of a solution, the pair sat in silence for an hour. Nothing was even said when, for a quarter of that period, the sound of a hammer banging a nail into something could be heard above. Eventually it was agreed that there was nothing for it but to go to bed. Sleep was not an option either, however.

Every quarter of an hour, there was the tapping of a broom handle on the floor or the sound of one of two different bells. Furniture was pulled back and forth along the floor. At one point, Drummond could be heard jumping up and down while moving around his flat. Then a heavy object was bounced down the stairs.

John Groves got out of the bed he was occupying in the spare bedroom, threw on some clothes and stormed towards the door leading to the porch. He was beside himself with rage. His mother heard him and got up, too. John flung the door open and saw that a small armchair had been hurled downwards, and that, just inside the front door, there was a pool of urine. John, who was now bereft of any self-control, pushed the armchair a foot towards the front door and shouted up the stairs: "Come down here, you little bastard! Come down here!"

The door upstairs opened, and Drummond called down: "What do you want, you creep?"

"What do you think you're playing at, you little bastard?!" John yelled.

Drummond bounded down the stairs in three strides. "What did you call me? Are you on the lookout for trouble again?" he asked, sneering.

"There's only one person who's causing trouble here … and that's you! I called you a little bastard because that's exactly what you are!"

"So," said Drummond, "you really DO want to have your teeth kicked in, don't you?!" Drummond moved a couple of inches forward so that the two men's bodies were almost touching each other, with Drummond's face at the same level as John's neck. Then, talking softly initially but raising the decibels every few seconds, he launched into yet another volley of insults. John tried to respond in kind but it didn't work. The insults, aimed at both John and his mother, became increasingly venomous until John lost the last vestige of his self-control.

He pushed Drummond backwards and aimed a punch at his head. Drummond avoided the blow easily and drove two short-arm hooks into the pit of John's stomach. John fell to the floor, and Drummond kicked him in the groin as he lay there writhing.

Drummond turned towards Mary Groves and snarled: "Now look what you've made me do, you silly old bag. It's lucky for the pair of you that I'm in a good mood! If you had caught me on a bad day, I would have fucking killed him! Now get that apology for a man inside before I change my mind and do some real damage!" Then, as he walked upstairs, he added: "You're pathetic! You're both pathetic!"

John got back inside his mother's flat as quickly as he could, though it had to be on all fours. Mary walked to where the telephone was and said: "Now I AM going to call the police."

An hour or so later, a car could be heard drawing up outside, followed by the sound of voices in the street. One of the voices sounded like Drummond's. The sound of footsteps on the stairs followed, and, a couple of minutes later, Mrs Groves's doorbell rang. Mary and John instinctively went to the front door together and, to their relief, a burly young policeman was standing there.

"What seems to be the trouble?" he asked, once inside Mrs Groves's sitting room. There was a faint look of amusement on the constable's young, pink face, which Mary and John Groves both found to be disconcerting. However, Mrs Groves did her best to recount what had just occurred. The policeman responded by saying that he had spoken to her neighbour already, and his version of events had been slightly different. He had said it "was just a neighbours' quarrel" and that Mr Groves had attacked him during an argument over rubbish left in the porch.

"Mr Drummond seems a bit of a funny little fellah to me," the constable conceded. "But, to his credit, he told me he was prepared to overlook the assault ... and he apologised for doing anything that might have wasted my time. I don't mean to criticise you but it's difficult for the police to become involved in a domestic dispute unless someone has actually suffered an injury, such as a broken nose or a cut lip at the very least. It would seem that, in this case, no one has been hurt. Am I correct in saying that?"

John Groves knew already that he was unmarked, save one small bruise on the stomach. He answered the constable's question with a resigned nod. As he got up to leave, the PC offered to call again "any time if there was real cause for concern." But the offer fell on deaf ears and drew no response. Once the policeman had driven off, silence reigned for several hours. Mary Groves went to her bedroom to lie down. John remained seated in the sitting room.

At around nine in the morning, a bell sounded above. Drummond could then be heard going out and John looked through the curtains to see him walking briskly towards Benson Street. His feeling of utter defeat and humiliation began to gnaw away at him. Anger took over. He paced round the sitting room, shaking with rage and throwing imaginary punches in the air. "I'm going to get you, Drummond!" he said aloud. The big question, of course, was how. Involving the police was not going to work. Neither was challenging Drummond to a fight!

So John proceeded to give serious thought to every option, however ridiculous, that sprang to mind. Should he hire a bunch of heavies? Or buy a pit bull terrier? Or run him over with a hired car? Or stab him with a kitchen knife? Or shoot him? Or lie in wait with a baseball bat? John began to think about the last of these options in detail … including where he would buy the bat and where he would lie in wait.

As he paced around the sitting room more and more frenetically, he could feel his heartbeat quickening. He began to feel sick. A tight feeling in the chest turned into pain. The pain started to travel down his left arm. The last thing he could do before collapsing and losing consciousness was to call out for help. Fortunately, the call was heard and his mother was able to get an ambulance to come round within minutes.

The crew took life-saving remedial action on the spot before taking him to hospital. Mary Groves remained in the waiting area all day while her son lay in intensive care and then, during the evening, in a room on his own in the cardiac ward. As always, the doctors and nurses were rushed off their feet.

Eventually, a registrar found the time to take Mrs Groves to one side and reassure her that her son was "out of immediate danger." However, the doctors wanted him to stay in for at least two weeks so that they could keep an eye on him. After that, rest and relaxation in a stress-free environment had to be the order of the day for some time to come. The registrar advised Mrs Groves to go home and make sure she had a good night's sleep. The suggestion was rejected. "I'm more likely to get that here!" she retorted.

However, Mary Groves knew she was only putting off the inevitable. She had to go back home some time, even if it was only to bring in milk and put some items she had shopped for in the fridge. And her next dose of medication was overdue. The new bottle of tablets, prescribed by Dr Eckersley-Wade, was in the bathroom cupboard.

So, at two o'clock in the afternoon, she left the hospital and took a bus that stopped outside it every 15 minutes and got off in Benson Street. The walk home from there was just over 400 yards. Unfortunately, though, the arthritis in her knee had suddenly worsened and every step she took entailed effort and pain. When she reached her front door, she discovered that the bottles of milk, delivered first thing that morning, had been smashed again.

Within minutes of her getting inside, there was a stamping of feet from above. Mary decided to make herself a cup of tea. In the absence of any milk in the fridge, it had to be black. A good cuppa might help her find some inspiration and, with it, a solution to her problems. In any case, she felt too tired to walk to the shops and buy more milk. Unfortunately, though, the black tea had only served to make her feel even more tense.

Every 10 minutes, either a bell sounded or a broom handle tapped the floor above. For much of the time, Drummond could be heard indulging in his customary "walkabout." Mary Groves decided to give the hospital a ring to see how her son was progressing.

The switchboard was busy but she was eventually able to make contact with a nurse she had met in person earlier. The nurse sounded harassed and her initial manner bordered on curtness.

However, when Mrs Groves' anxiety became apparent, the nurse's attitude changed. "There should be nothing to worry about as long as your son has plenty of rest and avoids stress," the nurse assured her.

The reassurance was obviously welcome, though it provided her with no clue as to what she could do about Drummond. So what was she to do? Call the doctor? Call the police? Call MAC Developments? Tap! Tap! Tap! Tap! It was now the turn of the broom handle. Mary Groves's head began to throb. The pain in her left knee became more acute than ever. "This just can't go on," she said to herself. There was nothing for it but to accept MAC Development's offer of money if she moved out, assuming that the offer still stood. What was there to stay for, after all?

As the firm was relatively new to the area, its name was not in the telephone directory yet. However, one of the two unsavoury-looking men who had called on her and tried to talk her into moving out had left a card. Mary remembered that she had angrily thrown it into either a wastepaper basket or the bin under the kitchen sink. She rummaged frantically through each of them in the hope that the card somehow remained in the bins, even though they all had been emptied at least once.

After emptying her two wastepaper baskets and examining the contents without success, she went into the kitchen and turned the bin in there upside down and emptied what was in there on to the floor.

"Please, please, please, let it be here!"

There were eggshells, empty tins, bottle tops yoghurt carton lids, left-overs from meals and, inevitably, pieces of paper and cardboard. Everything except what she was looking for.

Then, just as she was about to gather up the rubbish and return it to the bin, she noticed that two bits of cardboard were stuck to the bottom. One of them bore the words "CHRIS DOMAN, MAC Developments" and a mobile phone number. "Yes!" The feeling of relief was indescribable. It was also short-lived. Doman's mobile phone had been switched off, and she was back to square one.

Mary Groves rang the number again and again and again

without success. The bells upstairs, meanwhile, seemed to be getting louder, as did the broom handle noises. A large item of furniture being dragged across the floor sounded as if it might appear through a crack in the ceiling before crashing on to Mary's sitting room floor. She dialled 999 but put the receiver down before anyone could answer the call. What was the point?

After trying Doman's mobile phone once more, she considered popping out to the shops after all but the weather had changed suddenly and there was now a heavy rain storm. She wandered from room to room as if the answer to what she should do next would be written on a piece of paper for her somewhere. She went into the sitting room, the main bedroom, the spare bedroom, the kitchen and finally the bathroom She noticed that the bathroom cupboard had been left open, and saw the latest addition to its contents sitting on the top shelf. A new feeling of relief, a warm glow, swept through her. The headache, the arthritic knee and the noises above all disappeared from her consciousness. The relief for Mary Groves was immense, far stronger than when she found Doman's calling card. She now knew exactly what she could do ...

CHAPTER 15

APRIL MAY WAS RARELY out of Theo's mind. Business at Salter's was brisk, with plenty of inquiries coming in by telephone and in person, but hardly a minute passed without him hankering after her magnificent body.

The pair enjoyed many an extended lunch hour and, work commitments permitting, they coupled again as soon as their office doors closed for the day. Both had heavy workloads, though.

Theo, in particular, was sought out by a stream of potential house buyers and sellers every day. Many inquirers simply wanted to meet the new local hero. Some were aware that he was acting as selling agent for the great Wayne Benson ... and what was good enough for Benson was good enough for them! The ever willing Jenny Fitch was on hand to field many of these inquiries but even Jenny was beginning to feel the pressure. So Theo decided to advertise for a part-time helper in the office.

He was also concerned about the disappearance of Kelly, even though he was not sure what he was going to say to her about April! In the past, Kelly and Jenny had combined to provide effective back-up for Theo. He could do with her help now. The overriding issue, however, was whether she was all right.

So he told both Jenny and April that he was going to devote an afternoon to finding out where she was. Jenny reacted with a wry smile. April looked furious but said nothing initially. When Theo moved forward to kiss her, she turned her head away and said: "See you when I see you." She was clearly mortified. An air of insecurity and vulnerability that Theo had never seen before came to the surface. It made Theo yearn for her even more.

The most obvious first port of call was Rooker & Simpson, the insurance brokers' office. Edmund Rooker was, after all, the last person he had seen with Kelly. The premises were just a short drive away.

However, when he arrived the only person on hand was a young receptionist who said both partners were out and that she thought Mr Rooker was away on holiday. "Mr Simpson should be back in a couple of hours, and he should be able to tell you more," the receptionist told him.

So Theo then decided to telephone Sherry Munro, who he heard was au fait with local gossip and knew Rooker well, and this time he had better luck. "Yes, come round and have some tea with me. It will be lovely to see you," Sherry said.

Her home, with its sprawling gardens, was bathed in sunlight and looked as majestic during the daytime as it did on the night of the party. This time, though, there were no throngs of revellers, no security men, no floodlights and almost no parked cars. Hopefully, there were no thugs lying in wait nearby either!

A maid answered the door and led Theo to a small drawing room at the back of Sherry's, which had been kept locked while the party was in progress, and asked him to take a seat.

A couple of minutes later, Sherry appeared and greeted him warmly. She was wearing jeans and a long-sleeved top but did not look any different than she did at the party, when she had dressed up rather than down.

After pouring out some tea and offering Theo a biscuit, Sherry said: "I have a feeling I know why you're here. Are you still looking for Kelly Cheatham, by any chance?"

Theo nodded: "Well, yes. I have to admit that my call is not entirely social. The last time I saw Kelly was at your party, when she was dancing with Edmund Rooker, who I believe is a close friend of yours. I have got that right, haven't I? You do know Edmund well, don't you?"

Sherry sighed and said: "You could say that ... at least I THINK you could!" Then she added: "The trouble is that the last time I saw Edmund was ... well, have a guess!"

"You mean it was the same time as when I last saw them?"

"Yes, I'm afraid so. I had been hoping you might be able to shed some light on the subject. But it would appear that we are both equally in the dark." Theo told Sherry about his call to Rooker & Simpson, and said he would pay the office another visit before the day was out.

"Well, good luck," said Sherry. "I have only been able to get hold of a receptionist there, and she couldn't ... or perhaps wouldn't ... tell me anything."

Theo said he had decided to put the afternoon aside to concentrate on finding Kelly.

"We're obviously both in the same boat," he added. "It seems to me that we can help each other here. I will be going back to Rooker & Simpson, for a start, and I will, of course, let you know if I manage to glean any information."

Sherry said she had contacted a few friends and associates but had drawn a blank. "I just can't believe that Edmund would disappear like this, without even a 'by your leave'. He's such a stickler for correctness and propriety," she went on. "Mind you, he does have a naughty side to him."

"Really?"

"Oh, yes, you'd be surprised. He can be quite flirtatious, and he has a wicked sense of humour. He also has one of the sharpest minds I have ever come across. You'd have a job trying to pull a stroke with him, to outwit him, but I still can't imagine him doing anything underhand."

"Hmm!" Theo murmured. "The sooner I catch up with him the better."

Sherry then asked Theo if there was anyone else he planned to see about the missing pair.

Theo said he would have a word with the Bensons, because they were so influential in Camford and might have some further ideas about where to look, and then he would probably approach a few of his fellow estate agents.

Sherry sighed and paused for a moment, not entirely sure whether she should say what she wanted to say next. "Oh, that Wayne Benson!" she said at length. "I don't know how Lisa puts up with him! He's certainly not like Edmund Rooker."

"Why, do you mean that he is underhand in his dealings?" Theo asked. "Are you saying he's less than honest?"

"No, that's not what I'm saying really, not as far as I know anyway," Sherry said. "It's more a matter of him getting mixed up in things he shouldn't and getting out of his depth. And he doesn't half put his foot in it at times."

"Tell me more," said Theo.

"Well, I think the main thing to bear in mind about Wayne is that he's not very bright! In fact, there are times when he's as daft as a brush!"

"Well, I'll be blowed! He must have done something seriously daft to make you say something like that."

Sherry sighed again. "Oh, yes. There have been quite a few things. Some of them have been comparatively harmless, such as getting drunk, saying the wrong things and generally acting the goat. Unfortunately, though, there have been a few times when his stupidity ... and by stupidity I mean he is capable of being seriously stupid ... has got him into trouble."

Recent events had made Theo suspect this was the case already but he remained silent.

"He's run up gambling debts and been warned to pay up or else, and he also has this habit of driving without using a seat belt ... while over the limit, of course. On one occasion, he crashed into a car driven by Ray Williams while driving without a seat belt and, although I don't know the details ... these were carefully hushed up ... there was quite a bit of aggro over this."

Now Theo did speak. "I must confess to being amazed," he said, not entirely truthfully. "I've always had him down as a larger than life character but never imagined he'd step out of line to that extent. He is a councillor, after all."

Sherry winced, and sighed yet again. "Oh yes! And that was the biggest cock-up of them all, if you'll pardon my French! When his name was put up for a seat on the council, the public voted for him in droves. Then, before long, some bright spark put his name forward for the post of chairman of the housing committee. Within a month of him being appointed, the first of a series of highly questionable decisions was made, and I'm told that a number of his council colleagues were pretty relieved when, about a year ago, he suddenly resigned."

"What do you mean by questionable decisions?" Theo asked. "Are you saying there was some form of corruption going on?"

"I'm not sure, though there might well have been," said Sherry. "If there was corruption, it would have almost certainly occurred without Wayne being aware of what was going on. The only real certainty is that he was the most incompetent chairman of this or any other housing committee."

"What did occur?"

"Well, there's been the acceptance of a series of ill thought out planning applications, which should have either been modified before being allowed to go through, or rejected outright. In each case, Wayne was persuaded by people representing the developers to recommend acceptance and he was able to persuade the rest of the committee to go along with his recommendations. Some unsavoury characters involved in the building trade are known to have moved into the area, and it has even been suggested that Wayne had been bribed or put under duress in some way. No one can prove that, of course, and I doubt if anyone could imagine Wayne doing anything dishonest himself."

Theo was so intrigued by now that he had almost forgotten about his search for Kelly. "How were the planning applications ill thought out?" he asked.

"Well, the problems have ranged from inadequate parking provision to situations in which tenants have been harassed into quitting to make way for bulldozers," Sherry went on. "Some developments have caused traffic problems, some have been eyesores and out of keeping with the surrounding area and others have led to the appearance of undesirable occupants. You know that odious Ray Williams, don't you? Well, he's said to have made his presence felt in many an unwelcome way. We've had shady builders and other dubious characters turning up, and, as I said a minute ago, there have been tenants who have been forced out of their homes. There's even been a tenant committing suicide, I'm told."

"A suicide!?" exclaimed Theo. "Are you saying that Williams was responsible for this?"

"No, I don't know whether Williams was involved in that particular incident ... though it wouldn't surprise me if he was. He's said to have sailed pretty close to the wind in the way he has conducted business a number of times. He used to be a professional boxer based in London and, from what I've heard, he's still not averse to settling issues with his fists occasionally."

"Hmm, my first impression of him was clearly correct. But what about this suicide? How did it arise ... and where?"

"I'm not entirely sure," Sherry replied. "However, I believe it involved an elderly woman living alone on one of the developments that won approval via Wayne Benson. It happened very recently and the circumstances surrounding it are all hearsay at present, though it's been strongly rumoured that the developers had tried to get her to quit her home. That's all I know, I'm afraid."

Sherry then looked at Theo speculatively. "However, that's still more than I, or anyone else in Camford, I suspect, know about you. You've become more famous during the five minutes you've been in the town than most people manage in a lifetime. Yet none of us really knows anything about you."

"There's precious little to tell," said Theo casually. "It's nice of you to say that I've become famous but the truth of the matter is that I'm really rather boring."

Sherry was not ready to be denied ... not yet, anyway. "Where do you come from, for a start?" she asked.

"Oh, I made a decision to travel east," Theo said lightly. "You often hear of people going west, haven't you? Well, I made the momentous decision to do exactly the opposite! Exciting, isn't it?!"

Sherry began to protest mildly at this evasive answer but Theo gave a wave of the hand, shrugged his shoulders and, getting up to leave, said: "Many thanks for the tea, Sherry. Most enjoyable. Unfortunately time is marching on, I fear, and I'd better get over to Rooker & Simpson. If I glean any information from Edmund's partner or anyone else there, I will pass it on to you straight away. Oh, and if you're ever suffering from insomnia, let me know and I will provide a cure by telling you the story of my life!"

Theo was, in fact, genuinely pushed for time. He had stayed at Sherry's for longer than he had intended and, although what he had heard was both interesting and potentially productive, the whereabouts of Kelly remained a mystery. The visit to Rooker & Simpson, by contrast, turned out to be both brief and unproductive. Edmund's partner, Terry Simpson was back in his office but unable to help.

A small thin man in his thirties with prematurely greying hair, he told Theo: "I'm as much in the dark as you are, I'm afraid. My senior partner Edmund told me he was going away for a couple of weeks and did not want to be disturbed under any circumstances. It came right out of the blue, and on the day after he had been to a party at Sherry Munro's house. To be fair, though, Edmund had not had a single day off for nearly a year, so I can't really complain about being left holding the reins now. So I'm sorry, Mr Salter, but it appears that I can't be of any help to you."

Much of the afternoon had gone by now, though the brevity of his visit to Rooker & Simpson meant there was time to look up at least one other person.

Theo got on the phone to the Bensons, and Lisa answered. Wayne was out playing golf but she was available and would happily see him. The Bensons lived in Shakespeare Road, one of Camford's most prestigious locations and within five minutes walk of Sherry's. Lisa answered the door, looking as alluring as ever in figure-hugging black trousers and a black top.

The house was modern, detached and considerably smaller than Aggammenmon Hall, which had stood empty for six months … and would continue to do so until Sean McAvie moved in. The interior was filled with sporting trophies and other memorabilia, though Lisa had managed to find space for some old fashion photographs and other mementoes of her modelling days.

Lisa led Theo through the hall and into an open plan sitting room with polished wooden flooring and featuring leather armchairs, a piano and a long mahogany table. "I'm afraid I've no idea when Wayne will be back," said Lisa. "He's out playing golf, with the aid of a buggy, and, although George Bowes who he is with, is not a big drinker and will probably go straight home after the game, there will doubtless be plenty of others around who do like a drink. And, if that happens, Wayne will be spending more time at the 19th hole than anywhere else!"

"How will he get back here afterwards?" Theo asked.

Lisa gave an ironic little laugh and added, with some relief that Wayne did not drive to the golf course and would be brought home either by taxi or by a fellow golfer.

"At least he's got enough sense to do that." Lisa sighed in much the same way as Sherry had done earlier.

Lisa was talking in a vein that intrigued Theo enough for him to forget about the purpose of his visit. "You make him sound like an incorrigible drunkard!" Theo exclaimed. "He's not that bad, surely!?"

"Incorrigible is the word," said Lisa. "It could have been invented with Wayne in mind!"

Lisa went on to describe some of Wayne's escapades. Much of what she said tallied with what Theo had heard from Shelley that afternoon. There was a hint of desperation in her tone, making her appear even more vulnerable than when Theo first met her at the edge of that canal.

After a while, Lisa got on to the subject of Ray Williams and his unsavoury associates. "A couple of years ago, Wayne was driving home after a late night out with some of his drinking buddies. He was well over the legal drinks limit and, as was his wont, he had not bothered to put his seat belt on. He drove round a hairpin bend as if he was racing at Brand's Hatch, lost control and ran into a car coming from the opposite direction. Luckily Wayne has the fast reflexes you would expect being a top sportsman and he able to brake and lessen the impact of the crash, and no one was hurt," said Lisa. "I shudder to think what might have happened otherwise. Someone might have been killed … though I can't help wishing sometimes that the other driver had met his maker there and then."

She was close to tears, and Theo was hard put to resist the urge to put a comforting arm round her. "I think I'm ahead of you," he said. "The other driver was Williams, wasn't it?"

"Yes," Lisa said, half sobbing. "And that was when the real trouble began. Wayne was always getting in and out of scrapes but now he was in over his head."

Williams was able to see straight away that Wayne had not been wearing a seat belt, and it did not take him long to establish that he had been drinking.

"I could smash your face in and say it was you who started it ... and I've got witnesses," Williams had said, pointing at two companions sitting in his car, "or I could call the police. That would look good, wouldn't it? A famous sportsman and councillor getting fined and banned for what you've done!"

The damage to Williams' car was mainly to the bonnet and bumper and would have cost £200 or so to put right. Wayne wrote him out a cheque for £1,000 to cover the damage and, hopefully, to buy his silence. Williams snatched the cheque and said: "OK, that will do ... for now!"

"Something tells me that wasn't the end of it," said Theo.

"It certainly wasn't," Lisa replied. "A couple of days later, Williams, suggesting bygones should be bygones, invited Wayne to his house for an evening of playing poker. Anyone with even a smidgeon of common sense would have treated such an invitation with suspicion ... but not our dear Wayne. He fell for it hook, line and sinker!

"Williams had three of his mates round, too, and, at first, Wayne did well and made a bit of money. But, after he had been plied with a few drinks, he lost heavily and ended up £10,000 in debt. Williams and his friends had almost certainly been cheating but there was no proof, of course. Then the pressure began. There were hints at the possibility of unwelcome publicity ... not to mention having his legs broken. Unless ..."

"I can see where this is going!" said Theo, unable to conceal his excitement. "Williams coerced your husband into making him the selling agent for Aggammenmon Hall."

"That's right, and that's what was going to happen until the day you hauled him out of that canal," said Lisa.

Theo recalled his first confrontation with Williams at the great house and how Williams was less than effusive when he learned that Salter's was to be the selling agent.

"Good grief, your husband's generous to a fault ... at least he has been with me ... even it he does lack discretion at times," he said.

Lisa nodded. "But that's not all," she said. "Williams was livid about the agency thing and has threatened retribution. Wayne used to be the chairman of the city council's housing committee and I'm almost certain Williams and his associates got him to push through some very dubious planning applications. There was controversy over these projects, and Wayne suddenly resigned from the committee. I don't know for sure but am almost certain his committee colleagues eased him out."

"Isn't this something Wayne talks about?" Theo asked

"I'm afraid not. Wayne's the most open person I've ever met, which is one of the reasons I love him, but anything to do with Williams or his role on the council are banned subjects these days. He just clams up at their mention. There are now times when he has dark moods, and I just can't get through to him, can't talk to him, can't get him to open up. It's all so unlike Wayne."

A tear ran down her cheek.

Now Theo got up, moved to the armchair where Lisa was sitting and put an arm round her. Lisa squeezed his hand and kissed him on the cheek. Theo kissed her on the mouth. Lisa kissed him back but then pulled away, saying "No!"

An angry Theo stood up, grabbed Lisa's arms, hauled her to her feet and held her for several seconds.

"Let go, you're hurting me!" Lisa sobbed.

Theo did as he was told and apologised. "I'm sorry, I'm so sorry, I didn't know what I was doing. Please let me know if there's anything I can do to help you and Wayne overcome your problems," he said weakly.

Lisa was weeping uncontrollably. "Get out!" she screamed. "Just get out!"

CHAPTER 16

"OH GOD!" Theo said aloud.

He had been sitting at his desk at Salter's with his head in his hands for the best part of an hour. He had let Jenny field all the telephone calls and deal with the handful of callers. Jenny had asked him what was wrong but received no response. "Oh God! What have I done?" he groaned.

Jenny was becoming increasingly disconcerted. She had seen her boss have mood swings before but rarely anything like this. There had been the occasional loss of temper, and she knew he was capable of withering sarcasm. This time, however, Theo appeared to be on the verge of despair, and this worried Jenny. The last time he had been like this was when something had gone disastrously wrong following an error of judgement on his part. "For Christ's sake, Theo, tell me what's wrong. Please! I know you. Something's happened, hasn't it?"

"I'm sorry, Jenny, I can't tell you," he said, looking more crestfallen than ever.

Jenny got up, moved behind Theo and put her arms round him. "Is it something to do with Kelly?" she asked. "Come on, you know you can confide in me."

"I can't find Kelly and nobody seems to know where she is," Theo replied. "But it's not just that," he added after a pause. "Something else has happened. It's personal and I don't feel I can talk about it."

"OK," said Jenny. "But you'll have to snap out of it soon. Evelyn Knight is likely to be calling this morning. She's keen to see you, as you know."

Theo perked up slightly and said: "Thank you, Jenny, and bless you. You're right, of course." Perhaps Miss Knight would be the bearer of some much needed good news.

Jenny was, of course, right in suspecting that Theo had made a misjudgement. His treatment of Lisa had been unforgivable, a grave error of judgement and Theo was well aware that there would almost certainly be repercussions. He had misread the signals and allowed his sexual desires to get the better of him.

It was surely just a matter of time before Lisa would tell Wayne what had happened in his absence, and she would probably tell her best friend Sherry as well. He had behaved like a pig, and the two most influential people in Camford were about to find out!

He would cease to be the local hero. The queue of people vying for the privilege of shaking his hand, buying him a drink and doing business with him could disappear. Wayne had told him that he was his friend for life. Now he might well take a swing at him! Theo knew that he would have to be more circumspect with people, especially the opposite sex.

The telephone rang and Theo picked up the receiver for the first time that morning. It was Evelyn Knight, asking if it would be all right if she popped round for a chat. "Sure. Come over now, if you like," he told her.

She turned up wearing a twin set and high-heeled silver shoes … and precious little else! A large V at the front revealed ample cleavage, while the skirt left six inches of thigh exposed. Her auburn hair had been cut since he last saw her, and was now as short as his. "Hi!" she drawled. "I've been looking forward to having the chance to talk to you properly for some time, and I have a proposition to put to you that could be of mutual benefit." Theo wondered what she meant by "proposition" and could not conceal a smile. His visitor seemed to know what was in his mind and smiled, too. "Is there somewhere we can talk away from the big wide world?" she drawled, almost teasingly. Theo, who managed … though only just … not to say he would take her upstairs, led her up to his first floor office. Evelyn sat down and crossed her shapely legs.

"You've aroused my curiosity. What sort of deal do you have in mind?" Theo asked.

"Well," Evelyn said, her drawl more pronounced than ever, "I want to offload some of my clientele, and am thinking of winding up my business altogether. On the other hand, another idea might be to go into partnership with someone like yourself. What do you think about that, Theo? It is all right for me to call you Theo and not Mr Salter, isn't it?"

"Yes, of course. I hope it's all right for me to call you Evelyn?"

"Yah, naturally," said Evelyn. "And ... Theo ... does the idea of you relieving me of some of my clientele, or possibly even going into partnership with me, interest you?"

For a moment, Theo was genuinely gob-smacked.

"Well, don't look so shocked, Theo," Evelyn drawled. "Say something, please ... even if it's 'Get lost'!"

Theo WAS interested but his first response was to ask: "Why me? What about the other estate agents in Camford who you must know much better than me. You've known me for barely five minutes!"

Evelyn sighed and said: "Oh, yah, but the others are such a dull lot. I don't particularly like them and I want some excitement in my life! And you are anything but boring!"

Theo felt tempted to point out that the likes of Nathan Pike, George Bowes and Bernie Ratcliffe were not exactly dullards. Neither was Ray Williams, for that matter. But he kept his counsel. He knew from what he had heard that Evelyn Knight was given to following flights of fancy.

The daughter of a brigadier turned stockbroker and a mother who walked out on the family a couple of years after her birth, she had been packed off to an expensive boarding school at the age of nine. She soon earned a reputation for rebelliousness. Initially her misdemeanours were confined to the classroom, playground or sports field but by the time she was 14 she was inviting local lads round to the dormitory for late night parties. Eventually she become pregnant, had an abortion and was removed from the school at the request of the headmistress.

By then, Brigadier Knight, whose health was failing, had quit the Stock Exchange and set up the local estate agency Knights. A few years later, after Evelyn was expelled from another school, Brigadier Knight decided the only thing to do with her was to give her a job at his estate agency. She showed that she had a flair for the job and eventually became a partner in the business. A year later, Brigadier Knight died and Evelyn took charge. Before long, though, she appeared to be going off the rails again. The doors of her office started to be closed more often than they were open, and rumours abounded that she was having a secret tryst with a prominent local businessman.

"Why do you want to do what you're proposing?" Theo asked her.

"Oh, I want to try my hand at other things," Evelyn said with a wave of a hand. "I have only ever been an estate agent, and that's only because my late father gave me a job. I want to do something for myself, and if I shed some of my workload that should be possible"

"What sort of thing do you want to do?"

"I want to do more artistic things. I have always loved painting and poetry, and I also want to try my hand at writing a novel. You're not going to disappoint me and produce a damper, are you?"

"No, I wouldn't want to do that, though I think it's a bit premature to talk about partnerships just yet."

"Yah, that's fair enough. Maybe later, though."

"OK," said Theo. "If you want to offload some of your business, I might be interested. Obviously, though, I want to know what sort of clientele we're talking about and who gets what in terms of commission on house sales."

"Tell you what, why don't you take two or three of my clients for starters and see how we go from there?"

As it turned out, Evelyn only had a handful of potential house-sellers on her books. Theo listened intently as she described them, and then stated his preferences. One of the preferred clients was an elderly widower who had decided to emigrate to New Zealand to be with his daughter and son-in-law. His house had been on the market for two weeks but the owner wanted a quick sale. Another was an

American woman who had inherited a large sum of money and hit on the idea of buying and letting out a couple of properties in England as an investment. However, she had found the travelling and the work involved in being a landlady too much of a chore and wanted to pull out.

A third client had left the Camford area for Plymouth and had not been able to sell his village cottage. The property had stood empty for six months, largely because it had been over-priced. It was agreed that Theo should take over these three clients with immediate effect, let them know immediately and give Evelyn a slice of commission on sales achieved. The amount of work Evelyn had done in connection with each client so far varied to some extent, and so it was agreed that the percentages would vary, too. The arrangement was to be verified in an exchange of letters.

"So, that's all done and dusted," Theo said, once negotiations had finished.

"Yah, and thank God for that!" Evelyn replied, uncrossing her legs.

"What do you say to a celebratory drink somewhere?"

"Great idea!" agreed Theo. "But I've got three new clients to contact first and some other business to attend to after that. But some other time, by all means."

The pair went downstairs and shook hands, with Evelyn giving Theo's hand a little squeeze before departing.

"Well, well, well! You've perked up a bit, haven't you?" Jenny said as Theo returned to his front office desk with a smile on his face. "Have you made another conquest, by any chance?"

"Yes, you could say that, and it might turn out to be a very lucrative one," he replied. "Now I have some phone calls to make."

The rest of the morning and much of the afternoon saw the office buzzing with activity as Theo conducted business with his three new clients on the telephone and, along with Jenny, dealt with a stream of inquiries from other sources.

By four o'clock, an air of comparative calmness took over.

"Phew!" said Jenny. "Now we can relax a bit. I'm sure you'll be glad to do that, anyway."

Theo offered a hint of a smile and then his face darkened. "Not really," he said. "There are still matters to be attended to."

"Oh, sorry!" Jenny exclaimed. "I'd forgotten all about Kelly."

"That's not the half of it," Theo said quietly. "There are fences to be mended." And then, barely audibly, he added: "Starting with April."

CHAPTER 17

THEO WAS FEELING lucky again. He was back in his Ford Escort, heading for the coast with April May by his side. He had mended his first fence! Theo had found the task of convincing April that he still cared for her, despite his continued search for Kelly, easier than expected. "We go back a long way," he had told her. "Kelly's been part of my life for a long time. I can't just erase her from my mind, even though you're the one who matters now."

April accepted the explanation surprisingly readily, and the suggestion of a weekend away was even more acceptable. Theo had also told her about his new arrangement with Evelyn Knight, ensuring that she heard about it from him rather than someone else. "She's after a partnership is she? I can see I'm going to have to keep an eye on the two of you," April had said with a smile.

Theo's only immediate problem was one of concentration. April's hand, which had been straying up and down his thigh for the last 20 minutes, suddenly moved higher. Theo took the first turning on the left and headed a little way down a narrow gravelled lane flanked by a hedge and shrubs.

The pair stepped out of the car and into the sunlight, which was gathering strength. Theo unzipped the back of April's skimpy sun dress, letting the garment fall to the ground. A few seconds later, a naked April was lying across the car bonnet as Theo made love to her. The love-making continued for an hour, with main road traffic passing within 10 yards from the barely concealed parked vehicle. When Theo eventually suggested that they resume their journey, April's response was to pull down his trousers and take his manhood in her mouth. The lovers reached their destination six hours after setting off. The distance they had covered was 80 miles!

The place they were due to stay at was a small, homely hotel 50 yards from the sea front. It had room for just 20 guests. One of its attractions was a small bar, where snacks could be bought at almost any hour of the day, which is why it had been recommended to Theo by both Nathan and Bernie. Theo and April arrived at "The Nook" just in time for supper but decided to have a quick bar snack and then head for the beach.

Because the hotel was about 100 yards from the village of Sandley, the stretch of sand directly in front of it was virtually the preserve of the hotel guests. The shore line was known to be safe for swimmers and was especially popular among families with young children during the daytime. Later on, the beach tended to be deserted.

Outside, Theo and April were greeted by a red sunset, a warm, gentle breeze and the sound of minute waves caressing sand. The tide was almost in. A short flight of stone steps led to a 12ft wide strip of sand that remained dry in all but the stormiest of weathers. There was no one else to be seen. April disrobed and walked into the water before plunging forward and swimming powerfully away until she was barely visible in the half dark. After a few moments, Theo followed suit, leaving his clothes in a pile next to hers. He was a fine swimmer, a natural athlete, but he was still hard put to catch his lover up.

Once the pair had covered a couple of hundred yards, all they could see of terra firma was a light from the windows of "The Nook." A slightly stronger light could be seen in the opposite direction from a ship.

The lovers soaked up the scenery, caressed each other and frolicked until April suddenly said: "Bet you can't beat me back to the beach!" She was right. Theo summoned up all the power at his disposal but the strong, graceful strokes produced by April ensured that she won the race by about 10 feet.

"You're quite a gal, aren't you?!" Theo said at the end of it all. April managed to laugh, though both were short of breath.

Then, at that very moment, more laughter could be heard. Two voices, a man's and a woman's, could be heard a short distance away. The voices gradually grew louder until two outlines could be seen. Theo recognised one of them immediately. It was Kelly Cheatham. A minute later, four people froze. Kelly, slender but exquisitely shapely, stood there in the briefest of bikinis. Beside her was Edmund Rooker, also slender but surprisingly athletic looking in his swimwear. Theo and April were still naked.

The four eyed each other for barely a second before Kelly and Edmund, half walking and half running, headed in the direction of "The Nook," allowing the other two to get dressed undisturbed. The pair remaining on the beach gazed at the other two until they disappeared and then at each other, without saying a word. It was not until they were back in their hotel room that either of them spoke. "Well, blow me down!" April eventually exclaimed, almost in a whisper. "Is there no end to the surprises one can get through knowing you?"

"No one's more surprised than I am," was the reply. "Hopefully it's a welcome surprise?"

Theo, suspecting that April was fishing, said: "Well, at least I know she's all right, though, to be honest, I had just about given up on any hope of clapping eyes on her again."

A cynical smile swept across April's face. "Chances are you'll see her again at breakfast. The pair of them were heading towards the hotel when they left us. They might even be in the room next to ours right now!"

Theo grimaced. "Don't!"

Then April said, as much to herself as anyone else: "The big surprise for me was what a nice body that Edmund Rooker had!"

Less surprising was the fact that the planned night of passion away from the eyes and ears of Camford had lost its lustre. The love-making lacked the abandon of previous times.

April slept fitfully, Theo hardly at all. At six in the morning, Theo decided to wash, shave, get dressed and pop out for a walk on his own. He crept out of the room as quietly as he could and, once outside, headed towards the beach. Dawn had broken sufficiently for him to look seawards and observe a long expanse of flat, wet sand. The waves could be heard lapping over the shore line in the distance. Theo opted to walk along the path just above the beach towards Sandley and see what it had to offer. The village could arguably be described as a hamlet in a time warp. Its 300 or so houses had nearly all been built during the 19th century or earlier. "The planners must have kept a tight rein on developers here," Theo thought.

The houses came in a variety of shapes and sizes and, for the most part, were separated by narrow cobbled streets and alleys. A central High Street was the only road wide enough for two cars to pass each other from opposite directions. The High Street also sported a village stores which doubled up as a post office and a tiny pub-cum-restaurant

As Theo sauntered along the High Street, he could hear footsteps approaching from an alley nearby. The time was 6.20am, there was no else about and, recalling what had occurred while he was walking alone after Sherry's party in Camford, he stopped and braced himself in readiness for another nasty surprise. The surprise turned out to be Edmund Rooker. The two men eyed each other for a moment. Theo's first instinct was one of hostility towards the man who had taken his girl. But he quickly realised that he was in no position to preach fidelity! Edmund seemed to be reading his thoughts. "Great minds think alike!" he said with a half-smile.

"So it seems," Theo agreed.

"I didn't get much sleep either."

The men shook hands and agreed to walk together until it was time for breakfast. On the face of it, they were as different as chalk and cheese. Edmund, with his thinning grey hair, horn-rimmed spectacles and grey suit, white shirt, dark tie and black shoes, was socially correct at all times. The dark haired, younger Theo, wearing a tracksuit and trainers, had a casual, some might say dangerous, air about him. Yet any feeling of animosity or unease was dissipated almost straight away, though both avoided talking about Kelly. Theo discovered that Edmund had taken a master's degree in business studies and studied for a doctorate in psychology before entering the world of commerce. He had also excelled in sport at school, and was once a county squash champion. Much of their conversation was inevitably about sport in general and cricket in particular, though Theo soon learned that Edmund was equally at home talking about current affairs, religion, music and art.

His mind was so quick and incisive that he even managed to glean a few snippets of information about Theo's past. Edmund became the first Camford area resident to know that Theo's upbringing in the West Country had been a troubled one, with a domineering father and a couple of brushes with the police. However, like Edmund, Theo had always been a consummate sportsman, having represented his school at cricket, soccer, rugby, boxing and tennis.

Theo had always taken pride in his prowess at repartee, quick reactions and his ability to tell a joke or make a quip at the drop of a hat in any situation. Edmund, despite his austere appearance, was more than a match for him in these respects.

There was, in short, a lot more to him then met the eye … and it was not so hard to see how he could attract members of the opposite sex, such as Kelly and Sherry! It was a good hour before the two men decided to make their way back to "The Nook." As they approached the narrow road that led to the hotel, they saw two women sitting on the grass and conversing merrily near the steps to the beach. April and Kelly were chatting so gaily that they did not notice Theo and Edmund approaching until they were a few feet away.

"Couldn't you two sleep last night, then?" April asked, grinning broadly, once she had caught sight of them. "Have you got guilty consciences or something?!"

Kelly, smiling a little more coyly, said: "Perhaps a good breakfast together will cleanse all our consciences!"

CHAPTER 18

BREAKFAST AT "THE NOOK" was as convivial as any breakfast could be.

Edmund continued to surprise, this time with his skill as a raconteur. The only serious note was when he mentioned the suicide in Benson Lane and the suspicion that, somewhere along the line, Sean McAvie could have had a hand in it.

There was even talk of the two couples forming some sort of business alliance, with Theo and April perhaps forging a partnership, Kelly working for both of them and a system of referrals from Edmund's insurance business to Theo's and April's estate agency and vice-versa. Possible names for a new, merged estate agency were mooted, including April May & Salter and Salter & McArdle.

Later on, the quartet savoured the sea air, swam naked after dusk and retired to bed without the need to take an early stroll the following morning!

The idyll ended all too quickly. Back in his office, Theo had cause to fret once more. He needed to know more about the suicide in Benson Lane.

He needed to make his peace with Lisa and, if possible, avoid facing her husband's wrath by persuading her to keep quiet about his indiscrete move on her. He also had decisions to make over the clients Evelyn Knight had passed on to him. One possibility was for him to buy one of the properties for himself.

Yet another source of unease was Edmund. The multi-talented insurance broker had managed to winkle bits of information about him that he was not keen to divulge. Theo realised, on reflection, that here was a man with the ability to outmanoeuvre him and catch him unawares. The best course of action, he felt, might be to cool down this new friendship and give him a wide berth for a while.

Next on the agenda, though, was a visit to Benson Lane.

When Theo saw that the road was deserted, save a parked removals van, he asked one of the two removal men putting furniture into the van if there was any chance of him talking to the house's occupant.

"I'm afraid she's dead," the man replied. "Committed suicide, I'm told. Her son's inside but he's just come out of hospital, having had a heart attack."

Theo asked if he could talk to him, and the man went inside to find out. A moment later, John Groves came to the door and, on learning who the caller was, invited him in.

John Groves looked pale and frail and had lost weight. He made it clear that he had been ordered by doctors to rest and to avoid stress.

Theo expressed concern over what he had heard and explained that, although he had been appointed to market the properties in the new development in Benson Lane, he had played no part in any perceived malpractice.

"How do you know there's been malpractice?" Groves asked curtly.

"Just hearsay," Theo replied. "I don't know any details but rumour has it that attempts were made to force your mother to quit, and that concerns me deeply. I would like to know the truth."

John Groves gave a full account of what he knew, with particular reference to the problems with Derek Drummond. "Is he in the flat above now?" Theo asked.

"No, he's disappeared, and so have all his belongings. It's as if he was never in the flat at all! Do you know him, by any chance?"

"Yes, I believe I do!"

John Groves suddenly said he felt tired and needed to lie down for a while. So Theo apologised for disturbing him, voiced thanks for agreeing to talk to him, and departed. Theo's next port of call was the home and office of Sean McAvie.

McAvie lived 10 miles out of town in a house on a hill. The hill was one of just a few of any size in the entire region. The house, lent to him by an associate, was unique. Sitting on the brow of the hill and approached by a steep, narrow track, it featured walls constructed almost entirely of glass. When the lights were switched on in the evening, it could be seen shining like a beacon from afar. It was known as Lightner's Lighthouse, named after the owner, Seamus Lightner, who had upped sticks and left for Spain a few months earlier. Theo's Ford Escort was spotted long before it reached the asphalt parking area at the front. Sean McAvie appeared at the front door wearing a singlet, shorts and trainers. His body was lean and hard, despite his advancing years. "Hello, Theo. To what do I owe this honour?" he asked with a smile on his mouth but not in his eyes.

"I've just paid a visit to Benson Lane and had an interesting little conversation with the son of the woman who committed suicide there." Theo replied. "I take it you know about the suicide?"

McAvie eyed Theo thoughtfully for a moment before inviting him in. "And you clearly want to talk about it," he said. "But would you mind if I finish my daily workout first?" Without waiting for a reply, he led Theo along a corridor that bypassed a long through-lounge and kitchen to what he called the "recreational area," which consisted of an indoor swimming pool, sauna and finally a gym.

A brooding Ray Williams, who had obviously just had a swim and was now sitting in a robe by the pool edge, glared as Theo approached. The gym contained a treadmill, cycling machine, dumb bells, barbells, various machines designed to strengthen different muscle groups and an area for stretching and warming up and down. Chris Doman was jogging on the treadmill, Derek Drummond was doing press-ups and a skinny, sandy-haired woman called Fiona was pedalling away feverishly on the cycling machine. "Do try out any of this equipment, if you feel like it," McAvie said to his visitor. "I've still got a couple of sets of curls to do."

Theo, who was no stranger to weight training, declined on the grounds that he had no kit with him and would prefer to watch.

McAvie picked up a 70 pound barbell and lifted it up to his

chest and back down to waist height 12 times. After a minute's rest, he repeated the process. He then moved to another corner of the gym for 15 minutes of stretching and warming down before heading for a shower at the side. Doman and Drummond finished their workouts, too. Theo could not fail to be impressed. McAvie reappeared wearing a tracksuit, and asked the leotard-clad Fiona to make some tea and took Theo into the lounge.

Almost the entire length of the wall on one side of the room was glass, though this could be screened by shutters via the pull of a cord when required. A polished wooden tiled floor was partially covered by straw mats, while furniture included a leather settee, four leather armchairs, a pine table with six matching chairs, and another table on which stood a television set and stereo.

"Right!" McAvie said, once the two men were both seated. "You were asking about the suicide in Benson Lane. What have you heard?"

Theo told him about his meeting with John Groves and what he had heard about Drummond.

"I see!" McAvie exclaimed with a raise of the eyebrows. "That sounds highly unsavoury, highly unsatisfactory! However," he added, after a pause, "I must confess to some surprise, as I had heard a somewhat different version of events."

"You mean from Drummond?" Theo asked, with a hint of accusation in his tone.

At this moment, Fiona entered with a tray laden with tea, milk, cups, saucers, plates and biscuits, followed by Drummond, Doman and Williams. "You have come in at the ideal time!" McAvie said to them. Then, to Drummond, he added: "My friend Theo has just told me a most interesting version of the events that occurred before your friend Mrs Groves committed suicide in Benson Lane." McAvie took on an almost bloodshot look as he repeated almost word for word what Theo had told him.

Drummond looked sheepish and then angry. "That's absolute rubbish!" he rasped, glowering at Theo.

"I'm glad to hear it," McAvie said sarcastically. "I'd be most disappointed if you had stepped over the line. Are we to assume, then, that this story Theo got from Mrs Groves's son was a fabrication, a pack of lies? Was it all made up?"

"Of course it was. I tried to be friendly, and even invited her to tea, but she and her son gave me trouble from the moment I moved in. That's all I have to say," Drummond said. His self-control looked in danger of snapping any minute.

"Why would Mr Groves make such a story up?" Theo asked him coolly. "And why did you start living in the flat above Mrs Groves?"

Drummond's blue eyes flashed and his fists clenched. "How much more of this am I expected to put up with?" he demanded of McAvie.

"Now, now, now, let's stay calm," his employer replied. "Perhaps it would be best if you went into the garden to cool down while I try to answer Mr Salter's questions." Drummond got up and left, giving Theo a malevolent look as he went.

Ray Williams, who had remained silent until then, looked at Theo and said: "It seems to me that there are now two people who're itching to take a pop at you!"

"You be quiet!" Now it was McAvie's turn to be angry. "I've just about had enough of your antics. You're beginning to become a liability." Williams took this as a cue to leave the room, too. Once he had done so, the shifty-eyed Doman entered the conversation. "Why exactly are you so concerned about what happened in Benson Lane?" he asked Theo with a half-snarl. Theo couldn't help thinking that here was a younger, cockney version of McAvie.

"Well, apart from anything else, I like to be told what's going on," he retorted. "A suicide might mean nothing to you but I don't like the fact that it has happened at all. Loss of life might seem unimportant to you but I'm sure you're bright enough to realise that a suicide might be bad for business."

The conversation was in danger of getting out of control. "OK!" McAvie said, holding up a hand. "Now let's all calm down! Squabbling among ourselves is not going to get us anywhere." McAvie looked at Theo and added: "You have a point about being kept informed and I apologise for my failure to do so here.

"I can also understand your unease about what has occurred

in Benson Lane and, whatever the true version of events is, the whole situation leaves a lot to be desired. Drummond was living in Benson Lane because he had just come into my employ and I fixed him up with some temporary accommodation there. If I find out his behaviour has been out of order, I will make sure he is held to account."

Theo suspected that McAvie knew exactly what had gone on but could not, of course, prove it. "All right," he said, "but don't you think there should be some recompense for the Groves family?"

McAvie sighed. "Aye, I guess you're right. I could write a letter of condolences to John Groves and offer some form of compensation, perhaps offer to pay for the cost of the funeral." Theo nodded.

"Right, that's settled!" said McAvie. "I'm keen for us to do business again. "Is there anything that I can do for you, anything that I can do to show goodwill?"

Theo paused for a second and then said, through his teeth "Well, there is one thing ... it concerns that ape Williams ..."

A slow grin spread across McAvie's face. "Are you saying what I think you're saying?" he asked.

"Without a doubt!"

"Are you sure that's discreet?"

"Discreet! Yes, I'd prefer to be discreet. Williams and I have some unfinished business, and your place seems to be as good as any for settling it ... just the two of us ... discreetly!"

McAvie chuckled. "All right," he said. "And I know just the spot where the two of you can conduct your ... business!"

He took Theo to an area of garden surrounded by hedges at the back. A year ago, the land had been earmarked as the site for a new vegetable-growing project but the owner's sudden departure to Spain meant it was lying fallow instead. The plot was square in shape and much the same size as a boxing ring.

McAvie set off to find Williams.

When Williams appeared, sauntering along with a prize-fighter's gait and shadow boxing as he went, he made no attempt to conceal his smugness. Here was his chance to re-live his glory days in the ring and, at the same time, humiliate a hated adversary. Williams took off his shirt to reveal massive shoulders and arms that resembled sides of meat. But, although, he was still wearing a singlet, there was no disguising the sagging belly.

Theo took note and took off his own shirt, and Williams was forced to observe that there was no singlet and no flab. Williams was taller, wider and almost four stone heavier. However, the smug expression had gone.

Doman and Drummond then appeared, too, and McAvie said to them: "OK, I hope you enjoy the show!" Then, to the two combatants, he said: "Right! The pair of you have been itching to get at each other. Well, here's your chance! Get to it!"

Theo Salter and Ray Williams circled each other for a few moments before Williams threw a left jab. Theo moved his head to one side so that the punch whistled past his ear and aimed a left of his own at Williams' ample stomach. Williams blocked that punch with his right elbow.

The pair circled each other again before Williams feinted with a left and threw a thunderous right cross which Theo could only half avoid. Williams then staggered Theo with a left hook and drove him backwards with a flurry of blows from both hands. Theo avoided some of these by side-stepping and then standing in close and landing some blows of his own to the body.

Williams used his weight advantage to push Theo backwards and then landed a crunching right to the jaw. Theo's knees buckled momentarily but he was able to land a right to the mouth followed by a vicious left hook to the stomach.

Williams pushed Theo backwards again and slammed home another devastating right and Theo went down. Theo was hurt but he was an accomplished boxer in his own right, and he was confident that, as long as he could withstand the initial onslaught, he would eventually prevail.

If McAvie and the others had not been present, Williams would have been tempted to deliver a kick as Theo hit the ground. Instead he waited until his man was up, and then threw another volley of blows. But he received several in return, and he was beginning to breathe heavily.

The pugilist-turned-estate agent tried to keep the fight at long range. He tried to make the most of his extra weight and, every now and again, used his head, thumb and forearms and hit below the belt in an attempt to establish ascendancy.

These tactics failed to work and every foul was repaid in kind. Theo began to land the more frequently and more tellingly of the two and Williams realised that drastic action was needed to stave off defeat. His mouth was open and he was forced to grunt whenever a blow sank into his stomach. Williams suddenly backed away and lowered his guard, inviting his adversary to come forward. Theo advanced but only by a few inches so that when Williams aimed a kick at his groin, it lacked full power and, in any case, landed on a thigh instead.

The next part of Williams' ploy was to hurl himself on a doubled-up Theo and batter him once he had him on the ground. This tactic failed, too.

Theo turned sideways so that the onrushing Williams landed on his back following a hip throw. Theo was on top of him in an instant. "All right, you big fat shit! If you want to play dirty, that's fine with me!" he snarled, as he rained punches on to Williams' face. Theo's expression was one of uncontrollable rage.

Blood started to pour out of Williams' nose and mouth, and two teeth were spat out before the beaten man lost consciousness. Theo failed to hear McAvie shout "Oi! That's enough!" and he continued to slam home punch after punch until two pairs of hands grabbed him from behind and pulled him off.

"What the hell do you think you're playing at!?" McAvie shouted angrily. "Do you want us all to get mixed up in a murder case?" But Theo was not listening. He was looking at the two men who had rescued Williams and realising that there was still unfinished business to be resolved.

"All right, you had a score to settle and now you've settled it. Now clear off! Go home, and I'll be in touch in a few days. You might like to remember that there's the purchase of Aggammenmon Hall to be completed ... not to mention the little matter of how you're going to help me market the Benson Lane project. But right now, go home, for Christ's sake! Go on, fuck off!" Theo put his shirt back on and made to leave. But all he could think about at that time was the attack on the night of Sherry's party. Williams was not his only assailant, and it did not take much to work out who were with him that night.

CHAPTER 19

"WHERE THE HELL have you been?"

It was one of those questions that did not need an answer. Paul Shenfield, the deputy news editor was back late from lunch yet again. And Ivor Lewins, the new deputy editor, was well aware of where he had been.

"Sorry, I lost track of the time," the time-keeping transgressor mumbled feebly. His breath reeked of alcohol and his crumpled suit was covered with dandruff and stained with liquor, tobacco smoke and God knows what else. Ivor Lewins, younger by more than 20 years, stood over the figure slumped over his desk and glared down at him. The new deputy editor of "The Camford Daily News" had been appointed at the behest of the new managing director, Stephen Elkington, whose remit from the board was to introduce a new broom, bring in new, young talent and clear away the dead wood.

Ivor Lewins, who was nearly always clad in a navy blue blazer, grey trousers with knife-edge creases, a white shirt, gold cuff links, dark tie held in place by a polished brass pin, and highly polished black shoes, was just 28-years-old. His jet black hair had been brushed back, and there was not a solitary lock out of place.

Paul Shenfield was 52 and had clearly seen better days. He was once almost as thrusting and aggressive as the man standing over him. His all-round experience as a reporter was almost second to none. But a broken marriage and an excessive love of the bottle had gradually eroded the enthusiasm and drive that had once made him a Fleet Street high-flier. "I'll try to be a good boy in future," he told Lewins wearily.

"The editor wants to see you," Lewins barked. "And that means now!"

Paul Shenfield followed Ivor Lewins out of the newsroom and across a small, drab reception hall to the editor's office. His heart missed a beat when he saw that Colin Edwards, the editor, had the new MD with him. "Please sit down," the editor said to him as calmly as he could. The MD fixed a pair of gimlet eyes on him.

Colin Edwards was another ex-Fleet Street man. He was slightly younger and only slightly smarter in appearance than Paul Shenfield. His suit and shirt were of better quality but no better put on! Edwards and Shenfield had known each other in London long before they ended up in Camford.

Stephen Elkington, a newcomer to the town, was in his early thirties, had had a public school education and, after qualifying as a chartered accountant, had taken up a succession of executive posts on various provincial newspapers. He usually wore a Saville Row suit and he drove a Porsche. And he had already made it clear that he regarded journalists as a breed of habitual pub crawlers who spent more time writing out expenses claims than producing material for the newspaper.

"I'm sorry, Paul, but this just will not do," Edwards said at length. "You are spending far too much time in the pub and not enough at the news desk, where you should be directing reporters," he sighed. "We can't have people, especially key members of staff, abusing their responsibilities like this."

"I understand you have been late back from lunch yet again!" Elkingon rasped. "The paper is no longer making money and there have got to be changes. And it's about time some of you journalists got off your arses and did some bloody work!" Paul Shenfield went pale. So, too, did Colin Edwards. Elkington glared at both of them.

It was the editor's cue to speak again. "One of the first things we must do is improve the content of the paper and strengthen our news-gathering operation. To accomplish that, we must have a stronger news desk."

Paul's heart sank to his boots. "This can only mean the chop," he thought to himself. The editor had a resigned air about him. Was he heading for the chop, too?

"What we need is staff who can make money for us," Elkington cut in.

Edwards went pale again. "Jim Johnson has agreed to stand down as news editor and move to the subs' table, and a replacement will be coming over from one of our sister newspapers in Staffordshire," he told Paul. "We think it is time for you to have a change, too." The short pause that followed seemed interminable.

"I want to appoint Alan Carpenter to the post of deputy news editor. I know he is only barely in his mid-twenties but he is energetic, intelligent, enthusiastic and full of ideas. The paper needs a younger, more thrusting profile, and we have to make changes ... urgently."

Edwards looked nervous. The MD made little effort to conceal his contempt. Paul Shenfield tried to prepare himself for the worst. "Under the circumstances, we feel a change of roles is the best step forward for you. There are, in fact, two possibilities. You can either move to the sub-editors' table, where your experience of handling news would be invaluable, or you can take up a new post which we are about to create.

"Oh really, what's that?" Paul was beginning to feel exasperated over the way the details his fate were being kept from him.

"It's a very important post," said Elkington. "It entails staying sober, smartening up your appearance, getting on with an important section of our advertisers ... and helping to make money for the company."

Edwards then spoke in a more placatory tone. "We have decided to introduce two property sections, a weekly pull-out supplement and a monthly commercial property section dealing with shops, offices, factories, warehouses and so forth," he said.

"The two sections will contain advertisements from estate agents, builders, developers, building societies, solicitors and anyone else concerned with the buying and selling of property. Each section will require good, solid editorial matter, and you would need to liaise with advertisers ... estate agents in particular ... to get the right sort of material.

"The residential property supplement, which we expect to be the bigger of the two, could, for example, feature a piece about Aggammenmon Hall ... with not only details of its accommodation but also something about its history and its owners. Wayne Benson could be asked why he chose to sell it, and you could also contact the new owner and ask him what plans he might have for it in the future.

"The estate agent involved in its recent sale, incidentally, was Theo Salter, who, as you know, has been somewhat elusive with us up until now. He's bound to be a source of interesting material ... if you can get him to talk to you." After a few moments silence, the editor added: "Give yourself a day or two to think about it, by all means."

However, Paul Shenfield had made up his mind already. A switch to the subs' table, which entailed being glued to a desk and working on copy written by people other than himself did not appeal. Apart from that, he detested the chief sub, a trade union activist turned martinet, whose ability to toady to those with power and humiliate those without it was legendary.

"I'll take the property job," he said.

CHAPTER 20

"WHAT HAPPENED TO YOU?" Lisa asked coolly.

"Oh, I've just had a bit of an accident," Theo replied, his customary self-confidence conspicuous by its absence.

"What another one?!" Lisa's tone was decidedly icy now. "What do you want anyway?" Lisa was looking downwards from her open front door on to a visitor who was feeling decidedly small.

"We need to talk," said Theo.

"What about?"

"Oh, come on, you know what about! I want to apologise and I need to talk to you properly about what happened."

"Why? What is there to be said?" Theo was unused, to say the least, of such a frosty reception.

"I value your friendship, and I don't want it to be spoiled by one silly act of stupidity on my part. I value Wayne's friendship, too. Can't we talk about this and sort something out?"

Lisa's eyes hardened. "You value Wayne's friendship!" she echoed icily. "Is that what this sudden visit of yours is all about?" Lisa gazed at the swelling around Theo's left eye and the bruise on his right cheek. "Don't you think you should be showing your injuries to a doctor? You're a bit accident prone, aren't you?" Her questions were laced with sarcasm.

"Don't be like that!" Theo pleaded. "Can't you at least let me in so that we can sit down and talk? Surely you owe me that much?"

Just then, the phone rang. "Sorry, I'm going to have to go," Lisa said. Wayne's away at the moment. I haven't told him anything, if that's what you're worried about. And I probably won't," she added as she closed the door.

The phone call was from Paul Shenfield, who introduced himself at the new Property Correspondent of "The Camford Daily News." Paul wanted to talk to the Bensons about Aggammenmon Hall and its change of ownership. "My husband's away at present and I will talk to him about this as soon as he gets back," she told the journalist. "In the meantime, you might like to know that the new owner is the property developer, Sean McAvie. He's quite a character, by all accounts. You probably already know that the estate agent involved is Theo Salter. He's a bit of a character, too, of course … and you might just find out that there's more to him than meets the eye!"

Paul Shenfield thanked Lisa Benson for her help, and Lisa promised to get in touch on Wayne's return. On putting the receiver down, Lisa's thoughts turned to Theo. "Yes, there's undoubtedly more to him than meets the eye," she mused. "And Paul Shenfield's not the only one who'll be interested in finding out what it is!"

Theo, meanwhile, returned to his office with a heavy heart. His moment of indiscretion with Lisa had cost him at least one friendship, even if she did not tell Wayne about what had happened. He recalled the observation that Wayne was a friend for life, and doubted whether this could still be so.

Would Lisa tell all to Wayne? Or would she confide in a close female friend, someone like Sherry, instead? And, even if she told no one at all, how would Lisa conceal her hostility, even if she wanted to, when both were in the company of others? The only conclusion Theo could draw was that he needed to be more discrete from now on. It would certainly not help if his set-to with Williams became public knowledge either!

However, he was reasonably confident that McAvie would be discreet and that, hopefully, his associates would be, too. Whether it was discreet to associate with McAvie, a former Gorbels hooligan, was another matter! But that side of things was, hopefully, all in the past …

"Well, well, well! Have you been in the wars again? Are you all right?" The questions came from Jenny Fitch as soon as Theo got through his office door.

"Oh, it's a long story and I'm fine," he said wearily.

Jenny gave him one of her knowing looks and made no comment. She knew that this was a time to be diplomatic.

"Good," she said. "Anyway, I've got something to tell you. One of the Evelyn Knight clients is anxious about the Smith Street house and is willing to drop the price substantially to secure a sale."

Theo thanked Jenny, said he would deal with it and started to look for the file. But before he could find it, April May appeared. She was wearing a twin set, high-heeled shoes ... and nothing else. Theo turned to Jenny and said: "Perhaps this is a good time for you to look at those rental properties in Ackerman Street."

Jenny knew when to take a hint. "What have you been up to?" April asked, once Jenny had gone. "Have you been fighting again?"

Theo smiled ruefully. "I have just had a discussion with Ray Williams on the ethics of estate agency ... I think he eventually took my point!"

April tried, unsuccessfully, to suppress a broad grin. "You're a naughty boy, aren't you," she seductively. "I can see that I'm going to have to sort you out!"

"Are you going to take me outside, then?" Theo quipped.

"No, I'm going to take you upstairs. Lock the front door and follow me."

The pair went into the boardroom, where April disrobed immediately and pulled Theo's trousers down. "How am I going to keep you out of trouble" she asked as she grabbed his penis. The answer to that question had to be deferred for two hours.

Potential trouble was brewing, though. Lisa had decided to confide in Sherry and ask her whether she thought she should tell all to Wayne, and what should be done about Theo. Sherry listened intently as Lisa told her how Theo made a pass at her, how he reacted when she rejected his advances and how he turned up on her doorstep with his face marked.

"Hmm! Something tells me you might have seen a bit of the real Theo Salter come to the surface," she said at length. "None of us knows much about him, do we? The trouble is he's such a charismatic character that people want to know what makes him tick."

"That's very true," Lisa agreed.

"I have to say, though, that he's as attractive as he's intriguing," Sherry observed. "Every other woman I meet seems to fancy him … and I wouldn't be surprised if that includes a little bit of you!"

"Oh, come off it!"

Sherry noticed that Lisa was unable to look her in the eye. "I knew it, I was right. You DO fancy him!"

Lisa turned her head and looked at her best friend full on. "All right! We know each other too well to kid each other. I fancy the pants off him!

"But you must also know that I love Wayne and would never do anything to hurt him. I know he can be irresponsible at times. He can act the goat and even be a downright buffoon. But I know he's always been true to me, and I will always be true to him."

Sherry nodded. She was well aware that neither Lisa nor Wayne had been whiter than white in the past. But she also knew, as far as anyone could, that the pair were faithful to each other. "Are you going to tell Wayne?" she asked.

"That's what I've been turning over in my mind again and again. If I tell him, he'll go ballistic. God knows what he will do! On the other hand, if I don't I will be breaking the pledge that there would be no secrets between us."

"Well, yes, but who's going to find out if you don't tell anybody? If you do tell Wayne, all hell could break loose. There could be the mother of all rows, there could even be a public scandal … the public might even believe that you were having an affair with the knight in shining armour who rescued your husband from the canal!"

"Oh God!" exclaimed Lisa. "This is too awful for words! How can I tell him? How can I NOT tell him?!"

"Perhaps you should think about it for a while, before rushing headlong into something you might regret?" Sherry suggested.

"In the meantime, I don't know about you … but I would like to know a bit more about our new local hero. Where does he come from? Why is he here? What has he got up to in the past?"

"How an earth are we going to find that out?" Lisa asked.

"Well, one thing we could do is get talking to Jenny Fitch or Kelly Cheatham, or both. They clearly know more than we do. We could bump into one or both of them in the town centre, accidentally on purpose, and suggest meeting up for a coffee. Then we could try to subtly get some information about Theo from them."

CHAPTER 21

IT WAS PURELY BY CHANCE that Lisa managed to meet Kelly a couple of days later.

Paul Shenfield had been out on the three occasions she had telephoned "The Daily News" and, because she was loath to walk in the vicinity of Salter's, she had left the task of contacting Jenny to Sherry. Sherry, meanwhile, was reluctant to be over-friendly with someone who had gone off with her partner from under her nose.

Kelly had virtually disappeared from view since that not-to-be-forgotten party. Yet there she was looking at clothes for sale at the recently completed John Brewer Shopping Centre.

"Hello," Lisa said to her casually after walking up to her. "I haven't seen you for ages. How have you been keeping?"

Kelly smiled and giggled a little. "Oh, fine," she said. "There's been plenty happening in my life lately … and all of it good!"

Lisa smiled, too. "That sounds marvellous, not to mention intriguing. Tell me more! I'm thinking of having a coffee somewhere. Would you care to join me?"

"Yes, thank you. That would be nice," said Kelly.

Lisa suspected that, despite her raunchy appearance, she was a shy, insecure person.

"Tell you what, let's go to Auntie's Tea Room," she said.

The tea room, in the heart of the John Brewer precinct, was, as its name suggested, a place known for its gentility … with prices to match its up-market profile. It featured wall-to-wall carpets, round tables with lace table cloths and waitresses clad in black dresses and white aprons. Just the place to have a quiet, intimate chat without being disturbed … Lisa ordered coffee and scones with jam and cream for two, and the pair exchanged pleasantries about forgetting their diets, the weather and the merits or otherwise of Camford's shops, until Kelly said: "I don't come into Camford very often. The village I'm now living in is so lovely that I never want to leave it."

"That explains why no one seems to get to see you," Lisa responded. "I remember meeting you briefly at the hospital ... and then I saw you again at Sherry's party, though we hardly got the chance to talk then."

Kelly giggled. "Well, yes, what happened at the party, and afterwards, was all a bit unexpected. And that's putting it mildly!"

"It certainly was ... in more ways than one!" Lisa agreed. "You seemed to vanish into thin air! Some of us were worried lest something bad might have happened to you. But here you are ... and you're looking all right. So perhaps something good happened to you!"

Kelly giggled, and then guffawed. "You can say that again!" she said with a grin from ear to ear. "I met the man of my dreams!"

Lisa's eyes narrowed. "I had always thought the man of your dreams was Theo Salter ... the man you visited in hospital and came to Sherry's party with."

Kelly could not conceal a look of guilt. "I thought he was, too, but then I met Edmund. He may not look much but there's a lot more to him than you might think. You'd be ..."

Lisa, who wanted to learn more about Theo, not Edmund, cut in by asking: "How did Theo react when you dumped him?"

"Oh, don't!" said Kelly. "I owe Theo everything. He almost literally saved me from the gutter. I owe him my life. He's a wonderful man, and I will always be in his debt."

"My goodness!" Lisa exclaimed. "Our new local hero might just be a national hero to boot! What did he do? No, don't tell me, let me guess. Did he rescue you from drowning in a ditch? No? Did he save you from the clutches of a rogue estate agent? No? Oh ... perhaps he used a cricket bat to hit an arch enemy for six!"

Kelly giggled nervously. "It's a bit embarrassing, really. It's something I don't find easy to talk about."

"Don't worry about it," Lisa said, sounding as reassuring as she could. "If you don't want to tell me, I'm not going to pressure you. However, if you do want to talk you'll find I'm a good listener … and it will be in confidence, of course."

Lisa could sense that Kelly desperately felt the need for a female friend who she could pour her heart out to … perhaps the sort of friendship that Lisa had forged with Sherry over a period of many years. Tears began to well up in Kelly's eyes. Lisa took one of her hands and said: "Sorry, the last thing I wanted to do was upset you by opening old wounds."

Kelly began to weep uncontrollably. Lisa moved her chair until she was beside her and wrapped her arms around her small, frail body. The two women realised that one of the waitresses and a couple of the customers were watching them. They ceased their embrace, and Kelly wiped away her tears.

"I have had a very unsettled life," she told Lisa at length. "It was a life without love, affection or security until I met Theo … and then Edmund."

Kelly went on to describe how, at the age of four, she was taken into care because her drunken, violent parents were deemed incapable of looking after her properly. Two members of staff at the care home sexually abused her and went to prison for it. At the age of seven, Kelly went to live with foster parents, who showed her kindness but no affection. After three years, they could not cope any more because of ill health, and Kelly went back into care again. The new care home was miles away from anyone she knew and was run almost like an army barracks … with discipline that was both regimental and harsh.

At the age of 13, Kelly absconded, hitch-hiked to London and lived in the streets. "London's an easy place to get lost," she said matter-of-factly. "You can easily disappear and it's difficult for anyone to find you, even if they wanted to."

"That sounds horrible," said Lisa. "How an earth did you survive?"

"By begging and foraging mostly," Kelly replied.

"Anyway," she continued, "I remember doing this for several months and I remember celebrating my 14th birthday with a group of other beggars. They were all smashed out of their brains on meths … but it was still the best birthday celebration I had ever had!"

"What happened next?" Lisa asked.

"Well, it was not long after that I first met Theo. I did not know it at the time but my life was about to change … and I mean for the much much much much better … forever."

Lisa was on the point of asking how Kelly and Theo actually met when the aura of calm, for which Auntie's Tea Room was renowned, was suddenly disturbed.

A heated argument was taking place in a far corner between a customer and the oldest of the three waitresses. "There's no need to use language like that," the waitress could be heard to say.

"I'll use whatever language that fucking well fits," the customer retorted.

"I'm very sorry, sir," the waitress said stiffly," but I'm not prepared to serve you. We don't tolerate this sort of behaviour here, and I think the best thing for you to do is leave. Would you kindly depart, please?"

"No, I fucking well won't!" the customer bellowed. I came in here expecting some service and if you can't give it then fuck off and find someone who fucking well will!"

The waitress, who was accustomed to being prim and proper in any given situation, was beginning to lose her composure. "I will do nothing of the sort!" she replied angrily. "No one is going to serve you here, and you'd better clear off before the manager comes and throws you out."

As the waitress turned to walk away and leave the room, Lisa and Kelly could see that the source of the trouble was a red-haired man of about 30 with piercing blue eyes who was wearing a white shirt with green stripes.

"Just let him fucking well try!" he roared across the room. Derek Drummond could see that people were looking at him.

"What are you fucking well staring at?" he shouted at no one in particular. "Are you looking for trouble or something?"

Sean McAvie had just dispensed with his services and, although there had been a generous golden handshake, Drummond resented the notion of rejection. He was certainly prepared for trouble himself … preferably head-on!

However, most of the customers averted their eyes and turned their attention back to what was on their tables. Two people settled their bills hurriedly and left.

Drummond continued to glare at everyone in the room, muttering expletives as he did so. After a minute or two, the manager appeared. A tall, smartly suited man of about 40, he bristled with authority. "What seems to be the trouble?" he asked imperiously on reaching Drummond's table. Drummond was quick to pick up his tone.

"What seems to be the trouble?" he echoed, trying to mimic the manager's Yorkshire accent. "The trouble is that you need to change your staff and replace them with people who know how to serve their customers properly!"

"Perhaps you could tell me how my staff have failed you," the manager said with as much patience as he could muster.

"They're too fucking slow, that's how they're failing. When I come into a café and sit down at a table, I expect quick, efficient service and not to be kept waiting."

"I'm sure you do," the manager said with a hint of sarcasm. "So does everyone else. The waitress you saw fit to swear at was busy serving someone else when you came in and all you needed to do was to wait for your turn. I'm sure you wouldn't have had to wait for long."

"Oh, so it's a case of the customer NEVER being right, is it?" Drummond was snarling now, and his manner was becoming increasingly menacing.

The manager appeared to falter but there was no going back. "All right, that's enough!" he said sternly. "It's quite clear to me that you're nothing but a trouble-maker and I want you to leave … now!"

"Try making me, you cunt!" said Drummond, standing up.

The manager, an imposing figure at over 6ft tall, towered over Drummond. The two men eyeballed each other for a moment before the manager said: "Come on … out!" and tried to take Drummond's arm.

Drummond drove a right uppercut into the taller man's groin and head-butted him as he doubled over in pain. He then pulled the manager forward so that he was lying forward across the table, and rammed his head against the marble surface. The manager's face came into contact with the marble again and again until the table and surrounding floor area were spattered with blood.

The beating continued, with Drummond landing punches to the small of the back and groin. Then he turned him on to his back and rained blows to the face and all parts of the body. The customers fled screaming, as did two of the waitress. Only the older waitress had the presence of mind to run to a nearby shop and ask to use the telephone.

Eventually the manager slumped to the floor, giving Drummond the opportunity to deliver a series of kicks to the head and ribs. "That'll teach you to try and tell me what to do, you stupid cunt!" the red-haired man said sneering. Drummond aimed a final kick at the manager's groin before picking up a table and hurling it at a large mirror that hung on the nearest wall. The ensuing hail of glass turned red as it landed either on the floor or on the manager's comatose form.

Drummond kicked the exit door as hard as he could before leaving. The door, which happened to be open and was made of solid pine, was splintered and severely dented as a result.

A large waste bin stood 10ft away from the tea room, and Drummond kicked that, too. Startled shoppers gasped as the bin cart-wheeled across the precinct.

Lisa and Kelly had fled to a lingerie shop nearby and were now, along with the staff, watching from a safe distance.

"No one's going to tell me what to do!" Drummond bellowed at all and sundry. "Do you hear me? Fucking no one!" Drummond started to walk along the shopping precinct, glaring at anyone who came within yards of him and muttering expletives as he went.

"Nobody gives ME orders!" he roared. Nobody, do you hear?! Anyone who tries to tell me what to do or not to do is going to get his fucking teeth kicked in! It doesn't matter who you are, you'll get your teeth kicked in! I don't care who you are! I don't care if you're Sean McAvie, Chris fucking Doman, Mary Groves, that pathetic son of hers, Ray fucking Williams … even Theo sodding Salter! And I'm certainly not taking buck from some tuppenny halfpenny manager of a fucking tea room!"

A young couple, who had just entered the precinct from the opposite direction and had no inkling of what had been going on, almost collided with the swaggering Drummond. "Get out of my way, you stupid cunts!" he roared at them. The startled pair retreated into a nearby jewellers. The sound of an approaching police car siren was muffled by the abuse directed at the couple. Two burly uniformed officers arrived and approached the source of the commotion.

"Will you kindly be quiet, sir, you're creating a disturbance," one of them said.

Drummond's response was to aim a kick at the officer's groin. The policeman was quick enough to turn sideways, so that the kick landed on his thigh, but he was unable to avoid a head-butt and a punch to the stomach.

The second officer tried to put Drummond in an arm-lock. The attempt failed, and an elbow hit him flush in the mouth. The first officer recovered sufficiently to land a blow of his own and to put a handcuff around one of Drummond's wrists. But the struggle continued with Drummond lashing out with fists and feet and, when the opportunity arose, thumbs and teeth were used, too. The two officers, who were both bleeding copiously, appeared to be fighting a losing battle. Drummond tried to put a hand in the pocket of the one who had handcuffed him, in an attempt to find the key, and then the three men fell to the ground in an ungainly heap.

Another siren could be heard, and seconds later, two more policemen arrived and promptly sat on their quarry. As they telephoned for further assistance, Drummond bared his teeth and issued a further series of threats and expletives. "I'm going to fucking get you for this!" he kept on saying. He struggled furiously but, this time, to no avail. Eventually the struggling and abuse subsided and stopped.

Lisa and Kelly, and a crowd of others, watched and waited until, after about 10 minutes two more officers turned up with a straight jacket and a series of straps. A quiet period followed, during which Drummond was trussed up and taken to the Black Mariah that was waiting just outside the precinct.

The commotion had been such that few people noticed an ambulance crew arriving and taking the Auntie's Tea Room manager away on a stretcher. Lisa and Kelly looked at each other. "Well, it looks as if the show's over," Lisa said.

"Yes, and I'm afraid I'm going to have to go," Kelly replied. "I've arranged to meet Edmund at his office and I'm late already."

"Pity," said Lisa. "I enjoyed our little chat before we were interrupted. Perhaps we could meet up again some time?"

Kelly smiled warmly. "Yes, I'd love to," she said. "It would be nice if you could perhaps come round for tea."

"Great! Tell me when?"

"Tell you what, I'll have a word with Edmund and we'll see what can be arranged."

"I look forward to that," Lisa said as Kelly walked briskly out of the shopping precinct to keep her appointment with her lover.

Lisa made her way to a nearby car park with a view to heading for home. "What a day!" she thought. "What an unexpected turn of events! And what an interesting person Kelly is!" Kelly had poured her heart out to her, and revealed quite a bit about herself. Yet there were still quite a few questions to be asked …

CHAPTER 22

IT WAS JUST the sort of house Theo wanted. And he was getting it at a knock-down price. A detached property in Affleck Way, an area known to be going up in the world, it was an ideal investment.

Its elderly owner, Philip Jones wanted to join his daughter and son-in-law in New Zealand as soon as possible, and a quick sale was paramount. Carpets, curtains and most of the furniture were being left behind.

Mr Jones's wife had died a year earlier, and he could not bear to be on his own any more. The house, and its gardens in particular, had been neglected to some extent for a couple of years, and Theo was able to point to this neglect as a reason for getting the asking price down.

Mr Jones, originally a client of Evelyn Knight, could think of nothing but leaving and starting a new life. Selling the house for £230,000 instead of £250,000 was of little importance to him. The bargain buy meant Theo could move out of the flat secured for him by Kelly. Jenny had agreed to stay on in the flat and take over responsibility for paying the rent.

Theo was also pretty sure that, with a bit of judicious marketing, the property could have fetched between £260,000 and £265,000. And he knew that the housing market was so volatile at that time that, with the aid of a lick of paint and a lawnmower, the value could approach the £300,000 mark within months.

He was cock-a-hoop. "Glad to be of help, Mr Jones," he told his new client on the telephone at his office. "I will take steps to ensure that contracts are exchanged within the next few days."

After putting the receiver down, Theo threw the telephone two feet into the air and caught it. "How about that?!" he said to Jenny gleefully.

"It sounds as if you're expanding at the same time as the firm," his assistant said.

"You ain't seen nothing yet!" Theo replied. "Salter's is expanding fast. Evelyn Knight has given us more of a helping hand than she will ever realise, and we're going to be quids in! And you can rest assured that you won't be out of pocket yourself."

Jenny grinned. She knew that when Theo was in such an upbeat vein the portents were good for her, too. Theo now turned his thoughts to the other properties Evelyn had asked him to look after.

Firstly, there was a pair of semis, next door to each other, that had been turned into four flats. Their American owner, a Mrs Carter, had grown weary of being a transatlantic landlady. She had decided against employing a local estate agent to manage the flats, and found that the to-ing and fro-ing from New York was unexpectedly tedious. Evelyn had been given the job of offloading the properties as quickly as possible.

The other property was a picturesque cottage in the village of Kettlestone, eight miles to the north-east of Camford. Its owner, a Mr Northropp, had retired to Plymouth and instructed Evelyn to sell the cottage at a virtually impossible price. The cottage had been empty for six months. And, with house prices rising everywhere, the value was considerably closer to the asking price now.

Theo delved into a filing cabinet and took out the sales particulars and some photographs of each of the properties and laid them out on his desk.

He decided that displaying the information in the window was not a good policy now. It was time to get in touch with Joe Prescott. Joe, a chartered surveyor with a knack for seeing a strong selling point or a defect in a property at the drop of a hat, had been a valued associate for many years. What he lacked in charisma, he made up for in expertise, and the two men made an ideal business team. Joe had been contemplating a move to Camford, and Theo believed the Kettleford cottage would suit him admirably.

Joe's opinion on how Theo should dispose of the four Camford flats would be welcome, too. April May had already expressed the view that they had investment potential. Theo thought so, too, and he wanted an expert view on their condition and how they should best be handled.

Theo was just about to telephone Joe when a surprise visitor breezed into the office. It was Sherry Munro. "Have you heard about the murder at the new shopping precinct?" she asked Theo and Jenny breathlessly. They both shook their heads. "A man went berserk in the Auntie's Tea Room and battered the manager to death. An ambulance rushed the manager to hospital but he was dead on arrival. There's been no end of a commotion, and there have been police all over the place.

"I just happened to be in this neck of the woods and someone told me about it. In any case, I thought it was about time I popped in and said Hello. How are things going?"

Theo, who had a suspicion that Sherry was really visiting to ask awkward questions relating to the pass he made at Lisa, did not particularly want to talk to her just now. "Pretty good, thank you. The office has been extremely busy lately," he replied truthfully.

"That's great news," Sherry said. "I was going to suggest taking the pair of you out for a drink. Have you time for a quick tipple?"

"Tell you what," Theo said, "why don't you don't you take Jenny with you and I'll try to catch you up a little later ... I assume you won't be going to Auntie's Tea Room!"

Sherry turned to Jenny and said: "How about the White Swan?"

"Sounds good to me," Jenny replied smiling.

Sherry had cause to smile, too. "I've always wanted to meet you," Jenny told her, as they sat down with their drinks in a quiet corner of the pub. "I used to listen to your records all the time."

"Thank you, I feel flattered." Jenny went on to express disappointment that Sherry had made no records recently, and Sherry told her there was the possibility of a comeback.

"The pop industry can be pretty cut-throat at times and I wanted out for a while," she said. "I've seen people ruined because they can't handle the pressure that can go with fame. Some have been destroyed by drugs, others by drink, others by their own egos! I decided to take a step back, take stock of my situation and invest some of the money I made on property and other things. I also felt the need for a break. However, there's fair chance that I'll be getting some more work soon … which would be good in a way, though there wouldn't be much time then for drinks at the White Swan!"

Jenny laughed.

"But that's enough about me," Sherry said. "What about you? Your life's probably much more interesting than mine! Have you always worked with Theo, or have you done other things besides estate agency?"

"Oh, I've done a few other things."

"Like what? You've aroused my curiosity now. Are you one of Theo's conquests, by any chance?" Sherry knew she was pushing her luck with that question and prepared herself for a rebuff.

But Jenny chuckled a little and replied: "No, I'm not inclined that way!"

Sherry could see she was blushing and moved on the conversation by asking: "How did you meet Theo? He's quite a character, isn't he? And he's held in such high regard in Camford."

"Yes, he is! And quite rightly so!" Jenny agreed vehemently. "He's the best friend I have ever had, the best friend anyone could possibly have!"

Sherry knew she had struck a chord and was more curious than ever.

Jenny was reticent about going into detail but Sherry eventually managed to glean some sketchy information about her companion's past life. She had left her turbulent family home at 15, been arrested three times for shoplifting and twice for dealing in cannabis, and was on the brink of committing suicide when Theo came into her life. "I was on top of this motorway bridge in Birmingham and was about to jump into the road in front of loads of traffic when Theo came along and talked me out of it," she said. Tears were welling up in her eyes. "Then he took me in his car to lodgings and paid for me to spend the night there.

"The next day, a couple of drug dealers waylaid me, said I owed them money and started to beat me up. But before they could do anything much, Theo appeared again... and he sorted them out good and proper!

"He said he would give me a job if I was prepared to leave Birmingham and work for him in Gloucester. There wouldn't be much money in it to start with but he was sure I could be useful to him."

"I should imagine you accepted without much hesitation?" Sherry suggested.

"You bet I did! There was nothing for me in Birmingham except trouble, and I jumped at the chance to start a new life. You've no idea how grateful I am to Theo. I don't suppose he knows either."

The conversation had become so intense that neither Sherry nor Jenny noticed Theo enter the pub and stride towards them. "You don't suppose he knows what?" he asked quizzically.

"Never you mind!" said Sherry. "We've been having some good old fashioned woman talk in your absence ... though I'm sure there's nothing for you to worry about!"

Theo smiled. "I see that I'm not going to get anywhere here!" he said. "Let me buy you both a quick drink. It will have to be on the quick side, I'm afraid, because there's quite a bit of work piling up in the office."

CHAPTER 23

IF THERE WAS ONE person he wanted to see less than anyone else, it was Clive Matthews.

Yet there he was, looking perfunctorily at some of the Property for Sale particulars in a corner near the front. Theo and Jenny were both dealing with a stream of visitors, as well as fielding telephone calls, and Theo hoped beyond hope that the new arrival would disappear when he saw how busy he was. Or, better still, perhaps, Matthews was merely a mirage! No such luck! The short, stocky man in a raincoat with two days of stubble on his chin and carrying an old zip-up bag continued to hover patiently.

Theo carried on taking down particulars of properties that the callers wanted to sell, and of the types of properties that others wanted to buy. One home-hunter expressed a desire to buy a town flat of the type that Mrs Carter owned. But Theo had plans for the two semis that had been converted into four flats and simply said he would keep an eye open for such a property. Eventually the queue thinned out, the telephone stopped ringing and Jenny gave a sigh of relief. "Phew! It's been all go today, hasn't it?" she said.

Then she saw Clive Matthews emerge from one side and said: "Good afternoon, sir. How can I help you?"

"It's all right," Theo said, cutting in. "I'll deal with this gentleman. Why don't you pop out and do that bit of shopping you were talking about while things are quiet?"

Jenny needed no second bidding, and was gone in a trice.

Theo Salter and Clive Matthews stared at each other for a few seconds, before the latter said: "Nice place you've got here. You're really going up in the world, aren't you?"

Theo observed that Matthews was as shifty-eyed as ever and, if anything, even scruffier. "Yes, life's full of surprises," he replied coolly. "Things are working out for me quite well in Camford and I've no complaints. How are keeping yourself?"

Matthews shuffled from one foot to another and, before he could respond, Theo added: "Something tells me your visit is not just a social call. What can I do for you?"

Matthews put his zip-up bag on Theo's desk and said: "I need your help in disposing of something in a hurry." This was exactly what Theo had feared. He stood up, glared down at Matthews and, in the most forbidding tone he could muster, said: "We'd better continue this conversation upstairs."

Theo then locked up his premises and took Matthews into the smaller of the first floor offices. "Right! Perhaps you could kindly tell me what the hell you're talking about!!"

Matthews opened the zip-up bag and took out bundle after bundle of £10, £20 and £50 notes. "I want to buy a property, and, as you can see, I am a real, genuine cash buyer!" he said. "I've got £300,000 here. Count it, if you don't believe me! It will be the easiest sale you have ever had!!

Theo's face hardened even further. "You're a bit of a comedian, aren't you?" he snarled. "Where did that money come from? You're not going to tell me, are you? You don't need to. It's got HOT written all over it!"

Now it was Matthews' turn to take a tough stance. "Since when's that sort of thing worried you? Have you suddenly become an evangelist or something?" he sneered.

Theo's eyes were now resembling gun barrels. "Why, you nasty little weasel!" he said with his fists clenched. "You evil scumbag!" What makes you think I want to do business with YOU? Tell me, did you steal that money, or did you come by it through one of your nasty little scams?"

Matthews began to cringe.

"You can't tell me, can you! I don't do money laundering, for one thing. The law's been tightened up on it, and an estate agent being offered a large sum of cash is required to find out if the money has been acquired honestly. You can't tell me that, can you?"

Matthews was poised for flight.

"Yes, that's right, the best thing you can do is get the fuck out of here!" It was now Theo's turn to sneer. "I've got a good mind to throw you down the stairs," he added. "However, I am going to do you a favour. I'm going to give you the name of the one estate agent in Camford who's so crooked and stupid that he might just consider taking your money. But, tread carefully, my friend. He can be quite nasty if you upset him!"

Ray Williams was desperate.

Sean McAvie had disowned him and there were virtually no customers. He could not afford to employ staff any more, and his days were spent pacing round his empty office and trying to arrange pictures of the handful of properties he had for sale, or had sold recently so that they could be seen to best advantage. He put in a couple of extra boards emblazoned with the words "Williams, the Real Estate Agent" in the front window.

All this was to no avail, and the bottles of whisky that sat in his desk drawer and were once produced as a sop for certain associates, began to receive his undivided attention. Yet it was only a matter of weeks ago that he was poised to sell the prestigious Aggammenmon Hall on behalf of Camford's most famous resident. On top of this, there was his potentially lucrative liaison with McAvie.

But McAvie had gone "all respectable" on him and dumped both him and Derek Drummond, presumably because they had become an embarrassment.

Williams mulled over ways to get even with McAvie and, in particular the man who had been behind many of his current problems and had, a few days ago, humiliated him. "Drummond isn't a bundle on Salter either, come to that," he said to himself. "But he's been locked up for God knows how long ... and he's a bit of a loose cannon anyway!"

Ray Williams happened to be out when a rare morning caller turned up at the door of the "Real Estate Agent." Williams was taking desperate measures to improve his estate agency standing.

He had been out in a van in the small hours of the morning and, under cover of darkness, removed "For Sale," "Sold" and "Under Offer" boards that had been put up by other agents, and replaced many of them with "Williams" boards.

There was nothing new about this practice, of course. He had done it before himself, and heard about one or two other agents doing it, too.

However, no agent would admit to doing anything so underhand, and the official line was to frown upon such a practice.

Williams had concentrated on two areas he knew where there were lots of houses for sale, and brought along a van he had borrowed to bring along his own boards and take away others. He had a van of his own but did not want to use it because it bore his name. The expedition was, by and large, a success, though, towards the end, a confrontation with a terrier standing guard outside a house led to a torn trouser leg and a few lumps of mud on his suit as a result of tripping up afterwards.

So, when he got back to base, he was almost as dishevelled as his waiting caller. Williams drove the van round the back of his premises, so that it would not be seen, before greeting him. "Hello, sorry if I've kept you waiting," he said to Clive Matthews.

"Oh, it's all right, I've only been here a couple of minute. Are you Ray Williams, by any chance?"

Williams confirmed that he was and invited Matthews in. "What can I do for you?" he asked hopefully.

Matthews, who had, in fact, been hanging around the premises for almost an hour, replied: "I want to make a cash purchase."

He plonked the zip-up bag on a table in the middle of Williams' office and displayed the money.

Williams stared at it in disbelief. "Where the hell did you get all that cash from?" he eventually asked. "And who told you to bring it here?"

Matthews opted to answer the second question first... and dodge the first, if possible. "Your name was given to me by a certain Theo Salter."

Williams' face blackened. "Oh really?" he snarled.

Matthews looked afraid, then amused. "He's no friend of mine either, if that helps," he said.

"He turned up his nose when I went to see him. It seems as if he's trying to make out he's respectable. Well, I can tell you different! The bastard's got up to as many dirty tricks in business as anyone. But he's crafty. He covers his tracks and no one can prove anything."

Now it was Williams' turn to smile. "Is that a fact!?" he exclaimed.

He went to his desk, produced a whisky bottle and two glasses and said: "Why don't you take a seat and have a drink ... and tell me all?" Williams poured out the drinks and knocked his back in one. Matthews took a sip as he watched his host refill his glass.

"What do you want to know?" he asked.

"There's plenty I want to know," Williams replied. "Why don't you start by telling me about Salter. I get the impression you're not very fond of him."

"I have a feeling that makes two of us," said Matthews. "Have you had trouble with him?"

Williams winced, knocked back his second whisky and poured out a third. "I think it's safe to say he's not my favourite person," he said. "Some people in Camford think he's marvellous. He's even in with that cricketer Wayne Benson, and everyone seems to believe that Salter can do no wrong. But I bet he can and has, and you've just pretty well confirmed that."

"Oh, he's pulled his fair share of strokes," said Matthews. "But, as I said before, it's difficult to prove anything."

"Tell me about it anyway," said Williams as he reached for the bottle again.

"Well, one of his favourite tricks is to agree to put a property on the market and, if the vendor lives outside the area, he makes no attempt to sell. He just keeps the details tucked away in a drawer. The vendor, who might well have to move abroad soon, gets desperate and is persuaded to lower the price. Salter or one of his associates, using an assumed name perhaps, buys the property for less than its value and then, a few months later, sells it at a whopping profit."

Williams grinned. "That's what's known as ring-fencing. Dead illegal if you're caught! What else has Salter done?"

"OK, you'll love this one!" Matthews said. "Salter has an associate called Joe Prescott, who is a qualified chartered surveyor. When Prescott does a building society valuation, he will under-value a property, perhaps by several thousand pounds. As a result, the building society considering granting a mortgage on it can't advance the sum that has been requested and the sale falls through. The vendor ends up putting the house on the market again through a different estate agent … and Prescott engineers things to ensure that the agent concerned is You Know Who!

"And here's another one …" Matthews was warming to his task now. "One house buyer, who happened to be a Salter client, revealed that he planned to have an extension built once the purchase was completed. Salter recommended a builder … McAvie was his name, if I remember correctly … and the builder charged an exorbitant fee for the work. A slice of that fee went in Salter's direction. I believe the money was used to finance improvement work on one of his own properties … but I can't, of course, prove that."

Williams gulped down yet another glass of whisky.

Matthews decided it was time to re-focus on his bag of money. He had taken just a few sips from his glass, to ensure that he kept his head clear.

"So there you are. These are just three examples of what Salter has done for you to think about," he said. "What it all boils down to is that Salter is a hypocrite … wouldn't you agree?"

Williams nodded. A combination of the whisky and the meeting with a seeming kindred spirit gave him a warm glow inside. "Oh, yes! … And let me say it's been a real pleasure meeting you," he told his new acquaintance and potential friend.

It was now time for Matthews to ask the crucial question: "Does all this mean that you won't turn your nose up at my bag full of cash … that perhaps you will accept the cash in return for a property you have on your books?"

Williams gulped down his fifth glass of whisky and said:

"Trouble is I don't really know you. We've had a few drinks together, and I've enjoyed our conversation. In fact, I've more than enjoyed it. You've given me some extremely interesting information, which could come in useful for me some time. But I don't really know you. I like you but can I trust you?"

Matthews then came to the bit he had rehearsed in his mind several times. "Let me tell you a bit about myself," he said. "It might help you make up your mind. You could say I'm a bit of a chancer in life, a bit of a drifter. I work as a salesman from time to time and I'm pretty good at it. As an estate agent, you'll be a good salesman, too. I like to travel around a lot. I never settle in one place for long, and I like to try lots of different things. One of my hobbies is buying up old properties, giving them a lick of paint and smartening them up, and then selling them on at a profit. That's why I'm here now. But, of course, the main thing you want to know is where I got all that cash. Well, if that so-and-so Salter hadn't got on his high horse he could have had that money and made the quickest sale of his lifetime. Well, I'm glad he turned me down! I don't know you very well either but I would far prefer to do business with you than with him."

"Thank you for that," said Williams. "But, no offence, Clive … I hope it's all right for me to call you Clive … but I do need to know where the money came from."

"No problem!" was the response. "Another of my favourite pastimes is gambling. I like betting on horses, dogs, who's going to win the next election and so on, and I also enjoy a game of poker or a good roulette session in a casino."

"Me too," said Williams grinning. "Is that where the money came from, then?"

Matthews nodded: "Yes, I've really hit it big lately. It's not true what people say about gambling being a mug's game. There's money in it if you know what you're doing. A week ago, I took a Hooray Henry to the cleaners at poker and then multiplied my winnings several times over at the races. So what I want to do now is sink my winnings into something solid like a house with investment potential. How does that sound to you … Ray?"

Williams got up, moved to a filing cabinet and took out a set of house-for-sale particulars. The property was a large detached cottage in Haleford, a village nine miles to the north-west of Camford that had been built from scratch 20 years ago and now had 5,000 inhabitants.

"How about this one?" he said. "It's been on the market for a year and I have just had the price reduced from £325,000 to £300,000. It was too expensive before but now it's a bargain." Williams told Matthews a bit more about Haleford and its facilities and promised to look after the £300,000. What he did not say was that he had, in fact, cut the price recently from £300,000 to "offers in the region of £250,000." The vendor, who had left the area, had initially insisted on heavily over-pricing the cottage but, out of desperation, had just agreed to a more realistic figure. "I will get in touch with a conveyancer friend immediately and he will get the contract drawn up. And, since, there's no selling chain involved, we can get this all wrapped up really quickly. Tell you what, let me give you the keys and you go and take a look at the place while I get it sorted."

Williams poured himself yet another whisky. He was in a triumphant frame of mind once more. He had brokered a deal that would leave him £50,000 in pocket. That would be enough for him to quit Camford and start a new life elsewhere. He might even return to London … and then he could plot his revenge on Salter and his other enemies.

He did not, at that stage, even consider the possibility that the £300,000 could have come from somewhere other than what he had heard from Matthews. That was partly because of the feelings of desperation he had experienced. The whisky had a hand in it, too!

CHAPTER 24

"ARCHITECT-DESIGNED" means bloody expensive! "Within easy reach of a motorway" means bloody noisy! "Compact" means not enough room to swing a cat! Paul Shenfield was enjoying his new job at "The Camford Daily News" far more than he thought he would. The estate agents he came into contact with were, by and large, a convivial bunch. Even Theo Salter was starting to be helpful.

When he was not sharing jokes with the agents, Paul was doing the same with fellow reporters and even sub-editors at times. His news editing responsibilities were behind him, and he was no longer living on his nerves.

Paul had now been Property Correspondent for six months. Apart from the odd tipple with an agent or at a reception involving a new housing development, he was not hitting the bottle in the way he used to, and he had even spruced up his appearance.

Paul was currently sharing a joke or two about estate agents' descriptions of houses for sale with the subs.

A sub-editor on a newspaper, national or local, is an unsung breed of journalist who licks reporters' written work ... known as "copy" ... into shape, trims it, corrects it, watches out for anything that is libellous or wrong in some other way, writes headlines and designs pages. Subs, as they are known in the profession, are frequently at loggerheads with reporters, who might question what they have done with their copy ... and, on occasion, contend that there is no need for subs at all.

Paul was on better terms with the subs than he had ever been before and shared a joke with them at every opportunity whenever the chief sub was not around. "The term 'manageable garden' means the garden is the size of a postage stamp," he quipped. "'Scope for modernisation' or 'scope for improvement' means the house is almost falling down or is riddled with dry rot. If a location is described as 'popular', it is as common as muck! If the location is 'sought after' it's bloody expensive! If it's said to have 'farm land views,' what it means is that cattle or pigs can be heard in the small hours of the morning … and that there's probably an abattoir nearby as well!"

The passing of the Property Misdescriptions Act had, in fact, made it a criminal offence for an estate agent to give misleading information about a property for sale. But the way agents described homes in their sales particulars was still, rightly or wrongly, a source of comment and amusement.

The gales of laughter coming from the subs' table could be heard by Harry Brown, the chief sub, who had been interviewing a candidate for a vacancy in his department. He reappeared and, with a piercing stare, ensured that Paul Shenfield returned to his work station and that the subs returned to their work.

There was a note on Paul's desk. It related to a telephone call from Jenny Fitch, on behalf of Theo Salter. Paul had been invited to a party celebrating the merger between Salter's, April May and Knights. Theo Salter and April were partners in a sense already, and Evelyn Knight had offered to be a sort of "semi sleeping partner" providing cover when Theo and April were away.

The new partnership was to be re-branded SMK Estate Agents, and it was to operate from new premises, the venue for the party, in a prominent part of the High Street. The three partners wanted Paul to write a short piece for "The Camford Daily News" property section about the firm and who worked for it.

In addition, Paul would have the opportunity to meet Sean McAvie, who would talk to him about his plans for Aggammenmon Hall and the new development in Benson Lane. Up to now, the formidable McAvie had been even more elusive than Salter, and previous attempts to secure an interview had met with the response: "I am about to appoint a press assistant and he or she will be in touch with you in due course."

Paul was smacking his lips at the prospect of securing in-depth interviews with Salter and McAvie ... even though he had found both to be slightly intimidating ... when he was summoned to the editor's office. "I want you to start a weekly 'Meet the Estate Agent' column in the property supplement," he was told. "It will be a sort of personality profile series and I suggest you start with Theo Salter. You could do April May, Evelyn Knight and the others later on. In the first article, we can remind readers how Salter became a local hero six months ago and, with the impending re-branding of his new firm, now is the ideal time."

Paul nodded enthusiastically: "I've always wanted to get hold of Salter and do a proper interview with him but he's been so elusive up to now. He's an interesting character, for sure. And I've heard on the grapevine that his past is far from whiter than white. It might even be shady."

Colin Edwards winced and wagged an admonishing finger. "I can understand you wanting to know more about him but don't forget that our property section is a magnet for advertisers." Paul was about to protest when a wave of a hand stopped him. "I'm not saying we should lickspittle to advertisers but we must not upset them. If we do, the MD will be down on us like a ton of bricks."

Paul gave a resigned shrug. "I won't let you down," he said before departing.

He returned to his desk to find a pile of mail awaiting his attention. Most of it consisted of details of houses for sale from various local estate agents. One letter concerned a small housing development in a nearby village and another two were from firms offering advice on plumbing and dry rot respectively.

The letter at the bottom of the pile was in an envelope bearing a Gloucester postmark and addressed to the Property Editor. Inside was a statement typed in capital letters. It said:

THEO SALTER MIGHT BE LOOKED UPON AS A LOCAL HERO IN CAMFORD BUT HE IS NOT ALL THAT HE SEEMS.

HE HAS PLAYED EVERY DIRTY TRICK KNOWN IN ESTATE AGENCY AND A FEW MORE BESIDES. HE IS AN OUT-AND-OUT

CROOK, WHO HAS BEEN INVOLVED IN ROBBERY, DRUG DEALING AND MONEY LAUNDERING. ONE DAY HE WILL BE FOUND OUT AND, WHEN HE IS, HE CAN EXPECT TO SPEND A LONG TIME LANGUISHING IN PRISON.

The statement was unsigned. Paul felt the only appropriate course of action was to show the note to Colin. Unfortunately, however, the editor's office was now closed.

"He's having a meeting with the MD and the advertising manager," Colin's secretary told him. "He told me that it might well last for over an hour, and that he was not to be disturbed under any circumstances."

CHAPTER 25

THEO WAS NOW a major player in Camford's estate agency scene. His joining of forces with April and Evelyn meant SMK Estate Agents would be handling a higher turnover in terms of total house values than any other firm, apart from Trumpers and Pike & Pinkerton. Trumpers, headed by Paul Phelan and Ian Gathercole, was widely regarded as the "Rolls-Royce" among local estate agents and handled nearly all the most exclusive properties in the area … apart from Aggammenmon Hall. Nathan Pike and Reg Pinkerton, who previously worked for Trumpers, were cut from the same cloth and they, too, specialised in the "top end" of the market.

So Theo reasoned that the newly named SMK's impact on the market was strong enough to justify a "junket with a touch of class." April and Evelyn readily agreed.

The Mayor and Mayoress of Camford were to be there to declare the premises officially open for business. The chair and vice-chair of the council's housing committee were to be present, along with various business associates, including many of the estate agents, bankers and building society officials who took part in the epic cricket match of six months ago.

Sean McAvie would be there along with Chris Doman and McAvie's new press assistant, as would Joe Prescott and Paul Shenfield. So, too, would Kelly and Edmund and, of course, the trusty Jenny.

Three of the invited guests would be conspicuous by their absence, though. Sherry Munro had sent a short typed note saying that she would be out of the country on a singing engagement, while Wayne and Lisa Benson had declined the invitation without explanation. Lisa did eventually tell Wayne how Theo had made a pass at her. Her bluff and frequently insensitive husband had sensed something was wrong and reminded Lisa of their pledge to have no secrets from one another.

Wayne's first reaction on learning the truth was to go ballistic and talk about "knocking the bugger's block off." However, Lisa had managed to calm her husband down and persuaded him that his new "friend for life" should be someone to cold-shoulder from now on. As a consequence, contact between Theo and Wayne and Lisa, and Sherry, too, ceased to exist. One or two of the estate agents had also begun to have reservations about Theo. Much of that stemmed from professional jealousy. However, a few agents were beginning to feel that the new "local hero" was a bit too colourful for their liking. They felt uneasy about his associations with McAvie and, to a lesser extent, Prescott, and had even heard whispers that he had had a massive punch-up with Ray Williams.

However, none of the agents were sorry to learn that Williams had left Camford and, in that respect, they knew that they had Theo to thank for his part in getting rid of a man whose actions had done nothing but discredit their profession for years. Perhaps, because of this, nearly all the leading local agents had agreed to attend the party. And what a party it was! A four-piece band provided music for dancing, and a catering firm ensured that there were cocktails and canapés aplenty.

The SMK premises provided plenty of space for all this. The main reception area at the front was double the size of that at the old Salter's office. The carpet had been rolled back to reveal a pine floor. The front counter was big enough to accommodate much of the food and drink. Desks placed against the walls were used for this purpose, too. There was plenty of seating as well, and to the side and behind the main areas were doors to several small offices. Upstairs were more offices, a boardroom and even a bedroom. Theo Salter, wearing a tuxedo, looked at his most dashing as he greeted guests. Joe Prescott wore a tuxedo, too, but still managed to look gaunt and round-shouldered … even shabby. Jenny Fitch, in a close-fitting trouser suit, white blouse and bow tie, was quite eye-catching, on the other hand.

April and Evelyn, meanwhile, looked devastating, and outshone the other hosts and the guests alike with what they wore. April had opted for a black, skin-tight micro dress and boots … all chosen to highlight her magnificent thighs. Evelyn was clad in white. Her ankle-length dress featured a plunging neckline and a slit that went from from waist to foot on one side.

The first arrivals were Sean McAvie, Chris Doman and the new press assistant, who introduced herself as Sara Ponsonby-Stewart. All three were clad in pinstripes and they all carried briefcases, which turned out to contain details concerning the Benson Lane development, the alterations being made to Aggammenmon Hall and some promotional material extolling the virtues of MAC Developments.

The various bits of paperwork were placed on an empty desk at the side for guests to look at. The ice was broken when Evelyn and Sara recognised each other as former classmates at school, embraced each other and began to reminisce about some of their past pranks. The mayor and mayoress in official regalia and the other councillors arrived shortly afterwards, and were soon happily conversing with their hosts, while Joe Prescott shifted from one foot to another in a corner and McAvie and Doman stood over their project literature. Before long, the room was full, the glasses were empty and then full again, and the band was in full swing. George Bowes and his petite wife soon had everyone dancing, with George showing an ability to move with unexpected grace. Even Joe Prescott took to the floor after Evelyn grabbed a scrawny arm and coaxed him into ungainly action.

By then, Theo and April were having difficulty keeping their hands off each other. They never could for long. Not even after six months of being together!

The pair slipped upstairs and locked one of the office doors. Once they were inside, April undid Theo's zip and pulled her knickers down. The music downstairs was too loud and the conversation too animated for anyone else to hear what was going on.

When Kelly and Edmund arrived, Evelyn was on hand to greet them. Edmund was as dapper as ever, while Kelly looked demure in a long-sleeved, high-necked, ankle-length brown dress. But she was glowing nonetheless. "Where's Theo? We've got something to tell him!" the latter said.

"Oh, Theo and April are around somewhere, though you know what they're like!" Evelyn drawled. "They're probably having a quickie upstairs!"

Kelly giggled, and Edmund, with a wry smile, said: "Well, hopefully we'll catch up with them later." Before long, Kelly and Edmund were dancing, along with just about everyone else, as the band played everything from Victor Sylvester fare to rock n' roll.

Evelyn and Jenny ensured that even McAvie and Doman joined in. Sara Ponsonby-Stewart took a turn at dragging Joe Prescott on to the floor and, when the hapless Joe managed to give her the slip, she started to dance with Jenny.

About an hour later, Theo and April were disturbed by a knock on the door. "Who is it?" Theo asked.

"It's me!" The tone was slightly mocking and the voice belonged to Sean McAvie.

A hasty adjustment of clothing followed, and the door was unlocked. McAvie stood there grinning. "I didn't imagine there could possibly be anything better for you to do than make sure this party went with a swing," he said. "I was clearly wrong!"

"How did you know I was here?" Theo asked pointlessly.

"Oh, I just know you!" McAvie laughed. Then, a little more seriously, he added: "It's property presentation time!"

"OK, we'll be right down," Theo said. McAvie grinned again, even more widely. "I probably know you better than anyone else at this party, even better than Prescott knows you," he said.

Theo gave a wry smile before replying: "Maybe, but that cuts both ways ... doesn't it?" McAvie was probably the only person with an interest in Theo's whereabouts just then.

Everybody but everybody was bopping when Theo and April came downstairs. The mayor and mayoress were moving sedately, George and his wife were displaying their athleticism, and Kelly and

Edmund danced sensuously and close together while gazing into each other's eyes. Even Joe had decided to throw caution to the winds and was bopping in a quartet with Jenny, Sara and Chris Doman.

Paul Shenfield had just arrived and no sooner had he taken a sip from his first glass of champagne than he was half-coaxed, half-pulled on to the floor by the effervescent Evelyn. Evelyn had had more than one drink by then and was dancing with such gusto and gyrating with such mammary dexterity that there was a real danger of an embarrassing accident occurring. When the music stopped, it took Theo some time to gain the attention of the party-goers and it took several bangs on a desk with a gavel to achieve something approaching silence.

"Sorry to interrupt your enjoyment but we must now come to the matter of why you are officially here," Theo shouted above the hubbub. "However, we will keep the formalities as brief as possible … and the merriment can continue all night afterwards if that's what you desire. But first we have two important announcements to make. The first is to confirm that April May, Evelyn Knight and I are in partnership and that we are now officially trading under the name of SMK Estate Agents."

Theo, April and Evelyn each said a few words about their plans for the future before Theo asked the mayor to come forward and declare SMK officially open for business by cutting a ribbon that had been put up near the front counter.

Theo then announced that properties were now for sale at the MAC Developments project in Benson Lane, and introduced the head of the developers Sean McAvie. McAvie gave a short talk about properties on offer in the first phase of the project, and what would be available later on. He also talked briefly about his plans for Aggammenmon Hall. These included a small development of rustic looking cottages in the grounds, if permitted by the council planners.

McAvie announced the appointment of Chris Doman as deputy managing director of MAC Developments, with special responsibility for ensuring that the casino being built in Benson

Lane would be a success. Doman had, in fact been a croupier in earlier life, though this detail was omitted.

In the meantime, all inquiries concerning MAC projects should be directed to McAvie's newly appointed press assistant, Sara Ponsonby-Stewart.

"Thank you for listening," McAvie concluded. "That's the end of the commercial, and I trust you will all continue to enjoy the party."

The band was just about to start playing again, when Edmond Rooker stepped forward and shouted: "Just one minute, I have got an announcement to make myself."

Edmund motioned Kelly to come forward and join him before saying: "I have asked the woman I love to marry me and I'm delighted to tell you that she has said 'Yes'." There was a ripple of applause as the couple stood in front of the band and kissed.

"Come on, you can do better than that!" Theo roared. "This is stupendous news! Now, let's do this properly! I propose a toast to the happy couple, who are also great friends of mine … Kelly and Edmund!"

The revellers now responded in unison: "To Kelly and Edmund!" A tumultuous cheer followed.

Theo clapped and cheered along with everyone else, though his actual feelings were ambivalent. Kelly had been an important part of his life for a long time. And he had been even more important to her. He knew full well that there had been a time when, for Kelly, a life without Theo was unthinkable.

He had been her rock, someone who had saved her from the gutter even. But now he had been replaced by Edmund, and might even cease to be a part of Kelly's life altogether. "And now, with this wonderful news making this occasion even more special than ever, let the party recommence! I want everyone on the floor!" And everyone did dance, save two new arrivals who had slipped in unnoticed.

The younger of the two men tapped George Bowes on the shoulder and said: "Sorry to trouble you but can you tell me where I can find Theo Salter, please?"

Theo was dancing with April, with one hand sliding up and down the back of each of her thighs, when the younger newcomer tapped his shoulder and asked: "Excuse me, sir, are you Theo Salter?"

Theo could see straight away that he was a policeman. "Who's asking?" he replied curtly.

"I'm Detective Constable Fielding," he replied. "And this is Detective Inspector Jackman," he added, pointing towards his companion. "We need to ask you a few questions."

"What, now!?" Theo asked angrily. "Can't you see that there's a party going on?"

Now it was DI Jackman's turn to speak. "We are really sorry to disturb you, sir, but we need to talk to you urgently. We would like you to accompany us to the station."

"What the hell's going on?" demanded April. She was even angrier than Theo. "What do you mean by barging in on a private gathering like this. I don't know what you're here for … but surely it can wait until the morning, can't it?"

"Not really," DI Jackman replied wearily. "The matter is important and it would be far better to discuss it out of the way, at the station. It shouldn't take unduly long." The older officer was in his late forties and had the air of someone who had seen and done it all before.

Theo sounded a little weary, too, when he said to April: "Don't worry, love. I'm sure this can be sorted out quickly, and I'm sure you'd like to see me co-operate with the police. You and Evelyn can keep the party going while I'm away. But be discrete, don't tell anyone where I've gone!" He then asked DI Jackman if he could arrange for a lift back to the party once he had been interviewed, and this was agreed.

The car journey to the police station took just over 10 minutes, and, on arrival, Theo was immediately taken to an interview room. DC Fielding asked him if he would like a cup of tea. The offer was declined.

"I appreciate your courtesy but should be obliged if you would tell me what this is all about. I really would like to get back to my party before it ends," he told the two officers.

"Yes, of course," DI Jackman said. "I appreciate your co-operation but I have to ask you a question or two ... discretely, of course. Then, after a pause, he added: "Our colleagues in Gloucester have picked up a guy by the name of Clive Matthews. I'm told that you know him. Is that so?"

Theo's heart missed a beat. But he kept his composure. "Er, yes, his name does ring a bell. I know him slightly but haven't seen him for years."

"That's interesting. He's said that he met up with you in Camford quite recently."

"That's not so. Why would he say that? What's all this about, anyway?" Only Jenny knew of Matthews' visit to the old Salter's office, and even she did not know what was in that zip-up bag. DI Jackman remained poker-faced throughout.

"Clive Matthews was picked up by police in Gloucester yesterday as a suspect in connection with a bank robbery in the area," he said. "He is also suspected of being involved in money laundering and drug dealing."

"Good grief!" exclaimed Theo. "I didn't know he was like that! But what's all this got to do with me?"

The DI sighed. "Well, there are certain things he has said about you, which I can't ignore."

"Like what?"

"Well, he's basically been making out that you're a crook. He says you have indulged in a host of dishonest practices as an estate agent in Gloucester and that you have also been involved in robberies, drug dealing and money laundering. And, initially, he said he called round with a bag full of cash for you to launder."

"What?! That's absolutely ridiculous!" Theo said in disbelief.

"Well," the DI continued, "I must also tell you that Matthews eventually admitted to handing the money over to another estate agent in Camford by the name of Raymond Williams. We are keen to talk to him, too, but we don't know his whereabouts at present. Can you shed any light on this, by any chance?"

Theo shook his head. "No, the only things I can tell you is that he originated from London and that he used to be a professional boxer. But, as you doubtless know, his office is boarded up and, as far as I know, no one has seen him for months."

DI Jackman stood up, thanked Theo for his help and asked DC Fielding to drive him back to the party. However, just before Theo left, the DI said to him: "There's just one more thing, come to think of it. Jenny Fitch used to be into drugs … and she's now working for you, isn't she?"

"And so …?"

"Well, it could be argued that there is a link between the drugs allegation and yourself."

"It's a bloody tenuous link, if I may say so," Theo retorted a little testily.

"Yeah, yeah, sure!" DI Jackman conceded with a wave of a hand.

DC Fielding was a chatty companion during the short drive that followed. He joked about life in the police force and about the dubious reputation of estate agents, touched on the canal rescue of six months ago and even started a discussion about cricket. Theo let the policeman do most of the talking.

The party was still in full swing, with everyone drinking and dancing more frenetically than ever. It was due to be talked about as "the best bash in Camford for years." The only person not dancing was April, who was hanging around near the front of the office.

She looked relieved to see Theo back so soon. "Is everything all right, darling?" she asked anxiously.

"Yes, sure," Theo replied. "It's nothing of any consequence really. I'll tell you about it later."

April smiled one of those smiles that was reserved for one man only, grabbed Theo by the arm and said: "Come on, let's dance." Theo joined her on the floor. But much of his gusto had gone.

CHAPTER 26

BULLDOZERS GAVE WAY To "bubbly" in Benson Lane on the day the MAC Developments site office was officially opened.

Much of the work was completed, though there was still much to be done. However, Sean McAvie, via Chris Doman, had ordered the construction workers to take the day off so that the dust could literally settle and guests would not be disturbed by the noise.

The site office was effectively one of the three reception rooms on the ground floor of one of the houses, a sumptuous detached property built to a high specification. The house, in addition, had four bedrooms, two bathrooms and a kitchen to kill for. It featured oak doors with brass handles, a mahogany staircase, pine flooring, a huge inglenook fireplace, a Jacuzzi as well as a bath in the bathroom, and a host of modern appliances in the kitchen. The office itself had ample room for guests, almost as much as there was in the SMK Estate Agents office. Champagne and buffet meals were laid on, details of the development were placed on two desks, and Sara Ponsonby-Stewart was on hand to greet guests as they arrived. McAvie and Doman stood near the desks, and made themselves available to answer questions.

Theo, April, Evelyn and Joe were all there, having left Jenny to hold the fort at SMK, as were various local businessmen such as building society officials Ian Shawcross and Lance Perry, bank manager Paul Green and his secretary Di Black and that most respected of all insurance men, Edmund Rooker.

Paul Shenfield was, of course, present to represent "The Camford Daily News", along with a handful of journalists from other newspapers in the region. Members of the public were to be made welcome at the site office the following day, and the office was to be manned round the clock thereafter until all sales had been completed. A few people had, in fact, managed to slip in uninvited. One of them was John Groves. Sara was at her most gushing that day but her public relations expertise did not extend to spotting and repelling gatecrashers. Doman was the first to notice the hapless Groves, who saw him sidle up to McAvie and have a quiet word.

April and Evelyn did their best to make Paul Shenfield and the other journalists welcome, while Theo, who had an inbuilt mistrust of the press, was happier to chat about cricket to Lance Perry. After about half an hour, Sara rang a bell to gain attention and announced that Sean McAvie, the head of MAC Developments, would like to say a few words about the company's new project.

McAvie told the gathering that all the new houses in Benson Lane would be on the market tomorrow. Building work on some of them was incomplete, and it would therefore be possible to make some alterations to the original plans, if required ... subject, of course, to an adjustment in price. The casino and restaurant would be ready in three months time, and further details would be released then.

"Meanwhile, information packs prepared by my press assistant Sara, who you met as you came in, have been laid out on the two desks beside me and you are welcome to take one before you depart," he said. "These will give details of the prices and so on of each house."

McAvie was then interrupted. "What about the price of life?" a voice called out from the back. It was John Groves. Doman, who was standing beside McAvie, took a step forward ... looking as if he was intent on ejecting the intruder. But McAvie gave him a tap on the arm that made it clear he should stay where he was.

"Good afternoon, Mr Groves. I wasn't expecting to see you today!" he said.

"I bet you weren't!" was the retort. "Where's your friend Drummond?"

McAvie's eyes narrowed. But, well aware that members of the press were present, he said calmly: "Mr Drummond is no longer with us." Then he added: "I'm not sure what you mean by your questions but I'm sure that if you stay around and enjoy our hospitality we can have a chat and straighten out whatever problem you might have."

And, before Groves could say anything else, McAvie roared: "Right! That concludes the formal part of out little get-together. Now, please study our literature, have plenty to eat and drink and, above all, relax and enjoy yourselves." McAvie motioned Groves to join him in a quiet corner. Paul Shenfield made a point of being within earshot. His news sense might have diminished over the years but his hearing was as acute as ever!

He had always felt slightly intimidated in McAvie's presence but could not help noticing that the redoubtable developer was in conciliatory mode while dealing with Groves. "Look, I do understand how you feel," he was heard to say. "I do sympathise over your loss, I really do. I feel terrible about what happened. It's not what I wanted at all. It was the last thing I wanted. That's why I paid for the funeral. Is there anything else I can do for you? Can I arrange for you to have a lift somewhere today, for example?"

John Groves burst into tears. "No, I don't want anything … except perhaps the disintegration of this bloody development!" he sobbed. "It's cost me the life of my mother and it's put an end to my livelihood…. and you can go to hell!" Just one or two guests saw John Groves storm out of the building.

The only one to take any real interest was Paul Shenfield, who picked up his information pack and the press release that had been prepared by Sara and followed the distressed interloper outside. Paul caught up with him on the corner of Benson Street. John Groves was smartly turned out and his grey hair was well groomed. But he was walking with the sort of shambling gait that is more often associated with a tramp. "Are you all right?" Paul asked him. John Groves looked at him suspiciously, and Paul then noticed that his jacket hung loosely over a frail frame and that his loose-fitting trousers were held up by braces.

"Hello, my name is Shenfield," the journalist told him. "I'm Property Correspondent of 'The Camford Daily News'. I couldn't help overhearing part of the conversation you were having with Mr

McAvie just then. I was wondering if you would like to talk to me about it or, whether I can help by giving you a lift somewhere."

John Groves gazed at Paul for a moment and said: "Yes, why not? There's quite a bit I can tell you, as a matter of fact." Paul suggested they went for a quiet coffee somewhere off the beaten track, and he took John Groves in his car to a small café-cum coffee bar called Snacks on Camford's southern outskirts. "Snacks" was very much a haunt for locals and Paul knew they would not be disturbed there. Paul recalled that, following the death in Benson Lane, there had been a suicide verdict at the ensuing inquest. It soon became apparent that John desperately needed to confide in someone, to pour himself out. Paul recalled his days as a young reporter who was initially surprised at how willing bereaved relatives were to be interviewed following the death of a loved one. Paul and John got on Christian name terms as soon as they sat down.

John told Paul about his difficult childhood, warring parents, his mother's three nervous breakdowns, his father's affairs with other women, separation, an acrimonious divorce and how he left home as soon as he could and went to live at the opposite end of the country. However, John had felt compelled to visit his friendless mother from time to time. "She was neurotic with a capital N, and so difficult to get on with that no one else had any time for her," he said. Paul bided his time before attempting to ask any leading questions. He had heard rumours that attempts had been made to drive Mary Groves out of her home ... but they were only rumours, nothing more. "Did you all live in Benson Lane as a family?" he asked.

"No, we lived in a house in Willoughby Street, about half a mile away, then. My mother moved to Benson Lane after the divorce," John replied.

"So she must have been there for some time. Was she reasonably settled there?"

Paul's last question drew the response he was waiting for. John's pale, care-worn face turned scarlet. His eyes went misty but he somehow managed to hold back the tears. "Was she settled?

Settled! That's not a word I normally associate with my mother. But I suppose she was … or at least as settled as she was ever likely to be!" He went on to describe how two representatives of MAC Developments tried to persuade his mother to leave … and then that disastrous encounter with Drummond.

Paul asked John to describe the MAC reps. John said he had never met them personally but was able to give descriptions based on what he had heard from his mother. One of the men could easily have been Chris Doman, Paul felt. Not surprisingly, much of the conversation centred on "that madman who moved into the flat above." Paul listened sympathetically and subtly inserted a question when it looked as if John was about to break down. Eventually he was able to secure a virtual blow-by-blow account of what had occurred. He also cast his memory back six months before saying: "I'm almost certain that Drummond is the man who was jailed for murdering the manager of a tea room in the town centre and then sent to Broadmoor. I'll have to check this at our cuttings library when I get back to the office, and I'll certainly let you know if you would like me to."

John asked to be kept posted, and then Paul drove him back to a hotel near the railway station where he had spent the previous night. Back at the "factory", Paul could not wait to get his hands on those library cuttings. He was not disappointed. The man in the flat above Mrs Groves WAS the tea room murderer. Now he could show Colin Edwards that he still had a keen news sense after all. And the editor still had not seen that anonymous note about Theo Salter. The news editor was on holiday and his deputy was off sick that day, and the editor and deputy editor had been forced to leave their offices from time to time to oversee the reporters. So, under the circumstances, Paul was expecting a long wait before being seen. However, much to his surprise, he was called in within 10 minutes of speaking to the editor's secretary.

The editor, deputy editor and advertising manager were all waiting for him. "How did you get on at the MAC site in Benson Lane?" Colin asked.

"Oh, it went fine, and there's quite a bit I have to tell you …"

"Good!" the editor said. "That's good because I have some important news for you. We have plans to develop and expand our weekly property supplement, and I trust you're going to start appreciating the importance of your role on the newspaper. As a first step, we are going to introduce a New Homes section, which will appear in the supplement once a month and will entail the need for some editorial about new housing developments in and around Camford."

The advertising manager cut in, saying: "We are expecting it to generate extra advertising revenue."

The editor then added: "A piece about the new MAC site and an interview with the head of the firm would be a good way to get things started. Later on, we will be targeting letting agents, building societies, solicitors, conveyancing firms and so on, with a view to attracting more custom from them, too. ... and we might need special editorial material in connection with these, as well. Are you happy with that, Paul?"

"Yes, that's fine," Paul said. "But there's just ..."

"Oh, sorry, there's was something you wanted to bring up yourself. Well, go ahead ... fire away!" Paul told the meeting about the anonymous note about Theo Salter and then outlined what had happened at the MAC reception and what John Groves had told him afterwards. Colin Edwards frowned and looked uneasy. The other two men glared at Paul.

"That's pretty contentious stuff!" the advertising manager said. "It's the sort of stuff that could upset people."

Paul's hackles began to rise. "I take it you mean that by 'people' you mean people who happen to advertise with us and not the man in the street. I thought we were all working for a bloody newspaper, for Christ's sake!"

Colin waved a placatory hand. "Hey, hey! Cool it! Let's not get our knickers in a twist! "You might well have a good story. It might even be a cracking story ... and good stories sell newspapers! But you must, first of all, check out all your facts carefully. The last thing we want is a writ coming through our letter box! Meanwhile, we need some copy for the New Homes section."

The other two men nodded in approval. "But," Colin added, "please keep tabs on the other stuff and let me know how you get on."

CHAPTER 27

THERE WAS QUITE A BUZZ going round Camford Police Station.

An inmate at Broadmoor had escaped. He was said to be highly dangerous, and heading this way. More details were to be released as soon as they became available. DI Jackman was on his toes already ... with something else. He wanted to know more about Theo Salter. He had been in the business of catching criminals for long enough to know when an allegation made about someone was worth following up.

In this case, the person who had made them, Clive Matthews, was hardly the most reliable of sources. But Jackman had developed a nose that could smell the truth even when presented by a habitual liar.

On top of this, there was Salter's association with Jenny Fitch, a known felon, to be considered. Something was not right. Jackman had contacted his old friend, DI Tom Northfield, a former "beat" partner who was now based in Gloucester, to see if he could turn up anything interesting about Camford's "mystery local hero."

And, now he was turning his attention to Jenny Fitch. Helping him with this was DS Helen Smith, whose youthful appearance belied a talent for winkling information out of people ... especially young women.

DS Smith had called round at SMK Estate Agents while Jenny was on her own and gently persuaded her to meet her later that day for a coffee.

The agreed rendezvous was a small coffee bar-cum-delicatessen about 50 yards from the police station.

When Jenny arrived there, she found both DS Smith and DI Jackman were waiting for her.

She had seen the latter at the party and he was now formally introduced before she sat down. Jenny, who knew perfectly well that the two officers were not there to ask after her health, waited stony-faced until one of them said what they wanted.

After a few moments, DS Smith said: "Thank you for coming. We would like to have a quiet off-the-record chat with you because we believe you can help us."

Jenny, a little defensively, responded by saying: "How can I do that? I've done nothing wrong. I know nothing and all I do is work at an estate agency for a living."

DI Jackman cleared his throat. "Now that's not entirely true, is it?" he said. "We've been in touch with colleagues in Gloucester and you figure in police records."

"That was a long time ago!" Jenny retorted angrily. "I now keep out of trouble!"

"I'm glad to hear it. But the fact of the matter is that you HAVE broken the law in the past."

"So …?"

"We would like you to help us," DI Jackman said wearily. "We are trying to shed light on a number of events that have occurred recently and we believe you might be able to help us do this."

Jenny, recalling how DI Jackman and a colleague had turned up at the SMK Estate Agency party, asked: "Is any of this to do with my boss?"

DS Smith then said: "It's a possibility. At the moment, we don't know but certain allegations have been made and these might or might not involve Mr Salter. We are not able to go into detail, though we can say that we are not out to arrest you. We are simply asking you to assist us."

"How can I do that? Jenny asked suspiciously.

"Well, to start with, what's your association, if any, with Clive Matthews?"

"There's none at all, though I have heard the name."

"What about Terry Springett and Ralph Meekin?"

Jenny shuddered. These were the drug dealers who had started to beat her up in Birmingham before Theo came to her rescue.

"Yes, I do unfortunately," she said. "They are part of my past and not of my future. I never want to see them again!"

"You are not likely to … not for a while anyway. They are both behind bars." DI Jackman and DS Smith both looked at Jenny hard and long before the former asked: "Did you know that they were associates of Mr Salter?"

Jenny looked startled. Before she could respond, DI Smith produced an envelope containing several photographs showing Theo Salter in the company of either Springett or Meakin or both. One of the photos showed money changing hands between Theo and Springett.

Jenny's heart began to pound. She began to feel dizzy. She could not believe what she had seen. "Why are you showing me these? What are you trying to say?" she screamed. Staff and other customers looked round to see what was going on.

"Theo Salter is my friend. He's the best friend I've ever had or could hope to have! Have you any idea what friendship is? You're just trying to get me to get him into trouble … and I'm not having any part of it! You can both go to hell … and you can stick your coffee up your arses!"

Jenny kicked a chair across the room as she stormed out. DS Smith was about to try to persuade her to stay but her senior colleague said: "Let her go. We can always talk to her later on if we need to."

Just as the two officers were about to leave as well, DC Fielding appeared. "I had a feeling I might find you here," he said. "I've got some interesting things to tell you."

"Go on," said DI Jackman.

"Well, the first is that a reporter from 'The Camford Daily News' has been asking questions about Salter. He's got one or two things to tell us and he's keen to talk to someone in the know."

"No problem. What's the other thing?"

"The other bit of news is that the man who escaped from Broadmoor IS Derek Drummond. He has killed two members of staff there, and it looks as if he spent some time carefully planning his getaway."

"And does all this directly affect us?"

"Yes, it looks as if it could. No one knows for sure but people in charge at Broadmoor believe he could be heading this way He had been talking of getting his revenge on people he feels had done the dirty on him in Camford."

"Do we know who?"

"Well, he has left behind a notebook with a list of names in it. The list includes the names of the two people he killed at Broadmoor, and there are the names of the three police officers who arrested him for murder, one of the waitresses at the tea room where the murder of the manager took place, and ... here's where it gets really interesting ... Sean McAvie and Chris Doman, of MAC Developments and ... wait for it ... Theo Salter!"

DI Jackman's usually jaded demeanour became unusually animated. He had been in the business for so long that he thought there was nothing new left for him ... except perhaps retirement. "I want to see that notebook," he said. "I want to see exactly what he has written. I want to talk to someone in charge at Broadmoor, someone who can give me some insight into this madman's thought processes. I know it's not PC to say this but that's what Drummond is ... an out and out lunatic! And," he added after a pause, "I want to have words with that reporter. There are all sorts of possible links to be checked out here. And what really intrigues me is that many, if not all these links, seem to involve Salter."

DI Jackman was not the only person interested in detecting links. Jenny Fitch had originally intended to return directly to the office after her meeting with the two police officers. But now she was in a pub 100 yards away, sipping a pint of lager and agonising over their conversation. "It can't be true!" she kept telling herself. "He's my best friend. He's always looked out for me.

CHAPTER 28

WHOEVER SAID "A policeman's lot is not a happy one" must be barking mad, DC Fielding thought to himself. It was more like a bed of roses, the young man believed. He felt he was on a never-ending roll. There were three commendations in the bag already, the prospect of early promotion and the likelihood of a glittering career. At the moment, failure was a foreign word.

As a schoolboy, the young Richard Fielding had enjoyed an above average academic record and an outstanding sporting one. His jovial and at times forceful personality had been recognised by his school head and for the last two years he had been a prefect. A career in the police, where he could be true to his belief in maintaining law and order and, at the same time exercise authority, had been the inevitable next step. His quick brain and athletic ability had soon come to the fore and he had had no difficulty in shining at the college for police cadets in Hendon.

He was now happily married with two children, aged four and two and a third one on the way. His wife, Michele had been a police cadet herself. So she was well aware that the hours were frequently unsocial. The couple's relationship was nothing short of idyllic. One of his commendations had been for the way he had apprehended Derek Drummond shortly after the tea room murder.

There had been a furious struggle, during which the young officer's training in unarmed combat was tested to the full before back-up arrived.

DC Fielding knew he needed to be vigilant on hearing of the escape from Broadmoor and that if there was to be another confrontation between himself and Drummond, the outcome would by no means be a foregone conclusion.

Meanwhile, however, there were stripes to be earned. DI Jackman had put a good word in for him already but promotion was not a foregone conclusion either. The ambitious young Fielding felt the need for one more notable "pinch," something that would catch the eye of the force's top brass. So he decided to take a look at the affairs of Sean McAvie and, in particular, Theo Salter. McAvie was well known to the police already as a former Gorbels hard man who had "made good." He had spent a term in a young offenders' institution for his part in a knife fight and had been suspected of other criminal activities, including protection racketeering and running a cocaine ring.

However, all that was a matter of decades ago and, although there had been rumours of further shady dealings, McAvie had kept his nose clean for a long time. He had worked hard to establish a veneer of respectability.

Theo Salter was a different proposition altogether. There was no criminal record to be studied, just hearsay. But, as the experienced, albeit jaded DI Jackman had observed not long ago: "There's something not quite right about the bloke." So DC Fielding had made the decision to do some research in his spare time. The Derek Drummond escape alert was the top priority just now. But there was at least a bit of time for a little computer research.

No record of an estate agent called Theo Salter could be found, though. So the next step was to see if he could find out what agents were operating, or had operated in the past, in the Gloucester area. He started with Gloucester itself, and had no joy. Then he looked at the lists of estate agents in nearby towns. Still no joy. The only name that looked even remotely worthy of attention was Saltzman and Prestwick ... because Saltzman sounded vaguely like Salter ... in the small market town of Mottlesham. After a while, he had to relinquish the computer at the police station because another officer had a more pressing need for it

The eager young DC was now heading towards a car park near

the town centre. Twilight was beginning to descend and, if he was quick, there might be time to tuck the children up in bed before spending the evening with his beloved Michele.

It was to be the last time they would be together for a while, as Michele and the children were to leave the area the following day to be with relatives.

They were to stay away from the Camford area until the threat posed by Drummond had been dealt with.

By pure coincidence, DC Fielding was walking down the street where Drummond had been bundled into a Black Mariah on the day of the murder. But there was no commotion now, just the reverse. Most of the shops were closed and all but one of the shoppers in the street had left for home.

The one shopper left was a little old woman who shuffled as she walked with stooped shoulders. She wore a long overcoat, a shawl, a head scarf and flat shoes and carried a rolled up umbrella. The shopper shuffled towards DC Fielding and, in a croaked voice, asked: "Excuse me, sir, have you got a light?"

"Sorry, I don't. I don't smoke," was the reply.

"Can you tell me where I might buy some matches?" the shopper then asked.

The DC paused for a moment to think where the best place might be. The woman was standing just inches away from him.

All of a sudden, the policeman observed an area of shadow round the chin and a pair of cold, blue eyes. He felt a sharp pain as a steel blade was plunged between two of his ribs. The next moment, the DC was on his back, looking up at his assailant, who whispered with a sneer: "Die, yee bluebottle bastard! Die!"

DC Fielding was unable to move. He felt as cold as he was helpless. He had never been at anyone's mercy before, as far as he could remember, and he did not like it. He thought about his idyllic childhood, his burgeoning career and the loving family waiting for him at home. Who was going to look after Michele and the kids now? Well, at least they should be safe. They would be leaving first thing in the morning and they would then be out of harm's way ...

It was getting darker by the minute. An angry-looking black

cloud, appearing like a nemesis, was dominating what was left of the horizon. The John Brewer Shopping Centre was almost deserted.

The Auntie's Tea Room, like most of the shops, had closed its doors. However, behind the tea room doors Edith Parfitt was busy in an office near the kitchen, working on the latest accounts. Miss Parfitt was now the manager. Her employers had commended her on the way the then waitress had handled the situation regarding Drummond six months ago and, following the manager's murder, promotion was her reward. The tea room had closed for a month enabling repair work to be carried out and Miss Parfitt to have time off to mend her frayed nerves.

Now business was brisker than ever, partly because of the impeccable way the new manager had run things and partly owing to the fact that the grisly goings on at the tea room had attracted publicity and proved a magnet for customers. Edith Parfit was now mulling over those enhanced figures. She had worked at the tea room for 15 years and was now enjoying the prospect of a place on the company's board. "If the figures keep going up, the position is yours," the MD had told her. At her time in life, it was almost too good to be true.

Edith spent more time than usual poring over the books. She checked the figures again and again until she was as sure as anyone could be that they were correct. And there was no doubt about it: they were 15 per cent better than a year ago! She began to think about what clothes she should buy to look the part of a member of the board. "Meet the new power dresser!" she said aloud.

As she filed away her papers in her newly purchased briefcase and got ready to leave for home, she could hear a tip-tapping sound outside. It was the noise of fingers on glass. She moved into the main café area and towards the property's glass front door. At first she was unable to see who was making the noise. But then the outline of a woman appeared. "Sorry, we're closed!" the tea room manager called out. But the woman continued to tap the glass with her fingers, making it clear that she was demanding attention.

"All right, all right! Just give me a minute to find my keys,"

Edith Parfitt said a little irritably. She rummaged in her handbag, found the right keys, unlocked the door and frowned at the strange woman with a scarf over her head who stood before her. "What's the problem?" she asked curtly. No sooner had she spoken than a chill feeling swept through her entire body. Cold blue eyes were boring into her, and, all of a sudden, she knew who she was talking to.

Early the following morning, staff turned up at the tea room to find that there was no one around to let them in, and some time elapsed before a spare set of keys could be found. By the time they could gain entry, a number of customers were waiting, too. One of the waitresses went into the kitchen and, on seeing the office door unlocked, went in there as well. She screamed at what she saw. Edith Parfitt had been bound to a chair, gagged and tortured to death.

CHAPTER 29

NEWS OF THE TWO murders on the same day was common knowledge nationally within 24 hours. The likely link with Drummond's escape from Broadmoor meant a full-scale police alert, with virtually all leave for the officers cancelled. Some officers who had booked leave made the decision to cancel it themselves for two clear-cut reasons.

One was that one of their own ... and a highly popular colleague to boot ... had been brutally killed.

The other was the gruesome treatment meted out to Edith Parfitt. It was clear, even without forensic evidence yet, that she had been beaten and burnt all over with cigarette ends for a period of possibly several hours. The gentle Miss Parfitt was known to a number of the officers and their anger was such that they had been told to rein in their emotions and concentrate on finding Drummond.

But he was nowhere to be seen. No one had seen him come into Camford and no one, it seemed, had seen him since. If he was indeed the culprit, then he had clearly gone to ground somewhere. One of the first tasks for police was to contact the other people on the list that Drummond had left behind. The other constables involved in the arrest were told to never go out on their own. Members of their families were advised to leave town for a while. The other names on the list were Sean McAvie, Chris Doman and Theo Salter. All three were urged to quit Camford until Drummond was found and caught.

All three refused. McAvie could not conceal his concern when told about the two murders. He had taken a calculated risk in employing Drummond, and, if he ever had been under any illusion about him being a loose cannon, there was certainly no illusion now.

But the MAC Developments project in Benson Lane was now at a crucial stage. Work was well under way and there were regular visitors to the site office. To close down the office and disappear at this stage could be costly.

Under the circumstances, the police undertook to patrol Benson Lane regularly and McAvie told Chris Doman and Sara Ponsonby-Stewart that neither of them should ever be on their own at the site office, for any reason. In addition, he enlisted the services of Frank Austin, a night club bouncer and well known local "heavy."

Theo Salter's reluctance to leave town was also money-based. A number of lucrative deals were in the pipeline, and yet he was, at that moment, operating in the absence of both April May and Jenny. Both had been unexpectedly distant of late and both had decided to take some leave at the same time.

Jenny had been inexplicably curt, even hostile, the last few days. Instead of looking at Theo with adoring eyes, she was doing so with a squint. Theo had for long valued her trust and devotion and now feared he might have lost it.

So when Jenny declared that she was due for some time off, Theo offered her a month's leave, with full pay of course, as an olive branch.

April's change of demeanour was less pronounced. But, again, there was a suggestion of mistrust. The love-making had lost much of its intensity and was less frequent. On one occasion, April had expressed disappointment that the likes of Lisa and Sherry, not to mention some of the other estate agents, were not inviting them into their homes any more. But, apart from that, Theo could see no reason why anything should be amiss. He had been too busy to notice this perceived isolation, in any case. When April announced that she wished to spend a month with her parents in her native California, Theo felt it was probably for the best if she went.

So now he was operating with part-time back-up from Evelyn Knight, Joe Prescott and a recently appointed office junior.

He was therefore far too busy to close down, though he

promised to be vigilant and expressed thanks when told that there would be regular police patrols near the SMK Estate Agents office.

In addition, Sean McAvie promised to let Theo borrow "Big Frank" from time to time.

Meanwhile, Theo had other fish to fry. Some of them were big fish at that! The telephone at SMK rang at frequent and regular intervals and Theo got his new office junior, a gangling 18-year-old called Darren Hensby, to field most of these calls and tackle most of the routine inquiries. Evelyn Knight was present for much of the time, too, as was Joe Prescott, and they provided invaluable back-up while Theo tackled the trickier tasks.

The main focus of his attention at present was the unoriginally named Rose Cottage, owned by a Colonel Alfred Kelly and situated in the hamlet of Little Pocklington, seven miles west of Camford and three miles from the new motorway link to London. Rose Cottage was a gem of a property. Although seemingly remote because of the narrow, winding roads approaching it for the last three miles, the detached cottage was, in fact, attractive to both commuters and those seeking a weekend retreat.

The property had been extensively renovated inside and yet retained its "olde worlde" exterior. Apart from roses round the front door, there were a thatched roof, exposed timbers, leaded light windows and a garden featuring a variety of rare plants and a pond containing koi carp. Theo had got Joe to take a look, and both had agreed that here was the perfect opportunity to make a killing and enhance expansion plans.

The beauty of the situation was that Colonel Kelly, who had spent much of his retirement time licking the once run-down cottage into shape and making it saleable, had suddenly decided to spend the rest of his life in the Seychelles. His sister was living there already and the Colonel, who had spent much of his life living in various exotic locations, had bought a property close to hers. He was due to leave England in a few days time … and he needed a reputable estate agent to find a buyer for Rose Cottage.

The much publicised heroics of Theo Salter had captured the imagination of a man who was no stranger to adventure himself, and so Colonel Kelly approached SMK Estate Agents without even considering any of the firm's competitors.

Joe Prescott had gone round Rose Cottage and its garden with a fine tooth comb and told Theo what he thought it was worth. Theo then gave the Colonel a suggested sales figure. Photographs were taken and Theo promised to display them prominently within 48 hours.

The day before leaving Britain's shores for ever, Colonel Kelly popped in to SMK to inquire how the marketing of Rose Cottage was going. He saw there were no details on display and, when he expressed surprise, he was told that "photographic production" problems had led to a short delay. He was assured that the particulars and photographs would assume a prominent position in both the front window and inside within two or three days.

Colonel Kelly had now departed a week ago, and the particulars remained locked up in a drawer. Joe had told Theo that he reckoned Rose Cottage would attract considerable interest among potential buyers and that it should sell for £900,000, possibly more, on the open market. Theo had told the Colonel that a price of £850,000 was "achievable if things went well." He had already decided that this was a property that should be bought by SP Financial Services Ltd ... a company run by Theo and Joe. Rose Cottage was to be kept under wraps for a few months, and then Colonel Kelly would be sent an email advising him that, because a sale had not been secured, he should reduce the price to "offers around £800,000."

Then, after another month or so, the Colonel would be told of an offer ... the only offer ... of £780,000 from a firm of financial advisers.

The next step would be for SP Financial Services to put Rose Cottage back on to the market later on. Property prices were rising steadily at the time, and Theo was confident that a sale price of at least £950,000 was achievable within a year. The profit would be £170,000. And that was for just one property! Theo and Joe were well versed in the art of "ring-fencing." They knew that the two most important elements were to pick the right sort of customer ...

and not to get found out! Colonel Kelly was the perfect foil! Several other properties, including those passed on to him by Evelyn Knight, were being, or had been, handled in a similar manner. There were, however, times when a different approach was considered more prudent.

Sometimes it was politic to slightly under-price a home and then publicise it widely. This would tend to result in several potential buyers competing for it and submitting higher and higher offers until well above the normally expected selling price was achieved. Theo would often encourage vendors to agree to a low asking price for this reason, and his charm was such that they nearly always agreed readily to do so.

Another system for securing cash for the SMK coffers owed much to the valuation skills of Joe Prescott. Joe, a qualified chartered surveyor who had passed all his exams with distinction, had frequently been entrusted with the task in the Gloucester area of valuing houses and flats for mortgage lenders. He would make his assessment, after going round a property, and then deduct several thousand pounds. As a result, the mortgage offer the potential buyer had hoped to receive fell short ... and the vendor had to put the property back on the marker. When this happened, it usually meant a change of estate agent ... and, somehow or other, that other agent was nearly always Theo Salter.

Joe Prescott's surveying skills were now well known in Camford, largely due to a word here and there from Theo, and the Camford Building Society was beginning to make use of his services as a mortgage valuer. Sean McAvie was useful to Theo, too, though McAvie expected a trade-off in favours. The fact that Theo had been entrusted with the job of agent for the MAC Developments project in Benson Lane was no coincidence.

When Theo was operating in and around Gloucester, a client had asked him for the name of a reputable builder, who could work on expanding and improving a property he had just bought. Theo told him about MAC Developments, whose quote for the work was well in excess of what it would actually cost. The client had naively accepted the quote without looking elsewhere, and Theo Salter and

Sean McAvie split the profit and used the money for improvements to their own properties.

"What a sucker!" Theo mused afterwards. "Serves the silly sod right!"

One aspect of estate agency that Theo and his colleagues were particularly scrupulous about was the preparation of "property for sale" particulars. The Property Misdescriptions Act of 1991 had made it clear that providing misleading information about a home for sale was a criminal offence. A serious breach of the Act could even lead to prison. An estate agent could not, for example, refer to "breath-taking views" if there was a sawmill, abattoir or cement works nearby without mentioning it. A photograph was not allowed to be misleading either. So when April and Evelyn both stressed the importance of giving out accurate information, Theo's reaction was to declare righteously: "Well, yes, of course!" On the face of it, everything was "hunkey dorey!" But it was not quite. Theo was beginning to miss April, and he was worried about her recent attitude towards him. Her observation that Sherry, Lisa and the other estate agents seemed to be cold-shouldering the couple rankled.

Theo could understand Lisa's coolness and he assumed that she had told Sherry about that indiscrete pass he had made. Sherry was on tour for much of the time these days, though, and so she was less of a worry than she might have been otherwise. He could understand why Lisa, Sherry and Wayne, who had probably been told, too, had become distant.

What particularly concerned him, though, was the attitude of the other estate agents. During his early days in Camford, nearly all of them had been in regular contact, with invitations to dinner, a game of golf or simply to join them for a pint of beer somewhere. These invitations had all but dried up. George Bowes and Nathan Pike would agree to meet up with him occasionally. But the others had virtually frozen him out.

One factor, admittedly, was that Theo had often been too busy to socialise. But that was not the whole story, by any means. Some of the agents were undoubtedly jealous of his success and his rapid rise to being one of the big names on the Camford estate agency scene. But that was not the full story either. Theo could sense a feeling of mistrust among his rivals ... as if they had heard things he did not want them to hear. And then there was Jenny Fitch. What could be the matter with her? Had someone said something untoward to Jenny as well?

One consolation was the occasional get-together he and April would have with Edmund and Kelly. Every few weeks, the two couples had been meeting for meals at either an up-market restaurant or one or other of their homes.

Edmund, who had initially struck Theo as something of a dullard, never failed to surprise him with his wit, breadth of knowledge and sharpness of mind. He gave the impression that he could even outmanoeuvre Theo if he wanted to. This could be slightly unnerving at times, though Edmund's entertainment value more than matched the Rooker intellect. Kelly, who had grown increasingly demure since starting to be with him, appeared to be blissfully happy. And that had to be good to see! If Kelly was to be anyone's else's girl, then why shouldn't it be Edmund? After all, Theo did have April now. Or did he ... ?

In the meantime, there was plenty of work to be done. Theo could focus on this for now, and, at the same time, be constantly mindful of the police warning concerning Drummond.

He was, in fact, grateful for the support he was getting in the office just now. The new office junior was proving to be quite a find. He had picked up the work quickly and was soon carrying out tasks without needing to be asked. Joe, a surveyor rather than an estate agent, was chipping in with a bit of agency help and Evelyn was in the office far more than usual ... and was "going beyond the call."

It could be said that Evelyn was an attraction and distraction at the same time. Theo could not help wondering how many customers were being tempted into the SMK office by the ample cleavage on display rather than the pictures in the front window. And there were times when the young junior did not know where to look!

Sometimes she would get up from her desk and brush past Theo, run a hand along a shoulder from behind while walking to the other side of the room. When she returned to her desk and sat down again, the lower part of her dress slid upwards to reveal shapely, stocking-less thighs. Any doubts Theo might have had about Evelyn's intentions ended that evening, when the two of them were left on their own.

Evelyn locked the front door, turned off the lights, walked behind Theo as he sat at his desk and slid both hands down the front of his shirt. She then undid a couple of buttons and caressed his nipples and stomach. After that, she got Theo to stand up by pulling at his tie. "I've been waiting for this moment for a long time," she said in that low sensuous drawl as she undid the side of her dress and, almost simultaneously, opened his flies.

CHAPTER 30

THERE WAS STILL no sign of Drummond. A week had elapsed since the two Camford murders and all attempts to locate the Broadmoor escapee had come to nought.

The police officers, who had anticipated an early and possibly dramatic arrest, had been out and about in almost unprecedented numbers. Now they were becoming frustrated. There had been widespread searches and doorstep inquiries, and appeals via radio, television and newspapers for the public to report anything remotely suspicious. And there had been lots of waiting around in cars and on foot.

The homes and work places of those whose names appeared on Drummond's "hit list" were under constant surveillance. But there was no sign, not even a sniff, of a breakthrough.

News that Ray Williams had been arrested for suspected money laundering, in association with Clive Matthews, had alleviated the boredom to some extent. Williams, for long a man looked upon with suspicion by the force, had been picked up at Heathrow while carrying a suitcase full of cash.

But the Camford crime scene was dead apart from a spate of minor thefts from some shops in Benson Street. Many of the police officers felt shoplifters should be referred to social workers and therapists rather than the magistrates' court.

So, inevitably perhaps, the feeling of panic in the town receded. Perhaps the two murders had nothing to do with Drummond? Perhaps Drummond had fled to Scotland, which, after all, was where he came from, rather than Camford? There had been two murders, admittedly, but they might be unconnected with each other

... and no concern to anyone apart from the victims and their families!

Meanwhile Theo and his colleagues had work to do. There was also the annual estate agents' dinner/dance to think about. Evelyn wanted to go and she persuaded Theo to accompany her. As the agents were each allowed to bring a guest. Kelly and Edmund were invited to accompany them, and a table was booked in advance.

Joe Prescott could have gone, too, but he had a backlog of survey and valuation reports to write up, and these took priority.

Joe was anything if not thorough. Even a building society valuation, which entailed far less attention that a "full structural" was far more time-consuming than it was for the average valuer.

He sat at the long table that took up most of the larger of the top floor offices at SMK, where informal board meetings and discussions with some of the firm's higher-profile clients had taken place. The table had, unbeknown to Joe, also seen a different kind of activity ... firstly involving Theo and April and, more recently, Theo and Evelyn.

Joe carefully laid out his files on the polished wooden table top. He would deal with the valuations, which would basically tell the mortgage lender concerned whether it should lend money on a property and, if so, how much. Major structural defects would be highlighted but a lot of other detail would be omitted.

He would then look at the full structural surveys, which were carried out on behalf of potential house or flat buyers and were far more detailed. The unearthing of a serious structural fault could put paid to either a sale or a mortgage application. A minor defect, such as the need for a bit of re-rendering, might not stop a lender granting a loan. But it could put off a prospective buyer or, more likely, give the buyer ammunition to negotiate on price.

As he systematically and efficiently wrote up his reports, Joe began to recall the days when he first knew Theo and how, over the years, they had developed a bond. It was a bond that went right back to primary school days.

Joe was a sickly child, who had suffered pleurisy at the age of three and picked up a host of ailments since. If there was a cold to be caught, he would catch it. He was tall, gangling and painfully thin even then. A slight eye deformity meant that he appeared to have a permanent squint, and, to make matters worse, he had a nervous tic in the same area.

Inevitably, the hapless Joe became a target for classroom bullies and, although he was taller than most of them, he was simply too weak physically to fight back effectively. The only robust thing about Joe Prescott was the sound of his name.

His early years at primary school were a source of sheer misery. The only solace he could find was in the work, at which he excelled. He picked up the three Rs more quickly than anyone else and, even at the ages of five and six, he was burying himself in books at every opportunity. He would avoid going out into the playground whenever he could and, although there was no homework expected of pupils so young, he would, once at home, go over what he had learned in class and then see if he could expand on that knowledge.

Not surprisingly perhaps, his classmates looked upon him as the school swot, and this did not exactly endear him to them. No one wanted to befriend him, and the bullies became increasingly incensed by Joe's "creepy" behaviour.

Most of the bullying consisted of taunts, insults and the aiming of missiles, such as paper pellets propelled by rulers and elastic bands, behind the teacher's back. At other times, there was the odd push, slap or punch in the stomach which, again, went unnoticed by teachers.

Towards the end of Joe's third year at primary school, the bullying worsened. He was set on several times and had his head pushed down the toilet twice. Then, on the last day of the last term, four boys waylaid Joe on his way home and punched and kicked him repeatedly before picking him up and hurling him into a bed of stinging nettles.

When he got home, bruised, dishevelled and in tears, there was a modicum of sympathy but precious little else. His father was dying of cancer and his mother was so racked with arthritis that putting food on the table and keeping the house clean … with help from Joe … were hard enough for her to accomplish without having to worry about schoolboy transgressions. However, it was now the end of term and, as long as Joe stayed indoors most of the time and managed to avoid the bullies when he had to go out, there would at least be some respite.

During the school holiday, Joe spent most of his time reading anything he could lay his hands on … from Enid Blighton to Dickins.

For two weeks during that long summer, he stayed with Auntie Ethel and Uncle George in order to give his mother a break.

His uncle, a jovial, rotund man, was a chartered surveyor and, when his nephew expressed an interest, he took him round one or two of the properties he had to visit in the course of his work and showed what he did. Joe was enthralled and Uncle George soon became impressed with the youngster's powers of observation and eye for detail.

"I'd like to do this when I grow up," Joe declared. He was still only nine. His uncle smiled and said: "When the time comes, you can come and work for me!"

Young Joe's feeling of elation lasted for several days. It ended when the prospect of having to return to school loomed large once more.

A new year at school, of course, meant a new class and a new teacher. Unfortunately, though, there was only one new pupil and his four main tormentors were still there, sitting together in one corner. It was not long before they were giving Joe, who made a point of sitting as far away from them as possible, the evil eye.

However, the new boy attracted even more interest. Newcomers were rare in the close-knit village of Ampleford, where the primary school was situated, and the bullies switched their attention to him. The new boy, whose name turned out to be Theo, sat at a desk near the front, just a few feet away from Joe, and the teacher asked Joe to help Theo to learn the ropes. Sniggers could be heard around the classroom, though the teacher did not seem to hear. Before long, a missile, in the form of an elastic band, hit the newcomer in the face. Theo grinned and shrugged his shoulders. During playtime, Theo was jostled and subjected to a variety of taunts but took no notice.

On the second day of his first term at his new school, the bullies' ringleader, Sam Warren, walked up to Theo, who happened to be talking to Joe, and asked: "What are you doing talking to that creep?"

Theo looked at Sam in the eye and asked: "What's it got to do with you?"

Sam, who was easily the biggest boy in the school but not knowing enough to notice how toughly built Theo was, went red in the face.

"You want to watch it, you do!"

"Or what?"

"I'm going to bash your face in!"

"You and who else?"

"Why you ... !" Sam was just about to lunge at Theo when the bell rang for classes to resume.

The following day, Sam confronted Theo in the playground again ... and was soon made to regret it! The usual playground chant of "Fight, fight!" gave way to silence as the watching children saw the "toughest boy in the school" get comprehensively beaten.

Back in the classroom, Sam, who had a black eye and a bleeding nose, was obliged to tell the teacher he had tripped and fallen on to one of the playground swings.

From then on, Sam and his cronies gave Theo a wide berth. Initially, they turned their attention back to Joe. But not for long.

Joe, who had been giving Theo some help with his arithmetic, suddenly found himself being confronted by Sam while on his way to the toilets.

"Where do you think you're going, creep?" the bully asked him menacingly.

Joe tried to take avoiding action but Sam pushed him against a wall and pinned him to it. "I'm talking to you!" Sam said, snarling. "I asked you where you were going!" He then slapped Joe's face.

But then he received a slap himself, followed by a punch in the stomach that doubled him up. "You leave him alone!" said Theo, who had been walking unnoticed a few yards behind. "Any more trouble from you, and I'm going to really hurt you!"

And there was no more trouble ...

From then on, the two outsiders forged a bond, which continued when they moved on to a secondary school in Gloucester. They had a tacit understanding. Joe would help Theo with his school work, which sometimes meant doing homework in its entirety, and Theo would protect Joe from bullies.

It was the ideal arrangement. Theo quickly showed that, if he had to, he could get the better of boys two years older than him in a fight. Word soon got round that he was a scrapper not to be trifled with, and, at the same time, his all-round athletic prowess earned him respect among the other boys. The girls were not slow to notice either! Joe's academic prowess continued to shine, and his move into the school's academic "A" stream was automatic. With more than a bit of help from Joe, the determined Theo managed to make the "A" group, too.

The more extrovert Theo managed to make a few friends other than Joe, while the latter spent much of his time alone in the school library … poring over the books available for his own purpose, or simply doing Theo's homework! Much of Theo's time was spent on the sports field and he was, in particular, outstanding at cricket, soccer, rugby and boxing.

The friendship between Theo and Joe, who seemed to be poles apart, gave rise to some comment among other pupils. But no one considered saying anything about it to Theo's face! If it was not for the fact that the pair were known to have had dalliances with a number of local girls and a few more with the pupils of an expensive girls-only boarding school, the closeness of their friendship might have been questioned in a different way!

As it was, Theo's prowess with the opposite sex became legendary even at the age of 16. Joe's success was somewhat less spectacular, though, on the occasions he could be tempted away from his books, the influence of Theo made those forbidden fruits accessible.

Joe's academic record continued to be outstanding and, when the time finally came for him to leave school, he went straight to university. After gaining a first in maths, he secured a post with a firm of chartered surveyors and, in his spare time, set about the studies that would make him chartered himself.

Theo fared well enough at school to gain two A-levels but decided university was not for him. Instead he became a salesman, firstly in a garage showroom and later with an insurance company.

This, of course, meant that Theo and Joe parted company for several years, though they did keep in touch periodically. Then, all of a sudden, Theo made the decision to become an estate agent and the pair, now in their 20s, joined forces again

At this point, Joe had just become chartered and it became clear to him that there was no point in remaining with his current employers. The firm was a two-man partnership whose staff consisted of a secretary and a trainee ... namely Joe. He was a trainee no more and he needed to move on.

Had Theo not contacted him and broached the subject of setting up an estate agency, Joe would have almost certainly secured a post with a bigger surveying firm or perhaps with a building society. Either would have been impressed by his academic record and the fact that he had passed his professional exams with distinction. His personality was not impressive, though, and not all employers would have viewed him as management material. Theo, on the other hand, had personality in spades and this more than made up for his lack of technical knowledge ... which Joe had in abundance.

So, once again, the pair formed what seemed to be the perfect alliance.

Theo and Joe found a small office available to let in the village of Mottlesham and started to trade in the name of Saltzman & Prestwick Estate Agents. Theo, who had the more capital to sink into the business, was the senior partner.

Both partners considered altering their surnames ... Theo because he had no love for his father, and Joe because he thought such a change might help give him a new image. Theo decided to delay making such a change, while Joe found it to be of no use to him and reverted back to his real name later on.

Business was hard to come by at first. The area was already well served by a variety of established estate agents, and there was no obvious need for any more. So competition was stiff.

Considerable effort was needed at the outset, and Theo's contribution to the money pot was crucial. Joe would sometimes muse over where all that cash had come from, and he could only assume that Theo's forceful personality had brought him wealth as a salesman. Theo always did have charisma. He did not always say a great deal but his bearing and commanding presence forced people to notice, respect, listen to … and even fear him.

Little by little, the charisma, coupled with Joe's growing reputation as a skilled surveyor ensured that some of the house sales and surveying assignments went through under the Saltzman and Prestwick banner.

These were tough times but they were also exciting. Associating with Theo Salter could never be boring. The words "stagnant" and "mundane" were not in his friend's vocabulary.

Theo was forever coming up with ways to promote business and, at the same time, oust the opposition. Leaflets extolling the virtues of Saltzman and Prestwick would drop into letterboxes at regular intervals. Posters with the words "Saltzman and Prestwick … Real Estate Agents" would appear in the unlikeliest places at the most unlikely times. Most of this publicity-seeking was carried out after official office hours.

Joe recalled one particularly exciting week when, under cover of darkness, he and Theo removed as many "For Sale" boards that had been put up by rival estate agents as they could. The boards, once dismantled, were taken by van to a remote part of the countryside and either burnt or thrown into a river or pond

No one ever found out who did it!

It was regrettable that the partnership had to be wound up so suddenly, just as business was beginning to pick up in a big way. However, it was good to be back working with Theo. The latest parting of the ways had lasted for two lack-lustre years.

Joe gave a contented sigh as he finished off the last of his survey reports. He was back working with Theo but, at the same time, operating independently as a surveyor and valuer. He was happy enough to help Theo out when he was short-staffed, as he was now, but, for most of the time, he was surveying houses rather than helping to sell them ... and surveying was, always had been, his first love.

He was not sorry to have missed the agents' dinner/dance either. It was not really his scene.

Joe opened up his large, brown briefcase and started to pack away the files with their newly completed reports. Just after he had locked the office door and started to walk downstairs, his composure was shattered by the sound of a heavy object smashing into the plate glass window below. Joe, pulse racing, fled back to the big upstairs office, went in and locked the door behind him.

CHAPTER 31

THEO WAS A RELUCTANT reveller at the annual estate agency "bash." He was having misgivings about his fling with Evelyn, who had persuaded him to attend, and he knew there would be repercussions.

His immediate concern, however, was how others at the dinner/dance would receive him. Having Evelyn, instead of April, on his arm was not going to help.

Apart from the other agents wondering "How come?" there was the inescapable fact that April was popular and Evelyn was not. The latter was widely regarded as an "upper crust waster" who looked upon privilege as a divine right and did not take the profession of estate agency seriously enough. In addition, she was reputed to have the morals of an alley cat. Theo had been well aware of her reputation for some time and now he feared he had made another error of judgement.

The venue was the ballroom at the prestigious Exchange Hotel, close to where Theo had been ambushed and beaten up on the night of Sherry's post-cricket match party. Sherry, just back from a month's singing tour, was among the guests, as were Wayne and Lisa Benson.

When Theo and Evelyn arrived at the bar area, which led to the ballroom, the three of them were there, in the middle, chatting gaily to George Bowes, Terry Hatcher and their wives. Seven heads turned and seven pairs of eyes bored into the new arrivals

"Hi there!" Terry called out after a moment or two. "How are you doing?" was the George Bowes greeting.

Sherry, Wayne and Lisa looked at Theo coldly, turned away and walked through the ballroom door. Their four companions followed. About a dozen other people, in three groups, were talking earnestly among themselves.

Theo went to the bar to order drinks, all the time hoping to see a friendly face. In a while, Edmund and Kelly appeared and Theo felt more at ease. Edmund was on his best form and even a quip about how revealing Evelyn's dress was caused plenty of mirth and no offence.

The quartet made their way to the ballroom and then to their table. The room was just over half full, and quite a few heads turned as they entered. Evelyn and Kelly both wore mini dresses, and Evelyn was, in addition, displaying cleavage and areas of midriff. The sight of Evelyn, rather than April, hanging on to Theo's arm was reason for people to look more than once.

Nathan Pike and one or two others greeted the two couples warmly, though Theo sensed that they were receiving a generally cool reception.

There was a time when the people of Camford seemed to be queuing up just to shake his hand. As the two couples sat down, a three-piece band began to play.

Paul Phelan, who had been an estate agent in Camford for longer than anyone else, welcomed from the platform all those present, announced that dinner would be served in about half an hour's time and urged everyone to feel free to dance in the meantime. Evelyn, who had been busy caressing Theo's thigh under the table, urged her companion to take to the floor with her. The dance was a slow waltz and Evelyn pressed her body against Theo's and placed her hands on his buttocks.

There were only two other couples dancing at the time and, because everyone else in the room could see what was going on, Theo felt obliged to grab her hands and put the left one on his shoulder and the right one into his own left hand to assume a more formal dancing pose. Evelyn's eyes were dancing with mischief and Theo could sense that she was mocking him. After a couple of minutes, the band started to play ... or at least try to play ... some rock music. Theo was relieved. But not for long ... A uniformed policeman was standing by the table where he had been sitting.

"Excuse me, are you the proprietors of SMK Estate Agents in the High Street?" he asked Theo and Evelyn on their return to the table.

When Theo confirmed that they were, the officer said: "Well, I'm sorry to trouble you but there appears to have been at attempted break-in at your premises. Detective Inspector Jackman is there now and he would like to have a word with you."

Theo, who was quite happy with any excuse to leave, said: "Yes, we'll come over straight away." As it turned out, the front window had been damaged enough for a glazier to be called in to fit a replacement. The area was boarded up, in the meantime. There was no sign of entry, however.

Joe Prescott had telephoned the police from the upstairs office and got under the table and remained there cowering until they arrived.

DI Jackman, who was waiting outside the premises with two other officers, told Theo and Evelyn that no one had seen what had happened, though an elderly man living in a flat above a shop opposite had heard the sound of shattering glass and seen a woman walking away about 50 yards along an otherwise deserted street.

"Can you tell us what she looked like," the DI asked.

"No, I only got a glimpse of her back. All I can tell you is that she was quite small and had something like a shawl or a scarf over her head … And she was walking quite quickly!"

DI Jackman nodded and thanked the witness. The possibility that the woman could have been Drummond in disguise crossed his mind. But, for now, he kept his thoughts to himself.

Theo and Evelyn went inside to clear up the shards of glass that had fallen inside, and DI Jackman promised to make sure the premises were closely guarded until they were made secure again.

After the two partners had left, the DI turned to the other two officers and said: "I want these premises kept under observation day and night. I also want a constant watch kept on Salter."

Evelyn Knight lived in a barn conversion in Little Pemberton, a remote hamlet 10 miles to the south-west of Camford and five miles from the nearest village. It has been given to her as an 18th birthday present by her late father, and although ostensibly on her own, she was rarely without company in it.

Evelyn's string of lovers was reputed to include Nathan Pike, George Bowes, a local bank manager by the name of Ian Wellard and Sean MvAvie's sidekick Chris Doman. A young lady whose business acumen could not be faulted, she was best known for someone with a low boredom threshold and a constant yen for excitement.

Recent events had sent Evelyn's pulse racing and, as Theo drove her home, as he had arranged to do beforehand, she did not want the excitement to end. So, by the time Theo and Evelyn had parted company at her exquisite Little Pemberton home, it was almost opening time at SMK Estate Agents.

"I need to keep tabs on that glazier," Theo said a little wearily.

"I might be a little late this morning," his latest lover drawled.

CHAPTER 32

THERE WAS JUST ONE ROOM in the whole of Benson Lane that nobody ever went to.

The MAC Developments project was well under way. The bulldozers had done their work, much of the rubble had been cleared and visitors to the site could see something that looked like the picture on the brochure.

Some of the houses were occupied and others were attracting a stream of potential buyers. The restaurant and shops were up and running and the building that was due to house the casino was a hive of activity. Teams of plumbers, plasterers, painters and decorators had, in turn, been working flat out to ensure that an early opening was a safe bet ... and, now, the first of the slot machines were being delivered. A stream of applicants for the posts of croupiers, bar staff, waiters, waitresses and bouncers, all to be interviewed by either McAvie or Doman, added to the activity. Sara Ponsonby- Stewart, based in the housing site office, had the task of showing home-buyers round.

And, because of the warning concerning Drummond's escape, "Big Frank" was there to keep an eye open for anything that might look suspicious.

The well known local "heavy" would spend his time pacing up and down the street, one side of which had been newly paved and partially lined with a series of boxes containing flowers, shrubs or young saplings.

The project was Sean McAvie's pride and joy. He wanted Benson Lane to have that suburban, leafy look that would hopefully cement the veneer of respectability he craved.

The houses had small, neat gardens with painted wooden fences and gates in front.

The commercial premises had their own paved walkways. All the properties sported tastefully designed facades, all created with the intention of providing MAC Developments with its own up-market, genteel image.

"Big Frank" was deployed for the odd hour or two in the vicinity of SMK Estate Agents when it was known that Theo Salter or one of the others there was going to be alone. But, for the most part, he was employed as protector for McAvie and his minions and, when not pacing up and down Benson Lane, he was walking round every property in turn.

The only room that he ignored was a tiny basement area directly below the site office. The only access to it was a narrow flight of stone steps, which, at this stage, could only be reached by clambering over iron railings. The steps led to a tiny window. There had been an outside door to the basement once, some time before the original building had been razed to the ground to make way for MAC Developments, but this had been bricked up.

The window, nearly six feet from the ground, had no sill. So anyone wanting to get through it would have to clamber up the wall, grab the handle to open the window and enter head first in virtually one quick movement. No one even approaching the size of Big Frank would contemplate attempting such a feat!

The room itself was about 10 feet square, and permanently cold and dank. There were long-term plans to turn it into a wine cellar. The building housing the site office would be the last home to go on to the market, and only when all the other homes had been disposed of. At the moment, the walls and ceiling were bare and there was no lighting. Sunlight rarely reached the basement, and Derek Drummond needed all his ingenuity to make his period of occupation remotely comfortable.

The room contained a battered old armchair, a small stool and a rolled-up, threadbare carpet. The stool served as a table to place food on, and, initially, Drummond wrapped the carpet around himself to keep warm.

Little by little, he had added to his comforts by going out at night, after the site office had closed and everyone had gone home, and helping himself to items from some of the shops in the nearby Benson Street. He had taken food, clothes, blankets, a sleeping bag, a torch and a number of items of cutlery and crockery.

Some of the clothes were women's clothes, ideal for disguise. Some of the crockery could be used as weapons.

Drummond had always been a dab hand at picking locks. While in Broadmoor, he had struck up a friendship with a notorious cat burglar who had lost his marbles and, when not overcome by an adverse mood swing, had been able to give him tips on how to enhance and extend his "talents." Drummond now had the know-how to enter premises silently and without leaving clues.

As a result, any signs of entry into the shops were not detected until after goods were actually known to be missing.

Drummond was well aware that he had a short fuse. His violent temper had got him into trouble since he was a small child. He could recall one incident in which, at the age of four, he had used a toy train as a weapon and hospitalised a six-year-old at his first school. Foster parents, teachers and probation officers in Glasgow had all failed to get him to overcome his lack of self-control.

Broadmoor, on the other hand, had succeeded ... to a point. He soon discovered that straight jackets, padded cells and injections to the backside while being held down were to be avoided if possible.

As a consequence, Drummond discovered the virtue of guile. The anger never went away but it was kept just below the surface and, little by little, the staff felt able to be slightly less watchful. Drummond had even managed to befriend one of the younger nurses, who, in turn, had tried to persuade some of the others that he was not the dangerous man he was when first admitted.

Drummond had learned to bide his time. He made a point of learning when vehicles came and went, and where he could lay his hands on a weapon. Eventually he managed to steal a nail file from a handbag.

Then, one morning, just after a baker's van arrived to make its

215

regular bread delivery, Drummond used the file to stab a nurse to death before clambering through a small window and running towards the van. Another nurse who barred his path was stabbed as well. The van was round a corner, and its driver, who saw nothing of what had occurred, drove off with Drummond hiding under a sheet in the back. His careful planning had worked! The Broadmoor staff had been lulled into a false sense of security and, for one fleeting moment, taken their eyes off the ball!

However, Drummond did realise that he had just made one mistake ... when his pent-up fury boiled over to such an extent that he battered the plate glass window of SMK Estate Agents with an iron bar.

From now on, the police would be more vigilant. Someone might have seen the attack on SMK, and even his disguise might not help him any more.

All those thoughts were going through his troubled mind as he sat in the basement room in Benson Lane, munching a cheese sandwich and then two bananas. And, mistake or no mistake, the fury would not go away.

Drummond had spent hour after hour cooped up in that confined basement space. His time at Broadmoor had made him better able to cope with solitary confinement, though.

And he had been able to revel in the satisfaction of having wiped out two Broadmoor staff, that tiresome waitress at the tea room and the "bluebottle" who had played the leading part in arresting him and having him put away. But there was still work to be done!

First on his hit list was McAvie, the man who had given him a job and then taken it away. "You're going to suffer for that, you bastard! I'm going to get you good!" Drummond said in a whisper, as if there was someone in the room listening to him. Then there was that cockney cunt, Doman, who had managed to curry favour with the MAC Developments boss. Salter was going to "get his," too, for asking questions about that silly old bag Mary Groves and implying that his behaviour had been untoward. He had, after all, only been doing his job!

The two other arresting officers were also targets, though Drummond suspected that they would be difficult to locate and he could not remember exactly what they looked like. So, under the circumstances, any policeman or policewoman he could lay his hands on would be fair game.

Drummond's prime target was undoubtedly McAvie, the man who had deprived him of his livelihood. But he was also the most difficult, as he never seemed to be on his own and was frequently in the company of a "heavy."

The easiest target was Doman. Unbeknown to McAvie, or anyone else for that matter, the MAC Developments chief's cockney sidekick was having a tryst with none other than Evelyn Knight. Sometimes the pair would meet and make love in the site office after everyone else had gone home ... or discuss the question of where else they might meet.

Drummond had discovered a spot on the basement ceiling where the plasterwork had worn away, and had used a stolen screwdriver to create a hole, though which he could hear them talk. When he learned that Evelyn was seeing Doman behind Salter's back, he felt a glow of satisfaction. How he would love to ram that piece of information down Salter's throat!

Meanwhile, Drummond had a decision to make. Who should he go after next: McAvie or Doman?

This was a matter to be mulled over for several hours.

McAvie was the one he wanted the most but Doman was the easier. If he killed Doman first, McAvie would be more on guard than ever and getting at him would be even more difficult. On the other hand, the death of Doman would put the wind up his former employer. And, if he could wipe out his bodyguard as well, that would really get to him.

Drummond conjured up pictures in his mind of the former Gorbels hard man alone, helpless and pleading for mercy before retribution was administered. The method of revenge was mulled over, too. There were several options, though the priority was to fill McAvie with terror before executing him in the most painful fashion possible.

And so it was decided: Doman would go first, and then the "heavy," if necessary. Then, perhaps, the odd copper or two! McAvie would be reduced to a gibbering wreck before getting his comeuppance.

Yet another factor behind Drummond's decision was the gun that Doman carried in a hole in the heel of his left shoe. Drummond had acquired this knowledge by overhearing a conversation above. He had heard Doman brag about the fact to Evelyn. "Let me see, let me see it!" she had kept on saying until Doman eventually relented and showed it to her. "Where do you keep the bullets? Where are the bullets?" Evelyn had then asked. Doman had told her that he kept a small supply in the other shoe.

"Thanks for getting me that wee bit of info, Evelyn," Drummond said to himself. "Yee've been such a good gal that I'm not going to kill yee!"

Twelve hours later, Drummond began to formulate a plan. During the daytime, Sara Ponsonby-Stewart was in the site office, updating brochures, preparing press releases and greeting anyone who called round.

Drummond learned to both his amusement and disgust that Jenny Fitch, another Salter associate, had been calling in to see Sara and arranging romantic meetings of a different kind. But, offensive as such a relationship was to his Puritan instincts, the pair's antics did not interest him.

His next quarry, Doman, was now within his sights.

However, it was not until after Sara had locked up the site office and left at around six the next evening that Drummond got his chance. At twenty past six, he heard the door upstairs being unlocked, followed by a conversation between Doman and his secret lover.

Drummond heard them arrange to meet in the woods about a mile outside town. The exact spot was a clearing with a pond, a fountain and a couple of benches. During the daytime, ice cream and hot dog-sellers would ply their trade there. After dark, the spot was a haunt for lovers.

Evelyn Knight's Ford Sierra and Chris Doman's Citroen drew up side by side, just in front of the fountain, at exactly midnight, as had been arranged.

The neatly cut grass in the clearing was bathed in moonlight. The secret lovers were relieved to discover that there were no other vehicles in the vicinity ... and they were too preoccupied with romantic notions to notice a lady's sit-up-and-beg bicycle with a basket in front leaning against the nearest tree.

The couple embraced and began to disrobe. Then, suddenly, they became aware that they had company. The shape of a woman emerged from behind the tree where the bicycle was and approached them. "Excuse me, do you have the right time?" the stranger asked in a croaky voice. Chris Doman's trousers were around his ankles and Evelyn Knight had stripped down to her underwear. Both were nonplussed.

The stranger walked up to Evelyn and, without warning, knocked her senseless with a punch to the jaw. "What the ...!" Doman spluttered involuntarily. "What the hell do you think you're ..."

Before he could finish his sentence, a sharpened nail file plunged into his stomach. As he fell to his knees, he realised who his assailant was. The nail file plunged into him again and again ... into his chest, stomach, neck and face ... until he was lying motionless in a pool of blood.

By the time Evelyn had regained her senses and put her clothes back on, the assailant was long gone. Her head was throbbing, her jaw was bruised and swollen, and there were bruises on the back of her head and along the back as a result of her falling.

She could see at barely more than a glance that Doman was dead.

She staggered towards her car, fumbled for her keys, got in and sat down. Her head was spinning, and it was several minutes before she felt able to drive.

However, she also felt the need to get away from the scene of the attack as quickly as possible. All of a sudden, Camford had become just a bit too exciting ... even for her!

It was time to leave her home, after lying low for a while perhaps. Then, once her head had cleared and her bruises had gone down, she could leave Camford and continue her quest for excitement elsewhere.

CHAPTER 33

THEO WAS HAVING one of the blackest days of his life.

Two house sales in Benson Lane fell through on the same morning. Jenny Fitch and Evelyn Knight telephoned on the same day to say they were quitting both SMK Estate Agents and Camford. And the police called to say that another murder, probably involving Drummond, had taken place.

These bitter pills should have been sugared to some extent with the news, also received that morning, that April was on her way back from the States. But there was a frostiness in the message, received by "answer phone", that made Theo feel uneasy. To make matters worse, Joe Prescott had gone down with the flu and there was only the office junior, promising though he was, available to share his workload.

Doman's body had been discovered by a young couple out walking their dog early in the morning after the murder. A woman's handkerchief was found nearby but there were no clues as to its owner. DI Jackman had wasted no time in alerting both Theo and Sean McAvie about this latest incident, though, again, there was no hard evidence that Drummond was responsible.. Theo decided to take the rest of the day off, and perhaps the next day, too. He felt it was prudent to meet McAvie to discuss both the problem of flagging sales and the potential threat posed by Drummond. He needed to speak to Jenny and Evelyn as well, for different reasons and preferably before April got back.

His first port of call was the MAC Developments site office in Benson Lane. "Big Frank" was carrying out his duties of "sentry" with greater urgency than hitherto. Inside, Sean McAvie and Sara

Ponsonby-Stewart were having a heated argument.

"I'm frightened!" Sara was heard to say in her clipped upper class tones. She did not drawl in the way that Evelyn did but there was no doubting her privileged origins.

"There's no need to be," her boss replied unconvincingly.

"It's no good, I don't feel safe here!"

"Well, you can. What do you think I've hired Frank for?"

"You shouldn't need to. You shouldn't be in this sort of situation!"

"I can't help the situation. The circumstances are exceptional. That's why I'm taking exceptional measures."

"Exceptional measures, my foot! They weren't much use to Mr Doman, were they?"

The two then became aware of Theo's presence. Theo could see that McAvie was doing his utmost to appear calm and composed, though there was no doubt that he was every bit as tense as his press aide.

"Hi there!" McAvie exclaimed, trying to sound jovial. "I should imagine you can guess what we're talking about."

Theo replied: "It doesn't take an Einstein to work that one out!"

"Are you here to talk about the same thing?"

"Yes, very much so … and also about the fact that two sales have just fallen through."

"Hmm, do you think those failed sales could be more than just a coincidence?"

"I honestly don't know."

"What, if anything, do you think we should do next?"

Theo paused, looked at Sara for a moment and then said: "Well, I have shut up shop for a day. That's not just because of the murder. I have other things to sort out, too, and people to see, though I can't help feeling there's a case for battening down the hatches here for a while until the storm blows over."

"You might just have a point," McAvie agreed. "Potential buyers might identify Benson Lane as a trouble spot now. With Chris's murder, they might even feel we are all jinxed. Sara here is getting nervous, and employing Frank is costing me money. And, hopefully, it won't be long before that madman Drummond is under lock and key again." McAvie then turned to Sara and said: "All right, my love, you can have a few days off. I will close the site down for a while."

Sara sighed with relief. "Thank you! When the trouble's over I will be back like a shot."

"OK, I will keep in touch by phone. So don't leave the country just yet!" McAvie's attempt at humour was greeted with the trace of a smile, and, within seconds, Sara was gone.

"Where will you be, Aggammenmon Hall?" Theo asked McAvie.

"Yes, that's right. I can conduct my business from there for a while and a stranger to these parts like Drummond could never trace me to there. Few people know I live there, it's off the beaten track and those who do enter the premises uninvited would have to get past two Rottweilers ... not to mention my housekeeper!"

McAvie then asked Theo what steps he was planning to take.

"I'm not sure yet but I've got a few people to see and a few things to sort out, and I might even leave the area for while."

As the two men wished each other good luck and vowed to keep in touch and meet again as soon as possible, Theo's left foot was covering the hole in the floor that separated the site office from the basement.

Theo's next port of call was Evelyn's elegant barn home just outside town. With April due back any time now, the news that Evelyn had decided to quit the area was not entirely unwelcome!

If Evelyn really was going, there would be loose ends to be tied up, business-wise, of course, and this would cause some inconvenience. The sexual frolics had been fun, to say the least, and, in other circumstances they would be missed. However, Evelyn was not April. Theo longed for April's return ... and the prospect of re-establishing his place in her heart.

When Evelyn answered the door, she looked more frumpy than he had ever seen her. Her hair was matted and, her complexion, without make-up, was pasty. And there was a bruise on her chin.

Instead of the usual figure-revealing clothes, she was wearing baggy trousers and a shapeless top. "You'd better come in," she drawled with a lop-sided smile.

Evelyn motioned Theo towards an armchair in her front sitting room and asked him coolly: "Did you get my message?"

Theo tried to appear cool, too. "Yes, of course I did, and it came as something of a shock. But never mind that just now. Are you all right? How did you get that bruise?"

Evelyn pursed her lips. "I was walking in the woods, and someone leaped out from behind a tree and punched me."

"What were you doing in the woods in the first place?"

Evelyn now assumed a slightly mocking air. "That would be telling!" she said.

"Maybe ... but it doesn't take a lot of guessing! It wouldn't surprise me if you were with Doman just before he was murdered!"

"Oh ... you know! Well, why did you ask then?"

Theo's feeling of anger was overridden by the relief of being offered a way out of a tricky situation.

Evelyn, reading his thoughts, said: "I hear on the grapevine that April May is on her way back from the States. Is the grapevine correct?"

Theo nodded. Evelyn looked Theo straight in the eye and smiled broadly and mockingly. "Well, well, well! How very, very convenient ... for both of us! By the time April has returned to your outstretched, loving arms, I will be out of the way ... miles out of the way! And April won't know anything about anything! She won't hear a single word from me about our little liaison while she was not around. So that's one thing less for you to worry about, dahlink!"

Theo tried to interject but, before he could, Evelyn raised a finger and added, more seriously: "There's just one thing, though. I don't want any more questions about what I've been up to. You're not my keeper! We've had our little bit of fun but now it's over. And, after what happened to poor Chris, I don't want to be around these parts any more."

"Yes, I can see you have a point," Theo conceded. Evelyn's mocking expression returned.

"Mind you, I have no regrets," she said grinning. "You were pretty good … No, let's be honest about it, you were one of the best. You might have been even better than Edmund, come to think of it!"

Within another two minutes, Theo was back in his car. He did not even get to ask Evelyn where she was leaving for … and did not really care.

Next on his visit list was Jenny Fitch, who had returned from her sojourn and was back in the flat which Theo had originally occupied.

Theo could sense that there was trouble ahead. Jenny's recent behaviour, and her attitude towards him in particular, had been out of character.

The young woman who had in the past declared that Theo was "someone she would lay down her own life for" had announced she was going away without warning. She had not said where she was going and had not been in touch once. In the past, Jenny had been in almost daily contact whenever she was away from him for any length of time. Even when Theo had quit Gloucester for Camford, there had been regular communication.

Theo could also sense a coolness towards him that he had not experienced before Jenny answered the door stony-faced.

"Would you like a coffee?" she asked, without a vestige of warmth in her tone.

"That would be nice, thank you," Theo replied, trying to adopt the same cool manner he had used with Evelyn.

Jenny handed him his coffee in a mug and said: "Long time, no see. I trust you are well?"

"Oh, I'm fine," Theo replied sighing. "One thing's for sure, I haven't been bored while you've been away."

"So I've heard. Even without that madman on the loose and possibly after your blood, you would not have been bored … not from what I've heard, anyway!"

Theo decided it was time to change the subject. "Sure!"

"Now don't go secretive on me. Where have you been?"

"Oh, here and there." Theo could see Jenny was beginning to enjoy herself, though he wasn't sure why.

224

"Come on, Jenny! What's all this about? Where have you been?"

"Are you sure you really want to know?"

"Yes, I'm sure!" Theo was becoming visibly agitated.

"Well, my time away from you began after an interesting little meeting in a café near the police station. I met two police officers and had a most interesting little conversation. They asked me some interesting questions about you, and they showed me some extremely interesting photos."

"Why should they be interested in me?"

Jenny half smiled and half sneered. "That's a very good question," she said.

"Yes it is, isn't it?" replied an unsettled Theo. "Perhaps, now, you could give me an answer?!"

Jenny's face hardened even more. "I then went on a little jaunt to Gloucester and met a few more little people, who all showed more than a little interest in you!"

"What the hell are you talking about?" Theo's temper was in danger of getting the better of him.

Jenny, meanwhile, was icily cold. "Do you remember those two drug dealers you sorted out in Birmingham?"

"Yes, vaguely,"

"There's no vaguely about it! I'm talking about Terry Springett and Ralph Meekin ... and you already knew them before that so-called rescue, didn't you?"

"What makes you think that?"

"I've seen photographs of you with them. The police showed them to me, and one of them shows you handing over money to them."

"OK, what if I did know them before? I still rescued you from them, didn't I?"

"Yes ... but why?"

"What do you mean Why?! I was coming to the aid of a lady in distress. I was helping a friend, for Christ's sake. Don't you remember that you were on the verge of suicide before you met me? I mean ... bloody hell!"!

"Don't you bloody hell me!" Jenny was now snarling. "Those two apes came after me in Birmingham on YOUR orders, didn't they? Come on, admit it!"

"OK, OK, OK!" Theo began to adopt a soothing, placatory manner. "Let me explain!"

"I wish you would!"

Theo sighed heavily and said: "Look, the reason I was in Birmingham was to head them off. There'd been a spot of bother in Gloucester, and Springett and Meekin were about to drop me in it with the police. I followed them to Brum to tackle them about it, and it was not until later on that I realised that you were the person they were going to duff up!"

"I don't believe you."

"Jenny, Jenny, we're best friends, soul mates! Remember? If you can't believe me, who can you believe? Come on, I've rescued you from a couple of thugs who're now inside and can't bother you any more."

Jenny eyed Theo with more suspicion that ever.

"So you're telling me you are NOT a drug dealer, that you're NOT involved with drugs in any way and that you only ever had my interests at heart?" she asked in an expressionless voice.

"Naturally!" Theo replied. "Imagine the effect such a slur would have on my estate agency business." He then added pleadingly: "Your presence at SMK Estate Agents has been missed. You're coming back soon, aren't you?"

Jenny shook her head. "No, I don't think so," she said sadly. "It's time for me to move on. You have been an important part of my life but you are not any more. I don't trust you any more and never will again."

Jenny's eyes then narrowed as she said: "By the way, you might like to know that, apart from the police, a local journalist has been taking quite a bit of interest in you. It seems to me that your card has been marked!"

Then, more coldly than ever, she added: "Oh, and there's just one other thing. Your two druggy friends who you say you rescued me from are not very happy about what happened. I've just spent a few days back in Gloucester and heard on the grapevine that, although Springett and Meekin are behind bars, they have friends on the outside… and they're coming after you!"

And then, with hardly a pause, Jenny said: "You WILL close the door on your way out, won't you?" Theo skulked back to his car, feeling more down than he had felt for years. But there was worse to follow.

Theo was yearning for April more than he could ever have imagined. He yearned for the sound of that deep, soft, seductive voice with just the hint of a Californian accent, the feel of that thick black mane of hair, those intimate caresses from her long, slim hands and the closeness of that heavenly body.

"Oh boy, you certainly know how to make a bloke feel good!" He had said that to her many times after making love with her, and now he said it to himself.

At this particular time, Theo yearned for an ally, a best friend, a soul mate, someone to comfort him. He thought about how he would meet April at the airport, greet her with flowers and whisk her back home, where they would be intimate for days on end. April had other ideas, though.

She had spent the last month re-visiting her roots and re-appraising her values. She was born on a small ranch owned by her now ageing parents. The ranch was currently about half its original size, with just a dozen cattle, half a dozen chickens and a couple of horses remaining.

The atmosphere and lifestyle ethos were still much the same, though. The parents, Josh and Lily McCardle were devout Baptists who loved the land and all that was simple in life. They had clear ideas of what was right and wrong and instilled these ideas into April and her three older brothers from an early age.

As a young man, Josh McCardle had been an outstanding baseball player, American footballer and horse-rider. His wife had been a top swimmer and gymnast.

Not surprisingly, their three sons, Josh Junior, Tex and Rory were outstanding at sports, too, as was April. April was the only one with academic ability to match, though. She was also the most wilful. There were times when she would question her parents' values and act in defiance of them. But her biggest weakness, if that is what it could be called, was her inability to see bad in people and, on occasion, situations.

Fiery on the surface at times, she tended to be seen as someone who would stand for no nonsense from anyone and who should under no circumstances by crossed.

However, while it was certainly true that incurring her wrath was not to be recommended, the likelihood of her trusting nature being taken advantage of was greater. It had begun to dawn on her that all was not right with Theo Salter.

The man who came to Camford six months ago, became a local hero and captured her heart soon afterwards had a tarnished aura about him all of a sudden. The physical attraction, which moved her to romance him right under Kelly's nose, was still there. But she could not ignore the warning signs any more. Rumours that he had sought out and fought Ray Williams pointed to a violent nature. The interest shown in him by the police was worrying, too. There was also something a little strange, perhaps even a little shifty, about his three closest friends, Kelly, Jenny and Joe.

April, whose tendency was always to think the best of people, would have probably brushed aside any feelings of unease had it not been for the fact that Sherry, the Bensons and some of the other estate agents had cold-shouldered Theo. Why? April had needed her Californian break to mull the matter over. What was going to happen to their relationship and to their business partnership?

By the time the aeroplane she was in touched down at Heathrow, she had made the decision to spend a couple of nights in London, where she would look up friends and then move in with a cousin in Little Debham, a village 10 miles to the south-east of Camford. She would then contact the Bensons and perhaps one or two estate agents in an attempt to ascertain the cause of Theo's loss of popularity.

So Theo's hopes of a passionate reunion were dashed when he received a curt note telling him that April did not want to be met at the airport and that she would not be returning directly to their love nest. There was not even a hint as to where she might be or how he could contact her.

April, meanwhile, had the time of her life in a West End hotel, drinking, dining and dancing the nights away with old friends. She even had time to fit in a visit to a show, which happened to star Sherry Munro. Although weary from a heavy work schedule, Sherry greeted April and her companions warmly in her dressing room afterwards.

She told April that her suspicions about Theo were well founded ... and suggested she had a word with the Bensons.

So April made arrangements to visit them on her return to East Anglia.

First of all, though, she popped into George Bowes's office and tried to get him to say why he thought Theo no longer seemed to be "flavour of the month." She had known George and his wife for many years and felt she could trust them implicitly. George listened sympathetically but remained tight-lipped and April could see that, although there were questions in his own mind, he would not say anything against a man who had become a friend. The Bensons were a lot more forthcoming. An unusually serious looking Wayne came to the door when she arrived at their house and said: "Come on in, we've got quite a bit to tell you."

CHAPTER 34

FEAR HAD BEEN A valuable currency for Sean McAvie.

He was well versed in the art of instilling it into others. He had been brought up in a run- down Gorbels tenement. His late father, Sean McAvie Senior, had been one of Glasgow's most feared hard men, and the young Sean had no choice but to follow in his footsteps. His father had demanded it and so, too, did the various challenges he faced in the school playground.

Before long, the younger Sean built up a reputation of his own and, when his father died suddenly as a result of the ravages of excess alcohol, he took over the mantel.

His reputation became so fearsome that club owners, drug dealers and even other gangsters paid him money to be in his favour. Unlike his father, however, he used his ill-gotten gains to build a property and house-building empire.

He had left Glasgow a decade ago in a quest to leave behind his gangster's persona and establish an aura of respectability. He had formed businesses in London, where he met Chris Doman, and then Gloucester but still felt the need to engage in occasional acts of skulduggery to cement deals.

The MAC Developments project in Benson Lane, Camford, was the latest vehicle in his drive towards social acceptance. But now, perhaps for the first time since childhood, he was apprehensive.

McAvie, who was alone in his new home, Aggammenmon Hall, save for his housekeeper, Fiona, had, for reasons of thrift, decided to rely on his two Rottweilers rather than "Big Frank" for protection. He was aware that, although he was exceptionally fit for his age, he was no longer young and did not relish a face-to-face confrontation with Drummond. Employing that madman had been a mistake.

He was apprehensive despite the fact that the massive electronically operated iron gates leading to the grounds and house were now supplemented by closed-circuit television. McAvie could see anyone arriving at the gates, which could only be opened with the aid of a switch inside.

High, spiked railings made access to the property elsewhere almost impossible, and the well manicured lawns and gardens that surrounded the house were floodlit at night.

McAvie had intended to catch up with his paperwork from his newly created office on the ground floor. Instead, he found himself pacing up and down the magnificent mahogany staircase and around the various rooms. Much of the inside of Aggammenmon Hall had been refurbished. Problems such as damp, uneven floorboards and flaking wallpaper had been eradicated. Many of the rooms had been fitted out with modern heating and lighting appliances, new furniture, television sets and computers. One of the larger rooms had been converted into a mini-cinema, while the cellar had been spruced up and filled with some of the finest wines. The main hall, meanwhile, could now be used as a banqueting hall or ballroom fit to rival the one to be found at Sherry's.

Outside, the swimming pool and tennis courts were in working order, and the stables were due to be made fit for horses to live in once more. McAvie found some consolation in what he had accomplished at Aggammenmon Hall ... but not much.

It was mid-afternoon when he decided to give the two dogs, Jock and Hamish, some exercise. The fearsome pair, bought as puppies, had been trained as guard dogs and were kept in a wired outdoor enclosure that included a kennel when not being taken for a morning or evening walk.

Sean McAvie had taught them to treat all but a handful of humans as enemies. The exceptions included his estranged wife Aileen, his brother James, his housekeeper and his former right hand man Chris Doman.

Derek Drummond had never encountered Jock or Hamish, a

factor that made McAvie decide not to employ extra protection.

The man and his two dogs walked, ran and frolicked with abandon for almost an hour. The air was cool, clear and invigorating. The wind was gentle but strong enough to create a rustle among the many trees and shrubs in the gardens and grounds.

The wind and the barks of delight combined to muffle the sound of a vehicle approaching and then stopping 50 yards past the gate, on a grass verge near a screen of trees. Inside, Fiona was washing her hands and she did not see the car appear on the CCTV when it drew level with the gates, before passing out of sight.

McAvie tried to outrun his two dogs in a race around the perimeter fence. Hamish, the swifter of the pair, shot off into the distance. Jock paused to pick up a heavy twig and to wait for his owner to catch up. McAvie and Jock then half-ran, half-trundled side by side. At this stage, Hamish was nowhere to be seen.

Suddenly, a startled yelp, followed by howls of pain, could be heard. The howls continued unabated. McAvie could still not see Hamish, though.

Eventually Jock did. His brother was lying in a pool of blood beside a barn about a quarter of a mile from where McAvie and the two dogs started their race.

McAvie could see immediately that his beloved pet and protector had been shot, probably several times.

Jock began to growl the sort of growl that would greet an intruder. Seconds later, another shot, this time just audible, rang out and Jock fell in an inert heap. A bullet had gone into his head.

McAvie could tell that the shot was from above and he just had the time to look up at a massive oak tree branch that overhung the barn's roof before someone or something landed on top of him and a heavy blow to the back of the head knocked him senseless.

McAvie woke up to find himself bound to a chair and gagged inside the barn. His head was throbbing with pain. Standing in front of him was a figure in woman's clothing. But it did not take him long to realise who his assailant was. Those cold blue eyes staring down on him were unmistakable.

Derek Drummond removed the shawl to reveal neatly-cut

ginger hair and sneered. "Well, well, well! What have we got here?" he mocked. "I know what we've got. We've got a Gorbels hard man who's being held captive by a transvestite!" Drummond cackled with laughter, proud of his perceived sense of humour. "What I would like to know, though," he went on, "is whether you're really as hard as you make out you are!" he added.

Drummond loosened the gag and, almost simultaneously, struck McAvie with the back of his hand. The force of the blow caused the chair to fall backwards and almost somersault. Blood spurted from McAvie's mouth.

Drummond put the chair and its occupant back into an upright position.

"What have you got to say for yourself?" he asked, pushing his face forward so that it almost touched McAvie's.

McAvie spat out a tooth. "How the hell did you get in here?" he asked defiantly. Drummond cackled again.

"It wasn't easy," he said with a grin. "It was quite challenging, in fact. But I like a challenge! And I learned quite a bit about your security arrangements from conversations I overheard in Benson Lane. You didn't know I was hiding in a basement, did you? What do you think about that, Mister Hard Man?"

"You're a clever little fucker, aren't you?" McAvie retorted.

Drummond delivered another fearsome back-hander that sent the chair tumbling again and broke McAvie's nose. Before making the chair upright again, he kicked him in the ribs. "You're quite right, I am a clever fucker," Drummond said. "This clever little fucker was able to work out how and where to get over a fence and on to a tree branch above this barn. So your security was not as tight as you thought, was it?"

"Go fuck yourself!" said McAvie.

Drummond snarled. "There's just one thing, though," he said. "That barbed wire on top of the fence was not very nice, was it? It gave me a nasty cut on one of my legs … look." Drummond pulled up the dress he was wearing to reveal an ugly gash on his left thigh. He then landed a full-blooded punch that made the chair and its occupant turn a full somersault. "You cunt, you fucking bastard!"

he screamed. "What right have you got to do me out of a job and then have me locked up?" A further volley of expletives accompanied by a series of kicks followed, after which Drummond untied McAvie, jumped on him and sat astride him as he slammed punch after punch into his face. "Chris Doman's gun came in pretty handy, too, for that matter," he said, musing after stopping. But he did not stop for long. Before walking out of the barn, he landed about six mighty kicks to the head.

News of the latest murder reached the public domain the next morning, following a telephone call to the police from a hysterical Fiona. Her boss had been missing from the house for several hours and she had become concerned enough to search for him outside. The sight of the two dead dogs had made her scream. The discovery of McAvie's battered body in the barn had almost caused a heart seizure. At that point, Fiona had begun to fear for her own life.

However, by then, the vengeful Drummond, still dressed as a woman, and the car he had stolen were long gone.

CHAPTER 35

THEO'S WOES WERE far from over. His office junior, Darren Hensby, had announced that he had received an offer of the post of negotiator with the much respected firm of Trumpers from Ian Gathercole, and would not be coming back. There had never been any formal contract with SMK, and Theo had no choice but to let him go.

With Evelyn and Jenny gone and April away, he was sitting in SMK's main office on his own. The loyal Joe Prescott had agreed to come in and provide cover later on, though Joe was clearly not happy about it. Surveying was his passion. Selling houses was, to him, a necessary evil.

Theo cut a forlorn figure as he sat at his desk in an empty sales area. There were few incoming telephone calls, fewer visitors and hardly any house-for-sale particulars in the window or on the walls.

There was hardly any contact with friends or business associates either, though Edmund Rooker continued to keep in touch intermittently and occasionally met Theo for lunch or a drink.

Most of the houses for sale through SMK were those belonging to people who lived outside the area or were about to leave it. Luckily for Theo, this aspect of his business was, as it had been in Gloucester, the most lucrative. He had a particular talent for massaging prices. There were some properties, such as purpose-built two-bedroom flats or terraced houses in sought after areas that he knew would attract a lot of potential buyers. In cases such as these, he would price them lower than any other agent in town would ... and then wait for the offers to roll in. Competition for the homes would become so intense that the initial offer from a potential buyer would soon be topped, the second offer would be capped too, and a succession of new and increasingly higher offers would lead to a sale at a price well beyond what would normally be expected.

For some other properties, the "ring-fencing" tactic could be used. These properties tended to attract "specialist" interest rather than a stream of buyers and needed to be priced with care. Theo had the knack of knowing how much the property was likely to fetch at any given time. In some cases, he would keep the fact that he had such a house for sale on his books hidden from the public. After a few months, he would advise the vendor that a price reduction was needed to secure a sale.

His next step would be to buy the property at the lower price for himself or sell it to an associate at well below the market value. A few months later, the property would be re-sold at full market value and, with prices ever moving upwards at that time, there would be a substantial profit for Theo and his associates.

Having a "tame" surveyor in his pocket was another boon to Theo. His old school friend and associate, Joe, could be relied on to under-value some properties that were the subject of mortgage valuations from time to time. The properties concerned would be on the books of rival estate agents, who would lose a vendor's custom once an unexpectedly low valuation led to a mortgage lender refusing to grant a loan for the amount hoped for, expected and required for a purchase to go ahead.

The vendor would then feel obliged to look for another agent, and either Theo or Joe would ensure that the other agent would be SMK!

Joe had originally protested about being asked to indulge in such a practice. However, Theo was quick to remind him that it would not be good for Joe if certain homosexual and deviant sexual practices, which only he knew about but many suspected, ever came to light.

This side of the business had been shrinking lately, though … largely because Joe's long-standing association with Theo was now common knowledge. There was not much business in the offing generally, in fact, and Theo sat there wondering where the next bit of custom would come from … and whether anyone would even walk through the door.

Suddenly, two people called in, in quick succession. The first was Colonel Kelly, who approached Theo with a look of thunder on his face. The second was a somewhat sour-looking woman of indeterminate age who wore a long coat and a shawl over her head. Theo had an uneasy feeling about both of them.

"I want to know what the hell's going on!" Colonel Kelly bellowed.

Theo motioned for the Colonel to sit down and promised the woman he would try not to keep her waiting for too long. Once seated, the Colonel repeated his question: "What the bloody hell's going on?! My house has been on the market for yonks and there hasn't even been a sniff of interest. What are you doing about it?" His round, mottled face was growing redder by the second.

Theo took a silent deep breath before replying: "I'm glad you came in. I was about to contact you at your home in the Seychelles."

The Colonel went crimson. "The only reason I'm not in the Seychelles is because I'm here trying to find out why my house hasn't been sold by now. I haven't even had a single, bloody inquiry! I repeat: what the hell's going on?!"

Theo took another deep breath. "I've been trying to get in touch with you but without success. I've tried to contact you by telephone but you've always been out."

"Bollocks!" the Colonel roared. "I've been in regular contact with friends in Camford, and they've been in contact with me. They've told me that, despite all your bullshit about marketing, there have been no adverts in the paper and not even a solitary mention of my house in your window or on your walls. You haven't got any adverts in here at all, have you?"

Theo did his best to placate the Colonel. "The office was refurbished recently and we have had to take down all the photos and house-for-sale particulars while this was being done, he said, thinking on his feet the best he could. "The details have been displayed, I assure you, and they will be going back up again soon."

The Colonel wavered for moment and the redness is his cheeks went down … before returning again. "I don't believe a bloody word of that!" he said contemptuously.

Then, a little more quietly, he asked: "What do you intend to do now?"

"Well," said Theo, "we have had difficulty in attracting buyers and I fear this could be because the property is over-priced." Theo was about to suggest a new For Sale figure but was cut short.

"Bollocks!" Colonel Kelly's face was a deeper crimson than ever. "My house is worth every penny I have asked for, probably more, and I have no intention of bringing the price down," he said. "What I AM going to do is get another estate agent to sell it for me and do the job properly." The Coloner paused and sneered. "Your reputation as a local hero when you first came to Camford cuts no ice with me. You're nothing more than a cheap swindler, are you?"

As he stormed out, Theo tried to think about the second visitor of the morning and what he would say to her, especially in the light of what she had just heard. But the sour-looking woman was nowhere to be seen.

Standing just inside the entrance door, though, was a grim-faced DI Jackman. He told Theo how Sean McAvie's battered body had been found in a barn at Aggammenmon Hall.

"The only way the murderer … and we're pretty sure it was Drummond … could have got on to the premises would have been to climb the high wire fence near the barn, stand on top of the barbed wire that covered the top of the fence and jump on to the barn roof," he said..

"If it was Drummond, how could he know where to find McAvie?" Theo asked. "How would he know where Aggammenmon Hall was? The place is almost the back of beyond, let's face it!"

"It certainly is," the DI agreed. "How he knew where to go and how to find it remains a mystery, though we do have a theory."

"What's that? You could say I have more than a passing interest!"

"Well, we have reason to believe Drummond could be in

disguise … possibly as a woman. He must have hidden somewhere where he could overhear private conversations. At present, I have got officers looking round the MAC Developments site in Benson Lane to see if there are any places where Drummond could have hidden and eavesdropped."

DI Jackman paused for a moment before adding: "Meanwhile, I have made arrangements for an officer to keep an eye on you round the clock. As you know, Drummond wrote a little list while in Broadmoor. Your name is on it, and the others named on it have all been killed!"

Theo could see no point in arguing. A few second later, the DI was gone. The sour-faced woman had disappeared and Theo sat at his desk, head in hands. He was not one to brood for long, though. He had been in tight corners before, and, to some extent anyway, relished the challenge of getting out of them.

He thought about who was going to run MAC Developments in future, now that its two prime movers were dead. Were there other directors? Did Sara Ponsonby-Stewart have a stake in the business? He tried to contact Sara at the MAC site office but no one answered the telephone. He would have to try again later.

Theo then turned his mind to the question of whether the irate Colonel Kelly could be appeased in any way, and reluctantly concluded that here was a bit of business that had to be written off. His next step was to start poring through paperwork to see if he had missed any opportunities to attract new clientele. As he trawled through the contents of one of his filing cabinets, a thumping sound could be heard from above. It was if someone had picked up a hardback book and hurled it on to the floor. Theo had not forgotten the warnings that he could be in danger. But fear was a word that he had been brought up to treat with contempt.

He climbed the stairs to investigate with caution nonetheless.

When he reached the top, he could not help thinking he should have, perhaps, called the police first. But what the devil! He was upstairs now, and was well able to look after himself.

The first upstairs rooms were the cloakroom and then the small office that was used as a consulting room. Theo opened each door quickly and quietly and soon saw there was no one there. A small stock room that was more like a cupboard was empty, too. So that just left the main upstairs office, which had been earmarked for the role of boardroom but ended up much more often as a place where he could make love to April and, later on, Evelyn. The intruder, if there was one, had to be in there. Theo turned the door handle as quietly as he could and, with every sinew of his body poised for action, entered.

Only his lightning-fast reflexes saved him from being felled by a baseball bat. A barely discernible rush of air heralded the swing of the weapon, which had been aimed at his head. Theo ducked just in time and landed a straight left to his assailant's face. The assailant aimed a kick at Theo's groin. The kick was deflected and landed in the stomach instead. It still hurt. The two adversaries separated for a moment, and Theo could see that his attacker was, indeed, Derek Drummond. A long coat and a shawl had been flung on to the table in the middle of the room, and his face was in full view.

Drummond's hair looked redder than ever. He bared his teeth like a fox. His eyes were like blue bullets.

"It's time for you to get yours, you cunt!" he snarled, his visage a picture of hate. Theo saw Drummond reach for a gun in his pocket and flung himself forward, making the gun fly across the room.

The two men exchanged punches and, almost at the same time, tried to wrestle each other to the floor. Theo, who had never been hit so hard by a smaller man, took a couple of steps backwards with a view to maximising his longer reach.

He snapped Drummond's head back with a hard straight left and followed up with a thudding right to the jaw. Drummond took the blows without flinching. Theo landed another left and right to the face, followed by a wicked left hook … a punch he had perfected in his days as a schoolboy boxer.

Blood poured out of Drummond's nose and mouth. But he was still on his feet. Drummond aimed a second kick at Theo's groin. The kick missed again but the head- butt that followed did not.

Drummond leaped forward and sank his teeth into the side of

Theo's neck. Theo jabbed a thumb into Drummond's eye and hurled his enemy backwards on to the table. He banged Drummond's head down on to the wooden surface and rained blow after blow to his face.

But suddenly Theo yelped in pain as Drummond grabbed his testicles and squeezed as hard as he could. Then, with superhuman strength, Drummond lifted Theo off the ground and hurled him across the room and delivered a mighty kick as he landed on his back near a wall. Theo was able to grab an ankle to stop another kick, before getting up and pushing Drummond backwards. Drummond moved back still further and, before Theo could stop him, he was standing with the gun in his hand. Theo's body was wracked with pain, especially around the groin, and even standing upright was an effort. His face was cut and bruised, and blood was pouring out from the side of the neck where he had been bitten.

Drummond was an even sorrier sight. His face was a mask of blood. His nose had been broken, his jaw swollen and three teeth loosened. But he was the one holding the weapon.

"Right, you nasty, hard, keelie! You piece of shite! It's time for you to say your prayers, and to say goodbye!" A shot rang out and a bullet grazed Theo's left cheek before biting into the wall. Drummond laughed manically. "Oops, I missed!" he said cackling. "I am going to have to try again, aren't I?!" He used the pistol to fell Theo with a blow across the face.

"Now kneel, you cunt!" he sneered, before kicking him in the stomach. Theo, hardly knowing where he was, struggled to move from his prone position to obey the order just given to him. Once he had done so, there was another order. "Now look at me," said Drummond.

Theo looked up at a face so misshapen following the battle, and so contorted with rage to boot, that it resembled a gargoyle. Or perhaps it was the devil incarnate, ready to take him down to his domain. "Be prepared to meet your maker," Drummond whispered. Another shot rang out. But Theo was still kneeling.

Drummond was lying on the floor in a pool of blood, and an armed policeman was standing just inside the door. Behind the officer was DI Jackman.

"I told you that you needed to be careful, didn't I?!" the DI said.

The next face Theo saw was that of Staff Nurse Trimmington. He was looking up at her, and there was an involuntary "Ouch!" as he tried to move.

"Take it easy!" the nurse said. "You've taken quite a battering. But don't worry, you should be right as rain in a few days. It's important for you to get plenty of rest just now, and we want to keep an eye on you for the moment, just in case."

Then, with a wry smile that struck Theo as being surprisingly sexy, she added: "You're quite the man of action, aren't you? I remember when you came in last time, and had a feeling you were going to make things interesting around here!"

Theo managed a wry smile of his own and said: "It's good to know I've managed to get your attention!"

Staff Nurse Trimmington laughed. "Yes, I think she could be sexy!" Theo thought to himself.

"Have there been any visitors?" he asked.

"There have been a number of callers, both in person and on the telephone, but I have told them that you need to rest and that you should be left alone until tomorrow."

"Can you tell me who they were?"

The nurse smiled wryly again and replied: "I can't name names off the top of my head, though I can tell you that most of the inquirers were women. I can't imagine why that should be!"

The following morning, there were visits from DI Jackman, Kelly Cheatham, April May and, surprisingly, Lisa Benson.

The DI, on arrival, confirmed that Drummond, now dead, was almost certainly behind the recent spate of murders in and around Camford. Police had discovered Drummond's hiding place in Benson Lane, where various items of food and clothing and a couple of knives had been found. "Take care, we'll be in touch," he said as he left.

Theo's second caller of the day was Lisa. Theo was unable to conceal his astonishment.

"I thought I would pop in briefly to see how you were. You are, after all, the man who saved my husband's life … and I owe you that much," said Lisa.

"How is Wayne these days?"

"Oh, he's fine. He's calmed down quite a bit lately, and he's even on the wagon."

"That's a bit drastic!" Theo quipped.

Lisa smiled that smile that made men go weak at the knees. "You're quite incorrigible, aren't you?!" she said. "Anyway, I must go now. Let me know if you need any help with anything, like transport home."

Kelly's call was almost as brief. She sat by his bed, hardly saying a word. Theo noticed she was more demurely dressed than usual. He also sensed that all was not well with her.

"How's Edmund?" Theo asked.

"Oh, he's all right, I guess," Kelly said without enthusiasm. But she said no more and, after kissing Theo lightly on the forehead, was on her way.

A few minutes later, a concerned April appeared. Much of the concern centred on Theo's health … but not all of it.

"There's no need to hurry back to SMK." she assured him. I will hold the reins while you're indisposed and Joe is holding the fort at the moment. He's not particularly happy about this, as you can imagine, as he would far prefer to be out and about with his tape measure! Anyway, he sends his best wishes and will come over and see you later on. Meanwhile, it's good to see you're on the mend."

"I'll be fine," Theo replied. "What's more important is how you are. Did you have a good time while you were away? I have missed you."

April, clearly unconvinced that she had been missed, said she had had an excellent time. "I've had plenty of time to think," she added. "And, once you're up and about again, we're going to have plenty to talk about." April's visage grew sterner as she then said: "Incidentally, I've been looking through some of those files in the office … and they provide food for thought, too!"

CHAPTER 36

"WHAT'S ALL THIS about" April demanded.

"What's all what about?"

"Why have we got properties that have been on our books for months on end and never been advertised?"

"Sorry, I'm not with you," Joe replied. But he was unable to look her in the face.

"What the hell has Theo been playing at?!" April's visage was filled with thunder.

"I don't know and, now you're back, I'm off to see how Theo is. You don't need me here any more, do you?"

Joe was consumed with relief when April answered "No" and he was out of the office in double quick time. April glared at him as he went.

She sat there seething as she scrutinised three files from SMK's "For Sale" section in a cabinet. All the three houses involved were "top end" properties. All three vendors were now living abroad, having left England hurriedly. One of those vendors was Colonel Kelly.

"What the hell's going on?" she murmured to herself.

April then started to trawl through the "Sold" section and, before long, she discovered six sales, which Theo alone had been handling, had been long drawn out and unsupported by any form of advertising. All the vendors were living either abroad or at the other end of Britain. And all the properties were eventually sold at much reduced prices. They had then been re-sold after a few months at massive profits.

Before the re-sales, two of the houses had been owned by Theo himself and another by Joe Prescott. The other three had been in the name of SP Financial Services, a company with a head office address in the Isle of Man.

It did not take April long to guess where the S & P came from!

"I've got some questions to put to you, Mr Salter!" she said aloud. " … And you, too, Mr Prescott!" Worse was to follow.

April noticed that, in the course of another transaction, Theo had recommended MAC Developments when a purchaser asked for his advice on who to approach for some improvement work to be done. The builder had charged almost double the usual amount for the work, and attached to the file was a note indicating that Theo and Sean McAvie had shared the profit.

Then she saw how two properties had been on the market through another estate agent and been valued by Joe Prescott … after which sales had fallen though because insufficient mortgage finance could be raised. The properties had then gone on to SMK's books and been sold. More than a coincidence!

"Bloody hell!" she exclaimed.

"Ooooh! What language!" April realised she was no longer alone. Two visitors were standing directly in front of her desk, and she had an uneasy feeling they were not prospective purchasers.

"Sorry about that, you weren't meant to hear!" she said, a trifle ruffled.

"Ooooh!" And we have such sensitive ears!"

"What can I do for you?" April asked, trying to sound business-like.

"Now that would be telling!" the other man said, sneering.

April observed the two men for a second and did not like what she saw. The one who had spoken first was small, sandy-haired with blue eyes and had a Scottish accent. The other was slightly taller, thickset and with dark brown eyes. Both were clad in sky-blue suits and white shirts with ties like bootlaces. Both had gun barrel eyes.

"We're looking for Theo Salter," the Scottish one said in a high pitched voice.

"Where is he?" the other man asked in a deep voice. His accent belonged to the Gloucester area.

"He's away," April answered curtly. She did not like their manner.

"Now that's not a very friendly tone, is it?" the Scot said menacingly while circling April's desk. "I asked you a perfectly reasonable question and I expect an answer."

The Gloucester man placed his hands on the front of the desk and leaned forward until his face almost touched hers. "Come on, now, you must know where he is. Let us know where we can find him and we'll be on our way," he said.

"He's away at the moment. He'll be back in a few days," April said. "Perhaps you would like me to pass on a message?"

"We would rather give him the message in person, if you don't mind," the Scot said. "And, believe me, the matter it concerns is very personal indeed!"

"We will be back." The Gloucester man added. "I do hope you haven't been making anything up. That would make us feel quite put out." He then picked up the in-tray on April's desk and let it drop on to the floor, with its contents spilling every which way.

"Oh, yes, we'll be back all right. You can count on it!" the Scot said."

April had not felt so threatened since her confrontation more than six months ago with Ray Williams at Aggammenmon Hall.

Once the callers had gone, she put her hand on the telephone with a view to calling the police. She then put the receiver down before dialling, though.

What would she say to them? That two unpleasant men had called round, saying they wanted to see Theo? There had been no violence, just the hint of a threat.

In any event, did April want the police to take more interest in Theo's activities than they were taking already? There were times when April's tendency to think well of people, no matter what, bordered on naivety. But even she was aware that DI Jackman suspected that Theo was involved in shady practices.

Did April want Theo to get into trouble? At this moment, she did not know what she wanted. She had to confide in someone, however. Sherry was away and Lisa, although a good listener, was not likely to be dispassionate about a man who had made such aggressive advances towards her. After some thought, she decided to contact Edmund Rooker, someone she knew less well but was undoubtedly able to give good advice. Edmund agreed to see her in his office later that day.

The respected local insurance broker listened attentively as April described how she had received two unwelcome visitors and how she feared for Theo's safety.

Edmund asked for descriptions of the men and nodded when he heard them.

"I don't like the sound of these fellows. I'm going to try to find out a bit more about them and, in the meantime, I'm going to get someone to keep and eye on you. I also suggest you live away from home, in a hotel perhaps, for a while until this matter is cleared up."

"Good grief! Is it really that serious?" April asked.

"I think it might be. Now, you work out where you can stay while I make a phone call to someone who will protect you."

April used Edmund's office land line to book a room in a hotel, where friends had stayed in the past, 10 miles outside Camford, while Edmund got on his mobile phone. April told Edmund she had booked a room for three nights, starting that night, and Edmuind said: "Good. You will be getting a visit at the SMK office first thing tomorrow morning from Cecil. He's the most un-Cecil-like person you're ever likely to meet! He will be on hand all day, every day, until things have blown over and he'll drive you back to your hotel once your day's work is over. He will also act as your chauffeur if you need to go out anywhere and, apart from tomorrow morning, he will be able to collect you at the hotel and drive you to work."

The hotel happened to be on the road to Aggammenmon Hall, which was about three miles further on. April decided to close the office early that day and make straight for the hotel, which featured a swimming pool, sauna and gym along with the opportunity to have a massage afterwards. Her Californian break had proved to be a tonic but the subsequent stress following a long journey and other subsequent worries made the idea of a relaxing break particularly attractive.

So April spent the rest of the day pampering herself. The hotel was known for the quality of its food and accommodation, and the following morning saw her fit, relaxed and ready for anything that life could throw at her.

Although it was almost rush hour time, April encountered little traffic on the journey back to Camford. The road did not twist and turn as much as it did between the hotel and Aggammenmon Hall but it was narrow, the surface was uneven in parts and there were enough bends to make caution the bye-word.

After April had been driving for a couple of miles or so, she saw something that made her heart miss a beat. A Landrover was just a few feet behind her, and behind the wheel was a young man with a red face and massive shoulders.

It was the same man, with the same vehicle, who had menaced her while she was on her way to view Aggammenmon Hall for the first time.

This time, however, there was no rage and no horn-honking. The big man was wearing a thoughtful look and the Landrover was being driven at a steady speed and at a respectful distance from April's MG. He appeared to be following her, though April was, for some reason, curious rather than concerned.

The MG and the Landrover kept on the same route, firstly entering Camford and then travelling along the roads towards SMK Estate Agents.

At the car park, the big, red-faced man watched as April got out of her car and walked the short distance to her work place. April unlocked the SMK door, picked up some letter and walked to her desk. Just as she was hanging up her coat, there was a knock on the door … and in walked the Landrover driver.

"Good morning, I'm Cecil," he announced, "I believe you're expecting me!"

CHAPTER 37

THERE WAS A BUZZ Of excitement at "The Camford Daily News." News of the death of Drummond had filtered through, and the newspaper office was a hive of activity at all levels. The words "Hold the front page" were actually used. A meeting of all the top executives was hurriedly arranged.

"We must follow the story up with as much background material as we can get," the editor said.

"I'll get my best reporters on to it," the chief reporter said.

"We must increase our print run for the next day or so," the works manager said.

"We need to bring in a couple of extra van drivers and make sure the newsagents give the story publicity," the newspaper sales and circulation manager commented.

"We're going to need extra pagination," the chief sub-editor added.

"We must get someone to do a backgrounder on Drummond, to find out more about what made him sort of person he was," the features editor observed. "An interview with Theo Salter is also a must, or course."

It was agreed that the Drummond drama should be the subject of a special "pull-out." A short editorial conference followed.

"Right!" said the editor. "Once we've got the main story out of the way, we need to do some in-depth research concerning the case. We need to look at the facts that led up to the final showdown in the estate agent's office, and I suggest we feature profiles of the two main characters ... the hero and the villain. There are lots of people to talk to and there's lots of research to be done, and we need to set up a team to handle all this."

Colin Edwards turned to his recently promoted news editor, Alan Carpenter: "Alan, I suggest you put Philip in charge of the writing side, and, if he needs two or three other reporters to help him, make sure he gets them, please."

Then he turned to Harry Brown, the formidable chief sub-editor, to say: "Harry, the job of designing and sub-editing the pull-out sounds like a job for Charlie. What do you think?"

Harry nodded. "Yes, Philip and Charlie could do a good job here." He recognised, as his superior did, that Philip Cranford and Charlie Sedgeman were both highly capable journalists. More importantly perhaps, they were both known as volatile trade union activists who could be useful, rather than troublesome, if given special responsibility and the hint that promotion could be on the cards if they did well.

When Paul Shenfield, the property correspondent, heard what had been planned, he expressed a desire to be involved. Alan responded with a slightly contemptuous "No thanks, you're needed for producing copy for the property section."

Alan regarded the much older Paul not so much as a "has been" as a "never was!"

Paul, who, in many ways, was glad he had been "put to pasture" with his property-writing role, might well have accepted the rejection had it been delivered differently. But Alan's attitude riled him. "I'll teach the little upstart!" he thought.

Paul recalled how Alan first arrived at "The Camford Daily News" as a wet-behind-the-ears novice, how he helped him to learn the ropes and how Alan rose through the ranks by "making the right friends."

There were two pubs near the office. One, the Rose & Crown, was just 20 yards away on the same side of the road, while the other, the George & Dragon, could be found 100 yards away on the opposite side. The rank and file members of staff would traditionally spill into the Rose & Crown as soon as it was lunch time or close of play, while anyone at middle management level or above tended to gravitate towards the George & Dragon. It was not long before Alan, still a tyro, was frequenting the latter. "I'll teach the little bugger!" Paul said aloud. A couple of colleagues overheard but showed no surprise!

Another source of irritation for Paul was the fact that Theo Salter was going to be portrayed as a hero. He did not like the man, felt intimidated by him and had been in the newspaper business for long enough to sense when there was something shady about a person. Apart from that, he knew already that not all the other estate agents were happy about his presence in Camford. "Yes, it's time to do a bit of digging!" he said, again aloud. The two nearby colleagues looked up from their desks and exchanged knowing looks.

Paul had never been to Gloucester before, though he had often meant to. He had met two distant cousins, who lived in that neck of the woods, at a wedding reception in Shrewsbury 10 years ago, and they had both said he should come over and stay some time. Now, at last, he had got round to it. Paul had been due some leave and he had suddenly decided to ask if he could take the next week off. Alan had said "Yes, as long as you've got enough property copy written!" without hesitation. Paul's presence or otherwise in the newsroom was of little interest to him.

Paul had arranged to stay with Nigel, who was of a more similar age than Martin and lived in the centre of Gloucester whereas Martin's home was five miles outside the city. He intended to spend time with both cousins but felt that being based centrally would be better for the task in hand. Nigel, an insurance clerk looking forward to retirement, knew little about the world of estate agency. However, one or two of his friends were more au fait, as was the younger Martin, an architect.

"I've never heard of Theo Salter, or Joe Prescott, for that matter," Martin said to Paul on his second day in Gloucester. "However, I do recall that there used to be a firm called Saltzman and Prestwick, and I seem to remember that the two men running it were Theobald Saltzman and Joe Prestwick. The names aren't exactly the same, of course, but they are similar enough to be looked into."

"Do you know anything about them, or what they look like?" Paul asked.

"No, but my friend, Cedric Strudwick, who's an estate agent, should be able to tell you. Cedric is one of those straight-down-the-line agents for whom honesty is an article of faith. He detests agents who indulge in sharp practices and would have no qualms about exposing one who he knew to be guilty of them."

Then Martin asked: "Are you here to do a job for your newspaper?"

Paul sighed. "No. Well, not officially anyway," he said. "The people who run the paper are only interested in making money … and we must not, under any circumstances, upset the advertisers!" He could not conceal the bitterness.

Martin looked at Paul quizzically before reaching for his mobile telephone and arranging for Paul to meet Cedric. When Paul arrived at the office of Strudwick & Hawes the next day, Cedric showed him a photograph of Theo Salter and Joe Prescott standing outside the shop bearing the name of S & P Estate Agents. "They left Gloucester in a hurry and, although a lot of us were not exactly sorry to see them go, I am curious to know what he's up to now. The other estate agents here would like to know, too." Paul told Cedric how Salter rescued Wayne Benson from a watery grave just before he arrived in Camford, how he became a local hero and then how he fell from grace.

"There's something not right about Salter, or Prescott, for that matter," he concluded.

Cedric agreed vehemently. "There certainly isn't!" he thundered. "He's got crook written all over him. But no on can prove it."

"What's he been up to?" Paul asked.

"It's difficult to know where to start!" The very mention of the name Salter … or, to be more precise, Saltzman ….caused Cedric to be beside himself with rage.

"He's indulged in every sharp practice in estate agency under the sun … and more besides. You name it, he's done it! And that's just the tip of the iceberg," Cedric went on. "He's reputed to have been involved in drug dealing, bank robberies, blackmail, money laundering, protection and even prostitution."

"Presumably no one can prove any of it?"

"No, though the Gloucester police were thought to have been closing in before Saltzman suddenly disappeared."

"Streuth!" Paul exclaimed. "Where did you hear all this stuff?"

"A lot of it is hearsay," Cedric replied. "What is true, though, is that Saltzman … or Salter … or whatever his real name is … has been seen in some pretty unsavoury company … including local heavies, known drug dealers and a suspected bank robber."

Cedric paused and then asked: "Have you come across Kelly Cheatham, by any chance?"

"Yes, I believe she arrived in Camford at about the same time as Salter and lived with him for a short time before forsaking him for a local businessman."

"Well, well, well! Did you know she was a prostitute and that Saltzman was her pimp?" Paul was flabbergasted.

"No one can prove it, of course, but it's common knowledge among the estate agents in and around Gloucester. Some of their clients made use of her services and it's rumoured that two or three of the agents indulged as well!"

"Good grief!"

"That's not all," Cedric continued. "Have you come across Sean McAvie, the property developer who was murdered the other day?" he asked.

"I certainly have!"

Paul described what had happened and Cedric, who knew quite a bit about it from reading reports in the national press, then told Paul how McAvie had bought 10 run-down rented houses in a street in Gloucester, harassed the tenants into moving out, made minor improvements to the properties and then sold them for massive profits.

"He was suspected of doing something similar in Camford," Paul said.

"I'm not surprised, though let me tell you the police are rumoured to have been looking into his activities and were close to pressing charges, I believe."

Cedric paused for a moment before adding: "There's more still! Both McAvie and Saltzman are said to have been involved in drug dealing and protection racketeering. Saltzman's name is reputed to have been linked with at least one bank robbery, and there was almost certainly a time when he dabbled in money laundering. The trouble, of course, is that there's no proof. Once you get some, you should have a great story that can be printed!"

Cedric later introduced Paul to three other estate agents in Gloucester, who backed up what he had said. But the only evidence, if it could be called that, was the anonymous note about Salter that Paul had received in his post at the office.

However, Nigel had promised Paul he would introduce him to a couple of friends who might be in the know. One of them worked in a betting shop, the other in a pub.

Paul was firstly introduced to Len Smith, a former insurance salesman who now managed a branch office of Higgins Turf Accountants.

"I turn a blind eye to a lot of things," Len told Paul over a coffee. "There have been some conversations I should have probably told the police about. Trouble is, if I do anything to encourage the police to frequent our premises it would put off the punters and be bad for business ... and I would get the sack! I could also be in trouble with the local villains and, in any case, all I can offer is hearsay rather than proof."

"What sort of conversations have you heard?" Paul asked.

"We've had drug dealers coming in and either selling stuff to some of our clients or chasing them for money that they owe them. No money ever changes hands inside our premises, though I have seen deals completed just outside from our window."

"Was Theo Salter ... sorry, Saltzman ... one of the dealers?"

"Oh yes, and so was his property developer friend Sean McAvie. The most interesting story I have heard about McAvie and Salzman, by the way, concerns the opening of a new restaurant in the city by a retired couple from the North. On their second day of trading, just before closing time, McAvie and Saltzman are reputed to have strolled in and said 'Good evening, we are your new business partners!' The couple disappeared the next day and the property has been empty ever since!"

Paul found Len's revelations to be riveting and frustrating at the same time. He felt vindicated, too. But there was still no proof. There was still nothing that could be put into print. By way of a last throw of the dice, he asked Len if he could name any of Theo Salter's associates, apart from McAvie. "Well, there were Ralph Meakin and Terry Springett, who I believe are now banged up inside," he said. "Rumour has it that Salter dropped them in it with the police to save his own skin."

"Never heard of them," said Paul. "Anyone else?"

"Yes, there are a couple of other drug dealers who spring to mind … Jason Jones and a Scottish bloke whose name I can't remember. Jones is a big mate of Springett, I'm told. So … if rumours are correct, Saltzman won't be any too popular with him!"

"Anyone else?"

"The only other name that spring to mind is Clive Matthews," Len said. "Matthews is reputed to have taken part in a bank robbery. Saltzman is said to have acted as both getaway driver and money launderer. But, again, there is not a shred of evidence …"

Bobby Gentry, landlord of the River Boat Inn, was as wide as he was tall. Office workers who poured into his city centre hostelry for a lunch time or after-work pint looked upon Bobby as the most jovial mine host imaginable.

During the late evenings, though, when a different kind of clientele appeared, Bobby could and did display his tough side. A baseball bat lay to hand under the counter and even the local hard men who popped in from time to time knew they had to keep in line. He greeted Paul warmly. Much of what he said tallied with Len Smith's observations. "I like Saltzman about as much as you do, probably less so," Bobby said "I agree with what you say about there being something not right about him.

"He would sometimes be in here with other businessmen at lunch times, looking all respectable. We would also see him quite a bit late in the evenings, when he seemed to attract all sorts of unsavoury characters … pimps, prostitutes, thieves and especially drug dealers … I didn't want to see. I would sometimes see money changing hands and sometimes I would see transactions taking place in the street nearby. But Saltzman and his associates were discrete. Nobody misbehaved in any way … that's partly because everyone knew I would sort them out if they did … but there were lots of hushed conversations, sly looks and people suddenly disappearing to the toilet together or going outside."

"So you never saw anything illegal actually happen?" Paul asked.

"Well, I suspect the transactions taking place in the street were illegal but, without deserting my pub and actually standing over Saltzman and his friends, there was no way I could be sure or prove anything"

Paul started to clutch at straws. "What about conversations? Was there anything you ever heard that might be worth looking into?"

Bobby winced and rubbed his chin. "There is one possibility," he said at length. "But it's a long shot at best."

"Go on," urged Paul. "A long shot's better than no shot at all!"

"OK, here we go! The last time I saw Saltzman in here was just before closing time on a Friday night. Saltzman was sitting at a table in a corner with Terry Springett, who's as nasty a piece of work as you'd care to meet. I was clearing away glasses and I couldn't help hearing Springett saying to Saltzman 'OK, I'll leave it in the lock-up'. That's all I heard, nothing else."

"Hmm! Do you know what was meant by 'stuff' and have you any idea what lock-up he was talking about?" Paul asked.

"Sort of," said Bobby. "That little shit Springett made himself rich by peddling heroine and crack cocaine. I'm told Saltzman dropped him in it to save his own skin, and if there's one good thing Saltzman did do was get that bastard put behind bars!"

Bobby had grown red in the face.

"So we can be pretty sure the stuff Springett was talking about was hard drugs," said Paul. "What about the lock-up? That's not so easy. Is there any particular lock-up you have in mind?"

"I do but it is very much a long shot," said Bobby. "I happen to know the road where Springett lives and about 50 yards away, down another road, is a row of six lock-up garages. They're in a pretty run-down neck of the woods and I happen to know that quite a few low lives hang around there. I once drove past those lock-ups and I noticed that a thug by the name of Ralph Meakin, another nasty piece of work, was hanging around nearby ... as if waiting for someone."

"Any idea which lock-up they happen to use?"

"None at all. I have no idea which one and I don't know what, if anything, is inside any of them."

Paul had not felt so excited for years. "I'd like to have a look anyway. Would you be prepared to help me?" Bobby's face hardened before a slow grin spread across it.

"I'd be glad to," he replied vehemently. Then he added more calmly: "Mind you, we're going to have to be careful. If we mess up we could end up in a whole heap of trouble."

Shortly after closing time the following night, once all the punters at the River Boat Inn had downed their last pints and started to wend their unsteady ways homewards, Bobby unlocked the back door to let Paul in. He took him through to another door at the side, which led to a yard occupied by a nondescript black van. Bobby jumped in and motioned Paul to join him. The journey to the lock-ups took around 20 minutes, during which Paul noticed that the streets became increasingly bleak-looking. The lock-ups, covered in graffiti, had run-down tenements on one side, a block of high rise flats on another and waste land on the other two.

"Time to get to work," said Bobby. "Now remember, keep an eye on the van and throw a stone my way if you see or hear anyone coming."

Bobby, who had told Paul he once had an uncle who was renowned for his lock-picking skills and had passed some of them on to him, fished out a bunch of spindly-looking instruments. Some looked like keys, some like nail files.

One by one, he opened the lock-ups and shined a torch inside. Two of them were empty, one contained a couple of motor cycles and the fourth had a small car in it. However, inside the fifth lock-up were five bags containing a powdery substance that Bobby felt was unlikely to be flour! He told Paul to put them in the van.

Inside the sixth lock-up were a cardboard box filled with syringes and a couple of pipes, and a large tin with a padlock, which Bobby found more difficult to get to grips with than the lock-up doors.

Then Bingo! Bobby saw inside the tin a stack of £20 notes and a notebook containing lists of dates and names with sums of money written next to each of them. Among the names were those of Sean McAvie and Theo Saltzman. Saltzman's name appeared on five different pages. The sum of £10,000 was written on each page, with all but one of the figures with a tick next to them.

Inside the notebook, on a separate piece of paper, were the words "Ralph, make sure Saltzman gets his cut. Then kill him!" The message was signed "Terry." And on the floor were traces of dried blood. Perhaps the lock-up had been used as a place for meting out "punishment" to an addict who had fallen behind on payments for his "fixes?"

Bobby picked up the cash-filled box and the notebook and took them to the van. "Right, let's get out of here!" he said to Paul.

The search of the lock-ups had taken no more than half an hour, during which the area had remained deserted, but Bobby and Paul had no wish to push their luck and stay longer. Back at the pub, the pair took a closer look at what they had taken and discussed what to do next. Taking them round to the police in person was not an option as they had just committed the illegal act of breaking and entering.

So they decided to parcel everything up and send the contents, with a note revealing where they had been found, to the police in Camford.

"I don't know how to thank you for your help," Paul said to Bobby just before they parted company.

"Think nothing of it. It was my pleasure," Bobby replied. "A couple of years ago, my niece, who was only 14 at the time, got hooked on crack and she's now in rehab. I am almost certain that Saltzman and his friends were the ones who got her into the state she is in now … and I have been trying to work out the best way to fix the bastards while keeping my own nose clean ever since. So, let me tell you, Paul, I am the one who should be grateful!"

CHAPTER 38

THEO'S hand was up Staff Nurse Trimmington's dress when Kelly arrived at the hospital. Theo was about to be discharged and, despite his antipathy towards inertia, he had mixed feelings about leaving his bed.

The prim, severe-looking Angela Trimmington had presented Theo with a challenge to be relished. He was soon able to detect a sensuality behind the cool façade, largely thanks to some outrageous flirting. He suspected that she had been attracted to him when they first met at the hospital after the canal rescue.

Theo was now putting his theory to the test and enjoying every moment. He had already kissed and caressed her behind drawn curtains, and been pleasantly surprised by the shapeliness of her contours. He took his hand off Angela's thigh just before Kelly had time to notice.

"Ah, you have a visitor," Angela said crisply, and quickly assuming her matronly air. "I'll leave you to it!"

Theo watched her march purposefully out of the room before turning to Kelly to welcome her.

He could see that her appearance was more dishevelled than usual. Her clothes, although of good quality, had been hastily put on, her hair had barely been touched by a comb, the usually carefully applied make-up was conspicuous by its absence, and there was a bruise on her left cheek.

"You caught me just in time, I'm just about to leave," Theo said. "How are things?"

He could tell that all was not well.

Kelly looked at him imploringly and was about to speak. But

instead she burst into tears and wept uncontrollably, burying her head under Theo's chin as she did so. A strong, protective arm encircled her.

"What's wrong?" Theo asked kindly, once the weeping had stopped. "Are things not going right between you and Edmund?" He knew the answer already.

"No, I've made a terrible mistake," said Kelly, who started to sob again.

"You're not the only one," Theo said. "My relationship with April has gone pear-shaped."

"Really? What happened?"

"Never mind about that now. I'm getting over it. Tell me about your problems with Edmund, and I will help if I can."

"Can I come over to your place and stay with you?"

"Yes, of course you can. Now, why don't you tell me all about it?"

"All right but it's not going to be easy. You're not going to like what I have to tell you."

"Try me! Just take your time."

Kelly took a deep breath and said: "At first, everything was great. Edmund was brilliant to be with ... just as you were!"

"And then things went wrong?" Theo asked.

More tears welled up in Kelly's eyes. "Yes, everything went terribly wrong. Edmund started to find out about my past. He has a way of getting information out of people without them always realising and, when he found out everything, his attitude towards me changed. There was no affection any more, just contempt, and then he started to slap me around. He started to make me do things I didn't want to do and if I protested he would beat me. One evening, a couple of spivvy-looking blokes I had never seen before came round to the house and Edmund told me to do a striptease for them. When I refused, he tore my clothes off, tied me to a bed and whipped me with a leather belt in front of them."

"Oh my God!" Theo was livid. "I'm going to pay that Rooker a visit!"

"No, no, no, don't! Kelly implored. "He's dangerous! Everyone in Camford knows him as a respectable businessman but there's a lot more to him than that. I think he might even be a gangster! He has shady-looking people coming round to the house occasionally and he often gets me to deliver parcels to people and collect money from them. Some of the people I meet look really nasty. I've also heard Edmund do one or two deals … they sounded like drug deals … on the phone. Once I heard him give the order to have someone beaten up. I wasn't meant to hear, of course. I'm terrified of him now."

"I'm not surprised," said Theo. "You're coming home with me … no argument!"

A quarter of an hour later, the pair slipped away quietly … watched only by a wistful Staff Nurse Angela Trimmington.

Before long, they were inside Theo's new house. It was modern, detached and, as an estate agent would say, "built to a high specification." It was well furnished, too, and featured a variety of modern appliances.

Kelly gazed around the sitting room admiringly. "You haven't done badly for yourself, have you?" she observed.

"I'm not complaining," Theo replied. Then, after a pause, he asked: "You said at the hospital that you had told Edmund everything. By that, do you mean … everything?"

Kelly blushed. "Yes, I'm afraid so. But, as I said before, Edmund has this way of getting things out of people. And when he found out it made no difference that it was all in the past. Oh Theo, it is in the past. Please tell me that it really is all in the past?!"

Theo took her in his arms and kissed her gently on the forehead.

"Yes, it's in the past. From now on, you're mine … and mine alone!"

Kelly pressed her body against his and kissed him hard on the mouth. "Oh, you don't know how happy you're making me feel," she said. "We were always meant for each other, and now we're together again!"

The couple gazed into each other's eyes before Kelly suddenly said: "The only problem now is that I haven't got any clothes to change into."

"Don't worry about that for now. I'll pop over to Edmund's some time and collect your other things. In the meantime, why don't you pop upstairs and see what's in my wardrobe. You look good in a shirt, for a start!"

While Kelly was upstairs, Theo checked his telephone for messages and also opened his mail. The first message was from DI Jackman, who wished him a speedy recovery following the attack by Drummond and expressed a desire to talk to him again shortly.

The second was from Edmund Rooker, stating how April had encountered two unwelcome visitors at the SMK office and that he had laid on protection for her.

The mail consisted of two utility bills and a handwritten letter from Jenny Fitch. The letter, bearing no address, was short, terse and abusive. It stated, in no uncertain terms, that she now regarded Theo as someone who liked to manipulate people, that he never was the friend she thought he was, and that she hoped his drug-dealing activities would lead to an untimely and painful death.

Theo screwed it up, binned it and sighed: "Win some, lose some!"

A moment later, Kelly reappeared. She was wearing Theo's best white shirt, complete with bow tie, stiff collar, brass stud and cuff links ... and nothing else.

"The adverts say this kind of shirt looks better on a man!" she said. "What do you think?"

The bleakness disappeared from Theo's visage. "If people believe that, they'll believe anything!" he said with a smile.

His hand slid up a thigh before he picked her up and carried her back upstairs. The pair made love with as much intensity and abandon as they ever did. It was if they were being bathed in a shaft of sunlight that was reserved for them only.

However, Kelly, and Theo in particular, were blissfully unaware at that time of the storm clouds that were gathering.

DI Jackman had in front of him the anonymous note, stating that Salter was a cheap swindler. It had been sent to him some time ago by Paul Shenfield, and now the DNA test results showed that it had been handled by Clive Matthews. Yet Salter had denied ever having had anything to do with Matthews.

Even more exciting was the parcel he had just received from Gloucester. The contents would be DNA-tested, too, and colleagues in Gloucester could visit and examine the lock-ups where the drugs, syringes and cash were alleged to have been kept.

The DI was now confident he was closing in on his quarry. That was if he got there first …

Robbie Murray and Jason Jones were, in many ways, the perfect paying guests at The Falcon Inn, on Camford's southern outskirts. They were immaculately dressed, possessed impeccable manners, were punctual at meal times and displayed generosity with their tipping. Yet the proprietors, Jack and Jean Robson, felt ill at ease in their presence, as did the waitresses and other guests.

The two men had spent two nights at The Falcon Inn and paid for a week's accommodation in advance, saying that they were not entirely sure how long they would be staying.

When Jack Robson ventured to ask if they were in Camford for business or pleasure, the two men looked at each other before Jason Jones replied: "A bit of both." Their faces were flint-hard, even when their lips made the movement of a smile.

Robbie Murray, whose Scottish accent was tinged with a touch of West Country, said: "We're thinking of buying some property in this neck of the woods. I don't suppose there's an estate agent you could particularly recommend?"

Jean Robson tried to be jocular. "I'm not sure I'd care to recommend any of them. Estate agents are a load of crooks, as far as I'm concerned, though I suppose that fellow Gathercole, who runs Trumpers, isn't too bad."

Then, a little more seriously, she added: "They all operate in pretty much the same part of Camford, anyway, and I can give you a map which will show you where to find them."

"That's tremendous," Jason Jones said effusively. "We're most grateful to you."

Messrs Murray and Jones spent most of their time sitting in the inn's small lounge area, reading the newspapers, or going out for short walks. It was if they were waiting for something to happen or for a signal for them to make something happen themselves. On the third afternoon of their stay, Jones's mobile phone rang while the pair were in the lounge, and there was a short, animated conversation. In an instant, the pair were on their feet and out of the front door.

Their subsequent wait at Camford railway station was reminiscent of a scene from the film "High Noon", that classic Western, in which three villains waited for a train carrying their leader who was hell-bent on revenge against the town marshal.

In this case, however, there were two men waiting for an associate, someone they had never met before. The intent was much the same, though.

The train arrived on time, and one of the first people to get off was a burly man in a sky blue suit and with the face of a prize fighter.

"Are you Ray Williams?" Jones asked him.

Williams nodded. "Sorry to have kept you waiting," he said.

"No problem," Murray replied. "We hear you're keen to have a piece of the action."

Williams nodded again and grinned. "You can say that again!" he said.

"I understand you don't want too many people knowing you are here at the moment," Jones said to Williams as he drove towards The Falcon Inn, where a room had been booked in advance for the new arrival.

"That's right, I'm out on bail at the moment," Williams replied. "The filth tried to pin a bank robbery rap on me but couldn't make it stick. Clive Matthews is not so lucky, though, and he's being held on remand. In the meantime, the filth are still trying to get me for money-laundering."

"Is it true that Salter … or Saltzman or whatever his name is … dropped you in it?" Murray asked.

"Yes, it is. Clive saw Salter with his stash first. The two of them had done business before. But, this time, that bugger Salter turned his nose up and would have nothing to do with Clive. He referred him to me instead!"

"Our friend Salter's pretty good at dropping people in it, isn't he?" Jones observed icily.

"Oh yes! I owe Salter big time, believe me!" said Williams.

"So do we," said Murray. "Thanks to him, two of our best friends and associates are banged up inside. And they are going to be there for some time."

"But Ralph and Terry have friends on the outside," said Jones.

"And Salter has enemies!" Williams added vehemently.

"He certainly does," Jones agreed. "Let me tell you about the stroke he pulled with Ralph and Terry."

Jason Jones and Robbie Murray went on to explain how Theo Salter got Terry Springett and Ralph Meakin to follow Jenny Fitch from Gloucester to Birmingham and "punish" her for failing to pay money she owed to "the firm" over a drugs deal.

As soon as the pair had left, Theo plundered a kitty containing £10,000 that had been due to be split three ways and took all the cash for himself. Then, because he knew he was being watched by the police, he went to Birmingham himself and, because he knew where Meakin and Springett were staying, was able to keep them in his sights and intervene once they started to beat Jenny up.

"He gave them quite a pasting," Murray said.

"Yes, and that dyke Fitch became his friend for life," Jones added.

"And, to cap it all," Murray said, beside himself with rage, "he turned Ralph and Terry over to the filth."

"He did it to curry favour with the police, of course, and, at the same time, make them believe he was clean," said Jones.

"But this time, that shit Salter has made an error of judgement," Murray went on.

As the car reached The Falcon Inn, Williams commented: "Yes, and we're going to make sure that this has been a particularly painful misjudgement!"

"By the way," said Jones, "Robbie has another reason for wanting to get even with Salter."

"That's right," said Murray. "Do you remember Derek Drummond?"

"How could I forget him?!"

"I certainly can't. He was a cousin of mine!" Murray added.

CHAPTER 39

"I OUGHT to punch your erudite head in!" Theo told Edmund Rooker, as the latter opened his front door.

Edmund looked surprised rather than startled, and gave his visitor a hard, quizzical stare. "Good heavens, Theo! What's all that about?"

"I'm here to collect Kelly's belongings."

"Why?"

"Why? Why?! She's shown me some of her bruises, and she's told me some of the things you've been up to. You aren't quite the pillar of respectability that most of the Camford business community had been led to believe, are you?"

"Really?"

"Yes, really! You and Kelly are finished, and now she's back with me."

"What about April?"

"She's history. Now, are you going to step aside while I collect her things ... or am I going to have to flatten you first?"

A glint appeared in Edmund's eyes before he replied with icy coolness: "Come in and help yourself. I will show you where to find them."

Theo stepped into Edmund's elegantly furnished detached home and, with the help of Edmund and a muscular manservant with a bent nose, gathered together Kelly's clothes and other belongings and put them in the large cardboard box he had brought with him. The process did not take long. Kelly had always possessed either nothing or very little, and this was still the case.

As Theo put the box into his car and prepared to drive off, he waited for the expected parting shot.

"You're quite a guy, aren't you?" said Edmund. "I was all set to offer you a key role in my organisation. But it looks as if I was wrong to think of such a thing. You are clearly not interested!"

Theo could not resist responding by saying: "What sort of role is that? Head of crime? Or is it simply deputy chief sadist?!"

Edmund sneered. "The question is merely academic because you are never going to find out!"

Before going home, Theo decided to make a couple of calls elsewhere. First of all, he dropped in on the SMK office to open his post and to see if anyone was there. Since the attack by Drummond, the office had stood empty for much of the time, with Joe Prescott now his only business associate.

Theo's new plan was to install Kelly in the position previously occupied by Jenny, to cajole Joe into spending more time at SMK, and to consider whether current finances justified taking on another member of staff.

As it happened, Joe was there … sitting at the desk once occupied by April. He looked agitated.

"Hello Joe, what's up?" Theo asked.

"I've had a couple of very nasty visitors, and they're looking for you!" he replied.

"Earlier on, I had a phone call from April to say they had been here before and to warn you that they looked as if they were up to no good … and then they came round again!"

Joe went as white as a sheet. "They demanded to know where you were, and they started to threaten and manhandle me," he added.

"Did they give their names?" Theo asked.

"Did they leave any messages?"

Joe fumbled for a piece of paper on the desk and held it up. "Their names are Jason Jones and Jim Murray. Do you know them?"

"What did they look like?"

Joe described them as best he could.

"I think I know Jason Jones," Theo said. "If he's the one I'm thinking of, he's bad news. We'd better shut up shop for a while and work out what we're going to de next."

Theo's next port of call was Benson Lane. Joe decided to accompany him. Theo needed to know who was running MAC Developments following the murders of Sean McAvie and Chris Doman. A nasty surprise was in store for him. Theo and Joe arrived at the site office at 1.30pm and, much to their chagrin, saw a notice stating that the office was closed between 1pm and 2pm. Joe turned away and walked back towards the car. However, Theo noticed that the door was slightly ajar and, just before pushing it open, he heard the sound of love-making. A half-naked Sara Ponsonby-Lewis was lying on her back across a desk while another woman kissed and caressed her. The second woman was Jenny Fitch. Jenny saw Theo standing just inside the room first. Sara continued to lie there writhing for several more seconds until she realised she was being watched. She fled through a door at the back.

"Did you enjoy the show?" Jenny asked with a defiant curl of the lip.

Theo, who was well aware of her sexual orientation, replied: "Not really, I've seen it all before!"

"All right, what are you doing here?" Jenny's eyes were now filled with hostility, hurt and resentment.

"I have an interest in the property development here, remember?"

"Not any more, you don't!" It was Sara who spoke this time. She was back in the room, with both clothing and composure restored.

"Why not? Have you taken the firm over or something?"

Now it was Sara's turn to sneer.

"Well, I suppose the best way to put it is that recent events have made it necessary for changes to be implemented," she said mockingly.

Jenny sidled up to her, embraced her and kissed her hard on the mouth. "We have a new board of directors," she told Theo. The gloating was unmistakable.

"My father bought a stake in the business around the time Mr

McAvie took me on as his press aide," Sara said. "He gave me a small slice, too."

"Really, and who are the other directors?" Theo asked. Jenny laughed, in the most disconcerting manner possible.

"One of them is your friend, Mr Edmund Rooker," she said. "He put some capital in some time ago and he's so well connected that we're on the verge of being more of a going concern than ever. Another is Mr John Groves. Remember him?"

"I'm sure he does," Sara chipped in. "Mr McAvie was so concerned about what happened to Mr Groves's mother that he bought him a handful of shares and gave him a place on the board." The idea of McAvie having a conscience left Theo gaping.

"So there you are," said Jenny. "We've got Edward Ponsonby-Lewis as chairman of the board, Edmund Rooker and John Groves as directors and Sara as managing director.

"And," said Sara, "Jenny here is my general manager, and she will soon be a director, too." More kisses between the two women followed.

Then Jenny, with her most triumphal stare yet, added: "There's just one more thing. As part of the MAC Developments shake-up, we have appointed a new firm of estate agents to market the properties that remain for sale."

"You really like to put the boot in, don't you?" Theo said bitterly.

"It's nothing less than you deserve!"

"Fine! You will be pleased to hear that I'm now out of your life for good. So, just remember, if you ever get into any sort of trouble in the future, don't come crawling to me for help!"

The two women grinned. Theo then asked: "What firm of estate agents would want to work with a two-bit outfit like yours?"

Sara was the one to reply. "We've appointed Bowes & Ward for that purpose," she said. "They're a solid, reliable firm, and I'm sure they'll do us proud. I believe George Bowes is ... or perhaps I should say was ... a friend of yours."

Theo walked out without responding any further.

As he made his way towards the car, not knowing whether to feel angry, bemused, murderous or simply sorry for himself, George

Bowes approached the site office from the opposite direction. "Hello Theo, just the person I wanted to talk to," he said.

A red mist descended in front of Theo's eyes. "I don't want to talk to you, fuck off!" he said, pushing George hard in the chest with the flat of his hand. The push was with such force that the powerfully built rugby player was forced to stagger backwards, trip over a loose stone and land on the seat of his pants.

"What the hell do you think you're doing?" he roared as Theo got into his car and drove off.

George remained in the sitting position for a full minute. "All right, Salter, if that's how you want it, to hell with you!" he said. "From now onwards, you're on your own!" George had been on the point of proposing a merger between his firm and Theo's. Such a step would benefit all concerned, especially his beleaguered buddy, he felt. But not now. "To hell with you, Salter!" he roared after Theo's car had disappeared. "You're on your own now. And you're more on your own than you think!"

Meanwhile, a bemused Joe was asking Theo what had been going on.

"I've been shafted!" was the terse reply, and Joe knew it was not the time for questions.

Ten minutes later, Theo announced that he was going to pop into the office for a few minutes to check his emails. He would then close up for a few days and spend some time on the coast with Kelly. Joe reluctantly agreed to keep a "nominal eye on the place."

The only email of any interest was from Reg Pinkerton, circulated to the Camford estate agents en masse and announcing the team for the next annual cricket match between the agents and the bank and building society staff.

The name of Wayne Benson loomed large. The name of Theo Salter was conspicuous by its absence.

CHAPTER 40

APRIL MAY HAD had plenty of time to think.

She had mulled over her doubts about her relationship with Theo while in California, and had since had many of those doubts confirmed.

The two unwelcome visitors to the SMK office had amounted to more evidence that the former local hero had been keeping dubious company, to say the least. Her reluctance to believe there was bad in anybody had made it difficult for her to have doubts. Even Ray Williams had once been seen as a jovial ruffian!

Now, of course, there were the questions of what she should do with her life next and the more immediate one of how long she was going to need protection from those thuggish visitors. She had no doubts about them!

April had chatted to Lisa, Sherry and other friends, some of them estate agents, and they had all agreed that Theo was bad news.

If she took the seemingly inevitable step of leaving the area, she was going to miss them. The only thing she was going to miss more was the love-making with Theo. Oh, why couldn't life be a bit more straightforward ...?!

One thing for sure was that life in a hotel room did not suit her. Something had to change. April considered the imponderables for hour after hour until she suddenly realised what she had to do. She made a decision that flew in the face of logic. But logic be damned! There were questions to be answered!

April walked down the first floor corridor that led to Cecil's room and knocked on the door. Then she noticed the door was slightly ajar, and she could see Cecil, clad in a singlet and shorts, was doing one-arm press-ups on the carpet near his bed. He was built like a colossus.

"Could you take me to the SMK office, please?" she said nervously.

"No problem," her bodyguard answered. "I will be ready in five minutes." Unlike the man she had first encountered on the road to Aggammenmon Hall, he was politeness personified.

Just as April and Cecil began to set off, two fire engines and an ambulance, all heralded by sirens, whistled past Cecil's Landrover. A few minutes later, a police car passed as well. Twenty minutes after that, the cause became all too apparent.

The area looked like a war zone. The sounds of sirens, shouts and screams could be heard as Cecil negotiated his way through snarled-up traffic to get to the public car park. Onlookers, standing three or four deep, were lining the street at each end as emergency service officials did their best to maintain order.

Flames could be seen leaping into the sky, and April got Cecil to use his bulk to force a way through to the front of the nearer crowd. A cordon had been put up and three burly policemen were there to ensure that no one got through it.

"Oh my God!" April exclaimed, as she saw where the flames were coming from. The SMK office, until recently her workplace, had been bombed and burned. Windows were shattered, walls breached, and the street was littered with rubble, dust and shards of glass. The three fire engines were directly outside the office door. The ambulance was behind them. Four police cars were in evidence, too. Police officers were ensuring that the fire-fighters were able to do their work unimpeded by the public.

April could see hosepipes being trained on the building and sensed that some of the fire-fighters were inside. Then her heart missed a beat. Two fire-fighters emerged from behind a cloud of smoke. One of them was carrying a man on his shoulder. "Oh no!" April sobbed. Two ambulance men appeared with a stretcher, and, after a minute or two, April could see the man being placed on the stretcher and taken to the ambulance.

"Oh Theo!" April cried out. "I've got to see if it's Theo!" she screamed to Cecil. Before anyone could try to stop him, Cecil pushed his way towards the forefront of activity and gently propelled April towards where the stretcher was.

April uttered an involuntary sigh of relief. The man on the stretcher was Joe Prescott. He was unconscious and appeared to be seriously injured. As she looked down on the luckless Joe, a hand tapped her on the shoulder. "I can see you're relieved," DI Jackman said to her. "Are you all right?" April nodded. "Your friend Mr Salter doesn't appear to be in the building. Have you any idea where he might be? I need to talk to him."

"I would like to talk to him, too," April replied. "But I'm sorry, I haven't seen him for a while."

The DI looked at both April and Cecil speculatively before saying: "Pity!"

Then, after another pause, he asked: "By the way, did you know there has also been a fire at the new development in Benson Lane? No? The site office has been badly damaged, though fortunately there was no one inside."

"Good grief, I had no idea!"

"It does seem to be something of a coincidence, don't you think?"

"It certainly does, "April agreed.

The DI left April and Cecil to watch the blaze being brought under control. When it became apparent that there was not much else to see apart from a mess, the crowds started to disperse. "Where would you like to go next?" Cecil asked. "Perhaps we should go the hospital to see how poor Joe is," April replied.

One of her reasons for wanting to visit Joe was to see if he knew where Theo was. Unfortunately Joe was dead by the time they reached him.

DI Jackman, meanwhile, returned to his work place to muse once more about Theo Salter and the material that lay on his desk.

Apart from the package, which had been sent anonymously from Gloucester, there was the anonymous note that had been written by Clive Matthews, received by Paul Shenfield and sent on to Camford Police Station. Paul had not identified himself but it was clear to the DI that whoever the sender was felt the allegation that Salter was guilty of a catalogue of misdeeds warranted police attention.

And it was now established that the note had Matthews' DNA on it.

DI Jackman also had in front of him a cutting of the "Hero and Villain" feature which Paul had written in "The Camford Daily News," following the fight to the death at SMK.

The piece described how Derek Drummond, the villain, was born out of wedlock, had a deprived childhood, been in and out of care homes and young offenders' institutions and, later on, spent two spells in prison for assault causing grievous bodily harm.

Pleas from probation officers and psychiatrists for him to receive help in overcoming serious mental health problems had fallen on deaf ears. One psychiatrist had suspected Drummond was a paranoid schizophrenic, while probation officers had claimed he was so dangerous that the public needed to be protected from him.

Drummond was, the article said, a tragic figure who had never had a mother, father or lover, and could only ever connect with members of the criminal fraternity who would exploit his murderous "talents."

The "hero" piece recounted in detail how Theo Salter rescued Wayne Benson from the fenland canal and how he shone at the local cricket match. It stated that he hailed from Gloucester and ran an estate agency there before going on to describe how his estate agency had developed in Camford

DI Jackman found the feature frustrating. There were gaps galore and the information about Salter was, at best, sketchy. He could tell that Paul Shenfield had either not been granted an interview with Salter or, if he had, only been given minimal information. But, let's face it, that was par for the course with Salter! Little was known about the man and he was the last one to give anything away!

The most important item on the desk, though, was the package. Inside it was a note bearing the message "If you want to know more about Theo Salter, take a look inside the lock-ups in Spillman Street, Gloucester."

DI Jackman's colleagues in Gloucester were already on to it. The insides of the lock-ups were being scrutinised and DNA-tested. The contents of the package were to be similarly examined.

He telephoned his West Country counterpart, DI Tom Northfield, a friend he first knew during their police training days at Hendon.

"Great to hear from you again, Tom … especially when you're helping us reel in some of the big fish in our drugs scene," he said.

"Have you got anything on our friend Salter?" DI Jackman asked.

"Yes, his DNA's all over the place."

"How do you know it's his, Tom?"

"Oh, we know all right!" the Gloucester DI said. "We've had our eyes on the bastard for some time. We've had him in for questioning more than once and we've taken a DNA sample off him."

"But, until now, you've never been able to pin anything on him! Right?"

"Spot on, Tom!" Tom Jackman could detect a note of glee in the other Tom's tone.

His Gloucester counterpart continued: "The evidence we've garnered from the lock-ups tells us more about who the local dealers are, and some of it links Salter with them. The notebook in the package you received points to Salter's involvement, and the DNA shows that he had been inside the lock-ups himself.

"As you know, we had Meakin and Springett put away for dealing and now we know that Salter did business with them.

"You might recall how he rescued Jenny Fitch from them in Birmingham and then subtly let us know how we could find them with a supply of coke and a stash of ill- gotten gains in a warehouse. Meakin and Springett were arrested and jailed following the tip-off. However, the two of them maintained that they knew Salter and that Salter was the one who sent them to beat Fitch up. Presumably the idea was to throw you off Salter's scent?" DI Jackman asked.

"That's how it's looking. We were on the point of pulling Salter, who we suspected had a supply of heroin in his garden shed when we received the tip-off, and we're almost certain that the diversion he created gave him time to move the stuff and cover his tracks."

"So he can't be any too popular with Gloucester's criminal fraternity now?"

"You can say that again! Rumour has it that Meakin and Springett, and possibly others too, have a contract out on him."

DI Jackman's reaction of "bloody hell" was followed by the observation that there was much work to be done, both in terms of protecting Salter from would-be assassins and apprehending him. "Is there anything else you've got on him?" he asked.

"Not yet, though there are other things to be looked at. Apart from looking into possible criminal proceedings against him for fraudulent activities as an estate agent … and we've received quite a few complaints about what he has got up to … Salter is suspected of … wait for it … pimping and money laundering.

"His lady friend, Kelly Cheatham, who you might have come across … if you'll pardon the pun … is thought to have given some of Salter's business associates sex for money, with the proceeds going to you know who."

"How are you going to prove it?"

"We might not be able to, though there is an outside chance we'll get him for money laundering. We can now link him with Clive Matthews, who has been charged with involvement in several bank robberies … and on the question of where the money went to, Matthews is pointing the finger. Salter owns, or has a stake in, several companies said to be devoted to providing financial services and we are looking at how these companies are being financed."

After a pause, DI Northfield added: "So you and I are going to be in regular contact with each other for a while! And it looks as if you're going to have to get hold of Salter quickly, if only to prevent someone from killing him!"

CHAPTER 41

IF THERE WAS EVER a man who was wanted and not wanted at the same time, it was Theo Salter.

The police wanted to interrogate him and, if possible, charge him. His enemies wanted to apprehend him in an entirely different way. His business associates and former friends, meanwhile, wanted him out of Camford. The "local hero" tag had long gone and the local estate agents ostracised him. Theo Salter was, at best, seen as a loose cannon, at worst as a crook.

Even the notoriously harem-skarem Nathan Pike, who once regarded Theo as a drinking buddy and kindred spirit, was heard to say that he was "the sort of agent that the rest of us have to live down."

Much of the animosity was undoubtedly due to jealousy of Theo's conquests ... both business and sexual. When Jason Jones and Jim Murray started to make inquiries concerning his whereabouts, the agents they approached all said they had no idea and indicated that they were in no hurry to find out.

"We'll be glad to see the back of him," Nathan Pike said to Jones. "There used to be a rogue agent in Camford called Ray Williams. We were glad to see him go, too, though, if anything, this guy Salter is even worse!" Jones was hard put to conceal a wry smile. It was just as well that Williams was lying low just now, he thought. Jones and Murray knew they had to be careful, too.

The two bomb attacks, on the MAC site office and on SMK, had been designed to scare Salter, to harm him financially and to flush him out. They did not know that Prescott was at SMK at the time of the attack there, and his death would mean the police would be more on the lookout for strangers in the town than ever.

Yet Jones and Murray, and Williams, too, were becoming increasingly frustrated over not knowing where Salter was. Jenny Fitch, who might have been able to help them once, had reportedly left the area. Kelly Cheatham was nowhere to be seen either. Wayne Benson was approached as well. "I don't know and don't want to know!" he roared.

The most frustrated of all was Ray Williams, who had agreed with the other two that he should not stray beyond the hotel's confines. However, on the third day after his arrival back in Camford, the feeling of being cooped up became too much for him, and he increasingly felt the need to stretch his legs. The hotel was towards the end of a leafy lane that led to a park and recreation area in one direction and a fairly busy road in the other. Williams decided that an afternoon stroll in the park would do no harm.

On reaching one end of the lane, which at the time was secluded, he could hear the rumble of traffic and recalled that the busy motorway link was just a few streets away. Williams headed for the park, reached at the other end of the lane via a gate. The entrance was flanked by bushes and hedges and it was only after he had walked five yards beyond the gate that the park and "rec" came into view.

A few young children, some of them supervised, were playing on swings and roundabouts. No one else could be seen, apart from a man and a woman walking round the park's perimeter. Then, all of a sudden ... Bingo! Williams cupped his hands around his eyes to shield them from the sunlight and saw that the woman was April May. Her companion, a mountain of a man, looked familiar, too. He had seen him in the company of Edmund Rooker.

Williams stood behind a bush and a tree to ensure that he would not be noticed.

It looked for a while as if April and Cecil could be walking towards him. But instead they crossed a stile in a gap in a hedge and disappeared. After a few moments, Williams followed. He reached the stile just in time to see the pair turn left at the end of a tiny lane and into a street. He had to be careful. He could see that the man mountain was both athletic in appearance and vigilant. He might well be acting as a protector!

Using all the stealth he could muster, Williams followed them into the street and watched as they walked along it and then turned into the entrance of a hotel.

From that moment on, Williams, Jones and Murray kept the hotel under surveillance. Jason Jones and Jim Murray arrived in the street in a hired car and parked about 50 yards from where April was staying, and the three men took turns at using the binoculars they had with them.

After about an hour, April emerged, still followed by Cecil who opened the front passenger door of a Landrover for her to get in before getting in himself and driving off. The Landrover headed north, away from Camford and along a rural route that twisted and turned. April could see the route was familiar, and suddenly an eerie feeling crept over her.

"Where an earth are you taking me?" she asked, unable to conceal a feeling of unease.

"Mr Rooker has a surprise for you," Cecil replied grinning. "Have no fear. You'll find out soon enough!"

Before long, they were at Aggammenmon Hall. The gates were open and Cecil drove in. As he did so, a screeching of tyres heralded the presence of a battered Vauxhall Astra which passed the Landrover and stopped at right-angles in front of it. Three men, two of them carrying revolvers, got out.

"Hello, April May. Remember us?" asked Jason Jones.

"I'll give YOU something to remember in a minute!" said Cecil, whose expression now resembled the one April saw during her first encounter with him. "What do you think you're doing?"

"You'll do well to calm down and keep quiet, or you'll end up remembering nothing," Murray said as he pointed his gun at him. Williams, the one without a weapon, then appeared and walked towards April until just a few inches separated them.

"These two gentlemen need some information from you … and if you start playing up, I will take the greatest pleasure in beating it out of you!" he said to her.

"I have nothing to tell you except that you're a shit!" April declared defiantly.

Williams' eyes narrowed. "Where's Theo Salter? Tell me now!"

"I don't know and wouldn't tell you if I did. Go fuck yourself!"

Williams punched April in the stomach hard enough to make her double over. Murray felled Cecil with the butt of his revolver as the latter moved forward to confront Williams. "Tell us where he is!" Jones bellowed at April. "Or do you want some more?"

"Go to hell!" April retorted.

"All right, Ray, you'd better give her the full works!" said Jones.

"With pleasure!" Williams replied as he prepared to deliver another blow. But he was interrupted.

"That's enough!" a voice rasped. Edmund Rooker was standing there, flanked by two other men April had never seen before. Edmund was holding a rifle. "Throw those guns on to the ground ... now!" he told Jones and Murray. The pair obeyed and, as they did no, Cecil felled all three adversaries with a baseball bat he had taken from his vehicle.

Edmund turned to April and said: "I'm sorry about this. Are you all right?" April had a sore rib but she was tough and athletic.

"I'll survive," she answered ruefully. Cecil, who was standing over Williams, purple faced, was told to lock the three unwelcome callers in the cellar.

"They can stay there until I decide what we should do with them," Edmund said.

"Aren't you going to call the police?" April asked.

"Just leave them to me," was the reply. "Now," Edmund continued after a pause," I invited you here for a purpose ... but, first of all, you must come inside and have some tea and biscuits."

Edmund took April into the front lounge of Aggammenmon Hall and April could see that McAvie had had it tastefully refurbished. Edmund asked again if she was all right, and she nodded. One of the strangers appeared with a trolley laden with cakes, biscuits and a large tea pot. He perfunctorily introduced the other two men as Alan and Ken before explaining the purpose of the meeting. "As you may or may not know, I now own a major stake in MAC Developments," Edmund said. "Much of the business is conducted from Aggammenmon Hall, which I have bought as an investment. After a year or two, I plan to sell it on, and I would like you to act on my behalf in this respect. In addition, I would like you to act as joint estate agent marketing the development in Benson Lane, once things have been tidied up there and got up and running again. How do you feel about it?"

"I might be interested but you ought to know that I am on the point of severing my ties with SMK," April said.

"No problem. In fact, the severance you refer to is one of the conditions of my proposition. Theo Salter and I are not the close friends we used to be. I had, at one point, been thinking of offering him a place in my organisation … but let's just say we hit upon a snag or two!"

"A place in your organisation! What does Theo know outside estate agency? He knows nothing about insurance for a start."

Edmund gave a wry smile. "Oh, there are other fields, you know! But never mind about that, are you interested in my proposition?"

April felt uneasy and could only say: "I will need to think about it."

"That's fine, of course you do," Edmund said. "There's no great rush. For now, just relax and enjoy your tea and cake and I will then get Cecil to take you back to your hotel."

As April got up to go, Edmund turned to Cecil and said: "Once you've taken April back to the hotel, could you come straight back here, please? She won't be needing your protection any more."

By the time she had got into Cecil's Landrover, April had made her mind up about Edmund's business proposition. "Thank you for looking after me these last few days," she said to Cecil on arrival at the hotel. "Perhaps you could tell your boss I have decided to decline his kind offer. I have decided instead to return to the United States."

By the time Cecil got back to Aggammenmon Hall, Jones, Murray and Williams had been moved, while bound round the arms and legs, to a small room at the back of the huge house. The three captives had been placed on wooden chairs with Alan and Ken standing behind them and Edmund sitting behind a desk and facing them.

Cecil joined Alan and Ken behind the three chairs. "Right!" said Edmund. "Now everyone's here, the party can begin!" His expression was anything but jocular.

"I don't take kindly to people barging in on my property uninvited, especially when they're brandishing firearms and issuing threats," he said with a steely glint in his eyes. "What are you doing here? What do you want Salter for?"

"What's it to you?" Murray retorted.

Cecil slapped his face with the back of a meat plate-sized hand, sending chair and occupant cart-wheeling across the room. Blood seeped from Murray's nose and mouth. "I'm in no mood for pussyfooting around!" said Edmund. "Let's try again, shall we?" Cecil picked up the chair with Murray tied to it and put it back where it was.

But it was Jones who spoke next. "Salter grassed up two of our mates, and we've come over from Gloucester to settle the score," he said.

Jason Jones then went into detail about how Theo Salter had sent Terry Springett and Ralph Meakin to Birmingham to "punish" Jenny Fitch, beaten them up while they tried to carry out his instructions and then had them arrested to get the police off his own scent.

"Good, now we're getting somewhere! Now tell me who you work for."

Jones hesitated for a moment. "You heard what he asked. Tell him!" snarled Alan.

"Or do you want some more?" Ken asked.

Murray was the next to speak. "Our boss is Peter Price and he'll kill us if he finds out that it's us who's told you about him."

Edmund sneered. "You're caught between the devil and deep blue sea, aren't you?" he mocked. Then he picked up a telephone and a few seconds later, he could be heard talking to Peter Price. He moved to a corner, though, and the exact words were indiscernible.

After a seemingly interminable 15 minutes, Edmund put down the receiver and smiled. "All right, you can untie these two," he said to his aides while pointing at Jones and Murray. Then, to Jones and Murray, he announced: "You will be pleased to hear that your story has been confirmed. Peter wasn't particularly pleased about his name being divulged but he was very understanding, given the circumstances!

"You're going to be working with me for a while ... and, if you do a good job, you will be back in Peter's good books. You'll be in mine, too!"

Edmund walked over to a small cabinet in a corner and produced a bottle of wine and some glasses. "I think the forging of our little alliance warrants a celebration," he said benevolently. "Let's relax over a drink before deciding what we do next."

However, there was one voice of protest.

"Hang on a minute, what about me? You've still got me trussed up like an animal!" said a protesting Williams.

Edmund looked at him long and hard. "Oh yes, I almost forgot about you," he said sarcastically. "You've always been something of a liability for whoever you've worked for, haven't you? I don't really have any use for you!" He picked up one of the revolvers that was lying on the desk and fired two shots into the ex-pug's heart.

CHAPTER 42

"TIME FOR YOU to put on that wig," said Theo.

Kelly followed him obediently into the bathroom, where he clipped her long straw-coloured tresses with a pair of scissors until her hair was only slightly longer than that of an average boy.

Theo carefully gathered up what he had trimmed and put it all into a plastic bag, while Kelly fished out her wig, which was short and brunette, from her handbag.

Theo then used a bottle of dye to make his own hair grey, and put on a false moustache of the same colour. Their coastal sojourn needed to come to an abrupt end.

Theo and Kelly had been watching the television in their hotel bedroom, when they heard the news about the two explosions in Camford and the death of Joe Prescott.

The bulletin revealed that the police wanted to interview Theo Salter and there was little doubt that there were others who wanted to see him, too.

The hotel bill had been paid, and the couple slipped away quietly through the back.

The bag containing Kelly's shorn hair was burned on the beach, which, because it was six o'clock in the morning, was deserted.

"What are we going to do next, darling?" Kelly asked as she looked up into his eyes. She knew it was best not to press him too hard about what was going on, though, and she trusted him, in any case.

"We're going to head for London," Theo said. "We'll be less conspicuous in the 'smoke' and while we're there I can work out what to do next."

Theo drove to the city's outskirts, where he left his new Porsche in a long-stay car park, and the couple continued their journey by tube. At Finchley Road, they walked for 10 minutes with their suitcases to a hotel where a room had been booked via Theo's mobile phone. Theo had worked in the area briefly during his early 20s as a salesman and he knew both the area and the hotel well. The hotel was big, rambling and now slightly run-down, the sort of place where guests could come and go, wine and dine and have illicit affairs without attracting attention. The staff were mainly Eastern European, short-stayers in Britain whose mission was to send their meagre earnings back to their families at home.

The rooms were spacious, drab and dimly lit, with peeling floral wallpaper and furniture that was of good quality but looking as if it had not been changed since Victorian times. Theo and Kelly slept fitfully during their first night there, and the following morning decided to see a matinee performance at a West End theatre.

The play, a comedy, was light-hearted, undemanding and exactly the sort of entertainment they wanted. "How about a stroll along the river?" Theo suggested afterwards.

The sun was still out, the air still warm, and there was just the gentlest of warm breezes. Kelly agreed readily. However, it was a time when a large part of London was leaving work and heading homewards, and the streets bustled with activity.

Some of the people not heading for home clearly had no home to go to, though, and the "Big Issue" sellers, beggars and those who just sat or lay on the ground barely had their existence acknowledged. After a while, Theo and Kelly left the busy riverside and ambled along some of the side streets. Along one of them could be seen a trail of cigarette ends and dirty needles. Then the couple saw sitting in the doorway of what was once a shop a young man and woman. The street contained a host of shops, in fact. They had all ceased trading and an atmosphere of dereliction and despair prevailed.

The young man and woman looked up at Theo and Kelly with glazed eyes. Spindly arms and legs protruded from what passed for clothes. "You got any change, sir?" the man whimpered, as if he was expecting the inevitable rebuff. "We haven't eaten for three days."

Kelly shuddered. She could see that both the man and woman were almost certainly still in their teens. Both had rings through their noses and lips and both had a complexion associated with an outdoor life that was far from healthy. A couple of needles were lying on the ground a few inches away from where they sat, and there was the smell of cheap liquor. She turned to Theo to suggest that they move on as quickly and emphatically as possible. But instead Theo put his hand into a pocket and fished out a sandwich he had not got round to eating. "I haven't any money to give you," he said, knowing only too well what it would be spent on. "But you're welcome to this." Kelly stood open-mouthed as Theo handed over the sandwich, and she could not fail to notice the expressions of gratitude and disbelief combined of the recipients. The young man gave half of the sandwich to the woman and they devoured it as if they had not had a meal for a month.

Theo and Kelly watched them eat, and then Theo asked: "Are you going to be here for a while?"

"Yes, we'll be here," the young man said. "We're not going anywhere."

"We've got nowhere to go," the young woman added.

"OK," said Theo. "Stick around here and we'll be back."

Theo, followed by a confused Kelly, walked briskly out of the side street and back in the direction of the river. "Where are we going?" Kelly asked.

"Back to that sandwich bar we stopped at earlier." About 45 minutes later, Theo and Kelly were back in the side street, carrying half a dozen sandwiches with a variety of fillings and a stack of sausage rolls.

The young man and woman, looking a little more animated now, accepted the offering gratefully again. But there was a slight problem. Word had got round among the down-and-outs and the pair had been joined by six others.

Theo laughed. Kelly had never seen him like this before.

"There's nothing for it, we'll have to go back and get some more!" he announced. On returning from their final trip to the sandwich bar… and Theo stressed with a smile that this was the final one … Theo and Kelly were so heavily laden with "goodies" that they were hard put to carry everything.

The crowd had grown to 20, some of them young, some middle-aged, all desperate and all overwhelmed by this rare act of largesse.

Pipes, "smokes" and needles could all be put to one side … for the time being at least.

After a while, Theo said to Kelly: "Let's go." And they slipped away and headed for the nearest tube station. Kelly nestled up to Theo as they sat silently and contentedly on their journey to Finchley Road. Back at the hotel, they made love tenderly, almost languidly. "Things are going to be different from now on," Theo said gently. A minute later, he was asleep. Kelly lay there and watched until drowsiness overcame her, too. She had never seen Theo look so much at peace with the world.

It was a feeling of peace that was to be shattered the following morning, though. Dawn had hardly broken when the ringing of Theo's mobile phone, which he had forgotten to switch off, disturbed the calm.

The call was from a frantic-sounding April.

CHAPTER 43

"I THINK you're in danger!" April said. "I'm on the way to the airport and I'm going back to the States. I don't want to see you again and I don't know why I'm bothering to phone you. But I've got to!"

"Why do you think I'm in danger?" Theo asked, rubbing his eyes.

April described the drama ... the part she knew about at Aggammenmon Hall. "I have a horrible feeling that Edmund Rooker is involved in all this skulduggery," she said. "I didn't like the look of his two henchmen. They certainly didn't look like insurance clerks!"

Theo voiced his gratitude. "I owe you one," he said.

"Forget it!" April replied, sounding both angry and tearful. "I phoned you before returning home because you and I had something once. I used to care about you. Perhaps I still do, though God knows why! But that's it ... goodbye!"

Theo knew he had heard her voice for the last time.

Kelly had heard it, too. "Are we going to go back to Camford, darling?" she asked.

"I'm going to go back just one more time," Theo said. "But not you. It might not be safe for you."

"I thought we had agreed that wherever one of us went the other would go, too," she protested.

"I'm sorry," Theo said. "But this must be the exception. Now, there's one way you can really help me, and that's by describing Rooker's two henchmen."

Kelly said she knew both Alan and Ken slightly, and did not like them. "They give me the creeps," she added.

"I'm almost certain they're both drug-pushers, though I'm not supposed to be bright enough to guess such a thing. But I have overheard one or two conversations I wasn't suppose to hear. Some of them have been on the phone and some of them have been with Edmund, and I know they have been up to no good. One thing I do know is that if I ever suggested anything to that bastard Edmund, he would give me a beating!"

"Would he now?" Theo replied, before putting his arm round her slender shoulders. "Well you won't need to worry about Rooker ever again."

As Theo headed back towards Camford, he made two decisions. One was to arrive under cover of darkness. The other was to acquire an unfamiliar car.

On arriving at the town of Angleton, about 25 miles from Camford, it was mid- afternoon. So he parked his Porsche in a quiet side street and sought out a vehicle hire firm.

When he found one, its shifty-eyed proprietor said he had available a Nissan Micra. Theo hired it for a week. He did not trust the proprietor, he did not like smaller cars and he suspected that his hired Nissan was in less than pristine condition. But it served its purpose, which was to help him avoid being recognised.

Theo knew there were various items to be collected from his house in Camford, such as a portable computer, a book of cuttings highlighting his athletic prowess and several trophies. Somehow he had to slip in and out unnoticed, and it was logical for him to wait until dusk before doing so. What he did not know was what he would do next. Should he confront his enemies, or should he merely disappear?

In the meantime, he took the extra precaution of buying a heavy-checked sports coat and flannels and a green shirt. They were all clothes he would not normally be seen dead in. A little more grey dye was applied to his hair, and then he popped into a coffee bar and waited for the sun to go down.

Apart from a couple of waiters and an elderly couple sitting by the window, Theo had the place to himself. The waiters were looking bored and they had a small transistor radio switched on to keep them amused.

Suddenly the selection of bland pop tunes gave way to a news bulletin. It stated that the body of Ray Williams had been discovered in a shallow grave in a rarely visited part of the woods on Camford's outskirts. A dog had dug the grave up, and now the case was being treated as murder. The bulletin also drew attention to the two recent bombings and the fact that Camford was in the grip of an unprecedented crime wave.

It went on to say that the police were anxious to question the estate agent Theo Salter, who had disappeared.

"Hell!" Theo muttered. Now it would be even more difficult to slip into his house unnoticed.

The elderly couple got up and left. A small group of teenagers popped in and talked in animated fashion about their forthcoming exams, and then a group of office workers came in. The sky began to darken, and Theo knew it was time to make his move.

After one last look at himself in the cloakroom mirror to make sure his appearance was as un-Theo Salter-like as possible, he took to the road.

As he entered Camford, his heart sank. Police cars and fire engines were in evidence once more, and he instinctively knew why. As he got closer to his house, he could see billowing smoke.

Theo decided to park in a parallel road and approach his house via a linking lane on foot. His worst fears were confirmed. Flames were leaping from the top of his home, and two fire engine crews were battling to get the blaze under control. A police car was parked nearby, and a 30-strong crowd was watching from a safe distance.

Police officers and fire-fighters ensured that no on could get close … let alone gain entry. Theo joined the onlookers.

"That's one hell of a blaze, isn't it?" he said, trying to sound casual, to a man at the back.

"It sure is!" the man replied. "Rumour has it that the fire was started deliberately."

"How come?"

"Because the fire started so suddenly and fiercely that rumours are already going round that someone put petrol bombs through the letterbox."

"Good grief! It sounds as if the owner of the house has enemies."

"Yes, he has plenty by all accounts," the man said. "His name is Theo Salter. He's quite famous and you might have heard of him. He sounds like a right nasty piece of work!"

By the time these observations had been made, the flames had engulfed the entire property, and the fire-fighters had the difficult task of stopping them from spreading to nearby buildings. Eventually, though, the blaze was brought under control. But by then Theo's home was little more than a shell. Theo returned to his car and spent the next hour trying to decide what to do next. The most obvious solution was to cut his losses, return to London and then, with Kelly, disappear from danger. But looking for the easy option was not Theo Salter's way. He came to the conclusion that many, if not all, his recent troubles could be attributed to Edmund Rooker ... his so-called friend, who had sought out his company while others ostracised him. Now, it was apparent that Rooker just wanted to manipulate him, as he had sought to manipulate Kelly.

Theo recalled how, during their recent confrontation, Edmund had talked about finding him a place for him in his organisation. He was now beginning to understand the sort of on-the-quiet organisation Edmund was alluding to, and he could guess that whatever place he would be given in it would entail unsavoury practices.

He thought about the way Edmund had ill-treated Kelly.

And he felt the anger well up in him as his mind turned to the three bombings. The attack on the MAC Developments site might not have been Edmund's doing ... he did, after all, have a stake in the business now. But, one way or another, Edmund was undoubtedly behind much of the trouble which had caused him to lose out financially in a big way and to put his life in peril. "One way or another, you're going to pay for this, Mister Edmund snake-in-the-grass Rooker!" he said, glaring at the steering wheel.

CHAPTER 44

IT WAS NOT LONG before the fire-fighters were out again. The target this time was Edmund Rooker's insurance company.

A sheet covered in petrol had been pushed through the letterbox at the front of the building and a lighted match thrown in after it. Three windows had been smashed and petrol-covered sheets thrown through them, too.

The building was empty, save a security man who barely had the time to raise the alarm and flee. The damage was extensive. A few hours later, by which time it was 3am, there was a series of hard knocks on the front door of the Rooker household. The door was answered by Jason Jones, who saw a grey-haired man with a moustache, a stoop and a checked sports jacket.

"What the hell do want at this time of night?" Jones asked angrily.

The unwelcome caller responded by punching him hard in the stomach and banging his head against the wall. "Where's Rooker?" the man demanded.

Jones, who now knew who he was dealing with, said as boldly and defiantly as he could: "He's not here!"

Theo Salter felled him with a punch to the face and kicked him in the stomach as he lay retching on the front patio. "Wrong answer!" Theo said, kicking him again. "Now tell me where he is!"

"He's at Aggammenmon Hall for a few days. He left me here to keep an eye on the place."

"How very thoughtful of him! Is there anyone with you?"

Jones, not wanting to admit he was alone, hesitated.

Theo kicked him again. "Answer the question!" he snarled.

"Yes, yes, yes, I'm on my own!"

"Is Rooker on his own at Aggammenmon Hall? Now answer me truthfully, or I'll fucking kill you!"

"Jim Murray is with him, along with a couple of local guys called Alan and Ken."

"Anyone else?"

"No, not as far as I know," Jones answered, not knowing whether he would be kicked yet again.

"Good!" said Theo. "Now get up!"

Jones struggled to his feet and Theo pushed him inside and ordered him to sit on a wooden chair in the dining room. Theo bound and gagged him before knocking him senseless with a candlestick that was lying on the table.

Theo then went outside to his car and brought in a can of petrol, which he used to liberally douse the dining room, lounge, hall and staircase. He threw a lighted match into the hall as he left.

Edmund Rooker was too preoccupied to worry unduly about the fire at the insurance office. It was something that could wait until the morning.

In the meantime, he had a party to organise. Most of his guests were unknown to the people of Camford. None of his insurance personnel knew about it, as the party was very much for those engaged in other, more shadowy spheres. It was his way of thanking friends and contacts for loyalty and "services rendered."

A small band was being laid on, along with a couple of pornographic films and three "women of the night." Two rooms had been earmarked for gambling and another for "coke-sniffing." It was several hours after guests started to arrive that news of the attack on his home in Camford reached Rooker.

Agammenmon Hall was the perfect setting for such a party. The magnificent property with its expansive gardens and grounds, all off the beaten track, offered endless scope, not to mention freedom from interference. Alan and Ken guarded the gate to the grounds, and Cecil stood by the front door of the house. The grounds were floodlit and another henchman, Ian, was on hand to control a closed circuit television system that covered the entire premises.

About 50 guests from all over the country, including Jim Murray and two others from Gloucester, attended. The party, which was due to last the entire night and possibly the next day, too, did not get under way until nine o'clock. The cocktail cabinets were well stocked and drinks were handed out liberally. And it was not long before the guests were making full use of the gambling facilities, drugs, porn and women as well.

Half a dozen of the guests were soon engaged in a game of poker, in which the stakes were high and judgement fuelled by alcohol and drugs was erratic.

In another room a dozen or so others had been drawn to a roulette wheel, and were placing their bets even more extravagantly.

The three "women of the night" had plunged naked into a Jacuzzi, where they languished with their glasses of champagne and made their availability clear. Some of the guests were watching the porn, others were busy with the "coke" and a good number were consuming as much free booze in as short a time as possible, while exchanging yarns about their various misdeeds.

Edmund Rooker smiled benevolently while presiding over proceedings. He took care not to drink much himself, though, and he never took any form of drugs, in any case.

But Ian, the man given the job of keeping tabs on the closed circuit TV, was less discrete. Although ordered to "take it easy with the wallop," he had rifled a bottled of whisky and a glass from a cocktail cabinet and had somehow managed to consume the lot within a couple of hours.

It was around midnight when a disconsolate Alan and Ken suddenly had an extra visitor to vet. No one had appeared for an hour, no one else was expected and, at the time, the two Rooker henchmen were feeling bored, frustrated and excluded.

"Why do we have to be the ones to miss all the fun?" Alan asked Ken.

"I don't know, it's a bugger, isn't it?" his companion said. "I feel like going into the house and joining in."

"Yeah, I know what you mean. No one would notice us, would they?"

It was at that moment that a grey Nissan Micra appeared and parked about 10 yards from where the pair stood. A grey-haired man got out and shuffled over to where they stood.

"Good evening," the stranger said. "I'm sorry to trouble you … but I'm looking for Aggammenmon Hall. Could you possibly direct me to the place?"

Alan and Ken both looked at the grey-haired man sternly. "This IS Aggammenmon Hall," said Alan.

"That's marvellous, I've been trying to find it for ages!" the grey-haired man said. Then, pointing to the great wrought-iron gates and moving towards them, he asked: "Is that the way in?"

"Just a minute!" said Alan. "There's a private party going on in there, and all the guests have arrived. Who the hell are you?"

"Oh, I'm so sorry!" the stranger said. "I had no intention of intruding."

"Right!" said Alan curtly. "You'd better be on your way, hadn't you?"

As Alan moved forward to push the stranger towards his car, a steel blade plunged into his chest. Ken pulled a revolver from a pocket. But the stranger leaped forward, wrested the weapon from him and plunged the blade into him, too.

Unlike Alan and Ken, Cecil was happy with his lot. Nothing pleased him more then the opportunity to display his imposing presence and demonstrate his abnormal strength. Although given to fits of rage when bored or frustrated, the task of acting as doorman gave him a buzz. Long spells of inactivity in a job like this did not matter to him, as there was always the possibility of explosive action at any minute. He had no desire to drink or join in the revelries, only to greet and vet those who arrived at the door courteously and efficiently … and keep a constant eye open for any sort of trouble.

Under the circumstances, it was hardly surprising that Cecil was quick to spot the shape of a man running between a pair of fir trees that stood either side of the far end of the front lawn.

He took a pair of binoculars from a pocket and used them to scan the immediate environs. But the suspected intruder was now out of sight. By then, a few of the merrier party guests had lurched outside for a whiff of air or, in one case, some amusement with one of the women.

Cecil knew he had to consider that the man he saw near the trees might have been a party-goer. However, this was what he was here for, and excitement surged through his veins as he continued to use the binoculars.

A small stone whistled past Cecil's left ear and clattered into the wall near the door. Only Cecil heard the noise, which could not compete with the sounds of music and carousing.

"Who's there?" he demanded. Another stone hit the back of his neck. "What the hell are you playing at?" he barked.

Cecil walked towards a clump of bushes at the side of the lawn, from where the missile seemed to have been thrown.

When he got within 10 paces of the nearest bush, a man stood up with arms outstretched in front of him. Cecil could only see the outline but realised, too late, that the man was carrying a weapon.

Three shots rang out, all of them unheard inside, and the massive form of Cecil became a blood-stained corpse.

When the police called with the news that his home had been attacked, Edmund Rooker's face went purple. Jim Murray, who was standing by his side, said to him: "Perhaps we should have that talk after all."

"Yes, perhaps we should," Rooker agreed, talking through his teeth. Earlier on, Murray had expressed a desire to discuss "what to do next about sorting out Salter."

He had been told to "leave it for now and concentrate on enjoying the party."

Rooker led Murray to the back of the house to a small conservatory, which had just been added. They quickly agreed that the attacks on the office and house could only be the work of Salter.

"He needs a lot more than just a kicking!" Murray said. "The bastard's killed my cousin, grassed up two of my mates and now done this to you. He ought to have his bollocks cut off!"

"Oh, don't you worry!" Rooker said. "I'm going to make him pay for what he's done. I'm going to pay him back good and proper."

"Oh really?! And how are you going to do that?" asked a voice from the corner.

Rooker and Murray swung round and saw that the third person to step into the conservatory, a man with grey hair, a grey moustache and a heavy-checked sports jacket, was the man they had just been talking about.

"How did you get in here?" Rooker asked curtly.

"Oh, it was quite easy, really," said Theo Salter. "Your men at the gate and the front door presented few problems, and your guests were so welcoming that one of them pointed me in this direction."

"I'm going to kill you!" said Murray, who then pulled a knife from his jacket.

Theo produced a gun and shot Murray in the head. Then he spent two full minutes giving Rooker a pistol-whipping.

"This is for what you did to Kelly and for what you have done to my property," he said while doing so. "You have cost me a lot of money and caused me even more aggravation. So say your prayers!"

Rooker fell through the glass at the back and, as shards and smaller fragments cascaded on top of him, Theo shot him in the legs, stomach and finally the heart.

Theo then strolled out of the conservatory, closing the door behind him, and back through the great house to the front door. Looking casual posed no problem, especially as the guests were all semi-inert as a result of all the alcoholic, narcotic and carnal attractions that had been laid on for them. Once outside, however, Theo sprinted towards the massive iron gates and to the car that lay parked in the road not far from them.

The bodies of Alan and Ken were lying exactly where Theo had left them. His revenge was complete.

But now it was time for Theo to leave the Camford area, never to return, as quickly as possible.

CHAPTER 45

THEO KNEW IT WAS possible to be on the motorway in less than two hours.

The awkward, winding road from Aggammenmon Hall to just outside Camford had to be negotiated first, of course. But, once that had been done, he could head for London, pick up Kelly and flee to a far-away, though yet to be determined, destination.

The car he had hired from the shifty-eyed character on the edge of London, had left much to be desired, and he would replace it as soon as possible. He had yet to decide whether to go back to his own car, which might be spotted by police, or to simply play safe and switch to a second hired vehicle.

The Nissan Micra, meanwhile, had served its purpose or, at least, it had done so up to now ... The motorway link was just half a mile away when the engine began to whine. Then there was a rattling sound from under the bonnet, accompanied soon afterwards by a burning smell. The engine finally stuttered to a halt and the only way Theo could make the car move was to push it.

The road was deserted but fortunately for Theo there was a garage 200 yards away. His mechanical know-how did not match his muscularity, and once he got there he needed help. It was still only 5.30 in the morning, though, and Theo banged on the reception area door in the hope that someone would be there to answer it.

A light came on and a wizened old man in overalls appeared behind the glass in the door and spent a couple of minutes fiddling with the lock.

"We're closed," he said. "Don't you know what time it is?" his tone was of sorrow rather than anger.

"I need your help, and I'll make it worth your while," Theo told him.

The leathery face lit up, and the old man replied: "What have you got in mind?"

"My car's broken down and I need it looked at urgently. If you repair it now, I will pay for the cost and top it up with a hundred quid."

The old man rubbed his chin. "You'd best come inside and have a cup of tea," he said at length. Theo sat at a small table where a pot of already made tea sat, and the garage man went outside to look at the car. Ten minutes later, the man returned to tell him: "The fan belt's broken, there's no oil and half the plugs in the engine haven't been screwed down properly. These things can be fixed easily enough but there also a much more serious problem. The brakes are faulty and could go kaput at any time."

"How long will it take you to fix things?" Theo asked.

"The brakes need to be replaced and I won't be able to do that until late this afternoon at the earliest."

"That's no good," said Theo. "Can you do a temporary job on them?"

The old man sighed. "I can fiddle about with them to make them last a bit longer, and they should then be good enough to get you to Camford at least … probably further. But I can't make any promises," he said.

Theo produced £200 and said: "Take this and do what you can. But be as quick as you can, please."

"OK," the man said. "But do bear in mind that this is just a patch-up job … and no more."

"How long will it take you?" Theo asked.

"Give me an hour or so and I'll see what I can do," he was told. "Feel free to make yourself another cuppa while you wait."

So Theo sat alone, left with his own thoughts. He reflected on the enormity of recent events. He had suddenly become a mass murderer! He had never been in such trouble since his childhood. Unwelcome memories came flooding back, making Theo cringe at the thought of them. Theo realised he was wrong in believing memories of his parents had been consigned to the past. The figure of his late Austrian father, Gerhard Saltzman, leather belt in hand, seemed to loom large. Theo cowered in his chair as he imagined how the belt was about to come down on him ... again and again

His father, who was all powerful in the household, had made it plain that he wanted the best for his son, or, to be more precise, he wanted Theo to be best in everything he did. Failure to measure up resulted in a beating.

Any hint of protest would be punished severely.

"I expect you to be big and strong like me," his father would rant.

With this in mind, Theo was forced to run the two miles to school and back every day from the age of 10, eat steak or chicken breasts twice a day and take part in a training regime that included press-ups, sit-ups and various exercises with weights.

"There's no room for weaklings or losers!" Saltzman would bawl out during each session. Theo's mother, Ethel, an alcoholic, treated all this as a huge joke. So inebriated was she nearly all the time that she left every aspect of Theo's upbringing to his father.

Then, just a few days after Theo's 12th birthday, Gerhard Saltzman went berserk in a shopping precinct, attacked two passers-by and was committed to a mental institution, where he died a few years later. By that time, his English mother had died of alcohol poisoning and the task of looking after Theo went to Ethel's older sister, Eileen.

Eileen was a kindly widow who ensured that her nephew was always properly fed and clothed. But, unbeknown to family members and social workers, she was also a "merry widow" with an assortment of lovers. Neighbours knew what went on, though, and Eileen became something of a social outcast. Her reputation inevitably reached the school that Theo attended, and her nephew became the butt of jibes and jokes. The young Saltzman soon learned to fight his way out of trouble, and when he handed out a no-holds-barred beating to a boy who was three years his senior, he tended to be both feared and avoided. His athletic ability prevented him from being entirely ostracised, though. His only friendship in those days was with the clever but frail and socially inept Joe Prescott.

Theo would protect Joe from the bullies and, in return, receive considerable help with homework. Not surprisingly, Theo enjoyed a feeling of power over Joe and would at times get him to do things he do not want him to do, such as helping him cheat with work in the classroom. When Theo learned that Joe was having a homosexual relationship with a younger boy, he did not need to explain that he had even more power to make him do his bidding.

Yet now Joe was no longer on this earth. Neither were his aunt or parents, and he never saw the handful of other relatives. Jenny had forsaken him. Apart from Kelly, his sole soul mate, he had no friends and no associates.

A tear rolled down a cheek as he reviewed his wretched life.

Theo looked up at the kitchen clock and saw that it was just coming up to seven.

The old man reappeared and said: "OK, I've got the car more or less road-worthy apart from the brakes, which need to be seen to a.s.a.p."

Then, noticing Theo had been weeping, asked: "Are you all right, sir?"

"Yes, I'm sorry. I'll be fine," Theo replied, wiping an eye.

By the time he was back on the road again, Theo had decided his best course of action was to head for a car hire firm in Camford, dump the car he was using at present and then head for London post haste in another hired vehicle.

As he left, the old man said he had got the previously out-of-use radio working. So Theo turned it on to find out whether anything had occurred to make him consider altering his plans. What he heard made him realise that drastic changes were needed.

The bulletin announced that five dead bodies, including that of a well known local businessman, had been found. The deaths were all being treated as murder … and the police urgently needed to interview the Camford estate agent, Theo Salter.

The irony of the situation was not lost on Theo. The local hero had become the local villain … public enemy number one!

What he did not realise, though, was that DI Jackman had had him in his sights for some time, as had Paul Shenfield. The jaded old pros, engaged in two entirely different fields, were set to see the twilight of their careers covered in glory.

The DI, who had been contemplating retirement for some time, had been seen to be going about his business with a positive spring in his step. A commendation, perhaps even promotion, now seemed to be a possibility.

The veteran journalist, meanwhile, had garnered so much information on Theo Salter that he had had no qualms about interrupting a management meeting to discuss the need to cut reporters' expenses and state his case for writing a series of articles on the "estate agent from hell." The meeting not only consented to the project but agreed that it was likely to enhance circulation of "The Camford Daily News" and, above all, increase revenue.

It did not take Theo long to realise that there would be police road blocks on the motorway to London. The police would be out looking for him en masse, not only in Camford but possibly all over the country … including railway stations and airports.

First of all, he had to be as far away from Camford as possible, in as little time as possible. He decided to head West, initially in the direction of Gloucester, and then head for Bristol, Bath or perhaps Cirencester. Somewhere along the line, he would meet up with Kelly and then the pair would disappear to somewhere remote.

The news bulletin was followed by a severe weather warning. This, Theo thought, might work to his advantage. His journey now took him to Elmsleigh, best known to him for its hospital, and then along the same route that took him into the Camford area in the first place.

By the time he reached the outskirts of Elmsleigh, Theo could see the police cars were out in force. No officer had spotted him yet, no doubt due partly to his disguise and the fact that Theo was driving an unfamiliar car. In addition, the weather was deteriorating rapidly and visibility was poor.

Theo had little idea where he was going to end up. But he had no doubt that whether he and Kelly would be in Tiverton or

Timbucktoo, there were going to be changes. They were going to start a new life together, with no lies, no cheating, no violence, no power games and no exploitation of any kind.

Theo had visions of atoning for past misdeeds and burying himself in charity work, such as helping the homeless.

There would be no more ring fencing, no more misleading property-for-sale details, no misleading valuation reports, no money laundering and certainly no stealing of other estate agents' For Sale boards.

Meanwhile, there was no time to look around Elmsleigh for a car hire firm. Stopping off at this point was too risky.

So instead, Theo turned off the Elmsleigh road and headed west along the long, desolate fenland road he had been on when he first came to Camford.

He thought he heard the sound of a helicopter, perhaps a police helicopter, but the storm clouds were becoming so black and low-hanging that trying to see anything more than a few yards away was becoming a challenge.

The wind increased in ferocity, the flat fenland landscape offered nothing to blunt its force and each gust was like a battering ram being driven into one side of the car.

The car itself leaped and lurched as it met a series if potholes and loose chippings. Fearsome forks of lightning accompanied tumultuous thunder claps. Thankfully, though, when the lightning lit up the sky, there was no sign of a helicopter.

After a while, the wind dropped, the clouds opened and the rain fell in sheets. The road became increasingly slippery. "Thank God there's no one else on it!" Theo thought. As it was, he needed all his driving skill, not to mention strength, to maintain a speed of 50mph without skidding, veering to the side and landing in a canal. The canal, which had been almost empty at the start of the day, was now filling up rapidly.

At the moment, the road was straight but barely two car widths in some places. In a while, it would leave the canal and start to twist and turn. Visibility was so poor that Theo knew he had to be prepared for a sudden change in driving conditions shortly.

In normal circumstances, a speed of 50 mph on the straight section of the road was, with its pot holes and other hazards, considered just about acceptable. In the stormy conditions prevailing at present, such a speed was manic. But Theo just had to get away … not only from the long arm of the law but also from exposure of what he had done and, above all, being shown up as a failure. The cold, hard image he had worked so hard to cultivate was cracking.

The only answer was to leave his old life and embark on a new one.

All of a sudden, the big black clouds shrank and floated upwards, and the rainfall thinned to a mere drizzle.

Theo recognised where he was. It was the spot where Wayne Benson's car had plunged into the canal.

For one bizarre moment, he thought he saw Lisa, a picture of elegance and untouched by water, standing by the side and waving for him to stop.

Then, at almost the same time, he heard the sound of a helicopter above.

Theo instinctively slammed his foot down on the accelerator. The car, leaped, lurched and skidded and hit a pot hole surrounded by loose stones.

He then put his foot on the brake but there was no response. The edge of the canal beckoned. The engine screamed, Theo cursed and the thunder clapped simultaneously.

The black clouds descended once more and a bolt of lightning struck the edge of the car as it plummeted towards the water.

Half an hour later, the clouds were gone and the helicopter was able to land nearby. The crew, who saw a car submerged a few feet away from a reed bed, now had the unenviable task of trying to find a body.